PROFESSOR K:
THE FINAL QUEST

An action-packed historical medical mystery

Jack Rogan Mysteries Book 4

GABRIEL FARAGO

This book is brought to you by Bear & King Publishing.

Publishing & Marketing Consultant: Lama Jabr
Website: https://xanapublishingandmarketing.com
Sydney, Australia

First published 2018 © Gabriel Farago

Signup for the author's New Releases mailing list and get a free copy of *The Forgotten Painting** Novella and find out where it all began ...

https://gabrielfarago.com.au/free-download-forgotten-painting/

* I'm delighted to tell you that *The Forgotten Painting* has just received two major literary awards in the US. It was awarded the Gold Medal by Readers' Favorite in the Short Stories and Novellas category and was named the 'Outstanding Novella' of 2018 by the IAN Book of the Year Awards.

A Note from the Author

After the release of *The Hidden Genes of Professor K* – book three in the Jack Rogan Mysteries series – in 2016, I was somewhat overwhelmed by the reception of the book, especially in the US, Europe and Australia. The book, a medical thriller, resonated with my readers so strongly, especially in medical research circles, that it was suggested I consider writing a sequel.

Encouraged by several prominent scientists who had assisted me with the science before, and after speaking with many of my readers, I was persuaded to go ahead with the project. However, this turned out to be a much bigger challenge than I thought at the time.

Because all the books in the *Jack Rogan Mysteries* series are 'standalone' and not sequels as such, it soon became apparent that something was needed to link *The Hidden Genes of Professor K* to a sequel. I was working on a short novella at the time – *The Forgotten Painting* – which was intended as a free giveaway to my readers as a small token of my appreciation for their encouragement and support.

As it turned out, the novella became the perfect vehicle to connect *The Hidden Genes of Professor K* to the sequel – *Professor K: The Final Quest.*

For those of you who are not already familiar with the novella, or my previous books, I have included a synopsis of *The Forgotten Painting,* which I hope you will find entertaining and an interesting introduction not only to this book, but my work generally. Others may find it a helpful 'refresher', preparing the way for Jack Rogan's next adventure.

However, please note that this book – like all my others – does 'stand alone' in the Jack Rogan series and can therefore be read as such.

If you would like to read the novella in full, you can download it now for free by visiting my website at www.gabrielfarago.com.au and follow the prompts.

Gabriel Farago
Leura, Blue Mountains, Australia

i

THE FORGOTTEN PAINTING:
THE STORY SO FAR ...

Warsaw Ghetto: 15 May 1943

The audacious uprising of 19 April 1943 had been brutally crushed by the SS. Soldiers searching the ghetto for survivors discovered a family – the Krakowskis – hiding under the floorboards in the ruins of one of the buildings.

An SS major was about to execute the father – Berenger Krakowski – when he noticed a striking painting hanging above a sideboard in the room. When he questioned Krakowski about it, he discovered that the painting had been given to Krakowski by a famous artist in 1920. Instead of shooting the family, the major sent them to the railway station for deportation to a concentration camp. As soon as he was alone, the major dismantled the picture frame and stole the painting.

McCormack & Sons of London, auctioneers: December 2014

The much-anticipated auction of a precious painting – a rare, recently rediscovered Monet – was about to begin. The auctioneer told potential bidders he had a surprise in store for them that would throw some light on the unique provenance of the painting. He then introduced the owner of the painting – Benjamin Krakowski – who gave an account of its extraordinary history.

Krakowski told his spellbound audience that the painting had a name – *Little Sparrow in the Garden* – and that it had been presented to his father, Berenger Krakowski, by Monet himself in 1920. Krakowski continued to surprise his audience by telling them that the man in the picture playing the violin in the garden was in fact his father, Berenger, and then described the tragic events that followed: the

Warsaw Ghetto uprising of 1943; the arrest and deportation of his family to Auschwitz; the murder of his parents and his sister; and how he himself had miraculously survived after his brother had been killed during an unsuccessful escape attempt. Choking with emotion, Krakowski concluded by stating that he had seen the painting for the last time as he and his family were taken away by the SS and herded with so many others to the railway station; destination, Auschwitz.

As he left the podium, Krakowski announced that the entire proceeds of the auction sale would be donated to the Rosen Foundation – a well-known charity doing outstanding medical work in the Third World – in memory of his murdered family.

Delighted with this unexpected, emotional account of the painting's turbulent history, the auctioneer introduced his next surprise guest – celebrated author Jack Rogan – who could answer the question on everyone's mind: *Where had the painting been since it was last seen by Krakowski as a boy in the Warsaw Ghetto in 1942.*

Rogan knew how to tell a good story. He held up what looked like a small notebook, which turned out to be the diary of a German missionary – Brother Francis – that promised to answer all the questions.

Rogan's story began in outback Queensland in 1985, the year of one of the worst droughts in living memory. Rogan, then seventeen, was living on his parents' cattle station and had watched the cattle die as the relentless outback sun sucked the life out of the parched earth and turned the meagre pastures into dust bowls.

To earn some much-needed money during the devastating drought, young Jack had spent a few months working on a mission near the family's property, where he befriended Brother Francis. An elderly, enigmatic character, Brother Francis died soon after and left a tidy sum and a cryptic note he had written just before he died, to Jack. This unexpected inheritance saved the family from ruin at the time and sent Jack on his way to pursue a dream. Sadly, however, the family cattle station was lost during another heartbreaking drought later on.

Rogan held up the note at the auction and read it aloud:

Dear Jack,

By the time you read this, I will be in the Good Lord's hands. I realise we knew each other for only a short time, but the length of days has nothing to do with friendship. There are many things about me and my past you don't know, and when you do find out, you will be shocked and no doubt disappointed. Words cannot express the regret I have felt over the years for the things I have done.

As a dying man and your friend, I ask you to help me right a great wrong. I know this is a big ask, but there is no time left to explain it all. The best I can do is point you in the right direction and hope you will one day grant me this last wish. Just before I left Europe after the war, I buried something in a cemetery. If you follow the instructions on the back of this note, you will find all the answers, and a lot more ...

You are the son I never had.
Your loving friend,
Francis

Many years later, the journey took Rogan to a cemetery in Berchtesgaden in Bavaria on Christmas Eve, 2008, where he discovered Brother Francis's diary and an ornate key hidden in one of the graves. Slowly, line by line, Rogan began to piece together a tragic story about unspeakable atrocities and a fascinating, complex man overcome by remorse.

He discovered that during the war, Brother Francis had been a high-ranking Nazi officer in charge of putting down the 1943 Warsaw Ghetto revolt. He learned about the crimes committed by that officer and finally discovered the great wrong Brother Francis had asked him to set right: it was all about having sent the Krakowski family to a concentration camp to face certain death, and then stealing the only thing of value left in the ruins of their miserable home: a painting.

As the war drew to an end, the officer sank deeper and deeper into despair and consumed by guilt, he became obsessed with one particular subject: returning the painting to where it belonged; its rightful owner. Of course, this made no sense in light of what had happened, but by then he was no longer rational or coherent.

In June 1945 the war was over. The officer was on the run and was hiding in the Imperial Crypt beneath the Capuchin Church in Vienna, the final resting place of the German and Austrian emperors. With him, he carried the painting that was giving him so much grief. By now the Russians had complete control of the city and the officer realised he was no longer safe; he had to get out of Vienna. Before he left the Imperial Crypt, he opened one of the sarcophagi with an elaborate key provided by the Capuchin fathers who had given him shelter, hid the painting on top of the coffin containing the embalmed remains of the deceased, and then disappeared.

Imperial Crypt, Vienna: 2012

Translating and piecing together Brother Francis's diary entries had been a laborious, time-consuming task. Several years passed before Rogan – by now a celebrated international author – found time to revisit the subject. During a trip to Vienna, he decided to explore the Imperial Crypt under the modest Capuchin Church in the city centre.

Open to the public, the crypt was one of the little gems of Vienna. What made the Imperial Crypt so unique was the fact that with one exception, all one hundred and forty-five individuals buried there belonged to one family, the Habsburgs, and included twelve emperors and seventeen empresses. As a depository of European history, it was unparalleled.

Rogan had the relevant pages of the Francis diary referring to the crypt with him as he walked along the rows of magnificent sarcophagi, each a masterpiece of artistry and craftsmanship. Unfortunately, the pages had been badly damaged, and the remaining clues were insufficient to identify the sarcophagus mentioned in the diary. All Rogan had left to go by was the coffin key. Regrettably, that too turned out to be a dead-end, and that was where matters rested until he contacted Benjamin Krakowski in London and told him about the Francis diary and the crypt.

Rogan, a master storyteller, had the entire auction room spellbound. Instead of telling his audience what happened next, he asked the auctioneer to invite Krakowski back to the podium to reveal the final chapter in the painting's extraordinary journey.

Delighted, the auctioneer obliged and Krakowski then gave a brief, emotional account of how the painting was finally discovered hidden inside Empress Marie-Louise's sarcophagus in the Imperial Crypt. However, his story was vague and sketchy, and lacked detail. Important questions remained unanswered.

The auction

Realising that a high point had been reached and basking in the excitement all around him, the auctioneer reached for his gavel and began the auction. Bidding was fast and furious, and soon it became apparent that a new Monet record was within reach. *Little Sparrow in the Garden* was finally sold for a staggering thirty-five million pounds to an anonymous buyer, bidding over the phone.

After the auction, Celia Crawford – a journalist working for the *New York Times* – approached Rogan. Because Krakowski had left many questions unanswered, she sensed there had to be more to the story and decided to investigate. She cornered Rogan on his way out and began to ask questions about the Imperial Crypt and the painting's discovery. Instead of giving her a quick answer or fobbing her off, Rogan invited her to dinner at his hotel.

When Rogan met Celia Crawford later that evening at the Waldorf, an exciting partnership was formed leading to some extraordinary revelations about the painting and its turbulent history.

It turned out that Crawford knew a lot about Rogan. She had written several articles about his books and adventures, and was about to file another one about the lost Monet and the auction, but she wanted more information. Rogan enjoyed the attention of the attractive, intelligent journalist and felt instantly relaxed and at ease.

Over dinner, he told her about a violin recital in the crypt, a coffin key and a remarkable boy with psychic powers, and how destiny and fate had collided in the Imperial Crypt and led to the discovery of the Monet hidden in a sarcophagus by a desperate Nazi on the run at the end of the war.

Hanging on Rogan's every word, Crawford took copious notes. However, the evening ended abruptly, as she had to rush back to her hotel and call her editor in New York to file her article. She thanked Rogan profusely and was about to leave when Rogan dropped a bombshell: he asked her if she would like to find out who the mystery buyer was …

'You know?' asked Crawford, her eyes wide with astonishment.

'Aha.'

'Are you going to tell me?'

'I'm meeting the proud new owner for lunch tomorrow,' said Jack casually, sidestepping the question. 'You can come with me if you like.'

Rogan hadn't told Celia everything. He didn't tell her about the other intriguing item he had found under the painting in Empress Marie-Louise's sarcophagus. The reason he hadn't mentioned it was not because he didn't trust her, but something quite different. He was still trying to work out what it all meant. But something told him it was important, as certain cryptic references in Brother Francis's diary were beginning to make sense. All Jack needed was a little more time to investigate and follow the breadcrumbs of destiny.

The next day, Rogan took Celia to the famous Time Machine Studios, a converted bond store on the banks of the Thames, to meet a legendary rock star – Isis.

Inspired by Krakowski's generous donation of the proceeds of the auction sale to the Rosen Foundation, Isis, an avid art collector, had become the mystery buyer of the painting. Apart from inviting Jack to view the painting in her penthouse, Isis had also invited Krakowski and Dr Rosen because she had an important announcement to make.

Isis told her guests that the tragic loss of her family and her recent recovery from a near-fatal illness had changed the way she saw herself, her success and the world around her, and that she had decided to use her staggering wealth and influence to make a difference. Isis announced that she was about to set up a Time Machine Foundation to support certain cutting-edge medical research, and that *Little Sparrow in the Garden* would become its emblem.

'My friends, a toast,' said Isis. She walked over to the painting and held up her champagne flute. 'May the little sparrow in the garden turn into a Time Machine eagle for the future. I give you, *Little Sparrow in the Garden!*'

'*Little Sparrow in the Garden,*' echoed the others, visibly moved, and raised their glasses.

Looking at the closely-knit group of friends about to sit down to a celebratory lunch, Celia felt like an intruder. She mentioned this to Rogan, who assured her it wasn't so and that very soon she too would be part of this special family.

'What on earth do you mean?' asked Celia.

'Isis wants to go public with this right now and ... I suggested you.'

'Me? Why?'

'Because you are the right person for the job.'

'And this is okay with Isis?'

'She trusts my judgement,' said Rogan, smiling.

The old man in the Swiss mansion

Emil Fuchs, a wealthy, reclusive art collector in his nineties with a shady past, lived in a grand Swiss chalet with spectacular views over the Alps. Fuchs had made his fortune during the war in ingenious ways. As a young executive in his father's bank, he had acted as the contact point between the bank and the Nazis to facilitate the flow of much-needed money to keep the wheels of the Nazi war machine turning.

Temperamental, arrogant and demanding, he had only one passion left in life: his fabulous art collection, mainly paintings, which he kept in his home. A man of iron discipline and routine but confined to a wheelchair, reading the papers in the morning – especially the New York Times, his favourite – was one of his little pleasures and the highlight of his day.

Enjoying the warmth of the morning sun near the panoramic window, Fuchs let his eyes wander over the headlines until they came to rest on something extraordinary: an article by Celia Crawford.

> *Mystery buyer pays 35 million pounds for lost Monet.*
> *During an epic auction that lasted several hours, a mystery buyer bidding over the phone paid thirty-five million pounds for Little Sparrow in the Garden, an unknown painting by Claude Monet that has recently been rediscovered.*
>
> *The celebrity auction, which was well attended, made headlines around the world. This was due to the painting's colourful history, reaching back to Nazi Germany and the war ...*

Furious, Fuchs threw the paper on the floor and rang the bell on his wheelchair.

His housekeeper appeared almost immediately.

'Dictation; now!' fumed Fuchs, staring at one of his favourite paintings hanging on the wall in front of him. Little Sparrow in the Garden is over there! It's mine! Some idiot just paid thirty-five million for a fake! he thought, enjoying a long-forgotten feeling of a wave of excitement rushing through his fragile body.

The email from Gstaad

Rogan was having lunch with Krakowski and Dr Rosen at his hotel when he received a phone call from an agitated Celia. When she told him they had to meet – urgently – Rogan invited her to join them. A flustered Celia arrived half an hour later and handed Rogan a piece of paper, which turned out to be an email addressed to her editor. Jack read the email and paled, and then handed it to Krakowski who read it out loud:

Dear Sir

I must inform you that someone has just paid thirty-five million pounds for a fake. Why? Because the original painting, namely Claude Monet's Little Sparrow in the Garden, hangs right in front of me on the wall in my house here in Switzerland. (See photo).

I purchased the painting from Berenger Krakowski in 1942 in Warsaw. He wanted to sell the painting, and I bought it. It was a legal, arms-length transaction. He wanted to be paid in gold, which I did. I still have the original bill of sale. (See photo). I think it is important to set the record straight. Your readers are entitled to know the truth, and so is the unfortunate buyer for that matter.

Emil Fuchs.
Gstaad.

The outrageous allegations in the Fuchs email came as a great shock; the potential implications were serious and far-reaching. If Fuchs was right, Krakowski had just sold a forgery at auction, and Isis had paid a small fortune for a worthless painting. It transpired that Rogan knew a lot about Fuchs and his reputation, because their paths had crossed before during the famous Swiss banking controversy triggered by one of Rogan's books.

To avoid a sensational scandal that could seriously hurt all involved, Jack came up with an imaginative plan. And so began the final stage of the forgotten painting's remarkable journey.

Warsaw Ghetto: August 1942

The mass deportations from Warsaw were in full swing and had only one aim: to send thousands of Jews from the ghetto to Treblinka for extermination. In a desperate attempt to save his family, Berenger Krakowski decided to give the only thing of value he had left – the Monet – to the Germans, who were searching the camp for hidden paintings, especially by impressionists.

x

However, when one of Krakowski's friends – David Herzl, a talented painter and master forger who knew how much the painting meant to Krakowski – heard about this, he offered to copy the painting for him so that his friend had at least something left after the original had gone. Krakowski agreed, and Herzl copied the painting.

The copy turned out to be so perfect that Herzl decided to do something daring: he replaced the original painting in the Monet frame with his forgery, but didn't tell his friend.

Using a Jewish ghetto policeman as a go-between, a meeting was arranged with the SS and a wealthy Swiss banker – Emil Fuchs, a well-connected, eccentric art collector – who wanted to 'purchase' paintings in the ghetto.

When Fuchs saw the painting in Krakowski's flat, he was delighted and paid the pittance Krakowski was asking for it, in gold. A stickler for correctness, Fuchs insisted on getting a receipt.

The examination

Rogan's plan to avoid a scandal that could embarrass and humiliate his friends, was as simple as it was daring. He suggested that Celia interview Fuchs to hear his side of the story. When Celia's editor contacted Fuchs to arrange a meeting, Fuchs, a proud and arrogant man, agreed, and Celia travelled to Switzerland to interview him.

Sitting in front of the painting in the stunning chalet, Celia listened to Fuchs give his account of how the painting had been acquired by him. She then made a bold suggestion to resolve the conundrum: As there could obviously be only one original, the safest way to find out which of the two paintings was the forgery, she argued, was to have Fuchs's painting examined by a reputable expert. And when it came to Monet, there was only one man who counted: Professor Moreau, the undisputed world authority on Monet.

When Celia mentioned Moreau's name, a confident Fuchs instantly agreed, and arrangements were made by the *New York Times* for Moreau to come to Switzerland to view the painting.

Professor Moreau arrived at the chalet the next day and began his examination. Rogan and Celia were both present and watched as Moreau methodically went over the painting with a magnifying glass to determine its authenticity.

A smiling Fuchs was confidently waiting for the verdict, when Moreau cried out: 'Here it is! Just as I thought. Hidden in the lily pond; how ingenious!'

'What exactly?' asked Fuchs, and wheeled his chair over to the painting.

'Here, have a look,' said Moreau. He handed Fuchs his magnifying glass and pointed to a certain spot in the lily pond.

Fuchs raised the magnifying glass, bent forward and, for what seemed an eternity kept staring at the painting. Looking quite pale and shaken, he let the magnifying glass fall into his lap and turned around to face Moreau. 'Is, is this a p-prank?' he stammered.

'Far from it,' replied Moreau. 'It's a signature.'

'Are you telling me that what looks like a Star of David and a small heart under this rock here is a *signature?*'

'It is,' Moreau replied, elated. 'And not just any signature, but the signature of David Herzl.'

'Who is David Herzl?' demanded Fuchs, becoming angry.

'David Herzl was one of Europe's most accomplished forgers during the war. He always signed his work in ingenious ways, with a Star of David, obviously for David, and a small heart for Herzl, which as we know means heart in German. He lived in the Warsaw Ghetto and was killed during the uprising in 1943. If it's any consolation, Herr Fuchs, this is without doubt one of the best forgeries of a Monet I've come across. In its own way, it's a masterpiece.'

Six months later

Jack was visiting Tristan and Countess Katerina Kuragin at her chateau in France when he received a phone call from Isis.

'I just had a mystery parcel hand-delivered by special courier,' said Isis. 'Had to sign for it myself, in person.'

'What is it?'

'A surprise. You should really come over and see this for yourself.'

'That important?'

'It is.'

'I'll catch the Eurostar in the morning,' said Jack, his curiosity aroused. 'I need a break anyway. I've been working on my Fuchs interview notes for a couple of weeks now, trying to incorporate them into my book. It's tedious, but potentially quite explosive stuff, especially now that he's dead.'

Emil Fuchs had passed away in his sleep two weeks earlier after contracting pneumonia. 'My editor is on my back and my publicist is calling twice a day. I hate pressure!'

'Poor boy. That's what happens when you're famous. Don't let them rattle you.'

'Easier said than done. Any hints?'

'Little Sparrow in the Garden.'

'Now you've really got me intrigued,' said Jack.

'I'll send a car to pick you up from the station. See you tomorrow.'

Boris was waiting for Jack with Isis's black Bentley at St Pancras Station the next morning, and drove him straight to the Time Machine Studios. Isis's personal assistant Lola greeted Jack downstairs and took him up to the penthouse.

'What's all this about?' asked Jack, enjoying the familiar ride in the glass lift. Lola shook her head. 'Come on, you can tell me.'

'No way! She'll skin me alive if I let anything slip.'

'Oh. That serious, is it?'

'You'll see in a minute.'

Isis looked like someone who had just stepped off the catwalk. Her impeccable make-up, perfect hairdo and the latest creation by one of her favourite fashion designers told Jack that Isis was definitely back to her true self again. She hurried towards the lift, her high heels clop-clopping on the marble, threw her arms around Jack and kissed him on both cheeks, French style. 'You're in for a big surprise,' she said, pointing to the easel standing in the middle of the room.

'Little Sparrow in the Garden, still in pride of place, I see,' said Jack.

'It is, but what do you think is next to it?' asked Isis, pointing to another easel covered with a black velvet cloth.

'No idea. Something new you've bought?'

'No. I didn't have to buy it. It was a gift.'

'How interesting.'

'Any ideas?'

'No.'

'What do you think, Lola; shall we put this poor wretch out of his misery and show him?' asked Isis.

'Might as well.'

Isis walked over to the easel and began to slowly lift the black cloth like a magician revealing the impossible. The only thing missing was a drum roll. As the cloth inched closer to the bottom of the frame, Isis quickly pulled it off with a flourish and stood back.

'I don't believe it!' said Jack, completely taken by surprise. He walked up to the frame and looked at the familiar painting. 'How … did … you …?'

'Fuchs left it to me.'

'Incredible!'

'I received a formal letter from his executors. Oh, and this is for you,' said Isis. She handed Jack a sealed envelope with 'Jack Rogan' written across the front in spidery handwriting.

Jack opened the envelope, unfolded the piece of paper inside, and began to read:

Dear Jack

I enjoyed sparring with you during our recent interviews more than I like to admit. Facing the truth for someone like me is never easy, but you have always been fair and objective in your dealings with me, and for that I am grateful.

You have given me your word not to publish the story of the forged painting while I was alive, and you have honoured that pledge. By the time you receive this, you will have been released from that promise.

I have left my art collection to various galleries around the world. True works of art can never belong to just one person. We are but temporary custodians of other men's genius, which must be shared with the world.

As for my forged Little Sparrow in the Garden, I have thought long and hard about what to do with it. I believe the right solution here is to reunite the two paintings, as both share a unique history and therefore belong together. That is why I have left my painting to Isis. I know she has great plans and will use her painting to raise money for charitable causes. If my Little Sparrow in the Garden can in some small way contribute to this, perhaps as a curiosity, then I am content.

It has been a pleasure to get to know you, Jack. You have brought a little excitement and sunshine into an old man's life.

Emil Fuchs

'Come on, Jack, are you going to tell us what it says?' asked Isis impatiently.

'Sorry. Of course,' replied Jack, and then read the note out loud, his voice solemn, as if he were reading a Will, which in a way of course it was. When he tried to slip the note back into the envelope, he noticed that there was something else inside. He pulled out another piece of paper, looked at it and smiled.

'What's that?' asked Isis.

'I'll show you,' replied Jack, and held up the piece of paper. It was the receipt for the painting, reluctantly signed by Berenger Krakowski with a heavy heart in the Warsaw Ghetto on that fateful day in 1942.

Jack walked over to the painting and tucked the receipt behind the frame. 'This belongs with it,' he said and stepped back.

'You're right, it does,' said Isis. 'A turbulent piece of history has just been closed. Thanks to you, Jack.'

'Not entirely,' said Jack, enjoying himself.

'What do you mean?' asked Isis.

'There's more ...'

'There is?' said Lola.

Jack pointed to Monet's original *Little Sparrow in the Garden*. 'This wasn't the only thing found in Empress Marie-Louise's sarcophagus ...'

'I don't understand,' said Isis, looking puzzled.

'There was another painting ... under the Monet.'

'*What?* Are you serious?'

'Absolutely.'

'What kind of painting?' asked Lola.

Jack walked over to the elevator door where he had left what looked like a large garment travel bag. He placed the bag on the couch facing the easel, unzipped it, and pulled out a wooden frame. 'This one,' he said, and held up a small painting.

'How extraordinary,' said Isis, and walked over to Jack to have a closer look. She took the little painting from Jack and leaned it against the back of one of the chairs. 'Pity it's so badly damaged.'

'That's one of the reasons I didn't want to make a fuss about it at the time. It didn't seem important and would only have detracted from the Monet,' said Jack. 'Nevertheless, it's all quite intriguing.'

'Do you know who painted it?' asked Lola.

'Unfortunately, no. There may have been a signature here at the bottom, but that's where it's badly damaged. Water.'

'A good restorer could do a lot with this,' said Isis.

'Sure. But let me tell you what I've discovered so far. It's quite a story.'

'You and your stories,' said Lola, shaking her head. 'Not only are you an adventure junkie, you are a story magnet as well, revelling in excitement.'

'So, that's how you see me?'

'I'm not the only one.'

'I would agree with that,' said Isis, laughing. 'Tell us about the painting.'

'All right. It's a bit of a detective—'

'Why am I not surprised?' interrupted Lola, rolling her eyes.

'So, first, let's have a close look at the painting. It's all about two people: the man in the bed here, and the man standing next to it, looking up at him.' Jack turned to Isis. 'You know a lot about art. Could you give us an approximate date?'

'Well, the style, composition, the dress of the man standing by the bed, the colours, all suggest sixteenth-century; Italian I'd say. The man lying in the bed is wearing a cap – very distinctive. Clergy perhaps, or aristocracy. Yes, definitely late sixteenth-century I'd say.'

'What about the window?' asked Jack.

Isis walked over to the painting for a closer look. 'Ah, the view through the window. Interesting.'

'What do you think it is?'

'Pity about the damage but ...'

'Yes?'

'It looks a bit like St Mark's Square in Venice.' Isis pointed to the painting. 'Here, this could be the Campanile,' she said.

'Very good,' said Jack. 'I think you're right. It definitely looks like Venice. And when you take the angles into account and the perspective of the view through the window, it would appear that we are looking across St Mark's Square from—'

'The Doge's Palace,' interrupted Isis, becoming animated.

'Correct. That's what I think too. What else?'

'The man standing by the bed has his back turned to us. He is holding a book in his left hand and is pointing to the book with his right. He's facing the man in the bed who is looking up at him; rather anxiously, I'd say.'

'Excellent.'

'The man with the book is holding something in his right hand,' interjected Lola. 'Pointing with it.'

'Correct. The devil's always in the detail. He is definitely holding something ...' said Jack.

'Looks like a pencil; a knife maybe?' ventured Lola.

'Actually, it's a surgical instrument; a scalpel used at the time.'

'How do you know?' demanded Isis.

'Alexandra told me.'

'She's already seen this? When?'

'A couple of months ago when she came to France to visit her mother. She stayed at the chateau for a few days. I was working on

Fuchs's interview. I showed her the painting then. She saw certain things in the painting that wouldn't have occurred to me.'

'What kind of things?' asked Isis.

'To her it looks like a doctor visiting his patient. I suppose the scalpel is a significant clue. She also thinks that the "physician" as she called him, is pointing to a medical text to support his diagnosis while the patient is looking – rather frightened – at him. You must admit, the man in the bed looks quite ill, doesn't he?'

'Makes sense.'

'There's more. Have a look at the mirror over the fireplace.'

'Very clever,' said Isis, bending over the painting. 'The face of the doctor is reflected in the mirror.'

'What else?'

'The book he's holding is also reflected in the mirror. You can see the front cover.'

'Any writing?'

'Not really; it's badly damaged.'

'True, but there are a couple of letters. Can you see?' asked Jack.

'I suppose so ... *u* and an *n*? Right here.'

'Yes; that's it.'

'A good restorer could help us here,' said Isis.

'Good idea. But there's more.' Jack paused, and took a deep breath.

'Well, are you going to tell us?' said Isis.

'I have found references to the painting in Brother Francis's diary. In fact, it was Alexandra who gave me the first important clue when she mentioned the doctor-patient bit. It's quite a puzzle, but definitely worth investigating.'

'You think so?' asked Lola.

'Definitely,' replied Jack, grinning.

'You know a lot more than you are telling us,' observed Isis. 'Admit it.'

'Too early. At this stage it's only a hunch. But if it turns out to be what I—'

'And you are just going to leave us hanging here, in suspense?' interrupted Lola. 'Come on, Jack ...'

'There's a possible connection between Brother Francis, the painting, and Professor K. That's all I'm saying ... for now.'

'Are you serious?' said Isis, surprised.

'I am.'

'Based on what?'

'What I've found in the diary so far, and what Alexandra told me. There's something in Professor K's papers that could have a bearing on all this. But there's a lot more work to be done before—'

'How extraordinary!' interrupted Isis. 'So what's your next step?'

'I was hoping you could help me find a good restorer. Alexandra seems to think the book in the physician's hand is the key to all this.'

'I know someone who would be perfect,' said Isis.

'You'll help?'

'Sure, but only if we become part of your team.'

Jack walked over to Isis and held out his hand. 'Deal,' he said, grinning.

'Here we go again,' said Lola, shaking her head. 'Just look at you two. I thought you had enough excitement to last you for at least a couple of centuries.'

'Come on, you know Jack. He has a good nose for these things,' said Isis.

'That's what I'm afraid of. Look where it took us last time!'

'You don't mean that; admit it,' said Isis, giving Lola a stern look.

'I have a bad feeling about this ...' said Lola.

'Cold feet perhaps?' suggested Jack, raising an eyebrow.

'No! I can't wait,' replied Lola, laughing.

And so began Jack Rogan's next adventure – *Professor K: The Final Quest*. In unexpected ways, as usual. If you would like to find out more about this intriguing painting and its extraordinary story, all you have to do is read on.

Gabriel Farago

CONTENTS

PROFESSOR K: THE FINAL QUEST

Jack Rogan Mysteries Book 4

GABRIEL FARAGO

This is the second book that was inspired by, and is dedicated to, the many talented scientists who work at the Garvan Institute of Medical Research, in Sydney. In awe of nature, but not seduced by its beauty, or cowed by its terror, they are always on the lookout for inspired ideas to improve the journey of man.

To learn more about Garvan, what it stands for
and what it does, please visit
www.garvan.org.au

ACKNOWLEDGEMENTS

Just like writing *The Hidden Genes of Professor K*, researching and writing *Professor K: The Final Quest* was an ambitious project. Once again, the learning curve was both challenging and steep, because for a layman like me, exploring subjects touching on cutting-edge medical research and complex science is never easy and would not have been possible without the guiding hand and encouragement of experts.

I am particularly indebted to Professor Chris Goodnow FAA FRS, Executive Director of the Garvan Institute of Medical Research in Sydney, for helping me get my mind around the rapidly changing science, and patiently reviewing the relevant chapters to make sure I didn't stray too far from what is realistic and possible in light of what we know today. For me, factual accuracy in my writing is paramount. Great care has therefore been taken to ensure that all matters touching on science and medical research are based on fact.

A special thank you must therefore also go to Professor John Mattick AO FAA FTSC, for his encouragement and support in getting this project off the ground. Several of his ideas and suggestions have been incorporated into this book, and have become part of the storyline.

It would be remiss of me to leave out someone special here, who also works at the Garvan – Debbie Burnett BVSc, BSc – Debbie patiently explained what an avatar mouse is, how it is created, and what it can do for research. But that wasn't all. She took me on an exciting tour of her domain located deep in the bowels of the Garvan to induct me into the mysterious realm of avatar mice. A fascinating experience I will never forget.

Preparing a book for publication requires many skills; it is a team effort. I've once again been very fortunate to have a group of talented and dedicated specialists to help me deal with the many challenges of

1

a rapidly changing publishing landscape. Without their professional support and advice, this book would not have seen the light of day. There are too many to mention, but a few definitely stand-out.

First, Sally Asnicar, my editor. Her exceptional attention to detail and insights into the characters, the science and the multi-layered storyline, have been invaluable in bringing this project to fruition.

Who says we don't judge a book by its cover? In a way we all do, especially when surfing the Net for inspiration of what to read. The talented Vivien Valk has once again designed a captivating cover that is true to the storyline, and reflects the spirit of the book.

Then there is Lama Jabr, my publishing and marketing consultant, whose steady hand has patiently guided this project through the many challenges of a treacherous publication jungle. Her insights and expertise, especially when dealing with social media and complex publishing platforms, have been invaluable, because just writing your book is not enough. You have to get it out there, to connect with the market and your readers.

And finally, it would be remiss of me not to mention my wife, Joan, literary critic, researcher, patient sounding-board and cheerful travel companion – we visit all of the places mentioned in my books.

Thank you all for believing in me, and what I'm trying to achieve with my writing.

Gabriel Farago
Leura, Blue Mountains, Australia

FOREWORD

Late at night at the Garvan Institute of Medical Research here in Sydney, when the DNA sequencing machines and high performance computers blink away unattended and the PhD students rule the laboratories, I sometimes expect to turn a corner and bump into Professor Alexandra Delacroix. And out on the busy Darlinghurst street, I'm sure that's Jack Rogan coming my way!

The imagery and science captured by Gabriel Farago in his latest Jack Rogan Mysteries thriller is extraordinarily true to the real lives of the remarkable scientists and clinical researchers here at the Garvan. There are many goose-bump moments when the answer finally shows itself, as we pore over the DNA sequence of a patient with an unexplained disease we may be able to cure.

The only small difference is that the time spent interpreting the results is so much longer and more challenging, our characters less vivacious, and we don't get to meet His Holiness! *Professor K: The Final Quest* takes us as readers on an epic, page-turning journey into the very heart of clinical genome research and its surprising connections to all things historical, political and personal, as we share the dream of a visionary scientist with the power to change the future of medicine.

Christopher Goodnow FAA FRS
Executive Director,
Garvan Institute of Medical Research, Sydney, Australia
(http://www.garvan.org.au)

3

ENDORSEMENT

Professor K: The Final Quest by Gabriel Farago is a stand-alone thriller and part of the Jack Rogan Mysteries Series. Dr. Alexandra Delacroix, Nobel Laureate, wants to continue the work on genome-editing pursued by the late Professor Kozakievicz. She has a God-given opportunity when the Vatican requests her help to save the Pope who is dying of an auto-immune disease. It is imperative that he remains alive to enable the conclusion of a crucial peace process. However, the secret to unlocking his disease is hidden away deep in time. The story transports us back in history to the Ottoman Empire and the work of another physician who is inextricably linked to the modern-day da Baggio family. Lorenza da Baggio wins Top Chef Europe, but she barely has time to celebrate her success before she is kidnapped and drawn into a sinister game played by the mafia.

Gabriel Farago writes effortlessly to present an absorbing and intriguing modern-day thriller steeped in the rich history of Italy. I was impressed with the many complex threads which were expertly interwoven and brought together to form a very satisfying finale to the book. I loved the wonderful descriptions of Venice, including the art and the buildings, all of which lent a real depth to the storyline. The dialogue was expertly written and spoken by a dazzling array of very charismatic characters including the rather unpredictable and dangerous Jack Rogan. Professor K: The Final Quest is a literary delight brimfull of culture, politics, terrorism, the mafia, and medicine. I can't fault it. Superb!

~Reviewed by Amanda Rofe for Readers' Favorite

INTRODUCTION

Istanbul. Sparkling gem on the Bosporus, where East and West collide and Europe meets Asia. I can think of no other metropolis where diverse cultures, religions, and thousands of years of history intersect in such a dramatic way. The name alone conjures up images of bloody conquests, fallen empires, armies marching into battle and stupendous buildings reaching to the heavens, where the *muezzin*'s haunting call echoes through ancient squares, calling the faithful to prayer.

Our guide – a Turkish archaeologist – had just taken us through the Topkapi Palace and the Hagia Sophia, one of the most awe-inspiring edifices on the planet.

'There's one more thing you have to see,' he said, pointing to a beautiful small pavilion next to the basilica. 'It's a *turbe*; a tomb. The tomb of Selim II. What I'm about to show you is a reminder of barbaric times, absolute power and murder. Not just any murder, but the most horrific mass murder imaginable. It's a sad part of our history that's often overlooked and rarely talked about. Even the historians here would like to forget all about it.'

Curiosity aroused, we took off our shoes and followed our guide inside. Designed by Sinan – the famous Ottoman architect – and built in 1577, the stunning building, decorated with colourful Iznik tiles and marble that reflected the bright morning sun, hides a dark secret. Expecting to find the tomb of Selim II, son of Suleiman the Magnificent and sultan of the Ottoman Empire from 1566 until his death in 1574, I was surprised to see many additional graves.

Silently, we followed our guide along the solemn rows of sarcophagi covered in green cloth, some of them quite small. 'I can see you are a little confused,' said our guide. 'If you think this looks more like a cemetery than a tomb, you are right. It is. As you can see, Selim is not alone. There are many others buried in here with him. That may be curious enough, but who they are, and how and why

5

many of them died, is far more intriguing and it will shock you.' Our guide paused, no doubt to let anticipation grow.

'To begin with,' he continued, 'we have five of Selim's sons buried next to him over there. They were all murdered on the night he died in December 1574. Why? To ensure that his eldest son, Murad III, would succeed him peacefully and without being challenged.'

'By silencing possible rivals?' I asked.

'Precisely.'

'And who are the others?'

'Nineteen of them are sons of Murad III, who were murdered on the night *he* died in January 1595. They were all strangled with a silk cord by deaf-mutes.

'Are you suggesting that by murdering all his half-brothers, the eldest son secured his succession and became the next sultan?'

'Yes.'

As we contemplated his words in stunned silence, I looked along the rows of solemn graves, each a sad reminder of a life cut short by naked ambition, lust for power, and fear. Momentarily overcome by the sadness of the moment, my mind began to wander. *What if one of them had somehow been spared?* I asked myself. *What if one of them had managed to escape, and survived? What if ...?*

For some reason, I couldn't get these haunting questions out of my mind. They stayed with me and became the inspiration for this book.

Gabriel Farago
Leura, Blue Mountains, Australia

PROLOGUE

Topkapi Palace, Constantinople: 16 January 1595
2:00 am

Fear and apprehension had spread like a deadly poison through the silent corridors of Topkapi Palace during the night. Murad III, grandson of Suleiman the Magnificent, Caliph of Islam, Amir al-Muminim, Sultan of the Ottoman Empire and Custodian of the Two Holy Mosques, was dying.

Safiye Sultan, Murad's favourite consort and mother of Mehmed, his eldest son and heir, knew it was time. To secure her son's accession, all possible rivals had to be silenced, swiftly and permanently. Her own future and position at the palace depended on it. Upon Murad's death she would become valide sultan – the powerful "mother" sultan – and Safiye was determined to make sure nothing stood in her way.

Safiye summonsed Gazanfer Ağa, chief of the white eunuchs and head of the Enderun – the Imperial Seraglio – to her chambers. 'Murad will not see the sun come up,' she said. 'As soon as he ascends to paradise you must act, without mercy. You know what to do.'

Gazanfer Ağa smiled, bowed, and took his leave. He knew that once he had carried out Safiye's deadly orders, she would be forever in his debt. This would not only consolidate his already considerable power, but elevate his position to dizzying heights. Gazanfer Ağa had carefully prepared for this moment. Everything was ready and in place. He knew the feared deaf-mutes were standing by and waiting for his orders.

Fatma Hatun, Murad's youngest consort, lay awake in her bedchamber. Gripped with fear and worry for her only son, Osman, who had just turned 16, she realised the dreaded event she had feared since the boy's birth had arrived. Carefully, she removed the beautiful tile behind her bed and reached into a hole in the wall. This was her secret hiding place that contained the precious gems – gifts from a besotted Murad – that could save her son's life. It also held other treasures that she was about to give to him.

Legs crossed and looking tense, Osman sat on a cushion in front of his mother, watching. Blessed with striking good-looks and an agile, inquisitive mind that thrived on curiosity and learning, Osman had been groomed for this moment all his life. He knew exactly what he had to do. His mother had gone over every step a thousand times before, except one.

'This is for you, my son,' she said, and handed Osman a small silver cylinder. 'Keep it on your person at all times and guard it with your life.'

'What is it?' asked Osman.

'Your future; open it.'

Osman opened the container and emptied its contents onto the carpet. First, a heavy little leather pouch filled with a small fortune in gold coins and gems slid out. Next, he pulled out a tightly rolled-up little canvas and several sheets of paper. When he unfurled the canvas, he saw that it was a stunning portrait of his mother, which he had never seen before. Surprised, he pointed to the painting spread out on the carpet in front of him.

'This was painted by Marco Vecellio, Titian's pupil. Your father commissioned the painting soon after I was given to him as a present by one of his sisters. I was sixteen, the same age as you.'

'And these?' asked Osman, holding up a few sheets of paper covered in beautiful calligraphy and decorated with exquisite miniature paintings at the top.'

Fatma smiled as she remembered the passionate nights spent with Murad. She had succeeded where others had failed. She had managed to reignite the sultan's appetite for carnal pleasures. 'These are recipes of the sultan's favourite dishes,' she said. 'I copied them myself from the originals that belonged to your great-grandfather, Suleiman the Magnificent, and are still kept here at the palace. These dishes are the best in the empire and the reason you exist. They are treasures …'

'I don't understand,' said Osman, looking puzzled.

'You will. One day. Now, however, it is time; come.'

Fatma handed Osman a small porcelain cup and kissed him tenderly on the forehead. 'Drink it,' she said, tears in her eyes. 'For a short while you will sink into a deep sleep. When you wake up, you will be safe … You know what to do?'

'Yes,' said Osman, and drained the cup.

'There is one more thing,' said Fatma. She took off the beautiful signet ring she wore on her right index finger – her only remaining contact with a happier past – and handed it to Osman. 'This was given to me by my father in Venice just before I was captured by pirates and became a slave. It now belongs to you. It will open many doors and show who you are, and where you come from. Keep it safe.'

'I will,' said Osman, his speech slurred by the powerful drug.

'Goodbye, my son,' whispered the distraught mother. 'We shall never meet again in this life. Perhaps in heaven? Who knows …?' Fatma, a Venetian Christian, fell to her knees and began to pray.

Murad looked at his favourite dwarfs and buffoons sitting on the carpet in front of his divan one last time, their colourful costumes a cheerful reminder of the fun times he had shared with them in the palace gardens. Then, with his eyesight fading, he turned his face slowly towards Mecca, and died.

Gazanfer Ağa walked over to the divan to make sure that the sultan was dead. Satisfied, he gave the signal. The deaf-mute standing at the door nodded and quickly left the room.

The three Nubian deaf-mutes hurried through the corridors of the inner palace like black angels of death, their excited, sweat-covered faces glistening in the moonlight. Purchased as young castrated boys, they had been brought to the palace as special slaves to be trained as eunuchs. Later, they had their tongues split to prevent them from speaking, and their eardrums burst with hot needles to make them deaf.

First, they dispatched the babies and toddlers. Strangling them quickly with the silk cords used for executions was easy, and took only a few minutes. The teenagers were more difficult to deal with. The assassins had to work as a team to kill them swiftly, and placate their hysterical mothers.

Bribery and corruption in the palace were rife, and greed was a powerful tool used by the ambitious and the ruthless to hatch conspiracies and forge alliances. Because Topkapi Palace was built like a fortress surrounded by high walls and guarded by an army of fierce janissaries, it had become a confined hotbed of power, where deadly rivals were often separated by only a corridor, a small courtyard or a thin wall. The eyes and ears of spies and traitors were never far away, and trust was as precious and as rare as diamonds.

When the assassins entered Osman's room, they saw Fatma standing in front of her drugged son lying on the carpet. This was a deliberate and prearranged ploy, making him appear lifeless and limp and therefore easier to handle without arousing suspicion.

One of the deaf-mutes pointed to Osman. Fatma nodded, handed him a fistful of precious gems wrapped in a silk handkerchief, and stepped aside. The tall Nubian stuffed the handkerchief into his pocket, lifted the boy off the floor and carried him outside.

It took the deaf-mutes less than an hour to kill all of Murad's nineteen other sons, put the bodies into sacks and have them removed from the harem by trusted slaves before the household woke to the news that the sultan was dead, and had been succeeded by his eldest son, Mehmed. When the sacks containing the bodies were lined up in a row in a secret underground chamber, awaiting burial, no-one appeared to have noticed that one of them wasn't dead.

Sunrise

'It's done,' said Gazanfer Ağa as the first rays of the morning sun banished the darkness, giving the still waters of the harbour below the palace a pinkish glow. Safiye smiled. With her son's accession now safe and assured, she had just become valide sultan, the most powerful woman in the empire.

Deep in the bowels of the Palace, two dwarfs entered the secret underground chamber. 'Where are you?' whispered one of them.

'Over here,' mumbled Osman. Still a little weak and feeling disorientated from the effects of the powerful drug, he began to wriggle inside the sack.

One of the dwarfs untied the rope at the top and helped Osman crawl out. 'Here, put this on,' he said, handing Osman clothes usually worn by the cooks in the kitchens. 'Quickly! Everything is ready.'

Safiye Sultan sat in the walled courtyard garden that only a few days ago had been the late sultan's favourite place in the entire palace. Elated, she looked thoughtfully across the still waters of the Golden Horn and contemplated the dawn of a new era in which she and her son, Mehmed, would rule one of the largest empires of their time. Immeasurable wealth and absolute power were at last within her grasp and years of careful, dangerous plotting were about to bear fruit. The thought of her rivals cowering in fear as they awaited their fate that she, as the new valide, now held in her tiny hands, made her heart beat faster.

She was about to close her eyes to savour the moment, when one of Gazanfer Ağa's dwarfs approached. At Safiye's signal, the dwarf walked over to his mistress and whispered something into her ear. Safiye paled. 'Get Gazanfer Ağa; quickly!' she commanded, and hurried inside. If what the dwarf had just told her was true, her new world was under serious threat and could collapse at any moment, burying her dreams forever.

Gazanfer Ağa stood in the secret underground chamber and counted the sacks containing the bodies of the murdered princes. *Nineteen,* he thought. *It can't be!* He counted them again. 'Open them!' he barked at last. Two dwarfs stepped forward and opened the sacks. Gazanfer Ağa walked slowly along the row of bodies lined up on the stone floor and carefully looked at each of the faces. Some – sightless, glassy eyes bulging like the eyes of a curious fish and tongues hanging out of mouths wide open in silent terror – were so contorted by their sudden, violent death, that Gazanfer Ağa had to look twice before he could recognise the once familiar features. *One is missing,* he thought. *Osman isn't here!*

When Safiye heard the dreaded news, she knew exactly who had to be behind it all; Fatma, Osman's mother. She also realised that Fatma could not have acted alone. This was a carefully planned conspiracy involving officials at the highest level. Safiye knew there were many at the palace who despised her and Mehmed, and would prefer another sultan. She also realised that Fatma's plan was as simple as it was brilliant. By removing all of Murad's sons except Osman, Safiye had unwittingly placed Osman next in line after Mehmed. Should something happen to Mehmed, Osman would become sultan. That was the law. Safiye's head began to spin as one word throbbed through her aching brain and refused to go away: *assassination!* Her son was in serious danger!

'How could this have happened?' demanded Safiye, seething.

'We'll know soon enough,' replied Gazanfer Ağa calmly.

'You have a plan?'

'Yes. Osman must be hiding somewhere inside the palace, so much is clear. I have already alerted the guards, and my most trusted deaf-mutes are searching every corner of the harem right now. We'll find him. Not even a mouse can leave this place without being discovered.'

'What else?'

'The three deaf-mutes who carried out the executions are in irons …'

'And Fatma?'

12

'Being interrogated right now, persuasively. It won't be long before we know everything.'

'Good. I don't have to remind you that we are not safe as long as Osman lives. Mehmed is in great danger. We must protect him!'

'Already taken care of.'

Not entirely convinced, but feeling better, Safiye looked at Gazanfer Ağa. *He's the most ruthless and ambitious man I know*, she thought, *and therefore my best protection. He knows exactly what will happen if he fails ... And so do I ...'*

Gazanfer Ağa's janissaries – the sultan's bodyguards – searched the palace with ruthless efficiency, mercilessly interrogating anyone suspected of having information about Prince Osman's whereabouts. Soon, the trail of torture-blood led to the palace kitchens. There, in one of the huge, vaulted chambers, they discovered something ominous.

'We've found something,' said the captain of the bodyguards. 'Come.'

Surprised, Gazanfer Ağa followed the captain to the massive kitchens. 'Good news, I hope,' he said.

The captain did not reply. Instead, he pointed to a wretch lying in a pool of blood on the stone floor. Barely alive, the man – a cook – was staring at Gazanfer Ağa with his remaining eye, blood oozing out of the empty socket of the other, which had been gouged out.

'What did you find?' demanded Gazanfer Ağa impatiently.

'This,' said the captain, and pointed to a rope dangling from a hook in the vaulted ceiling next to a chimney high above the kitchen floor.

Gazanfer Ağa looked up at the high ceiling and the open chimney at the top – just wide enough for a man to crawl through. A shiver of unfamiliar fear tingled down his spine. 'Do you think he could have ...?' he asked, shaking his head.

The captain pointed to the man on the floor. 'He just confirmed it,' said the janissary.

'When?'

'Two hours ago.'

'The roof's been searched?'

'Yes.'

'And?'

'We found another rope.'

'Where?'

'On top of the palace roof, near the main gate.'

'To help scale the wall leading outside?'

'It would appear so.'

'And Osman?'

'Nothing.'

Venice: January 1597 – two years later

A dense winter mist hovering above the murky waters of the Canal Grande covered Venice like a shroud. *It should be right here, near the Rialto Bridge,* thought the young man sitting in the back of the small rowing boat. He watched the ghostlike facades of the palazzos glide silently past like elaborate sets in some exotic play. Visibility was poor, and even his thick woollen cloak could do little to keep out the bone-chilling cold. As the vessel scraped along one of the posts used for tying up boats, the young man caught a glimpse of a familiar crest set into a stone arch above him. He looked at the signet ring on his little finger, and smiled.

'Stop! We are here,' he shouted, pointing to a tall, ornate building rising out of the mist. The man at the oars rowed over and tied up the boat. 'Wait here,' said the young man excitedly. He climbed out of the boat and almost slid on the wet, slippery wooden steps leading up to a narrow, moss-covered stone landing. He looked up at the massive portal, and again at the crest set into the stone above it, and nodded. *This is definitely it,* he thought, and pulled his dagger out of his belt. Using its heavy hilt, he knocked on the iron-studded wooden door, his heart beating like a drum.

The destination he had been dreaming about for two long years was finally within his grasp. Yet, now that he appeared to have reached what he had yearned for, doubts began to claw at his empty stomach, churning up uncertainty and a little fear.

For what seemed an eternity he stood in front of the door in silence, and listened. Nothing. Then he knocked again – this time harder – and placed his ear against the door. After a while, he thought he could hear footsteps. Then a key turned in the lock and the heavy door creaked slowly open. A small, wizened old man, his face a creased map of a long life of hardship, looked at him with watery eyes. 'What do you want?' he growled.

'I would like to see Cosimo da Baggio,' replied the young man, a little taken aback by the somewhat hostile reception.

'He's not receiving; go away.' Before the old man could close the door, the young man took a step forward and blocked it with his boot.

'I think he will,' he said calmly, pulling the ring off his finger and handing it to the old man. 'Give him this.'

The old man looked at the ring, his eyes wide with astonishment. *'Who are you?'* he asked after a while.

'His grandson.'

'Wait here,' whispered the old man, and closed the door.

The grand da Baggio family palazzo had seen better days. Built in the early sixteenth-century to impress and flaunt the wealth of the influential merchant family that had produced two doges, several cardinals, one pope and even a saint, it was now in obvious decline. The large entry foyer and central atrium with its imposing staircase, which the young man had heard so much about from his mother, should have been adorned with paintings by famous Venetian artists like Giorgione and Titian. Instead, the palazzo was empty, with only a few lonely family portraits gracing the corridors. Cold and damp, evidence of neglect was everywhere, a sad but accurate reflection of the family's waning fortunes.

'Not exactly what I expected,' said the young man, following the old man up the stairs. 'What happened?'

The old man stopped in front of a tall door on the first floor, caught his breath, and opened it. 'You'll find out soon enough,' he replied. 'The master is dying,' he added sadly, before stepping aside to let the young visitor enter.

At first, the young man couldn't see anything because it was almost completely dark in the room. The windows were covered with heavy brocade drapes, a fire crackling in a huge stone fireplace on the opposite side the only source of light in the dank room smelling of sickness and decay. As his eyes became accustomed to the gloom, the young man could make out a huge four-poster bed in front of the fire. Otherwise, the room appeared to be empty.

'Come closer where I can see you,' said a surprisingly strong voice coming from the direction of the bed.

The young man walked over to the bed and looked at the gaunt face staring at him.

A bony, shaking hand held up the ring. 'Where did you get this?'

'It's a long story.'

'I'm a good listener; sit.' The bony hand pointed to a chair by the fireplace. The young man pulled the chair across to the bed and sat down.

'What's your name?'

'Osman.'

'Hmm ... I am Cosimo da Baggio. Now tell me all about yourself.'

Over the next hour, Osman told his extraordinary story. He explained who he was, where he had come from, and why. He spoke of his mother with tenderness and love, and described life at the court of the sultan of the mighty Ottoman Empire. He spoke of growing up in the harem at Topkapi Palace watched over by his mother, who had taught him Italian, brought him up as a Christian in a Muslim world, and had told him many stories about Venice and her childhood in the very palazzo they were in. He recounted events and places in surprising detail only a person intimately acquainted with the da Baggio family and its history could possibly have known – all proof of who he was, and the truth of what he was telling. Cosimo only interrupted once, when Osman described his dramatic escape from Topkapi Palace and the reasons for it.

'Are you suggesting that nineteen of your half-brothers were killed the night your father died, to ensure your older brother's succession to the throne?' asked Cosimo, the incredulity in his voice obvious.

'Yes.'

'*Unbelievable.*'

'He's telling the truth,' said a deep voice coming out of the darkness. Osman turned around, surprised. He had assumed there was no-one else in the room. Slowly, a tall figure emerged out of the shadows and came closer, the skullcap, black cassock, purple sash and heavy gold pectoral cross a clear indication he was a prince of the

Church. 'I've heard reports about that horrible event, and the new sultan's men were looking for a young courtier last year, right here in Venice.'

The bony hand pointed again, this time to the tall figure standing next to Osman.

'This is Cardinal Urbano,' said Cosimo, introducing his younger brother.

'One thing bothers me,' said the cardinal. 'The fratricide took place almost two years ago ... Where have you been during that time?'

'After my escape from the palace, I made it safely down to the harbour and went into hiding. My plan was to board a merchant ship and get away as soon as possible. This turned out to be much more difficult than expected. The sultan's janissaries were everywhere, looking for me. I was a great threat to the new sultan, you see. Because he had killed all possible contenders to the throne, I was the only surviving rival. Should he die without an heir, I would become sultan. That's the law. As long as I lived, he wasn't safe ...' Osman paused, collecting his thoughts.

'What happened next?' prompted Cosimo.

'After lying low in a warehouse, I managed to get on board one of the ships by hiding inside a barrel. The ship sailed the next morning, and I became a stowaway. I had some food and water that would last for a few days, and no-one came down into the hold in the bowels of the ship to inspect the cargo. For the first time since leaving the palace, I felt safe. However, this illusion didn't last long.'

'Why?' asked the cardinal.

'On the third day of the journey, the ship was attacked by pirates. Fierce fighting erupted on deck, and I decided it was time to show myself. This I did, and joined in the melee. I thought that perhaps by making myself useful in repelling the attack – I am a good swordsman – I could find acceptance among the crew. For a while things looked promising, but then the pirates gained the upper hand and took the ship. Most of the crew were killed—'

'But not you,' interrupted Cosimo.

'No. I was captured and taken to the slave market in Alexandria. I was young and strong, and the pirates thought I was worth something to them alive. I was sold to a spice trader and began to work for him in his warehouse. Looking back, I think this saved my life. The sultan's agents and spies were searching for me everywhere. They were sent to every corner of the empire and a huge reward was offered for my capture.'

'I heard about that,' said the cardinal, nodding his head.

'Inside the spice trader's warehouse, no-one gave me a second look. I was a slave toiling from sun-up to sunset. I was invisible. I stayed there for a year, until a fortuitous event changed everything.'

'What happened?' asked the cardinal.

'A fire broke out. It wiped out most of the neighbourhood. The spice trader's warehouse burned to the ground. Many were killed, but I managed to make my escape. After that, I reinvented myself, became a seafarer and joined a Spanish merchant ship. This wasn't too difficult in Alexandria. Merchants were always looking for crew. After many a journey, I finally made it to Venice and … here I am,' said Osman quietly.

He reached inside his tunic and pulled out the metal tube his mother had given him the night of his escape from the palace. 'Somehow, I've been able to keep this safe during all that has happened to me,' said Osman. 'No-one thought of searching a poor wretch like me for anything valuable. I managed to conceal this container on my person and keep it with me at all times, just as my mother had instructed me to do.'

Osman opened the container and pulled out the little rolled-up painting. 'She asked me to give you this,' he whispered, his eyes misting over, and began to unfurl the painting. Leaning forward, Cosimo pushed himself up on his elbows to get a better look; the cardinal came closer.

'What is it?' asked Cosimo, frowning.

'Here, see for yourself,' said Osman, and placed the exquisite little painting on the bedcover in front of his grandfather. 'Your daughter sent you her love … and me.'

PART I
AL-QANUN

"The best physician is also a philosopher."
Galen

'Ladies and gentlemen, the moment you've been waiting for has arrived. It gives me great pleasure to introduce the winner of the 2014 Nobel Prize in Physiology or Medicine, Dr Alexandra Delacroix,' said the announcer, and stepped away from the microphone.

This is it, thought Alexandra as she walked past the King of Sweden and other dignitaries and then slowly up to the microphone, trying hard not to be overwhelmed by the enormity of the occasion. She had prepared herself for weeks for this moment, but nothing could have prepared her for the long and lonely walk to the podium, knowing that the eyes of the world were following her every step. But what gave her comfort and confidence was the realisation that in some reassuring way, Professor K – her friend and mentor – was walking along beside her. She could feel his presence and see his encouraging smile. *Speak from the heart, Lexi*, she heard him whisper, *it's always the best way*. All the tension and anxiety just seemed to melt away, leaving her with a feeling of calmness and confidence. For a moment, Alexandra stood in silence, collecting her thoughts while the world waited.

Wearing a simple, elegant black dress that set off her stunning and beautifully coiffured red hair, and a lovely string of pearls given to her by her mother on her graduation day, Alexandra radiated modesty and class.

'Your majesties, royal highnesses, ladies and gentlemen,' she began, 'you will not be surprised to hear that I have tried to prepare myself for weeks for this day. I have agonised over every word I would say, and have carefully chosen what I would talk about, and why. Yet, as I stand here before you everything has changed, because I realise that you cannot prepare for something as momentous as this in advance. So, I have decided to tear up my mental notes and start again.

'Progress in science is a collegiate matter and breakthroughs do not happen in isolation. More often than not, we stand on the shoulders of others to connect with that spark of inspiration, or take that idea a step further, or in a different direction. This is certainly true in my case. I wouldn't be standing here tonight if it hadn't been for the groundbreaking work of my mentor and friend, the late Professor Kozakievicz, affectionately known as Professor K because no-one could pronounce his name.

'As scientists, we often stare into the darkness, in awe of nature and its baffling complexity. However, Professor K believed we must not be seduced by its beauty, nor cowed by its terror, but must always be on the lookout for inspired ideas to improve the journey of man.

'As we stare into the darkness, something extraordinary is now happening. A shaft of light is slowly banishing the darkness and lifting the curtain of ignorance. What is that light? I firmly believe it is the dawn of a new era in medicine as we explore a treasure-trove of evolution hidden in our genes. The secrets are all there.' Alexandra paused, her thoughts racing back to Professor K's letter that had explained it all.

'Professor K taught me that inspired ideas and true genius are immortal,' she continued, 'and the only reason I can glimpse that shaft of light is because I am standing on his shoulders; humbled, yet full of confidence for the future.' Alexandra paused again, raised her hands, and pointed to the spellbound audience in front of her in a gesture of embrace. 'Our future,' she added quietly. 'Thank you.'

For a moment there was stunned silence, then the room erupted in enthusiastic applause, honouring an outstanding young woman and her remarkable mentor.

Almost blinded by the cameras, Alexandra smiled at the king as she walked slowly back to her table and sat down. 'That was quite something,' said Jack as soon as the applause ebbed away. 'How do you feel?'

'Drained.'

'That will pass, but the memory will linger. This is your moment.'

'Thanks, Jack.'

'I have something for you.'

'Oh? What?'

'The answer to a puzzle. Look under your serviette.'

Alexandra took a sip of champagne, lifted her serviette and looked at the handwritten note in front of her. It only contained one word. '*Al-Qanun*?' she said. 'Ibn Sina's famous medical text? What's all this about?' she asked, surprised.

'Remember the other painting we found hidden in Empress Marie-Louise's sarcophagus?'

'In the Imperial Crypt in Vienna, under the Monet?' replied Alexandra.

'That's the one.'

'Yes, of course. You showed it to me; it was badly damaged.'

'It was. And you were intrigued by it, and frustrated because we couldn't read the writing on the book—' said Jack.

'Held up by the man standing next to the patient's bed,' Alexandra interrupted, becoming animated.

'You were sure it had to be a medical text because the man looked like a physician.'

'Yes, because of his clothing and because he was pointing to the book in his hand with what looked like some kind of scalpel, or surgical instrument.'

'At least now we know all about the book: it's *al-Qanun*,' said Jack, 'the same book Professor K mentions in his papers.'

'What! Are you sure?'

'No doubt about it. The restoration has revealed the writing: *al-Qanun*.'

'The book Professor K's father had been searching for during the war; amazing!'

'And so did the notorious Dr Steinberger in Auschwitz – remember?' said Jack.

'You are right; he did. So, what's the connection? How does all this fit together? Any ideas?'

Jack nodded, smiling.

'Come on Jack; tell me!'

'There was quite a bit of sleuthing involved here before I realised what the connection was. We knew the painting had to be important, but we had no idea why, and Brother Francis's diary was very vague about it all.'

'Are you trying to kill me with suspense,' said Alexandra, 'or are you going to tell me?'

'The answer is Brother Francis himself.'

'I don't understand.'

'Who he really was, before he left Germany after the war and became Brother Francis.'

'You know?'

'Yes.'

'Well?

'He was SS Sturmbannfuehrer Franz Berghofer. And do you know who one of his close collaborators was during the war?'

'Tell me.'

'Dr Erwin Steinberger.'

'The Auschwitz doctor. Those dreadful medical experiments. How extraordinary! So, that's the connection.'

'Yes, and don't forget, Professor K's father was there too,' said Jack.

'But what does it all mean?' Alexandra looked at Isis sitting opposite, nodding. 'You knew about this?' she asked.

'Yes, we worked on it together,' replied Isis. 'I have lots of contacts in the art world. Good restorers are difficult to find. But it was Jack who pieced it all together. He's the master detective.'

'You two make quite a team, I can see,' said Alexandra, beginning to relax. She picked up the piece of paper and looked at Jack. 'Do you know if the book still exists; and if so, where it may be?' she asked hopefully.

'I'm working on it, but there's a lot more,' said Jack. 'We'll talk about it later.'

'I too have something for you, Alexandra,' said Isis, changing the subject.

26

'Oh?'

'The Time Machine Foundation has decided to sponsor a chair for you at the Gordon Institute for five years to support your research. It's all arranged.'

'What a wonderful idea,' said Jack. 'Congratulations!'

'Has CRISPR inspired you?' asked Alexandra, referring to a recent groundbreaking discovery which makes it possible to edit the human genome.

'It's much more than that. You and Professor K saved my life,' said Isis, lowering her voice. *It's the least I can do.*'

'I don't know what to say,' said Alexandra quietly, her eyes misting over.

'Say nothing,' said Jack, 'and enjoy the moment. You deserve it.'

Reykjavik: 11 December 2015

It was twenty-below zero and snowing, and the trip to Stockholm Arlanda airport had taken longer than usual in the early morning darkness.

'Here we are,' said Jack, helping Alexandra out of the taxi, the cheek-numbing cold hitting her like an arctic blast. 'We must hurry!'

'When are you going to tell me where we are going?' asked Alexandra, unable to hide her anxiety. She had barely slept a wink since last night's celebration banquet, and was still on a high.

'Soon.'

'Why not now?'

'Then it wouldn't be a surprise, would it?'

'But we are at the airport.'

'I'll give you a clue: It's on your bucket list,' said Jack, enjoying himself.

'What is?'

'What we are about to do.'

'You do know I have to catch a flight back to Sydney in two days?'

'Of course; trust me.'

Unpredictable, disarmingly charming, but always a little reckless, thought Alexandra, shaking her head. But she had to admit that this was precisely what made being with Jack so exciting and so much fun.

With the Christmas holiday season approaching, Stockholm airport was exceptionally busy and the departure lounge was already packed with eager tourists.

'Gate two,' said Jack. 'Here we are.' He reached into his pocket, and handed Alexandra a ticket. 'You'll need this,' he added, grinning.

'Reykjavik? *We are going to Iceland?* You can't be serious!'

'You wanted to get away from the limelight and "chill out", right?'

'I said that?'

'You did; right after the banquet.'

'But I didn't mean literally ...'

'Don't worry. After all the glitz and glamour, this will do you good.'

'Chill out in *Iceland?*'

'Can you think of a better place?' said Jack, a mischievous sparkle in his eyes.

'Seriously, Jack, why Iceland?'

'Can't you guess?'

'Aurora Borealis – the Northern Lights?' asked Alexandra hopefully.

'You can always trust a Nobel laureate to get it right. Row three; lead the way.'

Alexandra realised her life had changed, but she was determined not to allow her new celebrity status to become a distraction and dominate her life. She knew that medical research was her destiny and she owed it to Professor K to pursue his legacy. She had made a promise. Her mother had returned to Paris with Countess Kuragin and the other guests after the award ceremony, and Isis had flown back to London with Lola, leaving her and Jack in Stockholm to have some quiet time together before her long flight back to Sydney – alone – because Jack was once again spending Christmas at the Kuragin Chateau.

Due to her heavy workload at the Gordon Institute, Alexandra had only managed to get away for one week to attend the award ceremony, give her mandatory Nobel lecture and receive the prize. Australia and the Gordon were waiting to welcome the Nobel Prize winner, with several television appearances already scheduled for the day after her arrival, followed by a dinner with the prime minister in her honour in Canberra on Saturday night. The two days with Jack were therefore particularly precious.

'This reminds me of our flight to Sydney,' said Alexandra, leaning back in her comfortable seat as the aircraft taxied along the runway, ready for take-off, 'just after we met.'

'When I asked you to become my flatmate,' said Jack, 'and you called me a dangerous man?'

'Very good. Nothing's changed.'

'What, I'm still a dangerous man?'

'No, in fact you are an incorrigible rascal, but I didn't know that at the time, did I?'

'That's a little harsh, don't you think?'

'And unpredictable, and a little reckless at times. Like right now, for example,' added Alexandra.

'Come on ...'

'Well, getting woken in the middle of the night to be told to quickly get dressed – without any warning, mind you – and pack some overnight stuff because we are going away ... somewhere. What would you call that, eh?'

'I don't remember any objections.'

'No. I was too tired.'

'Nonsense! You are the one who moved in with a dangerous bloke you had just met and became his flatmate, just like that – remember?'

'True, but I didn't know he was an incorrigible rascal at the time, did I?' countered Alexandra.

'But now you know.'

'I sure do.'

'Well?'

'Well what?'

'You fancy incorrigible rascals; admit it.'

Alexandra leaned over to Jack and kissed him on the cheek. 'Spot-on; thanks, Jack,' she said.

'You don't mind the trip then?'

'Wouldn't miss it for the world!'

'Women!' mumbled Jack, shaking his head.

'Did you say something?'

'We should drink to that,' replied Jack, deftly sidestepping.

'I like your style. Champagne at seven in the morning. You can always count on—'

'What?' interrupted Jack, laughing.

'Incorrigible rascals.'

'I give up!'

'That lecture of yours about exceptional responders the other day had the scientists spellbound,' said Jack. 'I watched them. It was one of the highlights of Nobel Week. The whole of Stockholm was talking about it and the media loved it.'

'If you say so. I was very nervous.'

'Could have fooled me. What exactly are exceptional responders, and why are they so important?'

Feeling relaxed after two glasses of champagne, Alexandra turned towards Jack and reached for his hand. 'Let me give you an example. Let's assume for the moment that you are an Olympic athlete; a gold medallist say, in cross-country skiing and, as it turns out, so is your younger brother, and your father was one too. Well, we would say that's just too much of a coincidence; there has to be more to this. Something biological, something in the genes that the family members have in common and gives them the edge. Perhaps something about oxygen retention in the blood, something like that. Definitely worth investigating from a scientific point of view, because that makes them exceptional responders and we would love to know what it is that makes them what they are. And the good news is, we can now do just that.'

'How?'

'By sequencing their genome and then interrogating the results to find out what they have in common that may be making the difference.'

'And this would be helpful?'

'Absolutely. But it doesn't stop there, and it's certainly not just about supreme athletes. Take that holy man in India who feels no pain, for example; why? Or that small group of Eskimos in a remote village who all lived to a hundred? Or that man in Chicago who smoked all his life, drank a bottle of whisky a day and is now in his nineties without having had one day of ill health. Or that little boy who responded to a certain drug in a most unexpected way, which completely cured his illness that had been considered fatal. Do you get my drift?"

'So, Oscar Wilde's Dorian Gray who never grew old would fit into this?'

'Not quite. We are talking about nature here, not the paranormal,' said Alexandra, laughing.

'Just kidding. You are searching for those hidden genes, right?'

'Exactly. It's the next step. Professor K was a visionary; he knew this. His papers make this very clear. He was looking at exceptional responders long before others thought about it. Of course at that time, we didn't have the capacity to sequence the genome, which is the key to all this. But now we have. With the Illumina X-Ten at Gordon, right next to my lab,' Alexandra added, becoming quite excited. 'It's the dawn of a new era. Exciting times.'

'As we stare into the darkness, something extraordinary is now happening.' teased Jack, lowering his voice.

'Stop it!' Alexandra punched Jack in the ribs. 'But it's true. Exceptional responders could turn out to be that shaft of light that is slowly banishing the darkness and lifting the curtain of ignorance. I had that in mind when I said that yesterday at the dinner. Professor K certainly believed that. This idea of investigating exceptional responders from around the world has unbelievable potential, and I intend to use my new chair Isis has so generously donated, for precisely such a project.'

'And your new status as a Nobel laureate should give it some additional gravitas?' interjected Jack.

'I hope so.'

'You should be able to involve some of the top scientists in the project. Everyone loves to rub shoulders with a Nobel Prize winner.'

'I suppose.'

'Perhaps you could call it *The Hidden Genes of Professor K*?' ventured Jack, a little mischief glistening in his eyes.

Alexandra nodded. 'Not such a bad idea, actually.'

'Let's drink to that.'

'Why not? Thanks to you, I'm already a little tipsy. One more won't hurt.'

'You are not an exceptional responder then – in the alcohol resistance department, I mean,' said Jack.

'I'm not, but you could be.'

Jack had arranged a private tour to take them from their hotel in Reykjavik to the best viewing area for the Northern Lights. Their tour guide, a young meteorologist, was confident. Apparently, the conditions were perfect and the viewing had been excellent for a number of days now, and he expected it to be the same that evening.

They didn't have to go far before the heavens lit up, presenting one of the most awe-inspiring spectacles on the planet. The guide stopped the car on a ledge above a rugged valley. As they got out of the car, they stepped into a magical world of enchantment and wonder, like something out of a winter fairytale.

'Wow!' Look at that,' said Alexandra, overcome by the ethereal beauty of the moment. She had seen documentaries about Aurora Borealis before, but the real thing was infinitely more spectacular than she could have imagined.

Alexandra reached for Jack's hand and for a while they stood in silence, watching the pale, yellow-green light dance across the clear night sky, like some extraterrestrial light show entertaining the gods.

'In awe of nature, but not seduced by its beauty, nor cowed by its terror,' whispered Jack.

'You remembered?' said Alexandra.

'How could I forget? Your speech was inspirational.'

'It's difficult not to be seduced by this beauty, isn't it?'

'Sure is.'

'Do you know what causes this?'

'A collision between electrically charged particles escaping from the sun and swept through space as solar wind, and gaseous particles in the earth's atmosphere.'

'Very good, and the colours?'

'This pale, yellowish-green is produced by oxygen molecules. On rare occasions you can see an all red aurora caused by oxygen much higher up in the atmosphere. You can also have a blue or purplish-red aurora created by nitrogen.'

'How do you know all this?'

'I wrote some articles about it as a young freelance journo a long time ago. I saw the Northern Lights for the first time in Finland. Never forgotten it.'

'You are full of surprises, Jack Rogan.'

Then, the spectacular shapes of the celestial light show changed again and created what looked like a stairway to heaven. Deeply moved, Alexandra remembered Professor K's last words: 'At least it hasn't been in vain ...'

'No,' whispered Alexandra, tears in her eyes, 'it hasn't. I promise.'

As she watched the shapes change again, Alexandra thought she could hear her mentor whisper something in her ear: *CRISPR, Lexi, CRISPR is the answer. Remember that!*

On the way to London: 12 December 2015

Jack and Alexandra caught the early morning flight back to Stockholm the next day. Alexandra was due to fly to Sydney from London; it was a tight schedule, but doable.

'You like living on the edge, don't you?' said Alexandra.

'I don't know what you mean,' said Jack, feigning surprise.

'That was very thoughtful of you.' Alexandra turned to Jack sitting next to her on the plane and kissed him on the cheek. 'Thanks for bringing me here; that light show was ... magical. You know, something happened to me last night.'

'Oh?'

'As we were watching that ethereal stairway to heaven out there in the freezing cold, everything became very clear to me.'

'What do you mean?'

'My research; my life; the way forward. Everything.'

'A little enlightenment?'

'Something like that. You know what I mean, don't you?'

'Aha.'

'You believe in destiny.'

'You know I do.'

'It was a moment of destiny.'

Alexandra looked out the window and watched the stunning rock formations on Reynisfjara Beach glide past below, conjuring up images of Viking boats rowing into battle, migrating whales ploughing the wild seas and volcanoes glowing in the dark like ancient beacons showing the way through a wilderness frozen in ice and time.

'Do you think we could have a look at the painting before I fly back to Sydney?' said Alexandra. 'I have a few hours to spare in London tomorrow.'

'Should be possible; I'll call Isis. But why?'

'I can't get the painting out of my mind.'

'Is it the book, *al-Qanun*?'

'Partially. It's what Professor K says about it that's haunting me.'

35

'What does he say?'

'He believed that something very important is buried somewhere in the text.'

'But Ibn Sina's *al-Qanun* has been known for centuries; it's certainly nothing new. Until the seventeen-hundreds, it was the main medical reference source used in European universities. Scholars have analysed it line by line; scores of books, treatises and articles have been written about it. The libraries are full of it.'

'True. You've obviously done your homework. But what do you really *know* about *al-Qanun*, Mr adventurer-detective?'

'Is this some kind of test?' asked Jack.

'Take it any way you like.'

'Okay. Here we go. I first came across Ibn Sina in Vienna a few years ago.'

'In Vienna? How come?'

'The inauguration of the Persian Scholar's Pavilion in June 2009 at the United Nations Office in Vienna.'

'I know the pavilion. You were there?' asked Alexandra, surprised.

'I was. Iran donated a delightful little stone pavilion showcasing classic Persian architectural features, especially the Chartaghi.'

'Chartaghi? What's that?'

'A sacred Persian concept. Among other things, it symbolises the four holy geographical directions. In essence, it's a shelter constructed of four vaults that stand on four pillars. Displayed inside the pavilion are the statues of four famous Persian scientists. Do you know who they are?'

'I do. Razi, the physician and chemist who discovered alcohol and sulphuric acid; Biruni, mathematician and astrologer – he discovered the rotation of the earth; Omar Khayyam, poet, philosopher, mathematician and astronomer who came up with the formula of Pascal's Triangle, and—'

'Wait. Ibn Sina, known in the West as Avicenna,' interrupted Jack and opened his notebook. 'Philosopher and physician. He lived in Hamadan and Jurjan from 980 to 1037 CE. Omar Khayyam taught philosophy based on his ideas for decades.'

'Bravo,' said Alexandra, impressed. 'But what about *al-Qanun*?'

'*Al-Qanun* is Ibn Sina's most famous work. Its full title is *Al-Qanun Fi Al-Tibb* – The Canon of Medicine. It was translated into Latin by Gerard of Cremona in around 1150 CE and became the main medical reference book in European Medieval schools of medicine for centuries,' Jack said, tapping his finger on his notes.

'Very good; what else?'

'*You want more?*'

Alexandra nodded.

'It is most appropriate that Sina is sitting next to Razi in the pavilion. You want to know why?'

'Tell me.'

'Because Sina was greatly influenced by Razi's monumental work on medicine – all twenty-five volumes of it – called *al-Hawi*.'

'Professor K talks a lot about *al-Hawi* in his notes,' interjected Alexandra. 'Do you know what it is?'

'A kind of compilation of Razi's medical notes and various Arabic texts used by him at the time on pathology, therapy, pharmacy and so on. An early Arabic medical encyclopedia assembled after his death.'

'Correct, and Professor K was particularly interested in the pharmacological sections. But Sina is even more important because his approach was much broader than Razi's and included many additional areas of medicine not dealt with in *al-Hawi*.'

'But surely this is all history and hardly relevant to cutting-edge genomics?' said Jack.

'Not so sure. Remember *De Medicina* and the Aztec medicinal plant that gave us Demexilyn and showed us the way to KALM 30?'

'Professor K's hidden gene. Point taken. Do you think the good Professor was onto something similar here?'

'Don't know. Steinberger was looking for *al-Qanun* too.'

'The Auschwitz doctor?'

'Yes. As you know, he was obsessed with ancient medical texts. He believed the answers to many of our vexing medical problems can be found in such writings.'

'Well, in some ways then he wasn't that different from Professor K, was he?' interjected Jack.

'Up to a point perhaps, but Professor K believed the answers are not necessarily to be found in ancient texts, but hidden in our genes ...'

'Footprints of evolution buried in our genome, telling us of problems recognised and solved along the way,' said Jack.

'That's very good, coming from someone like you.'

'Someone like me? What do you mean?'

'An enlightened amateur and hopeless optimist.'

'I can live with that. But something puzzles me here.'

'What exactly?'

'*Al-Qanun* has been well known for a long time. It has been freely available to scholars for centuries. It's in all the libraries. So why search for it? *What was he looking for?*'

'I hope the painting will be able to answer that.'

'You think so?' said Jack.

'Yes. The painting and Professor K's papers. I already have an idea. Unfortunately, Professor K's notes are difficult to follow at best. Most of the time they are cryptic like a puzzle. They reflect his thinking; no straight lines here, I can tell you. Only ideas, hunches and a lot of speculation; theories, possibilities, stuff like that. But always following a golden thread of logic and often taking us into hidden corners never before thought to be important. Inspired connections, I call them.'

'Genius at work?'

'Oh yes.'

'And you think there's more to *al-Qanun*?'

'I'm sure of it.'

'And the painting could help?'

'It could.'

'You know something, don't you?' Jack probed again.

'Possibly.'

'You're toying with me!'

'Perhaps just a little,' admitted Alexandra. 'Now, how about some champagne?'

38

'At seven in the morning?'
'Incorrigible rascals are excellent teachers.'
'Ah.'
'And I'm a fast learner.'
'I can see that.'

Time Machine Studios, London: 13 December 2015

Boris gave Jack a rib-crushing bear hug and put the luggage into the boot of the Bentley. 'Good to see you again, Jack,' he said, and opened the back door for Alexandra.

'You have friends in unexpected places, Jack. I'm glad he's on our side,' said Alexandra, and pointed to Boris's huge back.

'A gentle giant and a wonderful man,' said Jack. 'Former wrestler. He's been Isis's bodyguard for years. Good friend of Tristan's,' added Jack, lowering his voice.

'You're a lucky guy, you know.'

'I am?'

'You make friends easily. It comes naturally to you. You see people differently, and reach out,' said Alexandra quietly, and squeezed Jack's hand. 'Never change.'

'You mean that? After all the criticism and flack I copped lately ...'

'Oh, just shut up! Why can't you just accept a compliment?'

'See what I mean?'

'You're in for a real treat,' said Jack as they stepped into the glass lift taking them up to Isis's apartment on the top floor of the Time Machine Studios overlooking the Thames. 'I remember my first visit here; I was gobsmacked.'

'So, that's how billionaires live?' said Alexandra, enjoying the ride.

Isis was waiting for them at the lift door. 'What a pleasant surprise,' she said, and kissed Alexandra on the cheek. 'I didn't expect to see you so soon.'

'I hope you don't mind,' said Jack, 'but Alexandra really wanted to see the painting before she flies back to Sydney later today. She has a few ideas ... and a few questions. But we haven't got much time.'

'No problem; it's right there.'

Alexandra walked over to the painting displayed on an easel in the middle of the large room. 'Wow! What a transformation,' she said, letting her eyes wander over the painting and trying to take it all in, especially the writing on the book cover. 'I can't believe it's the same painting. It looks fabulous!'

'The restorers have done a marvellous job,' said Isis, obviously pleased with Alexandra's reaction. 'It's a fine painting.'

'But we still don't know who painted it?' said Jack.

'No, but we know a little more about it,' replied Isis.

'We do?'

'Absolutely. Drink?'

'Why not?'

'Champagne?'

'Sure.'

Alexandra turned around. 'I can see you two make a great team,' she said, 'like two peas in a pod.'

'Mr Mendel may have something to say about that; what do you think?' remarked Jack, laughing.'

'So what do we know about it?' asked Alexandra.

'The experts agree that the style, the dazzling colours, the compositions and so on suggest it was painted in the sixteenth or early seventeenth-century, which makes it a late Renaissance painting; Italian. In fact, it is a classic mannerist painting.'

'What's that?'

'Mannerism is an artistic style,' said Isis, 'which originated in Rome during the early fifteen-hundreds. In fact, this painting is an excellent example. See here the elongated limbs of the man standing by the bed; his thin, aquiline nose, undersized head and vibrant colours? The almost theatrical composition makes it a typical mannerist painting. Some of the best-known mannerists were Veronese, El Greco, Vasari and Bronzino. This painter has certainly been influenced by El Greco, and may even have been a pupil, but we don't know for certain.'

'So, does any of this help?' asked Jack.

'Not sure. The reason I wanted to see the painting is this ...' Alexandra pointed to the man holding the book, his thin, bearded face clearly reflected in the mirror above the bed. 'The key to it all is the man; this man.'

'Oh? Why?' asked Isis.

'Because if we find him, we may be able to find this here.' Alexandra moved her finger slowly along the man's left arm without touching the painting, and then pointed to the book.'

'But now we know what that book is. It's Ibn Sina's *al-Qanun*. The writing is clear.'

'So it is. However, there was a Venetian physician who not only used *al-Qanun* as a reference book like most of the physicians of his time but went a step further. He *added* to it, substantially. And he did this by annotating the text and inserting his own personal notes and observations. He created his own, unique, expanded version of *al-Qanun*.'

'Amazing. Do we know who the physician was?' asked Isis.

'Unfortunately, we don't. That's the really frustrating bit,' replied Alexandra.

Impressed, Jack looked at her. 'How do you know all this?' he asked.

'Because of what you told me, and because of what's in Professor K's papers,' replied Alexandra, enjoying herself. 'In fact, you gave me the important clue, although you didn't know it at the time.'

Jack shook his head. 'I don't understand,' he said.

'Remember you said that Brother Francis made some oblique reference to the painting in his diary?'

'Yes.'

'Can you remember what that was?'

'Of course. He mentioned a trip to Venice during the war. He was trying to find a certain book, some kind of medical text used in the Middle Ages. He didn't say any more about it, but he did mention Dr Steinberger and Auschwitz. That's how I made the connection,' said Jack. 'He didn't find the book, but he did locate a painting that apparently had some bearing on it.' Jack pointed to the painting. 'This one.'

'That's the link,' said Alexandra, becoming quite excited. 'Some parts of the physician's notes and annotations were known to

Farago

Professor K's father and to Dr Steinberger in Auschwitz. Somehow, they must have had access to at least some parts of his book, or some writings about it; enough to make them interested. Very interested. We just don't have any—'

'But what they *did* find was important?' interrupted Jack.

'Yes, but incomplete.'

'Important enough to keep searching for more?'

'It seems so.'

'Any ideas?' Isis asked.

'Professor K's notes can be very challenging. I'm still trying to piece it all together, but it appears to relate to a type of cancer or autoimmune disease, and some unique treatment that seems to have worked. Some kind of drug known only to the physician. I think that's what got Steinberger so interested.'

'A bit like that Mexican jungle plant?' suggested Jack.

'Yes, but that's only part of it.'

'What do you mean?' said Isis.

Alexandra ran her fingers through her hair. 'It's complicated,' she said.

'Try,' said Jack.

'Somehow, the disease described by the physician, and the treatment, sparked a certain train of thought in Professor K ...' Alexandra paused, trying to work out how best to proceed. 'An inquiry into something new and quite radical; revolutionary.'

'Do you know what it was?'

'Yes. CRISPR.'

'What's that?' asked Jack.

'A game changer. It is perhaps the most important medical breakthrough of our time. Something that could transform medicine as we know it.'

'Are you serious? How?' demanded Jack.

'By trying to rewrite the genetic code in humans to treat disease.'

'Wow!'

'Coming from someone who's just received the Nobel Prize for medicine, that's certainly something,' said Isis. 'Can you tell us more?'

43

'Sure. CRISPR stands for "clustered regularly interspersed short palindromic repeats". Until recently, only a handful of scientists around the world knew what this was.'

'And Professor K was one of them?' asked Jack.

'Yes, in a way. In fact, now that I have a better understanding of his papers, I believe that was exactly what he was working on when he died. Genome-editing. He called it gene-therapy.'

'What is it?' asked Isis.

'CRISPR is a biomedical engineering technique that allows us to locate and change almost any piece of DNA in any species, including humans.'

'Incredible!' said Jack. 'I had no idea something like this existed.'

'I'm not surprised. But the technology involved is based on a unique survival mechanism; a clever evolutionary stunt used by bacteria to fend off infection by viruses. It's been around for hundreds of millions of years.'

'And this is important now because ...?' asked Isis.

'Let me explain.'

'Layman's speak, please,' said Jack, wagging his finger.

Alexandra looked at her watch. 'There isn't much time. I have to leave soon.' she said.

'Boris knows all the shortcuts to the airport; don't worry,' said Isis.

'It's all about a war between cunning viruses and clever bacteria. Rather than developing their own reproductive system, viruses found another, easier way to propagate by inserting their genetic material into that of other cells. And that included bacteria. Not surprisingly, bacteria didn't appreciate this and fought back – effectively. How? Here comes the really clever bit,' said Alexandra, warming to her subject. 'With me so far?'

Jack and Isis nodded, fascinated.

'Think of this as a battle. Bacteria found an ingenious way to take hostages: they held on to bits of the virus's genes when they were invaded, or infected would be a better way to put it. Then what did they do? Like on a battlefield, the bacteria released their secret weapon.'

'What kind of secret weapon?' Jack asked, intrigued.

'A barrage of magic swords.'

'How fascinating,' said Isis.

'Wait, it gets better,' said Alexandra. 'Here comes the magic. These special swords only attacked and cut invaders, and they did so in a very targeted way. They only attacked the enemy, and never engaged in friendly fire.'

'How did they do that?' asked Jack.

'That's the ingenious part. They used the bits of the virus's genes they had obtained during the invasion as a kind of barcode.'

'What, like in a supermarket?' Isis said.

'Exactly! They used the gene bits as a mechanism to recognise the invaders, and then proceeded to destroy them.'

'Unbelievable!' exclaimed Jack.

'Sure is. They would attack the invaders – the lethal DNA bits – with their magic swords – a genetic sequence – which in essence would disarm or neutralise the invading DNA bits by cutting them out. Game over.'

'Magic swords, eh?' said Jack.

'Something like that.'

'And this is a game changer?' asked Isis. 'How?'

'It certainly is. Okay, so bacteria have this unique and effective defence mechanism to ward off invading viruses. The real breakthrough came in 2012 when it was discovered that not only bacterial DNA can perform this clever trick, but that *any* piece of DNA can do it. The implications are truly stupendous.' Alexandra looked at her watch again. 'There is a lot more to all this as you can imagine, but—'

'But Professor K died in 2011,' interrupted Jack. 'So, he wouldn't have known about this discovery?'

'No, but he was onto it. He was actually looking into this very possibility well before that discovery was made. He was a visionary, ahead of his time, and I would love to take his vision a step further and perhaps turn it into reality and make it his legacy.'

'How?' asked Isis.

'By testing CRISPR on humans.'

'Is that possible?' asked Jack.

'It's actually surprisingly simple and inexpensive.'

'So?'

'It's very controversial but medical communities around the world are looking into it, frantically. And so are big-time investors, right now. Pouring millions into CRISPR research. In fact, it's a bit of a race ... Once this genie is out of the pipette, there's no holding it back.'

'So, what's holding *you* back?' asked Isis.

'Red tape and funding; especially funding. This would have to be a privately funded project because official support isn't forthcoming. Certainly not for a while. Lots of obstacles, mainly ethical and moral. Very frustrating, but not really surprising. We are talking about a technology with the potential to change human evolution; powerful stuff and very dangerous in the wrong hands ...' For an instant, Alexandra looked quite dejected. 'But that's medical research, I'm afraid. I'm sorry; I really must go or I'll miss my flight.'

'What kind of funding are we talking about here?' asked Isis casually, as they walked to the lift.

Alexandra laughed. 'About twenty million or so would kick it off, I suppose,' she said, 'with no guarantee of any return. See what I mean?'

'If you had that kind of money – personally, I mean – would you put your money into such a venture?'

'Without hesitation,' said Alexandra. 'But I am a scientist, not a businesswoman.'

"The only thing necessary for the triumph of evil is for good men to do nothing."
Edmund Burke

1

St Peter's Basilica was packed with thousands of worshippers hoping to catch a glimpse of Pope Pius XIII celebrating mass. It was the highlight of the spectacular 2016 Easter celebrations, watched by millions on TV across the globe and in St Peter's Square outside.

After the sudden death of Pope Julius three years earlier, Cardinal Brandauer – hawkish Dean of the College of Cardinals – had been the frontrunner during the long, divisive conclave that followed. However, to everyone's surprise, Cardinal Marco Contarini, Patriarch of Venice, was elected and became Pope Pius XIII. He was known as a consummate diplomat and skilful politician who believed in a more proactive role and involvement of the Church in world affairs, especially in the bloody, devastating civil war in Syria that had raged for most of his pontificate and cast a disturbing shadow across the world.

Pope Pius had made it his mission to somehow broker peace in the troubled region, and was determined to build a "bridge" between Islam and the Catholic Church. He believed tolerance and constructive dialogue between faiths were the answer, not misguided world domination. This radical departure from traditional Church policy that believed in the separation of church and state had brought with it great controversy, many admirers, but also many enemies, especially among the cardinals – many of whom did not agree with this approach.

And they were not alone. Several world leaders, especially Russia's President Putin, didn't approve either and resented the pope's meddling in global politics. The whole Muslim world viewed the pope's peace overtures with suspicion, suspecting a modern-day crusade. However, they all knew that the pope had clout; lots of it.

When he spoke, billions listened, and he was not afraid to speak his mind and remind world leaders of the devastation and misery they were causing for political gain, self-interest and naked ambition.

Flanked by two cardinals, Pope Pius walked slowly towards the high altar. The long service was almost over, and the stirring music soaring up into the gigantic dome was reaching an emotional climax. Suddenly, the pope stopped, pressed his right hand against his chest and collapsed. As the TV cameras zoomed in on the pontiff lying in front of the altar, a stunned world held its breath.

Alerted by security staff, four Swiss Guards rushed to the altar and carefully lifted the unconscious pontiff from the floor. As they carried him towards a side entrance, surrounded by cardinals who had formed a protective circle around him, a sudden hush descended on the crowded basilica like a shroud. It began near the altar at the front and quickly rippled to the back as news of what had just happened spread through the ranks of the faithful. Many fell to their knees as the pope was slowly carried past them in what looked like some macabre funeral rite. As the strange procession approached the side entrance, hundreds were on their knees praying for a much-loved pontiff, overwhelmed by what had just happened. Something that should have been an Easter celebration of life and resurrection, had turned into a tragic reminder of mortality and the frailty of life.

By the time Professor Montessori, the pope's personal physician, arrived at his patient's bedside, the pope had regained consciousness. Montessori quickly conferred with the ambulance team and two emergency doctors and then examined the pontiff.

Cardinal Borromeo, the new Dean of the College of Cardinals, had taken charge of the situation and took Montessori aside.

'We have a crisis,' he said.

'I can see that.'

'How is His Holiness?'

'The illness is progressing. Just as we expected.'

'We must try to keep this out of the public domain for as long as possible.'

'I understand, but ...'

'His Holiness is due to address the United Nations in New York and Congress in Washington in a few weeks. I don't have to tell you how important that is.'

'I'm fully aware of that.'

'Hospital?'

'No. I think he will recover from this episode rather quickly, for now.'

'Will he be able to travel?' asked the cardinal, the anxiety in his voice obvious.

'I hope so. This disease is very unpredictable ... and we don't know much about it.'

'I realise that. We'll have to make an announcement.'

Montessori nodded. He was familiar with Vatican protocol. He was also familiar with the complex politics of the place and the power play behind the scenes.

'His Holiness fainted briefly due to exhaustion. Can we say that?' asked the cardinal.

Montessori shrugged. 'Like last time?'

'Yes.'

'I suppose so. But we can't keep this under wraps for much longer. The attacks will become more frequent.'

'We need time. Please do everything you can. You know what's at stake here.'

'I do.'

The pope had been ill for several months. What had begun with sudden episodes of uncontrolled bleeding, had developed into a chronic inflammation of his lungs and bowels, causing other complications and alarming weight loss. However, contrary to medical advice, the pope was determined to conceal his illness from all but his closest inner circle, and keep going. Most importantly, he refused to be hospitalised, which in effect prevented his medical team from properly investigating the disease and severely limited their treatment options. Apart from classifying it as some form of autoimmune disease, medical opinion as to cause and therefore possible treatment that may be available was divided. In short, without further extensive tests and investigation, the doctors were in the dark.

Also perplexing were the bouts of unexpected recovery. For days, even weeks, the inflammation would recede, the pope's strength would return and he would put on a little weight. This was in part due to his steely resolve to get better and no doubt the effects of some of the powerful drugs used to keep the inflammation under control. Unfortunately, these little windows of brief recovery were only temporary and would disappear without warning, or apparent cause, and the debilitating symptoms would return with a vengeance. Often worse than before. The pope's condition was gradually deteriorating and, shackled by his stubborn refusal to follow advice, his exasperated medical team didn't know why.

Pope Pius looked at his friend and confidant sitting by his bedside. 'How bad was it this time?' he asked, speaking slowly, his voice weak.

'Bad, Holiness,' answered Cardinal Borromeo.

The pope managed a wry smile. 'We'll just have to pray a little harder, don't you think?'

'I doubt whether that's possible.'

'What did Montessori say?'

'It will pass; this time.'

'Good.'

Pope Pius realised that a sick pope was an ineffective pope, and any peace initiative would certainly fail if word of his illness got out. His enemies would see to that. However, he firmly believed that making peace in the Middle East was the reason he was elected pope and he was determined to make peace the legacy of his pontificate – if necessary, against all odds – and no illness, however severe, would prevent him from fulfilling his destiny. His unshakable faith, steely resolve and trust in God kept him going.

'You know what we must do?' asked the pope.

'Yes, Holiness.'

'The United Nations and Congress. Everything depends on that.'

'I know.'

'I must be well enough to travel and deliver my speech.'

'You will, Holiness.'

'This is too important to fail.'

'The good Lord will not allow that, Holiness,' said the cardinal.

The pope looked at him gratefully. 'No, I don't believe He will,' he replied, and exhausted, closed his eyes.

Torn between logic and faith, the cardinal looked at the pontiff drifting into a restless slumber. Logic told him that urgent medical intervention was required if the pope's condition was to be improved. On the other hand, he admired the pontiff's faith that seemed to suggest the opposite. After a while, the cardinal's troubled features relaxed and a smile spread across his face. *Who am I to question the views of Saint Peter's successor? I have to accept that*, he thought. Relieved, he stood up, bowed and took his leave, secure in the knowledge that faith had once again carried the day.

2

Dr Amena Algafari looked at her watch; it was time to go and relieve her husband. She was wondering what horrors had occurred during the night, and what would be waiting for her at the operating table. Located in a dangerous, rebel-held neighbourhood in Aleppo, the field hospital was only a short walk away.

Amena reached for her handbag, adjusted her headscarf and watched her son Joram tie his shoelaces. Bringing up an eight-year-old boy in Aleppo surrounded by mayhem and bloodshed wasn't easy. Joram would come with her to the hospital to meet his dad, who would then take him to school on his way home. It was the only way that two overworked surgeons could manage some kind of family life in a city torn apart by a savage war. 'Ready?' asked Amena. Joram nodded and put on his little backpack.

The Reaper, the US Air Force's most sophisticated drone, had taken off from a base in Turkey. Armed with GBU-12 Paveway II laser-guided bombs, it was on course for Aleppo.

Operating the Reaper was complex. Pilots at the Turkish ground control station would launch and land the aircraft, but most of the flying would be directed from the Creech USAF Base in Nevada, USA, located thousands of kilometres from the combat zone. Sanitised war by remote control. Identifying the targets was also complex and often depended on intelligence obtained from agents and informants on the ground, often at very short notice and without sufficient time to verify the veracity of the information. The enemy was always on the move, and to be effective, strikes had to be swift and accurate, but war is full of uncertainty and risk.

Early that morning, information had been received that an enemy column was on the move leaving the city, and could be hit on the road. The intelligence seemed reliable. Directed from the ground, the pilot in Nevada punched in the coordinates as the Reaper approached its target.

Dr Sayid Algafari left the hospital, stepped outside into the square and, shielding his eyes from the glare with his hand, looked down the street, burnt-out car bodies and debris a stark reminder of the fighting that had erupted again the day before. It was already very hot and the ambulances still kept coming relentlessly, delivering the maimed and the dying after another deadly ambush during the night.

The fifteen-hour shift in the operating theatre had taken its toll. It had been a particularly difficult night, and several of Sayid's patients had died on the operating table, their horrific injuries beyond hope. Sayid felt exhausted and could barely keep his eyes open. But then, something cheered him up. He could see his son running towards him.

Amena saw her husband standing next to an ambulance, and waved. Sayid embraced his son and waved back. This was how she would remember them, the image of the two people in the world she loved with every fibre of her being etched into the recesses of her mind, never to be erased. Moments later, the laser-guided bombs slammed into the hospital.

Back at the Creech Air Force Base in Nevada, the pilot was looking for confirmation. What he didn't know at the time was that he had made one small, fatal mistake. He had misread one of the coordinates, which sent the drone slightly off target. Instead of obliterating an armed enemy convoy, it had destroyed a field hospital.

Amena opened her eyes. Darkness. She could hear muffled screams and shouting, but couldn't move; something heavy was pressing down on her from above. Then slowly, she began to bend, first her toes, then her fingers. But she soon realised she wouldn't be able to free herself. As an experienced surgeon, she knew the best thing to do was to lie still and hope that help was on its way.

Fine, gritty dust made breathing difficult, and the metal taste in her parched mouth told her she was bleeding, most likely internally.

Drifting in and out of consciousness suspended all awareness of time, and it was only the throbbing pain in her head that prevented her from slipping into the welcome cottonwool sanctuary of unconsciousness. Amena knew that could be fatal and was desperately trying to hang on.

Then an image of her husband and her son standing in front of the hospital drifted into her mind's eye. It only lasted for an instant and was banished by a bright orange flash and flying body parts. A silent scream rose from somewhere deep inside her and almost extinguished the fragile spark of life, becoming fainter by the second. Then, something happened. The heavy weight pressing down on her was lifted away and a shaft of blinding sunlight exploded all around her.

'This one's still alive,' Amena heard a voice call out from above as eager hands began clearing away the debris covering her broken body.

3

Lorenza da Baggio listened to the bells and was counting the hours. Time passes slowly when you are desperately trying to sleep, but can't. Her amazing victory the day before that had made her a finalist in *Top Chef Europe* was keeping her awake. Watched by millions, *Top Chef Europe* was Europe's most prestigious cooking competition. At twenty, Lorenza was not only the youngest competitor, but her cooking skills had stunned the judges and she had quickly become the darling of the program.

Instead of feeling elated, her unexpected victory against Kemal Bahadir from Istanbul, one of Europe's most celebrated chefs, filled her with dread. It wasn't winning that bothered her, but what had come later. When a smiling Bahadir embraced her after the judges had pronounced her the winner, he had whispered something in her ear she couldn't get out of her mind. *What did he mean when he said 'you will regret this; you are not as good as you may think?'* she asked herself over and over. *Perhaps I misunderstood?*

Covered in sweat, Lorenza opened her eyes and stared at the open balcony door as the first light of the new day crept hesitantly across the marble floor and began to banish the darkness. Feeling better, she got up, stepped out onto the terrace on the first floor of Villa Laurentius and looked down into Florence shrouded in morning mist. The familiar sight of Santa Maria del Fiore – the Duomo, with Brunelleschi's spectacular dome – seemed to calm her, bringing back memories of school holidays and lazy shopping afternoons with her grandmother. A smile creased the corners of her mouth as memories of her late mother flooded back with alarming clarity.

Lorenza realised that she had to prepare herself for the biggest challenge of her life: the grand finale in the evening. Now that her dream was within reach, nothing else mattered; she knew that any distraction could be disastrous. With that, she dismissed the disturbing thoughts, closed her eyes, turned her face towards the rising sun and dreamed of victory.

Villa Laurentius was a TV producer's dream. No expense had been spared by the TV channel to secure one of the most stunning Renaissance properties in the hills just outside Florence for the show. Famous for its spectacular gardens, sumptuous interior, library and art collection, it was the perfect setting for Europe's most popular cooking show. After football and Eurovision, *Top Chef Europe* was the TV program boasting most viewers.

Capable of accommodating a hundred guests in luxury and elegant comfort, the stables had been converted into five-star accommodation complete with restaurant facilities, swimming pool and tennis courts. Booked out for months in advance, Villa Laurentius was a sought after venue for hosting corporate events, conferences, and bonding retreats for high-flying corporate types, or mega-rich business tycoons to plan the next takeover or international pipeline deal. On this occasion, however, the coach house had been converted into a state-of-the-art kitchen with six separate workstations and a huge pantry. The large ballroom on the ground floor of the villa had become an elegant dining room seating fifty guests and was used to showcase the dishes prepared by the contestants. Sometimes, the guests also acted as judges and would vote on each of the dishes.

Each year, *Top Chef Europe* was hosted by a different country, which added to the show's huge popularity and appeal. This year, it was Italy's turn to showcase its culture and cuisine. Celebrity chef Matteo Monti, owner of the acclaimed Michelin-starred restaurant MM in Siena, had been chosen as the compere of the competition, which lasted three months and moved to several locations within the country. This year's highlights had included a spectacular cook-off in the Colosseum, an al-fresco lunch for one hundred on the beach in Positano, and a formal candlelit dinner party in an ancient villa in Pompeii. All cooked for and presented by the contestants.

Hundreds of hopefuls from all over Europe had auditioned for months to become part of the competition. After a rigorous selection process, thirty lucky contestants had been chosen to do culinary battle for the coveted prize: to be crowned *Top Chef* of the year, which would most certainly lead to an illustrious career for life. But there were also other prizes. This year, a staggering one million euros, a new Audi, a book deal and a TV show were the rewards waiting for the lucky winner.

Louis Fontaine was in his element. The big day, the grand finale, had finally arrived. As the producer in charge, he was the artistic director of the show responsible for just about everything. Flamboyantly gay, in his middle thirties with a perfectly trimmed designer beard and wearing a pince-nez instead of glasses, which he balanced precariously on the tip of his large nose, Louis was the go-between, the peacemaker, the shoulder to cry on. He was the man the contestants could turn to with problems involving the judges, the media, or the complex corporation that owned and ran the show as a mega-business.

Living together for three months in virtual isolation, cut off from family, friends and the outside world, the contestants were under a lot of stress. Louis would stroke bruised egos, cover-up hissy fits and do his best to avoid other major disasters that were inevitable in a pressure cooker environment like *Top Chef Europe*, where naked ambition rubbed shoulders with jealously defended reputations and egos as big and volatile as Vesuvius.

Louis had decided to use the fabulous library overlooking the gardens as the venue for the interviews with the two finalists who would do battle in the evening. The light was perfect, and so was the setting.

'You look absolutely gorgeous, darling,' said Louis, taking Lorenza by the hand. 'You wore the blue dress; excellent. It sets off your hair. Your hair! Movie stars would kill for hair like that, you know. Come, sit here by the window; perfect,' fussed Louis. 'How do you feel?'

'A little nervous, of course,' replied Lorenza, smiling. She liked Louis and got on very well with him.

'To be expected. But your performance the other night. Well that was really something. To win against Kemal Bahadir ... unheard of!'

'How did he take it?'

'Quite badly, actually,' said Louis, lowering his voice. 'He shouted at the judges after the show and stormed out in a huff. Celebrity egos! What do you expect – right? Quite a performance.'

'Am I on first?' asked Lorenza.

'Yes. As I told you, Matteo will conduct the interview. It will be quite short. We have done this before. Just relax and answer the questions with your usual charm, darling. Nothing to worry about.'

Lorenza wasn't so sure, but interviews were an important part of the show. They were usually screened at the beginning of the show to profile the contestants, build tension and prepare the audience for the contest to come. An interview just before the grand finale was therefore particularly important, and Lorenza knew that difficult, sensitive questions would be asked, most likely about her spectacular win against Kemal Bahadir the previous day. She was right.

Kemal Bahadir paced nervously up and down in his hotel suite in Florence overlooking the Piazza della Signoria and glanced at his watch. It was almost time. He poured himself another glass of wine and turned on the television.

'In a few hours, the two finalists, Lorenza da Baggio from Venice and Carlos Castellano from Barcelona,' said the announcer, 'will go head-to-head in the greatest culinary contest of the year. The winner will be crowned *Top Chef of Europe*. We now take you live to Villa Laurentius just outside Florence for an interview with the contestants ...'

'Good afternoon, I am Matteo Monti. It is my pleasure to introduce to you the lovely Lorenza da Baggio, one of the two finalists in *Top Chef Europe*,' said Monti, smiling into the camera.

The camera zoomed in on Lorenza sitting in the library next to a spectacular flower arrangement, perfectly positioned by Louis on a small marble table for maximum effect. Lorenza's face was a cameraman's dream. Her large, cornflower blue eyes, pale skin and stunning auburn hair that framed her beautiful face with luxurious curls bouncing off her shoulders made her look more like a movie star than a budding masterchef about to do battle in the kitchen to fulfil a dream.

'Your victory the other day against Kemal Bahadir, one of the great chefs of our time, put you straight into today's finale,' began Monti, coming straight to the subject everyone wanted to hear about. 'Were you surprised?'

'I certainly didn't expect to win,' replied Lorenza. 'It was a very difficult contest.'

'Because the dish you had to recreate was classic Ottoman cuisine, Bahadir's speciality?'

'No. That didn't concern me at all. In fact, I was pleasantly surprised. I thought it was destiny.'

'Destiny? How intriguing. Care to explain?'

'It's a long story.'

'Tell us; please,' urged Monti, enjoying himself.

Unable to take his eyes off the TV, Bahadir listened in amazement to Lorenza's astonishing story. At the end of the interview, he turned off the television and for a long moment kept staring at the empty screen. *This is a disaster*, he thought, anger churning in the empty pit of his stomach. Then he reached for his mobile and dialled a number only known to a privileged few. It was a direct line to Salvatore Gambio.

4

The counterattack by the Islamic State of Iraq and the Levant – ISIL (commonly referred to as IS) – against the advancing Free Syrian Army near the Turkish border came to a sudden standstill just before sunset. The rockets stopped coming and the guns fell silent. Death was taking a break.

Amena Algafari decided to make a run for it before it got dark. Having survived the deadly hospital attack with only minor injuries, she was one of the lucky ones. The border was very close. For most of the day, she had been hiding in a ditch next to the road and had watched a different army, an army of the homeless and the desperate, trying to escape from the merciless carnage and destruction that was Aleppo.

Women carrying children – many of them injured – boys carrying heavy suitcases, toddlers dragging bundles of bedding, old men barely able to walk, were all heading north towards the border. Thirsty, and feeling weak from lack of food, Amena joined the throng and an hour later crossed the border into Turkey near the once sleepy town of Kilis. This was the first point of safety for hundreds of thousands of refugees who had been made homeless by four years of brutal war.

Kilis had been overwhelmed by the relentless tide of human misery flooding across the border. The generosity of its Turkish inhabitants had won worldwide admiration and even a Nobel Peace Prize nomination, but the town could no longer cope. The main Oncupinar refugee camp was overflowing and resources, even water, were stretched to breaking point.

Set up in 2012 to house refugees escaping from the Syrian civil war disaster, the Kilis Oncupinar Accommodation Facility was one of six 'container camps' established by Turkey. They were called container camps because the refugees were accommodated in identical containers, several thousand of them, linked by brick paths. Ingenious, cheap and practical. In addition, the camps had schools, playgrounds and medical facilities.

Just before fleeing Aleppo, one of Amena's former colleagues told her to find a Dr Rosen. Apparently, Dr Rosen, founder and principal of the famous Rosen Foundation, had recently established a clinic near the camp, and was in desperate need of trained medical staff.

Dr Rosen looked at the three modified army containers that were her new clinic, and smiled. She had seen worse. The facilities were basic, but somehow it all worked. Her tent clinic in Dadaab, the world's largest refugee camp in Kenya near the Somali border, had been the same. *Benjamin would be pleased*, she thought, *that his generosity has been put to good use.*

Only a few months before, Benjamin Krakowski, celebrated composer and violin virtuoso, had donated a staggering thirty-five million pounds to the Rosen Foundation. The money represented the entire auction sale proceeds of a recently rediscovered Monet. The painting, *Little Sparrow in the Garden,* had belonged to Krakowski's father. Stolen by the Nazis, it had been lost for over seventy years before surfacing again in extraordinary circumstances. The record sale of the painting and its astonishing history had attracted a lot of media attention at the time, and created quite a storm in art circles.

Dr Rosen turned to Nazir Al-Kafri, her young assistant standing next to her. 'I couldn't have done this without you,' she said, putting her arm affectionately around the young man. Nazir beamed. After losing his entire family during an air strike in Damascus six months before, he had ended up in Oncupinar. He firmly believed that meeting Dr Rosen had not only given him hope and purpose, but most likely saved his life.

'All we need now is a couple of doctors and nurses and we are in business,' said Nazir cheerfully.

Dr Rosen nodded. 'I wish,' she replied wistfully. She remembered the day she had met the frightfully thin young man from Damascus very well. She had been searching for someone in the camp who spoke good English and could help her with languages. Fluent in Arabic, English and Turkish, Nazir became her right-hand man. Enthusiastic and intelligent, with an inquisitive mind and a good sense of humour, Nazir had all the qualities Dr Rosen needed to help her navigate the complex and often-confusing and exasperatingly disorganised refugee camp environment bursting at the seams with desperate people.

Exhausted but elated, Dr Rosen reached for her water bottle. As she was about to lift it to her mouth she noticed a dark shape standing in the shadows. Someone was watching her. 'Can I help you?' she asked, and waved towards the shape. 'Come; don't be afraid.'

Amena watched the tall, elderly woman with short grey hair turn slowly towards her. She instantly recognised something familiar in the woman's voice that reminded her of her late husband: empathy and kindness. It was the voice of a true healer. Feeling calm for the first time since leaving Aleppo, Amena stepped out of the shadows and said, 'Dr Rosen?'

'Yes,' replied Dr Rosen, surprised.

'I am Dr Algafari from Aleppo. I would like to work for you.'

5

Luigi Belmonte made sure he looked like all the other tourists enjoying the sunshine. Casually dressed in a pair of jeans, polo shirt and a linen jacket and wearing a straw hat and dark glasses, he certainly blended in well. But his appearance was deceptive. In his forties, shortish with a barrel chest and broad shoulders, he radiated strength and moved with surprising agility for a man with such a powerful physique. Belmonte looked at his watch, reached for his Campari and smiled. The location, a busy restaurant opposite the Palazzo Vecchio in the heart of Florence, was perfect – and so was the time.

His instructions were clear: it had to happen in a public place, today, between one pm and two pm precisely. Belmonte was a perfectionist who took his assignments very seriously and left nothing to chance. He had been following Mario Giordano, the eldest son of Riccardo Giordano, the head of one of the powerful Mafia families operating in Florence, for several days now.

Good-looking, in his late twenties, Mario was in charge of supplying drugs to a number of nightclubs popular with tourists. He had several girlfriends and liked to have long lunches before taking them back to his apartment above one of the nightclubs owned by the family. To the exasperation of his Sicilian bodyguard, who followed him everywhere like a shadow, he preferred to sit outdoors, usually in one of his favourite restaurants also owned by the family. This wasn't just careless, but showed a certain arrogance and disregard for his own safety and his father's specific instructions. Habits were dangerous and made you vulnerable.

As an experienced hitman, Belmonte knew that meticulous preparation was the key to staying ahead of the game; and alive. He always studied the habits of his subjects carefully, and planned his approach accordingly. He was the master of the unexpected and the audacious. He dared to do what others wouldn't contemplate. This was reflected in his success rate, reputation and astronomical fee.

Mario was flirting animatedly with an attractive young woman, an English tourist he had met in one of the nightclubs the day before. Sitting at the table next to him, his bodyguard was sipping his mineral water and frowned when Mario ordered another bottle of Chianti. *Another long lunch*, he thought, looking bored as he watched the tourists stroll past in the Piazza della Signoria to take selfies with Michelangelo's celebrated David in front of the palazzo.

When Mario got up to go to the bathroom, Belmonte made his move. He knew the bodyguard would follow Mario to the toilet and wait outside. He had observed this several times before, and knew the exact layout of the restaurant.

Belmonte followed Mario and the bodyguard past the busy kitchen at the back of the restaurant and watched Mario go into the toilet. When the bodyguard pulled a packet of cigarettes out of his pocket and was about to light up, Belmonte knew it was the right time.

For a moment, there was no-one else around. He quickly walked up to the bodyguard from behind and shot him twice in the back, the dull thud of the gunshots masked by the silencer the only sound in the deserted corridor. Shot in the heart, the bodyguard was dead before he hit the floor. Without breaking his stride, Belmonte quickly walked past him into the toilet.

Mario was facing a urinal with his back towards the door. Another man stood at the washbasin drying his hands with a paper towel. Otherwise, the toilet was empty. Belmonte walked up to Mario and shot him twice in the back of the head, blood splatters turning the white tiles crimson like an exploding sun. The man at the washbasin turned around, his eyes wide with terror and surprise. Smiling, Belmonte lifted his gun and shot the man between the eyes. Slipping the gun back into his shoulder holster, he pulled a white feather out of his pocket and inserted it into Mario's open mouth. Then he walked casually outside and looked around. The dead bodyguard was lying face down in a pool of blood; a young waitress was kneeling next to him on the floor, screaming.

People came running out of the kitchen towards her to see what the commotion was all about. *Confusion; perfect*, thought Belmonte. *No-one will remember a thing.* Having carefully studied the configuration of the restaurant before, Belmonte knew there was a back door next to the kitchen that opened into a laneway behind the restaurant where the deliveries were made. He also knew that confusion and fear were the best cover. When you added a dead body and lots of blood to this, you had shock and panic as well. *A perfect recipe for conflicting accounts*, he thought, as he walked quickly past the distraught waitress, opened the back door and stepped outside into the brilliant sunshine.

Salvatore Gambio looked at his watch and poured another glass of wine for his guest. As the head of one of the three most powerful Mafia families in Florence, he left nothing to chance. *It's probably all over by now*, he thought and turned to face his notorious visitor. It had taken months of careful planning and manoeuvring to bring this meeting about. It wasn't often that the heads of rival families fighting a bloody turf war agreed to meet to discuss peace. '*Salute,*' he said and lifted his glass. 'Are we agreed?'

'We are,' said Riccardo Giordano.

They touched glasses.

'To our alliance,' said Gambio, and kissed Giordano on both cheeks.

'*Alleanza,*' repeated Giordano. For reasons he couldn't quite explain, he felt uneasy in Gambio's company, or perhaps it was the opulent setting with all the impressive paintings and trappings of wealth that made him feel uncomfortable. A man of simple tastes with a long Mafia family tradition, Giordano was a cautious man. He had reluctantly agreed to the meeting proposed by Gambio, but only after elaborate arrangements had been made and hostages exchanged. This wasn't unusual in Mafia circles. The reason the meeting took place at Gambio's fortress-home was purely strategic. It would send a powerful message to the Lombardo family, their main rival.

The turf war that had cost the life of Gambio's father three years before had been costly for all concerned, and a resolution seemed as far away and elusive as ever. The powerful families were evenly matched. But if two were to unite, the third may be forced to make peace on their terms and lose territory and influence. That was the strategy behind the plan. Simple, but compelling. Self-interest above all else; classic Mafia.

Giordano felt the phone vibrate in his breast pocket, signalling an incoming call. Only a trusted few knew his private number and would only call if it was really important. Giordano pulled the phone out of his pocket and looked at the screen. 'This is urgent,' he said, 'would you excuse me?'

'Of course,' replied Gambio, carefully watching his visitor.

Giordano answered the phone, and paled. 'I-I must leave at once ...' he stammered, and got unsteadily to his feet.

'Something wrong?' asked Gambio, and stood up as well.

'My son; he's been hit ...'

'My God; is he ...?'

'Dead? Yes,' whispered Giordano. '*Mario ...*'

'Lombardo, you think?'

'Who else?'

'How can you be so sure?'

'The killer left something behind.'

6

Chief prosecutor Antonio Grimaldi put down the phone, his face ashen. *An assassination in the heart of Florence in the middle of the day*, he thought, shaking his head. *Three dead; what a disaster!* The police had secured the crime scene, and Forensics were on their way. What Grimaldi feared most had just happened: the simmering feud between the Mafia families operating in Florence had once again erupted into open war. Grimaldi knew better than most what that meant. Early in his career he had worked in Palermo and Naples and had witnessed the relentless bloodshed, kidnappings and brutal assassinations firsthand. He also knew what was needed now: prompt, decisive action to solve the crime quickly and identify those responsible before the trail went cold and the code of Cosa Nostra silence descended like a curtain, blotting out the evidence.

As a realist, Grimaldi realised he had a problem. With fear and corruption spreading their greedy tentacles into every corner of the police force and honest men being sidelined or cut down, Grimaldi understood it would be difficult to bring the villains to justice. He needed help. Help from the *outside*.

It's a long shot, but definitely worth a try, thought Grimaldi. He reached for his phone and called the commissioner.

As chief prosecutor in charge, Grimaldi insisted on being briefed at the crime scene before the bodies were removed. On this occasion, visiting the crime scene was easy. It was only a short walk from his office to the restaurant, which had been cordoned off by the police. He pushed his way through the excited crowd gathered outside. The officer in charge met Grimaldi at the front door and showed him inside.

Grimaldi had attended countless crime scenes and knew the routine. He also knew how to read the evidence. What he saw had all

68

the hallmarks of a professional hit, but carried out with exceptional daring and at high-risk in the middle of the day in a busy restaurant. Why? This alone was unusual and therefore significant and worth noting.

Cesaria Borroni, her face flushed with excitement, hurried towards the restaurant. News about the shooting had spread like a sex scandal through police headquarters, abuzz with speculation. But that wasn't the reason for her excitement. It was the phone call from the commissioner that had left her speechless – and a little scared. It wasn't often the commissioner called a junior officer and gave instructions for a sensitive assignment of great urgency and importance.

Cesaria found the chief prosecutor bent over the bloody corpse of the bodyguard in front of the men's toilet. He was examining the gunshot wounds with one of the men from Forensics.

Cesaria waited for Grimaldi to finish. As soon as he stood up, she walked over to him. 'The commissioner asked me to report to you, sir,' she said.

Grimaldi looked at her, surprised. He had expected someone older, not a strikingly attractive young woman in her twenties. Grimaldi knew the commissioner well. She had to be something special, otherwise he wouldn't have sent her. 'Come with me,' said Grimaldi, and quickly walked through the open side door out into the lane behind the restaurant. He lit a small cigar and looked at the young woman standing demurely by the door, watching him. 'Tell me about yourself,' he said. 'There isn't much time.'

'What would you like to know, sir?' asked Cesaria, surprised. It wasn't the question she had expected from the man with such a fierce reputation.

As a survivor of two assassination attempts, Grimaldi was a legend. He was known as a demanding taskmaster, a perfectionist and relentless workaholic. Fearless, and almost fanatical in the pursuit of truth and justice, he left no stone unturned in tracking down the culprits and sending them to trial. 'How long have you been in the police force?' he asked.

'Two years.'

'Education?'

'Apart from my training?'

'Yes.'

'I have a law degree.'

'Good.' *That explains the intelligence radiating from the girl*, thought Grimaldi, enjoying the tobacco rush, *and why he sent her*. Like the commissioner, Grimaldi knew that integrity and dedication to the job were far more likely to be found in the young, before temptation, intimidation and disillusionment could do their dirty work. And what he had in mind required both: unconditional trust and dedication – plenty of it. And besides, a woman's touch could in fact be quite useful, he thought. 'I would like you to do something for me,' he said. 'Something urgent and very important.'

'Yes?'

'I want you to persuade a man to do something he has vowed never to do again.'

Cesaria looked at Grimaldi, surprised. 'Oh?'

Grimaldi held up his hand. 'I'll explain later,' he said. 'You will have to drop everything and travel, straight away. Would that be a problem?'

'No. Travel where?'

'Palermo.'

'When?'

'Tonight.'

7

The plane circled the terracotta rooftops and familiar church steeples on its approach into Florence, giving everyone a splendid view of the city from above, and then lined up for landing. Countess Kuragin pointed down to the river below. 'There; just next to the Ponte Vecchio is my favourite little hotel. Can you see it? The building with the large roof terrace?'

Tristan craned his neck to get a better view. 'I see it,' he lied, trying to please the countess who appeared very excited to be back in Florence. 'An ideal location for a room with a view,' he teased.

'You can say that again! You are in for a treat, I can tell you. This city is special. To me, it's the most enchanting city in the world. After Paris, of course,' she added, laughing.

'Can't wait.'

Leonardo da Baggio, Lorenza's father, looked at the indicator board. The flight from Paris was on time and was due to land any moment. He was looking forward to seeing the countess again. He hadn't seen her since the funeral, although they had been in regular contact. His wife and son had been tragically killed in a motor vehicle accident near Siena the year before. After that, life changed, but the wounds were still bleeding.

Countess Kuragin had been his wife's closest friend and the da Baggio family had visited her at her chateau just outside Paris many times. She in turn had stayed often at the Palazzo da Baggio Hotel in Venice, run by his late wife. Countess Kuragin was also Lorenza's godmother, which was one of the reasons Leonardo had invited her to attend the *Top Chef Europe* finale that evening. She was a precious link to his beloved wife and as far as Lorenza was concerned, a link to her late mother.

When Leonardo had contacted the countess the day before – just after Lorenza had won the contest with Bahadir – and asked her if she would like to come to Florence for the grand finale, the countess had jumped at the opportunity. As she had promised Tristan a trip to Florence for some time, she asked Leonardo if she could bring him along. She was certain he wouldn't mind. It also meant she didn't have to travel alone.

As soon as the finalists had been announced, the organisers had contacted Leonardo and invited him to attend the contest. They had also asked him to bring some family members and close friends along, as this was part of the show and a surprise for the contestants. The grand finale would therefore take place in front of family and friends, which gave the show an appealing, personal touch.

Once the contest was over and the winner declared, a celebration gala dinner would be served in the sumptuous ballroom of Villa Laurentius as a festive conclusion to the program. The dinner would be personally cooked and presented by the judges – all celebrity chefs – as a special tribute to all the participants. The contestants who had been eliminated along the way had also been invited, and would be watching from the gallery above the kitchen and cheering on the two finalists. This was part of a long *Top Chef* tradition.

The countess was shocked. The man coming towards her at the baggage carousel, waving, barely resembled the confident, handsome man with the aristocratic bearing she remembered. He seemed to have aged a decade since she had seen him at the funeral, and had the aura of a broken man.

'Leo, it's been far too long,' said the countess and embraced her friend. *He's so thin*, she thought, trying hard to hide her concern and appear cheerful. The countess had known Leonardo since their student days in Paris.

'It has,' said Leonardo. 'And you don't have to pretend.'

'What do you mean?'

'Look at me ...'

'Oh, Leo,' said the countess, tears in her eyes, and squeezed her friend's hand in a gesture of affection.

'I still can't get over it.'

'I understand.'

'No, you don't.'

'What do you mean?'

'It wasn't an accident,' replied Leonardo, lowering his voice.

'*What?* Are you serious?'

'I am. I'll tell you when we get to the villa. We are staying with the grandparents. You don't mind?'

'Of course not! My God, Leonardo, *what are you saying?*'

'Later.' Leonardo turned to Tristan. 'You have grown. And changed,' he said.

'For the better, I hope,' replied Tristan.

'Last time I saw you at the chateau, you were a schoolboy. You have turned into a confident young man ...' *He's about the same age Antonio would be now*, thought Leonardo, remembering his son.

'Studying art history at the Sorbonne,' interjected the countess, pleased to be changing the subject.

'And occasionally going on risky adventure trips around the world with Jack Rogan, I believe.'

'You've read Jack's book?' asked the countess.

'Couldn't put it down. How is Jack?'

The countess shrugged. 'Jack is Jack,' she said. 'He's working on some novella at the moment to do with some painting he discovered. In fact, he's staying with us at the chateau.'

'He's bored, if you want to know the truth,' interjected Tristan.

'How can you say that?' asked the countess, frowning.

'He needs a new challenge. I know he does.'

'The last "challenge" as you put it, almost got him killed – remember? And you too!'

'Katerina keeps reminding me of Somalia,' said Tristan, turning to Leonardo. 'I still get into trouble for that. Regularly.'

'And with good reason,' chided the countess. 'I think a little boredom will do Jack the world of good. Perhaps he may even grow up a little. Perhaps both of you will.'

'See what I mean?' said Tristan, laughing.

Enjoying the banter, Leonardo was laughing too and for a moment left the ghosts of the past behind. 'We just have time to go back to the villa, say hello to the grandparents, and change,' he said. 'They've been invited too and are coming along. Then it's off to the grand finale at Villa Laurentius.'

'How exciting!' said the countess. 'You must be very proud. We've been watching *Top Chef* for weeks.'

'Compulsory viewing at the chateau. Even Jack got into it. Never missed an episode,' said Tristan. 'Lorenza has been amazing.'

Leonardo beamed. 'Yes, she certainly has,' he said.

'See, you *can* smile,' said the countess, and linked arms with her friend.

'It's really good to see you,' said Leonardo. The countess squeezed his arm in silent reply. 'Lorenza is all I have left.'

'I know.'

8

Cesaria looked like all the other tourists catching the evening flight to Palermo. No-one would have guessed that the young woman in the faded jeans, Iron Maiden tee-shirt with a grinning skull, and short leather vest was in fact a competent police officer embarking on a difficult assignment. The only thing that set her apart from the crowd was the fact that she was travelling alone. Cesaria picked up her duffel bag and left the airport terminal to catch a cab.

'Are you sure this is the right address?' asked the cab driver, looking concerned.

'Quite sure,' replied Cesaria. 'Why?'

'It's just that this neighbourhood isn't ... well, the safest, if you know what I mean. After all, this is Palermo. I certainly wouldn't want my daughter walking around here on her own ... especially at night.'

'I'll be fine,' said Cesaria, laughing.

'If you say so.' The cab driver wasn't convinced. He turned into a dark lane, slowed down and looked at the street numbers. 'That's it over there,' he said, pointing to a dilapidated building on the right. The faded sign above the open door said Osteria del Sole.

Cesaria paid the fare and opened the door. 'I can wait,' said the cab driver.

'No need,' replied Cesaria. She got out of the cab and walked confidently past a group of raucous young men making lewd remarks and undressing her with their eyes.

Osteria del Sole had seen better days. Located in a poor, working-class neighbourhood, it served cheap wine and simple food to a predominantly male clientele. Cesaria looked around the shabby, smoke-filled room full of men sitting at communal tables rubbed smooth and shiny by countless elbows propping up disappointment and despair. Some of the men were playing cards, others were reading the paper, all of them were drinking and talking loudly, the mood jovial due to an advanced level of intoxication.

Cesaria walked over to the bar at the far end of the dimly lit room. 'I am looking for Fabio Conti,' she said, addressing the barman.

The old man looked at her with undisguised curiosity. 'Who?' he asked, cupping his ear with his hand.

'Fabio Conti,' shouted Cesaria, trying to make herself heard. Suddenly, the room went silent, all eyes on Cesaria standing at the bar. 'Fabio Conti?' repeated the barman. Cesaria nodded.

'Come,' he said. Cesaria followed the barman into another crowded, smoke-filled room behind the bar. The barman pointed to a man sitting on a wooden stool in the corner. The man was leaning against a barrel – eyes closed, his mouth wide open – obviously asleep. His crumpled, red wine-stained shirt was unbuttoned to the waist and a cigarette between his fingers had turned into a column of ash.

Good God, thought Cesaria, assessing the situation. The man in front of her in no way resembled the man described by Chief Prosecutor Grimaldi as a hero and one of the most fearless Mafia hunters in the country. Cesaria turned to the barman standing next to her. 'Do you know where he lives?' she asked.

'Right here, upstairs,' replied the barman and pointed to the ceiling.

'Could you please make us some coffee, and could someone help me take him to his room?'

'Sure,' said the barman, impressed. 'I'll help you. I do this almost every night. Pasquale, give me a hand!' he shouted. A young man came out of the kitchen and helped the barman take Conti upstairs.

Smelling of vomit and stale cigarette smoke, the tiny room above the bar was a total mess. The wooden floor was littered with crumpled clothes, empty bottles and newspapers. An unmade bed with dirty sheets and a torn blanket, an open wardrobe full of empty coat hangers – some of them broken – and a small table and chair were the only furniture in the room. A cracked washbasin with a cracked mirror above it, the tap dripping, was filled with underwear waiting in vain to be washed.

'He wasn't always like this,' said the barman, and lifted Conti onto the bed. 'Relative of yours?'

Cesaria shook her head.

'I'll send up some coffee.'

As soon as she was alone with Conti, Cesaria opened the window, picked up a towel from the floor and held it under the tap.

What could make a man sink this low? she asked herself and began to wipe Conti's flushed face with the wet towel and a tenderness that surprised her. Well-built, in his late forties with a shock of unkempt black hair badly in need of a haircut and a face that may have seen a little too much of the dark side of life, Conti was, even in this sorry state, an impressive man. Cesaria put the towel aside and began to massage Conti's temples.

After a while Conti began to groan as Cesaria's strong, practised fingers began to penetrate the stubborn alcohol fog numbing his brain. Conti opened his eyes and stared straight-ahead, his gaze blank. Then slowly, as his bloodshot eyes began to focus, Cesaria's face swam into view. 'Who are you?' he whispered, his speech slurred.

'I'm Cesaria Borroni from Florence … police,' replied Cesaria without interrupting the massage.

'What are you doing here?'

'Chief Prosecutor Grimaldi sent me.'

Conti sat up with a jolt and looked at Cesaria sitting on the edge of the bed next to him. 'Why?'

'To remind you of something ...'

'He sent you all this way to remind me of something? Remind me of what?' demanded Conti.

'A date.'

'I don't understand,' said Conti, looking confused. 'What date?'

'The seventh of January 2014,' said Cesaria quietly.

Conti nodded as images of the fatal shooting came flooding back with alarming clarity. He saw the motorbike approach in slow motion and watched the man on the pillion seat raise his right hand holding a gun – and fire. The bullet intended for Conti entered his wife's forehead instead, killing her instantly. After that, all Conti could see was blood.

Conti closed his eyes, trying in vain to banish the ghosts. 'What else?' he asked.

'He needs your help,' replied Cesaria.

Conti's heart missed a beat as a sense of excitement he hadn't felt for a long time began to well up from somewhere deep within. The ghosts receded. 'I must apologise,' said Conti.

'What for?'

'For looking like this. I'm not always … I haven't—'

'No need,' interrupted Cesaria and stood up. 'We all have our demons to fight.'

'You are right about that. Unfortunately, I've been losing the fight lately.'

'Perhaps it's time to fight back?'

Conti looked at Cesaria. *What a remarkable young woman*, he thought, no longer feeling quite so embarrassed.

'Perhaps it is. But first I need a shower. Please go downstairs and wait for me.'

Cesaria walked to the door, opened it and turned around. 'I've seen worse,' she said, giving Conti her best smile, and left the room.

9

Matteo walked into the change room behind the large kitchen in the converted coach house, which was buzzing with activity and excitement. Make-up artists, all kinds of wardrobe people and producers were busily at work preparing the finalists. 'This is it, guys,' he said. 'We're on in ten minutes. Are you ready?' Carlos looked at Matteo, raised his right hand and gave him a high five.

Lorenza put on her white *Top Chef Europe* apron with her name embroidered on the front and walked over to Carlos, her opponent. It was almost time. Lorenza was in awe of Carlos's talent and ability. Ten years older than her, Carlos, an architect with a passion for cooking, was a natural. Not only was he in command of all the necessary cooking skills and techniques, his instincts were exceptional. He didn't just visualise a dish, he could *sense* it. He didn't cook, but *create*. To watch him in the kitchen was to observe an artist at work.

However, his biggest asset was something quite different and totally unrelated to cooking. He was incredibly likeable. Completely devoid of arrogance, affectation or pride, which were so common among contestants at that level, he often admonished himself for making silly mistakes and then made jokes about it. His honest, self-depreciating manner had endeared him to viewers and judges alike. In short, he was a formidable opponent. Lorenza liked him a lot, and if she was to lose, she didn't mind losing to him.

Lorenza realised there was one vital area where she had the upper hand: taste. Taste was her ally, her friend, her secret weapon. She was a master of creating interesting and unique flavours in unexpected ways and combinations that made the tastebuds dance and the senses sing. *At the end of the day, my girl, in cooking, taste is everything*, Lorenza

79

heard her mother lecture her. *Never forget that.* She was certain that it was taste that had secured her win against Bahadir. The judges had said as much. No doubt her youth, glamorous looks and charming manner helped, but they didn't do the heavy lifting; taste did that.

Lorenza had first learned about taste in her grandmother's kitchen as a five-year-old. Her mother, an excellent cook with a passion for Ottoman cuisine, had introduced her to the subtleties of creating sophisticated, exotic dishes where taste was always the hero. In the da Baggio family kitchen in Venice, Ottoman cuisine had been a tradition for centuries. Handed down from generation to generation, the recipes were jealously guarded family secrets reaching all the way back to the court of the sultans in Constantinople.

However, as far as taste and flavour were concerned, spices were of course often the key, and Lorenza knew a lot about spices. The most expensive spice used in Ottoman palace cuisine was the sweet-smelling musk extracted from the male musk deer. This precious spice was used to perfume desserts and popular sherbets and many of the exquisite savoury dishes served at the sultan's table. Saffron and black pepper were indispensable and were used in almost all dishes as the basis for flavour creation. To this the palace cooks, who were held in high esteem and had a lot of influence, would then add cinnamon, cumin, or coriander, depending on the composition of the dish and their own individual cooking style.

Ottoman cuisine is an art, and the few precious recipes that survive from those early times are only guidelines, rarely specifying quantities or the exact spices to be used, and therefore do not give away all the secrets that were only known to the admired palace chefs working for the sultan.

Lorenza had memorised many of the recipes and had perfected them over the years. This was often done as a contest, a little game she had played with her mother as a teenager; how to recreate those complex dishes from memory and if possible, improve them. The family sitting around the dinner table on lazy Sundays would act as judges and vote without knowing who had created what dish, and then declare the winner. In a way, this wasn't so different from how *Top Chef* worked.

Carlos walked over to Lorenza and gave her a hug. 'Good luck. Show them what you can do!'

'Thanks, Carlos. Good luck to you too,' said Lorenza, tears glistening in her eyes.

A breathless Louis burst into the room. 'Ready? We're on; come!' he said excitedly. Dressed in a spectacular tartan tuxedo, platform shoes to give him a little extra height, and a polka dot bow tie that would have made Liberace envious, he looked more like a circus director than someone in charge of a TV show watched by millions. 'Good luck, guys,' he said. 'Go and dazzle them!

Gambio's driver collected Bahadir from his hotel just before the show began and drove him to the Gambio family villa in the picturesque hills outside Florence. Ironically, the spectacular sixteenth-century villa, which had once belonged to one of the prominent Florentine aristocratic families, was very close to Villa Laurentius. To save time, Gambio had suggested they watch the grand finale together, as Bahadir's little 'problem' was directly related to it.

Shielded from prying eyes and the outside world by a high garden wall, electric fence and dense hedge, the villa was both a fortress and the elegant home of a wealthy businessman, as Gambio liked to call himself. Armed guards at the ornate wrought-iron gates, sophisticated alarm systems and trained guard dogs provided privacy and safety, and ensured that Gambio could conduct his business affairs without being disturbed or, God forbid, overheard.

Three years before, Gambio's father had been gunned down in an ambush as he was getting out of his car to go to church, the brazen killing igniting a bloody turf war among the three Mafia families operating in Florence. The outraged authorities had been powerless to stop the bloodshed, and one prosecutor after another was either killed, or gave up in despair and left. After his father's violent death, Gambio had returned to Italy to take over the running of the family business in Florence. Prior to that, he had been in charge of the family's operations in Chicago for ten years.

Bahadir had worked for Gambio in the US for years, mainly running restaurants and brothels. As a celebrity chef with his own restaurant in New York frequented by the glitterati, he had a high-profile and was famous for his Ottoman cuisine. Known as 'The Turk', Bahadir had a fearsome reputation and had served as Gambio's eyes and ears and trusted right-hand man.

When his boss left the US, he did too, and returned to Istanbul to establish a new restaurant – Sultan's Table – which he turned into one of the leading restaurants in Turkey serving classic Ottoman cuisine. After that, he set up a very successful restaurant chain – also called Sultan's Table – which became all the rage with the well-heeled elite chasing the latest trend.

As a talented, trained chef and experienced businessman, he knew how to promote his restaurants and his reputation, and after operating his restaurant in Istanbul for only two years he won a Michelin Star, which was almost unheard of. It was rumoured that all kinds of influences had been at play to make this possible. With a number of cookbooks to his name and his own TV show, Bahadir was a well-known celebrity not only in his native Turkey, but in wider Europe as well. Ambitious and fiercely proud, he liked to think of himself as the leading authority on classic Ottoman cuisine, and promoted himself as having the oldest, most authentic Ottoman recipes in the world. His reputation and all his cookbooks rested on that claim.

Gambio's affable manner was deceptive. He liked to appear casual, easy-going and friendly. This was quite intentional and designed to put everyone at ease and make them lower their guard. But his eyes never smiled. They *observed*, radiating ruthlessness, cunning and danger. Especially danger.

'You are looking swell, buddy,' said Gambio, patting Bahadir on the back, the familiar, rasping voice of his former boss bringing a smile to Bahadir's face. While they had stayed in contact and done business together since leaving the US three years before, they hadn't met in person. This was by no means unusual, as Gambio preferred to do business that way. He was paranoid about security.

'It's been what, three years?' he said. 'Let's go into my study and watch the show.' Shortish, a little overweight, especially around the waist and thighs, with thinning black hair brushed straight back and a pencil-thin moustache that gave his pudgy face an almost comical appearance, he looked more like an Italian greengrocer than the head of one of the most feared Mafia families in Tuscany.

The inside of Gambio's villa was palatial. No expense had been spared to restore the villa to its former glory. Furnished to impress, antiques, stunning Roman antiquities and paintings by Donatello, Titian and Giorgione spoke loudly of staggering wealth, power and influence, and Gambio had plenty of all three and liked to show it. He ruled his criminal empire like a dark prince who made his own rules, bowed to no-one and eliminated his enemies with ruthless efficiency. Those were the main reasons he was still alive at fifty. But all was not well in the Gambio empire ...

The huge study on the ground floor was the nerve centre of Gambio's world. He ran his vast business interests from there and rarely left the villa. When he did, he travelled either in his armoured car with a small army of bodyguards around him, or in his helicopter, which took him from his front lawn straight to the airport and his private jet. Divorced from his second wife, an Italian who lived in the US with their three young children, Gambio lived alone, and liked it that way.

The reason Gambio had invited Bahadir to his home, which was a rare honour bestowed only on a privileged, trusted few, was because Bahadir was exactly the man he needed, and had been looking for. And as coincidence would have it, it all related to something quite extraordinary that would take place later that night. Gambio didn't believe in coincidences, only opportunities, and he was a master of turning opportunities into success.

Gambio turned on the television. 'There, see, they've just started,' he said, and reached for the bottle of Chivas Regal on the table in front of him.

As the compere of the evening, Matteo Monti had just introduced the contestants and the three judges – all celebrity chefs from various parts of Europe – and began to explain the rules of the grand finale, which would be held over two consecutive nights.

'The contest tonight will consist of three rounds,' said Monti, addressing the contestants. 'Each of the judges will present a dish – one of their signature specialities – which you will have to recreate. You will be allowed to taste it, but there will be no recipes. Each round will be worth ten points, and the judges will score your dishes out of ten. The final round, which will form part of tomorrow's contest, will be worth thirty points. The contestant with the highest score out of sixty will be declared the winner.'

Gambio turned to Bahadir and handed him a glass of Scotch. 'Cheers,' he said, 'I like cooking shows. Looks like we'll have plenty of time to have a chat. Now, tell me, what's this little problem of yours?'

10

Day one of the *Top Chef Europe* grand finale finished with only one point separating the contestants. It had been an exhausting, nail-biting contest. Lorenza's early lead in the first round evaporated in round two. Carlos won convincingly with a spectacular recreation of a complex, classic French dish and was an astonishing three points in front. Then came round three.

Josef Weindorfer, an Austrian chef from Vienna with a Michelin star under his apron, was famous for his Austro–Hungarian cuisine. He presented one of his signature dishes – *Eszterhazy Rostelyos*, 'Steaks Eszterhazy' – for the contestants to replicate. This hearty, rustic dish named after an illustrious Hungarian family appeared deceptively simple, but it wasn't. What set the dish apart was the subtlety and finesse of the sauce with its elegant flavours, and the delicate vegetable garnish.

Apart from cooking the meat perfectly, it was all about flavour. Chopped onions, chopped garlic, ground allspice, bay leaves, peppercorns, thyme, lemon peel, salt of course, and lemon juice all had to come together in harmony without dominating to make a mouth-watering sauce that made the tastebuds dance with excitement, craving more.

Lorenza was in her element. Not only did she identify the individual flavours making up the sauce, she got the proportions right. This earned her a perfect score of ten and reduced Carlos's lead to only one point. The contest was therefore wide open, and it all came down to the final round scheduled for the next day.

'She's really something,' said Gambio, nodding appreciatively. 'And so young; amazing. She could win this.' He turned off the television.

'I know,' said Bahadir, looking glum.

'Don't worry. If she does, we go ahead.'

'Are you serious?'

'Absolutely. But you will have to do something for me in return.'

Bahadir wasn't surprised. He knew his former boss too well. Nothing was free in the treacherous world of the Cosa Nostra. 'What's on your mind?' he asked.

'A business proposition.'

'Can you tell me about it?'

'I can do one better.'

'What do you mean?' asked Bahadir, looking confused.

'I'll show you how to make three-hundred thousand euros in three hours; come,' said Gambio, laughing.

'Where are we going?'

'Not very far.'

'At this hour?' It was almost midnight.

'Oh yes. This show is strictly for night owls and starts after midnight. And I can promise you, you've seen nothing like it.' Gambio stood up and walked towards the door.

'I'm intrigued,' said Bahadir.

'You should be. Let's go.'

It took them less than half an hour to reach the ruins. Located on a remote property outside Florence, the little chapel had been destroyed by fire in the eighteen-fifties and had been abandoned ever since.

'We are almost there,' said Gambio. 'When we get out of the car, put this on.' Gambio handed his guest a black woollen cloak, a tricorne – a hat popular in the eighteenth-century – and a golden mask made of papier-mâché.

'Some kind of theatre?' asked Bahadir, surprised.

'Of sorts. It's a disguise actually. People who come here want to remain anonymous. And with good reason,' added Gambio, smiling. 'You'll see why in a moment.'

The driver parked Gambio's armoured car under some trees a discreet distance from the ruins, lit up by floodlights like a stage. The picturesque ruins were located in a hollow surrounded by densely wooded hills, well out of sight of nearby villages and homes.

'I bought this property last year,' said Gambio, putting on his cloak, 'especially for what you are about to see; come.'

As they walked towards the ruins, they were joined by several others wearing identical cloaks, hats and masks. They had arrived earlier in a fleet of black limousines from Florence. Bahadir noticed that some of them had a white number pinned to the front of their cloaks; otherwise, everyone looked the same.

'What's with the numbers?' asked Bahadir.

'They are the golden punters as we like to call them; I'll explain later,' said Gambio. 'Stay next to me at all times. Watch and listen.'

Bahadir adjusted his golden mask to see better, and followed Gambio through a stone arch into the chapel. Inside, they were greeted by a tall man dressed just like them, but wearing a red mask. 'Welcome,' said the man, his voice muffled, and ushered them towards a row of pews arranged in a semicircle facing a stone altar. As Gambio turned around, Bahadir noticed that he had the number thirteen pinned to the front of his cloak. They took a seat at the very back. All the others were seated closer to the altar in front of them.

The inside of the chapel was lit by torches, the flickering flames sending crazy shadows dancing across the stone floor. Soft music echoed eerily through the chamber with no roof, adding to the strange, tense mood that made the hairs on the back of Bahadir's neck tingle with excitement and a little fear. 'A black mass?' he asked.

'Of sorts; only better. And much more lucrative,' said Gambio, laughing.

Once everyone was seated, the man with the red mask walked up to the altar and turned around to face the twenty or so guests seated in front of him. The music faded away. 'Welcome to *Ars Moriendi*,' he said, speaking slowly, his voice solemn like a priest's. 'Many of you have taken part in this unique event before, but for some of you, this is your first time. So, let me explain the rules. But before I do, allow me to introduce the combatants.'

The man turned around with a flourish and pointed to a gap in the crumbling wall behind the altar, the silence in the room electric. Suddenly, two shapes appeared out of the darkness as Mozart's exquisite requiem began to float across the ruins, conjuring up images of mourning, funerals and death. Softly at first, but becoming louder as the two shapes came closer, materialising and stepping into the circle of light in front of the altar. Two young men wearing black masks and only loincloths like messengers of the gods in some ancient Greek play, walked up to the man with the red mask from behind and stood next to him; one on his left, the other on his right.

The mesmerised spectators gasped as concealed spotlights illuminated the slim, pale bodies of the two young men from above, the strange, mauve lighting adding to the mystery.

'Composed by a Dominican friar in about 1415, *Ars Moriendi* – 'The Art of Dying' – is a Latin text offering advice on how to die well,' continued the man with the red mask. 'And these two young men standing before you, ladies and gentlemen, will show you how it's done.' The man paused, letting the tension grow. 'And I give you the opportunity for the ultimate wager: your money, against their lives. Here then are the rules: Each one of you has deposited a hundred thousand euros. This is your stake, the amount you can wager,' his voice droned on. 'I will call out the odds before each round and explain what will happen and how it all works.'

Bahadir turned to Gambio sitting next to him. 'What is this?' he asked.

'The biggest game in town with the highest stakes: life and death. Here, right now.'

'Who are these people?'

'High rollers. Mainly Russian billionaires and their girlfriends looking for the ultimate thrill.'

'Are you serious?'

'Deadly; watch.'

The man wearing the red mask finished explaining the rules and held up a silver coin. 'Heads or tails?' he asked, addressing the young man on his right.

'Heads,' said the young man. All eyes were on the coin as it rose up high, twinkling in the torchlight before hitting the stone floor with a sharp clang. 'Tails,' pronounced the man behind the red mask. Then he reached under his cloak and pulled out a gun like a magician introducing his next trick.

'This, ladies and gentlemen, is a .357 magnum Colt Python, one of the most famous and powerful revolvers in the world,' continued the man and held up the gun for all to see. 'You may have already seen the gun in an episode of *The Walking Dead*. If not, you will soon be introduced to its devastating power.'

The man reached into his pocket again and produced a single bullet. 'And this here is a .357 magnum, an awesome bullet.' The man loaded the gun, handed it to the young man on his right and stepped back. The young man spun the cylinder and handed the gun to the other young man. Having won the toss, he would begin and take the first shot.

'Russian roulette?' whispered Bahadir.

'We start with one bullet,' replied Gambio. 'Each of the players gets three shots. They alternate. If they are both still alive after six goes, we progress to two bullets and so on until ...'

'Jesus!'

'I give you ten to one, ladies and gentlemen. Ten to one, if the gun goes off. One bullet in a drum of six. These are good odds. Please place your bets. Call out your number and the amount you would like to wager. My assistants will record your bet. We will begin with number one. Your bet please.'

'Number one; ten thousand,' called out a voice in the front row.

'Number one; ten thousand,' repeated the man in the red mask.

'Number two; thirty thousand,' said a voice in the second row.

It only took a few minutes for all the bets to be placed. 'Are you all done?' said the man and stepped away from the altar. 'Let it begin.'

The young man without the gun climbed slowly onto the altar, crossed himself, and lay down on his back, his masked face staring at the stars above.

'I don't understand,' said Bahadir and shook his head. 'Why are they doing this?'

'Risking their lives? Prepared to die? It's complicated,' replied Gambio. 'Drugs, money and fear. A powerful cocktail.'

'What has all this to do with me?'

'Later; watch.'

The young man with the gun walked up to the altar and held the revolver against the temple of his opponent, the cold barrel with the silencer touching the skin. The young man lying on the altar began to tremble; chest heaving, his breathing heavy. Tiny beads of sweat appeared on his brow and glistened in the torchlight like diamonds on a tiara.

'When the music stops, count slowly to three and fire,' came the instructions from the man behind the red mask standing in the shadows like a demon, watching. The Sanctus of Mozart's *Requiem* rose to a crescendo and then stopped abruptly, lingering for a moment before fading into deathly silence.

'One; two; three,' called out the young man with the gun, his voice sounding distant and hollow, and then pulled the trigger.

11

For a while, Gambio and Bahadir sat in silence in the back seat of the armoured car, each digesting the consequences of the extraordinary drama they had just witnessed. A Land Rover with three bodyguards was following behind. Bahadir had seen violent death before, but nothing could have prepared him for what happened when the .357 Magnum entered the young man's head at point-blank range, shattered the skull and blew his brains apart. The amount of blood alone, gushing out of the huge wound and spilling onto the stone altar like some pagan sacrifice to appease angry gods, was enough to make even a cast-iron stomach churn in disgust.

Trying to calm himself, Bahadir looked out the window and watched the lights of Florence twinkle seductively in the distance, promising familiarity and safety after a night of unexpected horror. He still couldn't work out how he fitted into all this.

'An excellent night,' said Gambio, breaking the silence. 'Did you see that betting frenzy when we reached three bullets? That doesn't happen often, I tell you. The gun usually goes off well before that. The odds were certainly in our favour tonight. You brought us good luck! There was no stopping the punters; amazing. It's not just about the money here, you see. I own several casinos in the States. There, it's all about money. Here it's all about excitement and the ultimate thrill. We provide something the punters can't get anywhere else, and they are attracted to it like moths to a flame; especially the women! We made six-hundred thousand euros tonight; a record! The house always wins. But there is more; much more ...'

'What do you mean?'

'You'll see in a moment; we are almost there.'

'You still haven't told me about your proposal,' said Bahadir. 'Where do I fit into all this?'

'It has to do with what I'm about to show you. What you've seen so far is only half the story.'

'I don't understand,' said Bahadir, shaking his head.

'Patience; here we are.'

The car turned into a dark, narrow driveway leading to a farmhouse set well away from the road.

'Another one of my properties,' said Gambio.

Behind the house was a large wooden barn overgrown with ivy. The car pulled up in front of it. The driver got out of the car and opened the back door for his boss.

'A farm? How curious. What are we doing here?' asked Bahadir, getting out of the car and looking baffled.

'We harvest something,' said Gambio, laughing. 'What else?'

'Harvest what?'

'I'll show you; come.'

Gambio pushed the wide barn door open with his shoulder and stepped into the bright light inside. A semi-trailer with its back doors wide open was parked in the middle of the large barn. Hunched over a steel table, two women wearing plastic gowns and surgical masks were assembling something that looked like a container of sorts. The place was humming with activity.

'What's going on here?' asked Bahadir.

'What does it look like?' Gambio walked up the ramp leading into the back of the trailer and pointed inside. 'What do you think this is?' he asked.

Bahadir followed Gambio up the ramp and looked inside. 'An operating theatre?' he asked, nonplussed. 'I don't understand.'

'Yes, a mobile one. Have a closer look.'

A man wearing a surgical gown was bent over what looked like a body lying on a narrow operating table with bright lights trained on it from above. A woman, obviously a nurse, stood next to him holding a tray. The chest of the body had been opened wide. When Bahadir looked at the head facing away from him – what was left of it – he almost threw up. 'Good God!' he said, feeling ill.

'You are not squeamish, are you?' said Gambio, laughing. 'You've recognised our unlucky loser from earlier then? Within a few hours his heart and kidneys will be on the way to Saudi Arabia. You would be surprised what price a healthy young heart, expertly extracted by an experienced surgeon and safely delivered in state-of-the-art medical transport containers, can fetch these days. What we are harvesting here are healthy, young organs for transplanting; nothing is wasted.'

As the enormity of what was happening around him began to sink in, Bahadir couldn't help but admire the ingenuity of Gambio's daring enterprise. To come up with a bizarre murder–suicide gambling ritual earning hundreds of thousands of euros was unique. But to then use the corpse of the hapless loser to make more money by harvesting his organs, was genius. 'Extraordinary,' he said, shaking his head.

'Impressed?'

'I am,' conceded Bahadir.

'You are dying to ask what all this has to do with you – right?'

Bahadir nodded.

'I'll tell you,' said Gambio. 'Sun's coming up. Let's go back to the villa and have breakfast. I'm starving.'

Gambio tapped his driver on the shoulder and told him to make a short detour into Florence. The car turned into Piazza della Republica and stopped in front of a café. The driver knew the drill. He got out of the car and went to a side entrance because the café was still closed. Moments later, he returned with a cardboard box and handed it to his boss.

Gambio loved his food. He opened the box full of flaky cornetti, crostata, and savoury puff pastries. 'My favourite breakfast,' he said and pointed to a little brioche. 'Here, try one of these. Filled with sliced egg and truffle paste; delicious!'

Bahadir watched Gambio devour his third cornetti with gusto. 'Enough,' said Gambio and closed the lid, 'or we'll have nothing left to have with our coffee.'

Gambio turned to Bahadir sitting next to him and patted him on the arm. 'When I returned from the US three years ago to bury my father, I found the family business here in a dreadful mess. Lack of control, lack of loyalty, greedy fingers in the till, stuff like that had given our rivals a free hand to carve up and dominate the profitable drug business. I changed all that,' continued Gambio, laughing. 'I brought some of our loyal soldiers across from Chicago to teach these arrogant pricks here a lesson. They soon found out there was a new kid on the block who meant business. A few bodies in the river later, things began to change, but it became clear that we needed a new income stream.'

Gambio opened the box again and took out another cornetti. 'I first came across *Ars Moriendi* in Venice,' he continued, munching happily. 'I heard about it on the gambling grapevine and went to check it out. What I saw blew me away; forgive the pun,' he said, laughing. 'The guy who was running it, a small operator from Palermo called Belmonte, had come up with a winning concept. You saw how it works. Even with only a handful of punters, he was making a fortune in the basement of one of the old palazzos. Great setting. The punters arrived by gondola in the middle of the night. However, there was one main problem: supply.' Gambio paused and wiped his mouth with the back of his hand, caster sugar clinging to his stubble like a white moustache.

Bahadir was wondering where all this was heading. 'Supply?' he asked. 'Not enough gamblers?'

'Not at all. That wasn't the problem. He needed more combatants; young men prepared to risk all. Safe ones with no ties. That was the real key to the whole operation, you see. He had his sources, backpackers mainly, but they were risky and uncertain. I came up with something much better, and we became partners. Ah, here we are,' said Gambio as the car pulled up in front of the villa.

They went to the conservatory behind the dining room overlooking the garden. Gambio put the box with the pastries on the table and asked the maid to bring some coffee. 'Good solutions are all about imagination and balls,' he said pensively, and opened the box. 'My source was better, and the supply – at least for the time being – plentiful and much more reliable.'

'What kind of supply?' asked Bahadir.

'Asylum seekers. They arrive by boat from North Africa by the thousands. Once they set foot on Italian soil they are in Europe with the door wide open, but usually nowhere to go. They have risked all to come here, and have nothing left but hope. We give them that hope, if you know what I mean.'

'How exactly?'

'You've seen the game. They agree to play, and we promise the "winner" a lot of cash and a new life; simple. These are desperate young men used to risking all, usually with no family or ties of any kind. For a while we put them up in luxury beyond their wildest dreams. Everything is at their fingertips: food, drugs, booze, sex. Lots of sex. Their testosterone goes mad. They get a taste for what could be while we groom them for the game – and they are prepared to do anything we ask.'

'And you let the "winner" go?' asked Bahadir.

'Don't be naive; of course not. Only parts of him,' added Gambio, laughing.

'What about the bodies?'

'We dispose of them. Acid leaves no trace and organs cannot be identified. You've seen our mobile operating theatre? It's a converted refrigeration truck. I own a trucking business; the semi-trailer is part of the fleet and can go anywhere in Europe. Very handy, I can tell you.'

'So, what's the problem?'

'The punters, especially the women, didn't like black players. They got tired of Africans. We needed new, different players. Fair-skinned ones. We began to look east, towards Syria. The massive wave of asylum seekers sweeping across from Turkey into Greece opened up new possibilities. As you know, all of them want to go to Germany, Merkel country; the promised land, welcoming all. So we promise to help them get there; you get my drift?'

'Sure, but where do I—?'

'I'll tell you,' interrupted Gambio. 'Until recently, I had a very good agent with an excellent network. He identified suitable targets – hungry young men eager to get to Germany – and brought them here to Italy by boat.'

'What happened?'

'He got too greedy. Somehow, he found out what we were doing and demanded part of the action. He was trying to blackmail me, would you believe. Stupid bastard. He ruined a good thing. We blew up his boat with him in it. So, that was the end of our new supply line. Since then, we've had nothing but problems sourcing combatants.'

'I see.'

'So, here's the deal …'

Bahadir sat up and looked at Gambio with obvious anticipation.

'Tonight we'll find out if the beautiful Lorenza will be Europe's new *Top Chef*. If that happens, I will at once put our plan into action,' said Gambio, sipping his café latte, 'and get you what you want.'

'You think you can do it?'

'Come on, you know me better than that. I don't promise what I can't deliver.' What Gambio didn't tell Bahadir was the fact that the daring plan involving Lorenza fitted perfectly into his own strategy to consolidate his influence and power.

'How will you do it?'

'You just leave that to me.'

'And in return?' asked Bahadir.

'We go into business, pal; the *Ars Moriendi* business.'

'Oh? How?'

'Quite simple really, and that's the beauty of it. You have a large restaurant in Istanbul – right?'

'Yes.'

'You employ a lot of staff?"

'About a hundred.'

'And many of them are young asylum seekers from Syria, desperate to get into Europe?' said Gambio, carefully watching Bahadir out

96

of the corner of his eye. 'You have recruited in the camps along the Turkish border?'

'How do you know this?'

Gambio smiled. 'Never mind. I know you offer them a job and bring them to Istanbul where they work for you for a pittance. Well, there we can keep an eye on them, get to know them, select the right ones and then bring them to Italy; final destination *Ars Moriendi*. Their entry into the promised land,' added Gambio, laughing.

'Human trafficking ... I don't know,' said Bahadir.

'Come on. The money involved will make your head spin; promise. Easy money. And don't worry, you won't be alone.'

'What do you mean?'

'You'll have someone to help you with all this. Someone who knows the ropes, knows how to recruit the right guys, groom them and so on ...'

'Who?'

'You've already met him, this morning,' said Gambio, enjoying himself.

'You're making me curious; who?'

'Luigi Belmonte, my business partner from Venice ... the man behind the red mask.'

12

Cesaria sat in the deserted courtyard of Osteria del Sole watching the sun come up. Two dogs were asleep under the table and a handful of chickens were scratching around in the pen watched over by a proud rooster, crowing from time to time to greet the morning. The barman was making coffee in the kitchen and Conti was still in his room.

Conti had promised to give Cesaria his answer in the morning. She had pleaded with him well into the early hours to take up Grimaldi's offer and accompany her to Florence. But what Conti had told her about his past had not only kept her awake, but he had made it clear that his was by no means an easy decision to make. Cesaria had barely slept a wink in the tiny, claustrophobic room in the attic she had shared with the barman's daughter. After tossing and turning restlessly in the narrow, uncomfortable bed, she had finally drifted into a restless slumber for a couple of hours only to wake just before sunrise. Despite several carafes of cheap wine the night before, she felt surprisingly clear-headed and refreshed.

Cesaria heard the kitchen door open and turned around. Conti stood in the doorway with a tray in his hands. 'The baker just dropped these off,' he said, 'still warm.' Conti walked over to Cesaria and put the tray down on the table in front of her. 'The best crostini for miles,' he said. 'That's one of the reasons I live here,' he added, smiling. 'Have one.'

What a transformation, thought Cesaria, watching Conti with interest. The grumpy, dishevelled drunk from the night before had turned into a clean-shaven man wearing a freshly ironed shirt and a tie.

'Ah, here comes the coffee,' said Conti, pointing to the kitchen door. 'I think we can both do with some.'

'You are right about that,' said Cesaria, and thanked the old barman. For a while Conti and Cesaria sat in silence, sipping the hot coffee and enjoying the delicious crostini. *Give him time*, thought Cesaria, and decided against asking the obvious question. But she reasoned that the shirt and tie were encouraging signs.

This girl is good, thought Conti, appreciating Cesaria's tact and self-control. *She probably thinks she already knows the answer.* Conti took another sip of coffee and watched Cesaria. *I wonder how she'll react when I tell her?* 'I promised to give you my answer in the morning,' began Conti. Cesaria looked at him, alarmed by the sad tone of his voice. 'I'm afraid the answer is *no*,' he added.

'I see,' said Cesaria, unable to hide her disappointment. 'And you dressed up just to tell me this?' she said, the sarcasm in her voice obvious.

'No. I dressed up, as you put it, because I respect you and would like to take you to the airport.'

Cesaria pushed her plate aside. She had lost her appetite. 'I think you are making a big mistake.'

'That's a little presumptuous, don't you think? You don't know me. You don't know anything about me.'

'You're right; I'm sorry,' said Cesaria, realising she had gone too far. 'It's just ...'

'I know.'

'Do you?'

'You care,' said Conti.

Cesaria looked at Conti, surprised. 'Yes, I do. And yet—'

'It's complicated,' interrupted Conti.

'Simple things often are.'

'This isn't simple. After my wife died, I promised myself *never* ...'

'Perhaps it was the wrong promise,' ventured Cesaria.

Conti shook his head and looked melancholy.

'You would rather wallow in self-pity in this godforsaken place than do what you do best?'

'That's a little harsh.'

'Is it?' Cesaria pressed on. 'You are wasting your life here; a man like you ... just like my father,' she added quietly.

'What do you mean?'

Cesaria waved her hand, the gesture dismissive. 'It's nothing ...' she said.

'I told you a lot about myself last night. More than I have told people in years. Now it's your turn. Fair?'

'My father was a judge in Rome,' began Cesaria.

'Oh?'

'He was abducted by the Mafia during a high-profile trial. They kept him in a cellar for six months and demanded certain undertakings from the government.'

'What kind of undertakings?'

'The release of two prisoners, with pardons.'

'What happened?'

'The government refused.'

'And?'

'My father was found in the boot of an abandoned car in front of Castel Sant'Angelo. Surprisingly, he was still alive, if only just. They had cut off his ears and broken his fingers,' whispered Cesaria.

'I am so sorry.'

'But that wasn't the worst of it. He survived, but gave up and resigned. They had broken him.'

'And you are blaming him for that?'

'No, not anymore. I used to at the time; I was very angry.' Cesaria paused and turned to face Conti. 'But I'm blaming you.'

Conti looked at Cesaria, surprised. 'I don't follow,' he said.

'You are not a broken man like my father; far from it. Yet, you *choose* to do nothing. My father had no choice; I can see that now. And not a day goes by when I don't regret having blamed him ...'

'It's not as simple as you think,' snapped Conti.

'It is to me,' whispered Cesaria, tears in her eyes.

Conti realised it was time to change the subject. He glanced at his watch. 'If you want to catch the morning flight, we better get going.'

Palermo airport was already full of tourists and the security queues were long. Progress was slow and several planes were delayed. 'What made you decide to join the police?' asked Conti.

'Something that happened at my father's funeral.'

'Oh?'

'I was just finishing law at the time,' said Cesaria, 'following in my father's footsteps, you see. A long family tradition.'

'So, what happened?'

'As my mother walked past the open coffin in church, she slipped something inside.'

'What?'

'A small plaque my father used to keep on his desk. It had an inscription.'

'What did it say?'

'*The only thing necessary for the triumph of evil is for good men to do nothing.* It's what my father believed. Before they broke him,' she added sadly.

Conti stopped, his face ashen. 'Good God!' he whispered.

'You know what it is?' asked Cesaria.

'A quote from Edmund Burke, the eighteenth-century Irish statesman. When things got really tough, my wife used to remind me by using the same ...'

'Yes?'

'Never mind. Do you still have that ticket?'

'The one I rather naively brought with me, for you?' asked Cesaria, perplexed. 'I have it right here.'

Conti nodded. 'Good. Give it to me.'

'I don't understand; why?' stammered Cesaria.

'Because I'm coming with you.'

13

Lorenza's grandparents, Carlo and Amadea, lived in a fifteenth-century villa overlooking the Boboli Gardens and the river below. The villa had been in the Medici family for generations and still retained many of its original features and furnishings.

Countess Kuragin, an early riser, listened to the pealing of the church bells drifting across the river, the familiar sounds bringing a smile to her face as she remembered the endless summer holidays in Florence with her parents a long time ago. Gelato after church on Sundays followed by a pizza treat for lunch, elaborate picnics in the country and countless visits to art galleries and museums with her father were the stuff of happy memories to be treasured. Most of her friends flocked to the Riviera for their holidays, but not her father. He referred to the Riviera as *a sunny place for shady people* and preferred cultured Florence and its way of life.

The countess stepped out onto the terrace and took a deep breath. Shielding her eyes from the glare of the morning sun, she gazed down upon Florence, which looked like a painting.

'You're up early,' said Leonardo da Baggio, joining the countess on the terrace.

'So are you,' replied the countess, enjoying the first private moment with her friend since her arrival the day before. Part one of the grand finale had been exciting and tumultuous. Watching the long contest and the nail-biting culinary battle had taken its toll on everyone. The grandparents were exhausted by the end of the long evening and everyone had retired to their rooms as soon as they got home just after midnight.

The countess put her hand on da Baggio's arm. 'You must be very proud of her,' she said. 'That was an amazing performance last night, especially by someone so young. I wonder what they have in store for them this evening for the finale.'

'Whatever it is, I'm sure she'll do well. She is very determined and resourceful; well ahead of her age. She *wants* to win.'

Da Baggio paused and looked dreamily down into the city. 'She's doing it for her mother, you know,' he said quietly.

'I understand … What did you mean when you said yesterday it wasn't an accident?'

Da Baggio took his time before replying. 'Look at this city,' he began. 'Spectacular, isn't it?'

'Sure is.'

'Underneath all this beauty, culture and history is a dark side, brutal and very violent. This is a dangerous, corrupt place ruled by an untouchable elite. A criminal elite.'

The countess looked at da Baggio, surprised.

'Come on Leo …'

'I'm serious; the crash that killed Lucrecia and Antonio was no accident. The car was run off the road by a truck – deliberately.'

'How can you say this? There was an investigation …'

'It was a cover-up.'

'How do you know?' demanded the countess.

'It was supposed to be a warning, not a fatality.'

'*A warning?* Why?'

'Carlo and Amadea own a lot of property in Florence, as many of the old families do. There was this development proposal for a new hotel by the river. Spectacular views, right in the heart of the city, great location. Only one thing stood in its way …'

'What?'

'An old historic building owned by the grandparents, and they refused to sell. That's when it all started.'

'Started what?'

'The threats, the intimidation.'

'Come on …'

'I'm serious. You know Carlo, he isn't one to be pushed around. He refused. That's when they ramped up the pressure.'

'Who?'

'The Mafia. The Mafia rules this city with an iron fist. Three families. All the locals here know this. The authorities are corrupt and in Cosa Nostra pockets. The rule of law is compromised here right up to the highest level.'

'Are you serious?'

'Absolutely. After the accident, they approached Carlo again. They tried to make him sell and referred to the "accident" … That's when everything became clear and fell into place.'

'What did he do?'

'He told them to go to hell! Ironically, by killing his daughter and his grandson they had gone too far; a warning gone wrong. There was no more pressure. In the end they realised this and gave up. The development didn't go ahead.'

'And no-one did anything about this?'

'No. There was no way to prove it, and the inquest finding was as clear as it was final; it was an accident. Guess who owned the truck that ran them off the road?'

'Tell me.'

'The Mafia family behind the development. Things are that brazen around here.'

'My God, Leo; how dreadful!' said the countess and threw her arms around her friend. Now, everything began to make sense: Leonardo's appearance, his dejection; everything. 'What about Carlo and Amadea?'

'What do you think? They are devastated, they blame themselves …'

'How awful. But it's not their fault!'

'Try to tell them that.'

'Does Lorenza know?'

'No. And I hope she never finds out. It would destroy her. You can see why the possibility of winning *Top Chef* means so much. To us all …'

'We'll know tonight. Are Carlo and Amadea coming along again to watch?'

'They wouldn't miss it for the world.'

Preparations for the grand finale had reached fever pitch at the Villa Laurentius. Neither Monti the compere nor artistic director Louis had slept a wink since the nail-biting contest the night before. The show that would be watched by millions was about to get underway. *One point the difference*, thought Louis. *This is anyone's race; how perfect!* The two finalists, Lorenza and Carlos, were a producer's dream. The whole of Europe loved them.

Louis knocked on Lorenza's door and entered. 'Ready?' he asked. 'We are on in ten minutes.'

'As ready as I'll ever be.'

'You look absolutely gorgeous, darling,' said Louis, and adjusted Lorenza's hair.

'Has my family arrived?'

'Yes. Wonderful people. And your nonna; what a star! The audience loved her, especially her stories about your adventures in her kitchen as a toddler … You are very lucky!'

'I am.'

Apart from a fleeting embrace at the beginning of last night's show, Lorenza had had no other contact with her family. Phones were strictly forbidden. But she did manage to catch glimpses of them in the audience as they watched the contest from the gallery above the kitchen arena.

'How do you feel?'

'Elated, but a little scared.'

'Good. Scared is good. It brings out the best in people in situations like this. I've seen it many times. Just take a deep breath and stay calm. You can do it!' Louis prattled on. He gave Lorenza a hug and kissed her on the cheek. She was his favourite and he hoped she would win. 'Get ready. I'll be back in five minutes to get you.'

Lorenza walked out onto the balcony, took a deep breath, and listened to the church bells. Then she pulled a small photograph out of her apron pocket and looked at it intently. It had been taken in her mother's kitchen in Venice on her tenth birthday. It was a snapshot of her mother handing her a cookbook, her first. Lorenza lifted the photograph to her lips and kissed it. 'This is for you, Mum,' she whispered, tears in her eyes.

Moments later, Louis burst into the room, excited. 'Are you ready?' he shouted.

'I am,' replied Lorenza. She slipped the photograph back into her pocket, adjusted her apron and followed Louis out of the room.

14

Villa Laurentius, Top Chef Europe Grand Finale,
day two: 21 May, 7:00 pm

'Good evening, Europe,' said Monti, grinning into the camera. 'This is it! By the end of the evening, Europe will have a new *Top Chef*. Who will it be? Will it be Carlos' – the camera zoomed in on Carlos standing in front of the judges, waving – 'or will it be the lovely Lorenza? During the past few weeks,' continued Monti, 'both contestants have dazzled us with their extraordinary talents and have impressed and surprised the judges with their creativity and skills. But there can only be one winner!'

Sitting alone in his study, Gambio turned up the volume on the TV, poured himself a glass of wine and sat back. He was only interested in the outcome of the contest for one reason: should Lorenza win, he would implement his plan as promised, and bring Bahadir into the business. For Gambio, that would be the best outcome. And then there was an added, unexpected bonus … Gambio smiled as he remembered seeing the old couple – Lorenza's grandparents – in the television audience the night before.

At first he had refused to believe what he saw. But then, as the old man was introduced and began to speak, Gambio knew there was no mistake. This was the same man who had so stubbornly refused to sell and had caused him so much trouble with the hotel. To some extent, Gambio blamed himself. The botched accident had effectively killed the deal. However, fate had somehow dealt him another hand, and he intended to use it to win this time. And Gambio knew exactly how he would do that. All he needed was for Lorenza to be crowned *Top Chef Europe*.

Superstitious and a passionate gambler, Gambio enjoyed the excitement caused by uncertainty and firmly believed that fate would once again point him in the right direction; go ahead, or walk away? He was ready to do either.

Back in his hotel room, Bahadir was hanging on Monti's every word. Part of him was hoping Lorenza would lose, which would to some extent at least repair the damage inflicted by his earlier, crushing defeat. But to his surprise, part of him was hoping she would win, which would allow him to embark on the daring plan Gambio had proposed. This would open up totally unexpected possibilities and allow him to vindicate himself and heal his wounded pride in a most dramatic way.

After introducing the judges, Monti turned to the contestants and began to explain the rules. 'Tonight, the judges have decided to depart from tradition and do something quite different,' he announced with a flourish. 'You have already demonstrated your technical skills, your vast knowledge and insights into cooking and your ability to work under pressure. You have shown us that you are not afraid to explore something new, and know how to improvise and create. So, what's left? What is left here to explore?' Monti paused to build suspense. 'What is left, is *you*. You will have to show the judges who you are, what cooking means to you, and why. So, how will that be done?' The camera zoomed in on the faces of the two contestants standing side by side – looking serious and tense – and stayed there.

'You will be asked to create a dish of your choice that best represents your cooking style and personality,' continued Monti. 'As part of your presentation you will have to explain to the judges why you have chosen the dish, and what it means to you. This will form part of the score, as the dish will have to reflect that. The final element is time. Among other things, this is a pressure test. You will have unlimited access to the pantry, but only an hour and a half to prepare the dish. Each of the judges will score your dish out of ten, which will be added to yesterday's results. The contestant with the highest score out of a total of sixty, will be declared the winner.'

Lorenza's heart missed a beat when she heard Monti explain the rules. With the tips of her fingers resting on her mother's photograph inside her apron pocket as a painful, yet precious link to the past, she closed her eyes and smiled. '*Hunkar Begendi*,' she heard her mother whisper in her ear. *Yes, Mum, I'll cook the Sultan's Delight!* she thought and opened her eyes, her face exuberant. She had created the spectacular dish many times before, and knew every intricate detail of the complex recipe by heart. The dish had already impressed one of the legendary rulers of the mighty Ottoman Empire, perhaps it would impress the judges as well. And then of course there was the story …

'Contestants, are you ready?' asked Monti. Both Carlos and Lorenza nodded and smiled into the cameras. 'Your time starts *now!*'

The countess turned to Tristan, sitting next to her in the gallery. He was watching Lorenza hurry into the pantry with a basket under her arm to collect her ingredients. 'You are very quiet,' said the countess. 'Something wrong?'

'She is going to win,' replied Tristan, speaking softly.

'I hope you're right,' said the countess.

'I don't.'

The countess looked at Tristan, surprised. 'Why do you say that?'

'Because this victory will come at great cost.'

'How come?' asked the countess, frowning.

She knew from experience that dismissing Tristan's remark as a curious observation would be a mistake. She had witnessed his remarkable psychic powers many times before. Part Maori with an extraordinary, painful past, Tristan had inherited his gift from his mother, a Maori princess who died in tragic circumstances after saving the life of the countess's daughter, Anna. Tristan had featured in two of Jack Rogan's bestsellers, *The Disappearance of Anna Popov*, and *The Hidden Genes of Professor K.* Whenever Tristan's psychic powers came into play, the countess remembered his mother's words: 'His gift is much stronger than mine; he can hear the whisper of angels and glimpse eternity.'

When Tristan was orphaned as a teenager, the countess gave him a home and took him into her heart. He became part of her family and had a special bond with her daughter, Anna, which had grown stronger over the years.

Bahadir watched the contest with growing anxiety and concern as it became clear from the ingredients Lorenza had chosen that she was once again turning to Ottoman cuisine as the theme for her dish. She had already demonstrated her extraordinary knowledge of Eastern spices and how to blend them into flavours that made the Western palate, unfamiliar with their exquisite properties, sing.

Damn her! thought Bahadir, clenching his fists in frustration. This was bound to once again focus attention on his humiliating defeat, especially if she was to win.

To entertain the viewers and tease some information out of the contestants that would throw some light on the dishes they had chosen, Monti conducted a casual, humorous interview in the kitchen, and asked questions about the dishes, the cooking process and the ingredients. Carlos had made seafood his theme, and was preparing a paella with a twist.

'Carlos, from what I can see,' said Monti, bending over the frying pan, 'the hero of your dish is obviously seafood.'

'Correct.'

'It looks like a paella.'

'It is, but with a twist ...'

'Can you tell us a little more about that?'

'A Moorish twist,' said Carlos, lowering his voice, the tone conspiratorial.

'How intriguing ... Anything else?'

'It's all in the taste ...'

'Ah ...'

Monti walked over to Lorenza's workstation.

'Smells good,' he said, examining the fragrant contents of the iron pot bubbling on the stove in front of Lorenza.

'I hope so.'

'And what is your dish?'

'A taste-bridge between East and West. Byzantium meets Venice.'

Momentarily taken aback by Lorenza's cryptic remark, Monti looked at her, surprised, the camera zooming in on his face. 'How intriguing,' he said. 'Care to tell us a little more about this?'

'No, not really,' said Lorenza, laughing. 'I will let the taste tell the story.' She dipped a wooden spoon into the broth, lifted it to her mouth and closed her eyes. 'A little more cumin and cardamom, I think,' she said, smacking her lips. 'That should do it.'

15

'Five, four, three, two, one!' counted the excited spectators, cheering on the finalists. Looking down into the kitchen from the gallery above, the countess squeezed da Baggio's arm. Da Baggio looked at her and smiled in silent reply.

Unaffected by the excitement erupting all around him, Tristan stood in the background, watching. He was trying to make sense of the disturbing images that kept assaulting his agitated brain every time he looked at Lorenza from above. *What does it all mean?* he asked himself, and attempted to piece the images together into some coherent sequence. But to no avail; it was like chasing shadows.

Down below, Lorenza put the finishing touches to the presentation of her dish. She knew that the eyes prepared the way for taste. The appearance and presentation of the dish were therefore of critical importance. First impressions counted, a lot. Lorenza sprinkled some finely chopped parsley on top of the eggplant, wiped the side of the plate with a cloth and stepped back. *Done! Let Hunkar Begendi weave its magic,* she thought, and waved to her father and grandparents applauding in the gallery just above her workstation.

'Time's up,' said Monti, his face flushed with excitement. 'Very soon, ladies and gentlemen, we'll know who will be Europe's new *Top Chef.* The contestants have done their part, now it's all up to the judges. Ready judges?' The judges stood up and waved.

Carlos was first. Smiling into the camera, he carried his dish confidently over to the judges, and placed it on the table in front of them. The dish, a seafood paella presented in a large, flat copper pan, looked spectacular.

'Tell us about your dish,' said the French celebrity chef on the panel.

Carlos was ready for the question. He described his dish with great precision and flair, listing each item of seafood used and how it had been cooked. He then turned to the gother ingredients and described their specific roles and how they influenced the taste. He then spent some time talking about the importance of texture, especially in the rice. However, he had cleverly saved up the best for last: taste. His was a paella with a Moorish twist, he explained, and this was reflected in the all-important spices he had used. Because he had grown up in Malaga, the use of certain exotic spices brought across from North Africa gave the dish a unique quality only found in southern Spain.

The judges looked impressed. 'Let's taste,' said the French judge. He reached for a large wooden spoon and began to serve the dish; one small plate for each of the three judges.

Lorenza's spirits sank as she heard Carlos's impressive description of his dish, delivered with eloquence and style. She had no doubt that the taste would match the description and spectacular appearance of the dish. She had to admit that by comparison, her dish looked rather modest. But as usual it would all come down to taste. And then of course there was this additional element, a very personal one, which would form part of the score: the connection between the dish and its creator. Feeling better, Lorenza smiled. She was very confident about taste, and she knew she had quite a story to tell about the unique dish, what it meant to her, and why. She was ready to surprise the judges, and had worked out exactly how she would do that.

The countess turned to Tristan. 'Don't look so glum,' she said. 'I know he was good, but she is better, you'll see.'

'I'm sure you're right,' said Tristan, still feeling uneasy, and unable to make sense of the disturbing images. Then, it all came together in a flash of recognition. All the images had one thing in common: *danger!*

Not bad, thought Bahadir as he watched the judges taste Carlos's dish. *He could win this.*

Joseph Weindorfer, the Austrian chef, pushed his plate aside and looked at Carlos standing in front of the judges' table. 'Please tell us why you have chosen this dish, and what it means to you,' he said, and sat back.

Bahadir listened intently as Carlos spoke about his childhood and what it was like to grow up in Malaga, about going fishing after school with an old man he had befriended, and then cooking the catch over a driftwood fire on the beach with the other fishermen, as tradition demanded. Carlos charmed the judges with his description of his early attempts at cooking and mastering the spices, and entertained them with stories of his spectacular failures and modest triumphs, until the connection between the dish he had chosen and his passion for cooking became obvious and easy to understand.

After conferring briefly, the judges reached for their scorecards, scored the dish, and then put the cards aside. The scores would be revealed at the end.

Now it was Lorenza's turn. Feeling exhausted, Louis wiped his brow with a handkerchief as he watched Lorenza carry her dish to the judges' table. *What a remarkable young woman,* he thought. *Carlos was outstanding; she has a hard act to follow.*

Lorenza gave the judges her best smile, and placed her dish on the table in front of them.

'We were intrigued by your remark,' said the Italian judge, 'that your dish is a taste-bridge between East and West. 'What exactly did you mean by that?'

'Byzantium meets Venice?' interjected the French judge.

Lorenza smiled. The judges had just given her a great opening. 'I grew up in Venice. In fact, I still live there. My family – the da Baggios – were traders who made their fortune importing spices from the East, from Byzantium. These spices had a profound influence on Venetian cooking through the ages. Their influence can be seen to this very day and give Venetian cooking that special, almost exotic edge, unique to the region.

'The dish I have chosen is called *Hunkar Begendi,* the Sultan's Delight,' continued Lorenza, 'and it clearly reflects this. The original dish dates back to the sixteenth-century, but has been modified through the ages, especially by my late mother,' she added, the sadness in her voice obvious, 'and by me. We added certain Venetian aspects to the dish ... and often joked that perhaps now it would delight both the sultan and the doge.'

The judges nodded appreciatively.

'Tell us about your dish,' said the Austrian judge.

'This dish has two heroes,' began Lorenza, 'lamb, and aubergine. Instead of competing, as heroes tend to do, they complement one another and are bound together by a unique blend of Eastern spices usually found in the bazaars of Istanbul rather than the markets of Venice. What makes this dish so unique are the spices, and it must have been the spices that delighted the sultan and gave the dish its name. In essence, this is a lamb stew served on a bed of creamy roasted aubergine puree. But the simplicity of the dish is deceptive. The flavours are sophisticated and subtle. Cumin and cardamom rub shoulders with saffron and black pepper and the other spices to tease the tastebuds, but in a harmonious way without one dominating the other.'

Very clever, thought Louis. *She makes your mouth water with words.*

The judges looked at each other.

'Gentlemen, let's taste,' said the Italian judge, and began to serve Lorenza's dish.

16

'Quite a girl, don't you think?' said Gambio, and poured Luigi Belmonte another drink. Gambio didn't believe in wasting time. He had invited Belmonte to his home so they could watch the *Top Chef Europe* final on TV together. In the event that Lorenza turned out to be the winner, they could refine the audacious plan and work out the best strategy.

'She lives in Venice, did you hear?' said Gambio, laughing. 'Right in the middle of your patch. Certain things are meant to be, buddy; cheers.' They touched glasses.

Gambio knew that in Belmonte he had the right man for the job. The daring assassination of Mario Giordano the day before had been the final test. Belmonte had lived up to his reputation: he had carried out the assignment with professionalism and imagination that had impressed Gambio. And most importantly, he hadn't made any mistakes. Had he done so, he would be floating somewhere in the river by now, instead of having a drink with the capo.

Third generation Mafia from Palermo, Belmonte was loyal to a fault, and ruthless to the core. In short, he had an impeccable criminal pedigree. Having grown up in a family where murder was discussed at the dinner table, and extreme violence was considered normal, he had no formal education to speak of and was barely literate. However, what he lacked in education, he more than made up in natural cunning and fearless common sense that had kept him alive and had earned him the respect of men like Gambio. And what Belmonte craved more than anything else in the world was respect.

After several audacious assassinations in Palermo reaching to the very top of the judiciary and the police, he had become "too hot" even for the Mafia, and had to leave Sicily before the outraged authorities caught up with him. He had changed his name from Raffaele Bangarella, the notorious "Archangel of Palermo", to Luigi Belmonte, and ended up in Venice where he had set up his own unique gambling "business" that had brought him to Gambio's attention.

'So, what's on your mind?' asked Belmonte, carefully watching his business partner – boss would have been more accurate, but Gambio was happy to let the relationship rest on a little fiction to pander to the man's ego. In the end, Gambio held all the cards and pulled all the strings. He was content with that. For a habitual gambler like him, risks and high stakes went hand in hand, and Gambio needed both, or he quickly lost interest. Gambio had lived his entire life as one big gamble, only the stakes got higher with age, and the risks more daring.

'I'll tell you, but only if she wins.'

'And if she doesn't?'

'We walk away.'

'Why?'

'You have to ask? She only gets the million euros if she wins; simple,' replied Gambio, laughing. 'A target without big bucks is not a target we want, right?' Gambio didn't mention Bahadir and the other reasons. There would be plenty of time to introduce that subject later. For now, money was enough.

'Of course,' said Belmonte with a broad grin. Money was something he understood very well. 'We'll know in a few minutes. Salute!'

Locked away in his hotel room, Bahadir couldn't take his eyes off the TV screen. He watched the expressions on the judges' faces as they tasted Lorenza's dish. What he saw told him everything. *Hunkar Begendi,* he thought, anger and frustration churning in his stomach like two evil worms, fighting. *The bitch had to choose my signature dish!*

The Italian judge put down his fork and looked at Lorenza standing demurely in front of the judges' table, waiting. 'Now please tell us why you have chosen this dish, and what it means to you,' he asked, posing the identical question he had put to Carlos earlier.

Lorenza had been expecting this, and was ready.

'To give you an accurate answer,' she began, tossing back her luxurious hair, 'I have to take you on a little journey into history ... family history.'

The judges looked intrigued.

'Something remarkable happened in 1595 that has a direct bearing on this dish and what it means to me. Cosimo da Baggio, one of my ancestors on my father's side, was dying, without an heir. The family had fallen on hard times, but just before he passed away something extraordinary occurred that changed the future direction of our family: the grandson he didn't know he had, appeared on the doorstep of the da Baggio palazzo in Venice.' Lorenza paused, collecting her thoughts.

'Cosimo's daughter, Catalina – a striking beauty,' she continued, 'had been abducted by pirates eighteen years earlier. She was presumed dead, but was in fact sold into slavery and ended up in the sultan's harem in the Topkapi Palace in Constantinople, as Istanbul was known at the time, and became one of sultan's favourite consorts. She was given the name Fatma Hatun. To cut a complicated story short, upon the sultan's death, all his sons except his heir, Mehmed, were murdered to secure Mehmed's succession. However, one son managed to escape: Osman, Fatma's son. Two years later, he presented himself at Cosimo's deathbed, and became his heir.' Lorenza paused again, her face flushed with excitement. She was desperately hoping she wasn't boring the judges with her story. She needn't have worried. The judges were captivated, and so were millions of viewers. Taking a deep breath, Lorenza pressed on.

'However, Osman didn't come empty-handed. His mother had given him something rare and precious to take with him into his new life. A set of secret recipes she had copied personally from the originals that had belonged to Suleiman the Magnificent, the late sultan's illustrious father. These recipes were fiercely guarded palace treasures that had been gathered from every corner of the empire to please the sultan and enrich his kitchen.'

'One of those recipes was Hunkar Begendi, the dish I cooked for you tonight. It was my late mother's favourite,' said Lorenza, choking with emotion, 'and the first dish I remember cooking with her and my grandmother in our kitchen in Venice as a little girl, where generations of da Baggios had prepared similar exotic dishes for the family table.'

For a long moment, there was complete silence as the camera homed in on Lorenza wiping away a tear rolling down her cheek. The judges looked at each other. Then the Italian judge began to clap and the others joined in. It was a spontaneous gesture of respect for a brave young woman who had opened a secret corner of her heart to the world for all to see.

Gambio turned to Belmonte sitting opposite. 'What do you think?' he asked.

'She's got it in the bag, I'd say.'

'I agree with you. Here comes the verdict ...'

Monti realised he had to step in to make sure the show stayed on track, and on time, and followed the script. 'The moment you've all been waiting for,' he announced, 'has arrived. The judges are about to reveal their scores. Carlos, please step forward.'

Carlos embraced Lorenza standing next to him. 'Good luck,' she whispered and kissed him on the cheek. 'And to you,' he replied, and stepped forward.

Carlos's dish received a lot of praise from the judges. They singled out his technical excellence and imaginative blend of flavours that gave his dish a unique quality with echoes of North Africa. They commented on his charming story of the old fisherman and how the dish perfectly reflected that relationship and obvious influence on Carlos's passion for cooking. Carlos received a stunning combined score of twenty-six from the judges, which gave him a grand total of fifty-one points out of sixty.

The countess turned to Leonardo da Baggio, who was staring down into the kitchen.

'She may be losing her dream,' he whispered. 'She needs at least twenty-eight out of thirty to win. An almost impossible task.'

The countess squeezed his hand. 'Never say never,' she replied, smiling. 'Tristan believes she will win and he is rarely wrong in such matters.'

'I wish ...'

'And now it is the lovely Lorenza's turn,' said Monti, by now bursting with excitement. 'Please step forward.'

Louis looked at Lorenza and crossed his fingers.

Lorenza straightened her apron with a few battle-splotches of sauce splattered across her chest, and did as she was asked.

The French judge spoke first. He began by commenting on the originality of the dish, the perfectly cooked lamb that melted in the mouth and the unique blend of spices. He gave her a nine.

Then came the Austrian judge. He focused on taste and commended her on her exemplary technique of cooking each of the ingredients perfectly to retain integrity of texture, and praised the subtle flavours that surprised the palate in unexpected ways. He also gave her a nine.

It was now all up to the Italian judge. To win, Lorenza needed a perfect score of ten. For a while, the judge just looked at Lorenza and said nothing. Lorenza squeezed her mother's photograph in her apron pocket until her nails dug into the palm of her hand – drawing blood – but she held his gaze.

'All the obvious qualities of your dish like taste, blend of flavours, cooking style and so on have already been adequately commented on and evaluated by my friends. I have nothing to add in that regard,' began the judge. 'I would like to focus on something quite different; the *soul* of the dish. By sharing the unique history of this dish with us you have given it a new dimension; an intensely personal one. Cooking is much more than technique and experience. Every now and then, someone exceptional comes along. An artist who takes cooking to a different level.

'In my long career, I have only come across a handful of people who had this gift, this instinct to bring out something special in a dish only they can see. This is an art, not a science, and you, Lorenza, have this gift. You give your dish a *soul*; it becomes an extension of you … and that is why I have scored your dish … ten out of ten,' said the Italian judge, and held up his scorecard.

Stunned silence … then the room erupted in deafening cheers and applause, as Europe saluted its new *Top Chef.*

17

Amena took off her surgical gown and looked at Dr Rosen. 'I can't do any more, Bettany,' she said, exhausted. 'We must have done ten hours straight today. Bedlam again over the border.'

Pregnant women, children – some of them just babies – and the elderly, most of them with horrific injuries mainly caused by shrapnel, had arrived in a relentless convoy of misery from the border. Carried on improvised stretchers by relatives or complete strangers, they were deposited in front of Dr Rosen's container surgery in neat rows, hoping for a miracle.

Dr Rosen handed Amena a glass of water and put her arm around her new friend. 'I haven't seen surgery like this before – ever. You are truly amazing,' said Dr Rosen. 'You can do anything. Where did you learn all this?'

'From my husband, mainly. Necessity is a good teacher, he used to say. When someone is on the table in front of you, in desperate need, you do the best you can.'

Amena covered her face with her hands. 'If the world could only see this,' she sobbed. 'So many dead. We must have lost at least a dozen today.'

'Today was terrible, I agree,' said Dr Rosen, trying to comfort her friend. 'But we did manage all the emergencies. That's something at least, don't you think?'

'I can't forget that little boy with the missing leg. He reminded me of my son.'

'Come, let's have something to eat,' said Dr Rosen changing the subject, and opened the door.

As she stepped outside, two men carrying someone on a stretcher staggered unsteadily towards her. 'This one is in a bad way, doctor,' said one of the men, barely able to speak. The men put down the stretcher. 'Are you Dr Rosen?'

'Yes,' said Dr Rosen, surprised.

'We found him near the border. He asked for you.'

'He won't make it to the morning; please ...' said the other man.

Dr Rosen looked at Amena. Amena shrugged and pointed inside. 'Put him on the table,' she said, and stepped aside.

'Allah the Merciful will reward you in this life and the next,' said one of the men as he walked past.

Dr Rosen looked at the man on the operating table. Hallucinating, barely conscious and covered in dust, his thinning hair and grey beard encrusted with blood, it was obvious he was close to death.

'Do you know him?' asked Amena, and began to cut away the man's blood-soaked shirt.

'No,' replied Dr Rosen, and peeled away the torn fabric. 'Bullet wound just below the shoulder, right here; tricky spot. Lost a lot of blood. He's well into his sixties. Look at all these scars. This man has been in the wars. Must be very strong.'

'Or determined to stay alive,' said Amena, beginning to clean the wound. 'The will to live can be very powerful; I've seen it many times. Are you sure you don't know him? He asked for you.'

Dr Rosen had another look at the man's face and shook her head. 'How do you feel?' she asked Amena.

'I'm fine. If we don't take care of him now, he won't be with us in the morning, even with the strongest will to live. We have to get the bullet out and he needs an urgent blood transfusion.' Amena turned to the two nurses standing behind her. 'Let's get to work.'

Due to unexpected complications, it took Amena and Dr Rosen more than two hours to remove the bullet. 'I'm surprised he made it,' said Amena, beginning to sew up the wound. 'You're right, he's very strong, and very lucky.' Amena pointed to the wound. 'Another centimetre to the left, and he would have died instantly.'

'What do you think?' said Dr Rosen.

'If he gets through the night, he should be fine.' Amena looked at Nazir watching her. 'Take him next door into recovery,' she said. 'I know it's full, but you have to find him a corner somewhere. I'll look at him again in the morning.'

'I'll find something; don't worry,' said Nazir, glad to have been asked. He was eager to learn and always ready to assist.

Dr Rosen helped Amena take off her gown.

'What a remarkable young man. I don't know what we would do without him,' said Amena.

'You're right, but if we don't leave now, you'll be next on the table,' said Dr Rosen, laughing. 'Come, let's go.'

Amena and Dr Rosen were up at first light and doing the rounds in recovery before starting surgery again. More wounded had arrived during the night, needing urgent attention.

'What did I tell you?' said Amena, pointing to the man with the bullet they had saved the night before. 'Look at him.' Nazir had washed the man's face and combed his hair and beard. The man's eyes were wide open, and he looked remarkably refreshed and alert.

'He's a fighter,' said Dr Rosen, and walked over to the patient. 'How do you feel?' she said, and reached for his wrist to take his pulse.

'Thanks to you, Bettany, quite well, and back with the living,' said the man, and turned his head towards Dr Rosen.

Dr Rosen looked at him, surprised. He had called her by her first name. 'Have we met?' she asked.

'You don't know who I am, do you? Not surprising.'

'I don't understand,' said Dr Rosen, looking perplexed.

'The last time you saw me, I was in a deadly whirlpool with Marcus, deep inside a cave in Ethiopia,' said the man calmly, a twinkle in his eyes.

Dr Rosen let go of the man's wrist and kept staring at him, as her memory began to reconstruct the features of his face and slowly, surprise turned into recognition. 'Naguib?' she stammered. 'It can't be. Naguib is dead. I saw him drown.'

'Did you? Perhaps he survived?'

The voice too, sounded familiar. 'Good God, is it really you?'

'It is. I am Naguib Haddad, formerly Chief Inspector Haddad of the Cairo police force.'

'You saved Marcus's life; I saw it.'

'I owed him that, especially after Luxor.'

'I still can't believe it!' said Dr Rosen, obviously struggling. 'He doesn't know you're alive?'

'No-one does.'

'But how? Why?'

'Jack would call it destiny.'

Dr Rosen smiled. 'He would,' she said, and reached for Haddad's hand to reassure herself that he was really there. 'How did you find me?'

'That was easy. You have quite a reputation. The whole of Aleppo is talking about the healer just across the border who never turns away someone in need, never asks questions and never judges. Only saves lives.'

Dr Rosen shook her head, obviously a little embarrassed by the compliment. 'Where have you been all these years?' she asked.

'In prison mainly, but still hunting villains. It's a long story.'

As an experienced surgeon, Dr Rosen was used to dealing with the unexpected and was quickly coming to terms with the fact that the little man in front of her was really Naguib Haddad. The only thing unclear at that moment was how it could be possible.

'You are not going anywhere in a hurry,' she said. 'We'll have plenty of time to talk. Now you must rest, and I have to start surgery.'

'I have a lot to tell you,' said Haddad, smiling for the first time.

'I bet you have. Now rest. Doctor's orders.'

18

Grimaldi often worked on Sundays. The office was quiet, the corridors deserted, the phone silent. It was the best time for some clear thinking. And besides, he had already missed a whole day by attending a friend's funeral the day before. Grimaldi sat back in his chair, lit a small cigar and looked at his whiteboard when his phone rang. It was Officer Borroni.

'He told me I would find you in your office on Sunday, sir,' said Cesaria.

'Who told you?'

'Your friend, Fabio Conti.'

'*He is with you?*' asked Grimaldi, surprised.

'Yes, we are having breakfast just across the road from your office. I was looking for you yesterday, but—'

'Come to my office now,' interrupted Grimaldi. 'I'll meet you in the foyer.'

'Yes, sir.'

I don't believe it, thought Grimaldi. *She pulled it off! Amazing.* Grimaldi reached for his coat and hurried to the elevator.

Conti watched the elevator door open with some trepidation. He hadn't seen his friend for two years. For years they had been inseparable, like brothers in their fight against the Mafia in Sicily. But after the shooting that killed his wife, they had parted company on terms that could only be described as strained.

Grimaldi too, had mixed feelings about the meeting. He couldn't understand Conti's decision to throw in the towel and give up after the assassination. Deep down, he never forgave him for that. It was

126

handing victory to a common foe they had been fighting for years. Grimaldi was a crusader in the middle of a war and he had looked at his friend as a warrior with a similar commitment and conviction. While the horrific murder of Conti's wife was a great tragedy, he had expected Conti to come out fighting like never before. Instead, he had handed in his badge, resigned from the police and sank into obscurity.

Cesaria sensed the tension in Conti and stood back as the two men walked slowly towards each other in the deserted foyer. She realised this was an intensely personal moment between two friends who had known each other for years and been through a lot together. She also sensed a great deal was riding on this meeting, which could have a serious impact not only on her career, but on her personally. Cesaria watched the chief prosecutor's face as he approached his friend. With each step, his expression became more relaxed, until a hint of a smile crept across his rugged face. *They need each other,* thought Cesaria, as the two men embraced without saying a word.

In the lift, Grimaldi turned to Cesaria. 'I don't know how you did it, and I won't ask,' said Grimaldi. 'Thank you.'

I didn't have to do very much, sir,' replied Cesaria. 'It was all in a quote.'

'A quote? How curious.' Grimaldi looked at Conti. 'Is that right?'

'It is. And I'm sure you know which one.'

'Let me guess,' said Grimaldi as the lift doors opened. '*The only thing necessary ...*'

Cesaria looked at Grimaldi, surprised. 'It's what we believed in,' he said.

'Still do,' interjected Conti, 'perhaps now more than ever.'

'And that's why I need you,' said Grimaldi, 'and that includes you, Officer Borroni.'

For the first time since joining the police force, Cesaria felt something she hadn't felt before: belonging. Somehow, the extraordinary bond between the two men next to her was reaching out to her, including her in a strange, unexpected way. Cesaria realised this was a watershed moment not only in her career, but in her life. As she followed the two men into the room she made a promise: she would never let them down, whatever the cost.

Grimaldi walked over to the whiteboard by the window and got straight down to business. He knew that Conti would like that, especially after their unexpected reunion stirring up buried emotions and painful memories, almost forgotten. There would be plenty of time to get drunk together later and reflect on the past. But for now, there were far more pressing matters to deal with.

Grimaldi pointed to a series of photographs of Mario Giordano's bloody corpse lying in the restaurant toilet. 'This here is our problem,' he said. 'I'm afraid in a way it's like the assassination of Archduke Ferdinand in Sarajevo, and we all know what happened after that ...'

'World War One,' said Conti, reaching for his cigarettes.

'And this murder can do the same. Right here, in Florence. In fact, I believe it was intended to do just that.'

'Are you serious?' asked Conti, and lit his cigarette.

'I am. This city is a powder keg. All that's needed is one spark to blow it all sky high.'

'Go on,' said Conti, inhaling deeply.

'Three families rule this city with an iron fist. The Gambios, the Lombardos and the Giordanos.'

'All from Palermo,' interjected Conti.

'Correct. And that's one of the main reasons I need your help. You know more about them than anyone else I can think of.'

'A deadly bunch.'

'They sure are,' said Grimaldi, and pointed to a photo at the bottom of the whiteboard. 'Since the assassination of this man here – Luciano Gambio – three years ago, a bloody turf war has been simmering just below the surface, waiting to erupt. In fact, since this man here' – Grimaldi paused and pointed to another photo – 'Salvatore Gambio took over the Gambio family business after his father's death, things have become very—'

'Salvatore is here? In Florence?' interrupted Conti again.

'Yes.'

'Then we really have a problem ...'

'Oh?'

'He's one of the most ruthless Mafia capos still alive. Rivers of blood follow him everywhere he goes. I thought he was in Chicago.'

'No; he's right here, and I believe he's behind this murder. At this stage it's just a hunch, but you know how these things start.' Grimaldi turned around and faced his friend. 'But we can discuss all this later. This is what we have in mind for you ...'

'Oh?'

'I have already spoken to the commissioner. He wants to appoint you acting chief superintendent in charge of the *Squadra Mobile*. You will be based at police headquarters in Via Zara. This will give you all the authority you need.'

'What about the present super?'

'Resigned two months ago ... cold feet.'

'So I get helicoptered in?'

'Something like that.'

Conti nodded. 'That will cause a lot of bad blood,' he said.

'Very likely,' Grimaldi agreed. 'Is that a problem?'

'Not really. As long as I have a few capable officers I can rely on.'

'You will; but perhaps just a handful, if we're lucky.' Giordano pointed to Cesaria. 'One of them you already know.'

'A good start,' said Conti.

'With such a strong Mafia presence, we have the usual problems: corruption, fear, intimidation ...'

'I understand.'

'Interested?'

'I wouldn't be here otherwise.'

Grimaldi walked over to his friend and embraced him. 'Thank you,' he said, 'For the first time in years, I no longer feel so alone.'

'Neither do I,' replied Conti, and patted his friend on the back.

19

Papal Apartments, Vatican City:
23 May, midnight

Cardinal Borromeo was nervously pacing up and down in front of the pope's bedchamber. Professor Montessori was inside, examining the pontiff who had collapsed again just after supper. The pope's condition had rapidly deteriorated after the dramatic Easter Sunday episode, and the exasperated medical team looking after his health was running out of options. And so was the cardinal.

The cardinal heard the door open and stopped. Montessori stepped into the corridor, looking worried.

The cardinal hurried over to him. 'How is His Holiness?'

'Not well, I'm afraid.'

'You did raise the hospital issue again?'

'Of course.'

'And?'

Montessori shook his head. 'His Holiness won't hear of it.'

'This can't go on for much longer; *we must do something!*'

'I agree.'

'Any ideas?'

'As a matter of fact, yes.'

'Tell me.'

'As you can imagine, I've done a lot of research about this disease. Left no stone unturned. I've also spoken to several experts in immunogenomics, and they all agree that the symptoms strongly suggest we are most likely dealing with some kind of autoimmune disease, most probably somatic mutations.'

The cardinal stopped and put his hand on Montessori's shoulder. 'Please explain,' he said, 'and remember I'm a man of the Church, not the lab.'

'It's a very complex subject, but there have been some dramatic breakthroughs recently involving certain drugs in this very area. In fact, a team of scientists at the Gordon Institute in Sydney headed by a Nobel prize winner, has recently conducted some groundbreaking studies and published a very interesting paper in *Nature* and *The Lancet,* causing quite a stir—'

'And this could be helpful?' interrupted the cardinal. *Why are doctors always so long-winded?* he thought.

'Possibly, but there's a problem.'

'Yes?'

'So far, all we have is deduction and speculation; about the disease, I mean. Before we can go any further we would have to know exactly what we are dealing with. We have to know the *cause.*'

'We've been down this path before. His Holiness refuses ...'

'I know, but there may be a way.'

'What do you mean?'

'The breakthrough by the Sydney team was only possible because of one thing.'

'What?'

'Genome sequencing. The Gordon Institute is one of the few places in the world with the necessary equipment and expertise to do this; quickly and efficiently. This is cutting-edge science.'

'But this is all just hypothetical, surely,' said the cardinal.

'Not necessarily.'

'What's on your mind?'

'Well, if we could sequence His Holiness's genome, the experts seem confident that we could quickly diagnose this autoimmune disease, or eliminate it altogether to give us other options.'

'But His Holiness—'

'I know what you are going to say,' interrupted Montessori. 'All we need is a blood sample. And we have plenty. We've carried out dozens of blood tests.'

'But His Holiness would have to agree.'

'Of course. But that's your job,' said Montessori, laughing. 'His Holiness wouldn't have to leave the Vatican, and of course confidentiality would be a given.'

'Interesting ...'

'But there is one major hurdle.'

'Tell me.'

'Because we have so little time, we would have to somehow involve the team at the Gordon Institute in Sydney in this. Anything else would unduly complicate things and take too long.'

'And we could do all this from a distance; *from here?*'

'Yes. But we would have to make contact with the institute, explain the situation and get them to agree to come on board. Quite a challenging task, I would have thought,' said Montessori, 'considering what's at stake here. The delicacy of the situation, the timing and the high-profile patient we are talking about.'

'Sydney, you say ...' The cardinal looked at Montessori. 'You can leave that to me,' he said, a reluctant smile spreading across his worried face. 'This is definitely a matter for a man of the Church.'

'And are *you* that man?'

'No. This is a job for a Jesuit.'

'A soldier of God? Poverty, chastity and a special vow of obedience to the pope?'

'Exactly, and the man I have in mind has all these qualities, and a lot more. I'll call him in the morning.'

'Excellent! A collaboration between Church and lab perhaps?' joked Montessori, feeling a little more confident for the first time that night.

'Something like that.'

'Incidentally, the name of the Nobel laureate your Jesuit has to bring on board is Professor Alexandra Delacroix, one of the world leaders in genomics. I understand she's quite formidable.'

'So is he.'

'A soldier of God and a queen of the lab. Should be an interesting encounter, don't you think?' said Montessori, smiling.

'I'm sure of it. By the way, he has one more important quality.'

'Oh?'

'Charm.'

'Let's pray it works.'

20

For the first time since winning the *Top Chef Europe* grand finale on Saturday, Lorenza felt free. Her father had secured tickets to the Uffizi Gallery for her and Tristan. Becoming an overnight celebrity had come at a price. The entire Sunday and Monday had been taken up with back-to-back television appearances and interviews, and the eager paparazzi were following her like hounds chasing a fox. However, on Tuesday morning, Lorenza and Tristan managed to give them the slip by leaving her grandparents' villa early in the morning through a concealed gate at the back of the garden.

'I think we've done it,' said Lorenza, looking anxiously over her shoulder. She was surveying the deserted back street behind the villa leading to the Boboli Gardens. Tristan glanced at her and laughed. 'You look like Sophia Loren in one of those schmalzy Italian films of the sixties,' said Tristan, 'but it seems to have worked. There's no-one around. All we need now,' he added, lowering his voice, 'is Marcello Mastroianni on a Vespa to come and get you.'

Wearing a headscarf and a pair of large, dark sunglasses, Lorenza felt quite silly in her disguise, but she didn't care. A little freedom was definitely worth it.

'Stop it!' she said, and took off the scarf.

'Is that wise?' teased Tristan. 'Your hair is like a paparazzi magnet; just wait.'

'Don't care. Let's have some breakfast first, and then it's off to the gallery. And you can be my guide. Let's see what the Sorbonne has taught you.'

'You're on, *Top Chef.*'

'I can't tell you how pleased I am that you and Katerina are coming with us to Venice tomorrow. It's been too long ...'

Lorenza and Tristan had known each other for years. They first met at the Kuragin Chateau during one of the many da Baggio family visits when they were both fourteen. Countess Kuragin and Lorenza's mother had been friends since their university days in Paris and visited each other often during the holidays. Lorenza still remembered the shy boy with the long, spindly legs and sad eyes who could read thoughts and looked right into your soul. Fascinated by Tristan's amazing story – he had been in a coma for years after an accident – and the tragic circumstances of the death of his parents, Lorenza had been drawn to him since the moment they met.

'Something bothers me,' said Lorenza, as they strolled hand in hand down the hill towards the river.

'What's that?'

'You didn't seem very happy to see me win. I saw it in your eyes on Saturday night. You looked decidedly ... sad.' Lorenza stopped and looked at Tristan. 'Why?' she asked.

'Sad? Quite the opposite. I can't tell you how proud I am of you,' Tristan replied, sidestepping the question. 'Your performance, especially on the final night when you told them about Hunkar Begendi, blew me away ...' Tristan stopped and kissed Lorenza tenderly on the cheek. 'Truly; it was amazing.'

'That's not what I asked. The look on your face reminded me of something.'

'What?'

'That summer we spent in our villa on Lake Como; when Maria drowned ...'

'Oh.'

'You looked so sad, so troubled, the day before it happened. You had the same look on your face on Saturday.'

'I could never hide anything from you,' said Tristan.

'That's better. And?'

'I sensed something during the contest ...'

'*Sensed?* What?'

'Danger.'

'Can you be more specific?' asked Lorenza, becoming serious.

'No. Believe me, I tried.'

'The whisper of angels again?'

'Something like that.'

Lorenza took Tristan by the hand. 'It will pass; come.'

'I hope so,' said Tristan, unable to shake off the feeling of unease and apprehension that had troubled him for days.

As they crossed the Ponte Vecchio, Tristan stopped in front of a jewellery shop.

'A sudden interest in a girl's best friend?' asked Lorenza, tongue in cheek.

'Something caught my eye.' Tristan pointed to the shop window.

'Oh? What?'

'The bracelet; right there.'

'It's gorgeous.'

'Let's go inside and have a look.'

'Don't be silly. This is for rich tourists ...'

'I insist.'

Tristan opened the door and pushed Lorenza gently inside.

The man who had been following them stopped on the opposite side of the bridge. With his back turned to the jewellery shop, he pulled out a packet of cigarettes and lit up. Inhaling deeply, he watched the shop behind him reflected in the window he was facing.

Unlike the paparazzi camped in front of the grandparents' villa, Belmonte, a thorough man, had the whole property under surveillance. One of his men saw the couple slip out the back and alerted Belmonte, who had been watching the front.

Belmonte was on a high. The breakthrough he had longed for so desperately, had suddenly and unexpectedly fallen into his lap: Gambio had taken him into his confidence and he had become part of the trusted, inner circle. In fact, Gambio had gone one important step further. Obviously pleased with Belmonte's daring assassination of Mario Giordano, Gambio had admitted him into the family, an honour bestowed on only a privileged few. After Lorenza's victory,

Gambio explained what he had in mind, and why. But before mentioning Bahadir and the Syrian refugee connection, he had proposed Belmonte's admission into the family. Taken completely by surprise by this unexpected honour, Belmonte had eagerly agreed. Two of Gambio's senior lieutenants were at the villa and had witnessed the traditional initiation.

As the most prominent member of the family, Gambio officiated. He handed Belmonte a picture of a saint and then pricked Belmonte's finger with a needle until blood began dropping onto the face of the saint. One of the lieutenants then set the picture alight and Belmonte recited the oath of loyalty to the Cosa Nostra as the picture burned in his hands. After that, they toasted Belmonte's admission with copious quantities of cognac, and Gambio told Belmonte about the rest of his plan, and the part he expected him to play in it. By the time the sun came up, they had sealed a deadly pact that was as daring as it was audacious, promising riches and glory beyond Belmonte's wildest dreams.

Belmonte was carefully watching the young couple inside the jewellery shop until some kind of purchase appeared imminent. That was when he made his move. Once again, dressed like one of the many tourists crossing the bridge, Belmonte adjusted his straw hat and dark glasses, and entered the shop. He told the shop assistant who greeted him that he was only browsing, and began looking at a display cabinet with his back turned to Tristan and Lorenza, standing at the counter.

Lorenza held up her wrist and admired the bracelet. 'This is very sweet of you, Tristan. I don't know what to say.'

'Say nothing. Wear it, and we'll always remember this day.' Tristan then pulled out his credit card to pay for it.

Excellent, thought Belmonte and slowly turned around. As Tristan handed his credit card to the shopkeeper, Belmonte activated the scanning device in his pocket.

'Thank you, Mr Te Papatahi,' said the shopkeeper, and handed the credit card and receipt to Tristan. Lorenza kissed Tristan on the cheek, linked arms with him and they left the shop. As Tristan passed Belmonte standing by the door, he felt a sudden chill run up his spine, casting a disturbing shadow over the happy moment. It only lasted an instant, and disappeared as soon as they stepped out into the sunshine and joined the tourist throng crossing the bridge. *Another warning*, thought Tristan. *How strange*, but he chose not to mention it to Lorenza.

Belmonte smiled; he now had everything he needed. Within a few hours he would have access to all the information on Tristan Te Papatahi's credit card. He already knew all about Lorenza and her plans. The recent interviews had seen to that. She was planning to open a restaurant in Venice in the da Baggio family palazzo, and publish a cookbook using ancient Ottoman recipes that had been in her family for centuries. Soon, he would know all about her companion as well. *Venice, of all places,* thought Belmonte, hardly able to believe his luck. The fly was coming to the spider. Fate had dealt him another winning hand.

'*Amore*,' said the shopkeeper, and sighed as he watched the young couple leave the shop.

'*Si, amore*,' said Belmonte. He nodded to the shopkeeper as he opened the door and then slowly walked away without looking at Tristan and Lorenza who were strolling in the opposite direction.

21

Alexandra was addressing her research team in the Gordon library when the CEO sent her a message, requesting an urgent meeting. *I wonder what he wants,* she thought, *that's not like him,* and asked one of her post-docs to continue the briefing. She excused herself and hurried to the lift.

The CEO was waiting for Alexandra in front of his office. 'Apologies for the interruption,' he said, 'but this is really important. Let's go inside.'

Alexandra thought the CEO looked quite agitated, which was decidedly out of character. The CEO hurried past his secretary, ushered Alexandra into his office and closed the door. 'I just received a most unusual phone call,' he said.

'Oh?'

'From Cardinal O'Brien, personally.'

'Really?'

'He requested an urgent meeting, *with you.*'

Alexandra sat up, surprised. 'With me? Did he say why; what?'

'Apparently it's something highly confidential, and he is asking for our discretion.'

'How intriguing. It's good to see that the Church is taking such an interest in what we are doing here,' said Alexandra, smiling. 'Any idea what this is all about?'

'None whatsoever. I'm as nonplussed as you. Be that as it may, I don't have to tell you how important this is. He's one of the highest ranking members of the Catholic Church in Australia, and very close to the pope. As you know he has quite a reputation, and a huge amount of influence, not only in this country, but in the Church generally. He goes surfing with the premier, and plays tennis with the lord mayor. That's the sort of guy he is. So, be on guard,' came the warning.

'Are you sure it's me he wants to meet?'

'Absolutely.'

'Did he say when?'

'Yes. This afternoon at three.'

'Where?'

'Here.'

'*He is coming here?*' asked Alexandra, looking incredulous.

'Yes, he insisted on it.'

'You will be there, of course.'

'No; he wants to meet you alone.'

'Are you serious?'

'Absolutely, and he would like to see the Illumina X-Ten.'

'He asked for that?'

'Specifically.'

Alexandra shook her head. 'The plot thickens,' she said.

The CEO shrugged. 'You can rearrange your afternoon?'

'Do I have a choice?'

'Not really.'

The cardinal's car pulled up in front of the Gordon Institute at three pm sharp. The driver got out and opened the back door. The CEO met His Eminence at the entrance and took him straight to a conference room to meet Alexandra. The whole institute was abuzz with excitement about the unexpected visit and was wondering what it was all about.

Alexandra stood up as soon as the cardinal and the CEO entered the room. The CEO made the introductions and withdrew. Alexandra pointed to a chair, but the cardinal waited for her to sit down first before taking a seat.

'Firstly, allow me to congratulate you, Professor Delacroix. The Nobel Prize, what a wonderful achievement,' said the cardinal, 'and a great credit to the institute.'

'Thank you, Eminence.' *He's much younger* ... thought Alexandra, watching the cardinal with interest. She had expected someone much older. Tall, athletic, in his late fifties with greying hair around the temples and a tanned, youthful face that had seen a little too much sun, he looked more like a former tennis star keeping in shape than a prince of the Church. However, his most striking feature by far was his eyes: penetrating, ice-blue, and smiling. *Classic Celtic looks*, thought Alexandra, impressed.

Dressed in a simple black suit and shiny black shoes, the white dog collar and pectoral cross the only clues hinting at his high office, he looked totally at ease sitting in his chair with his long legs crossed, and filled the room with his presence. A balanced blend of modesty, authority and charisma, impossible to ignore.

What an impressive man, thought Alexandra, feeling completely relaxed.

'You must be wondering what this is all about,' began the cardinal, leaning back in his chair.

Alexandra smiled, but didn't reply.

'I am not exaggerating,' said the cardinal, speaking quite softly, 'when I tell you that I am here on one of the most important missions of my ecclesiastical career.' The cardinal, a skilled negotiator, paused to let this sink in.

'That's quite a statement, Eminence,' said Alexandra, her curiosity aroused even further. 'And what may that be?'

'To persuade you to help save a life.'

Alexandra looked stunned. It wasn't the answer she had expected.

'My help? Persuade me? I don't understand!'

'I have read your recent paper on *Deep Sequencing*, the quantum leap needed if we are to successfully fight deadly autoimmune diseases that only emerge in middle age or later,' said the cardinal, changing direction.

'You have read my paper, Eminence?' asked Alexandra, showing disbelief and surprise. 'You are interested in this subject?'

'I have to let you into a little secret,' said the cardinal, the tone of his voice turning almost conspiratorial. 'I was hoping to become a surgeon before I joined the Jesuits. I have a medical degree, but it's all about souls now rather than bodies, I'm afraid,' he added, his eyes sparkling with humour.

'You are full of surprises, Eminence,' was all Alexandra managed to say.

'What I'm about to tell you, Professor Delacroix, is in strictest confidence, and until you give me your answer, it must remain only between us.'

'Understood.'

'Should you agree to go ahead with what I'm about to suggest, then you will have to decide who should become involved and therefore privy to the information I'm about to disclose. However, the strictest confidentiality must be maintained. The entire matter depends on it. You will see why shortly.'

'I must say, you have made me very curious, Eminence. Exciting matters like this rarely happen in our world. This sounds more like something out of *Mission Impossible* than a science lab. We get excited about discoveries, not mysteries. And what we are talking about here, sounds suspiciously like a mystery to me.'

'It is. A big one at that. But science could help us solve it, and that's where you come in. But first, I must tell you who is in such urgent need of your help, and why.'

'Who, Eminence?'

'His Holiness, the Pope.'

Over the next hour, Cardinal O'Brien gave Alexandra a detailed, step-by-step account of the pope's illness and his stubborn attitude towards it that had caused so much controversy in the Vatican and frustrated his medical team. He explained the importance of the pontiff's upcoming visit to the United Nations and the US Congress, what was riding on that and why the pope's illness had to be kept secret. He explained what the pope's medical team was suggesting, and why. He could see from the expression on Alexandra's face and her body language that she was following the story with a mixture of fascination and disbelief.

He then outlined what Professor Montessori and his team had pieced together as an interim diagnosis of the pope's illness, and the way they were proposing to deal with it.

'In short, Professor Delacroix,' said the cardinal, 'it would appear that the pope's illness we are faced with here is some form of adult autoimmune disease like the one you are about to explore with Deep Sequencing.'

'I understand. As you would be aware, we have recently been able to make a successful diagnosis of the cause of a severe autoimmune disease in children using genome sequencing ...'

'Germline Mutations,' the cardinal cut in, 'and you came up with some life-saving treatment that worked and saved young lives.'

'Correct, but we still have a long way to go. There are serious side effects ...'

'And you are hoping to do the same for adults with Somatic Mutations?'

'You *are* well-informed Eminence,' said Alexandra, surprised by the cardinal's extensive knowledge of the complex subject. 'Yes, we are, with the use of Deep Sequencing, but first we have to determine the cause. We believe it's all in the genes. That's the challenge at the moment.'

'I know this is a lot to take in,' said the cardinal, 'but I'm sure you can appreciate the urgency and importance of all this.'

Alexandra nodded.

'Time and discretion are of the essence here. I believe that science – you in particular – can make not only a huge difference here, but can also make history and show us the way. Especially with your CRISPR project—'

'You know about CRISPR, Eminence?' interrupted Alexandra, her eyes wide with astonishment.

'I have followed your project from the very beginning. From the day the generous Time Machine sponsorship was announced a year ago that made it all possible.'

'You would therefore be aware of the many bioethical issues we are wrestling with at the moment,' interjected Alexandra, becoming quite excited.

'I am.'

'May I ask you a personal question, Eminence?' said Alexandra, hoping she wasn't going too far.

'Please go ahead.'

'Do you approve of what we are trying to do here, Eminence? Do you approve of CRISPR?'

The cardinal took his time before answering. He realised he was almost there. 'I do,' he said. 'Just as I approve of stem cell research. As you can see, I am on your side, Professor Delacroix. But the ethical issues are complex and have to be approached carefully and with caution. And in the right way, by the right people ...'

The cardinal smiled. The conversation was unfolding precisely as he had planned, and Alexandra's reactions were exactly as he had hoped. He was on the home stretch. His proposal was about to become irresistible. The cardinal knew from long experience that an arrangement – especially one as unusual and sensitive as the one on the table – can only work if both parties want it to succeed. And that would only happen if there was something important in the arrangement both parties wanted. The cardinal could see that by raising the CRISPR project, and hinting that he was prepared to assist in resolving the sensitive bioethical issues that had plagued the project from the beginning and had almost brought it to a standstill, would "seal the deal". Church and science would become allies of necessity and self-interest. History was full of examples.

'I think this is perhaps as far as we can take this for now, Professor Delacroix,' said the cardinal, backing off.

'I will need some time to consider all this,' said Alexandra, 'and discuss it with the institute and some of my team.'

'Of course. Perfectly understandable. Please give me your answer when you are ready. However, should you decide to go ahead, Professor Montessori, the pontiff's personal physician, will brief you with the details and make sure you have everything you need. He will be the main contact point between you, the institute and the Vatican. And needless to say, my door is of course also always open. And please don't hesitate to contact me to discuss those bioethical issues ... I already have a few ideas that may help.'

'Thank you, Eminence, I certainly will.'

'Now, do you think it would be possible for me to see the Illumina X-Ten, and perhaps meet some of your team?' said the cardinal, and stood up.

'Of course, Eminence,' replied Alexandra, her head spinning as the implications of what had just taken place began to sink in.

22

Haddad was making excellent progress after his life-saving operation and was already well enough to walk around a little and help Nazir with simple chores. Dr Rosen's surgery had been overwhelmed by a relentless wave of injured new arrivals needing urgent medical attention. At the end of the day, Dr Rosen and Amena would fall into their camp beds, exhausted, just to do it all again the next morning, starting at sunrise.

It was already dark by the time Dr Rosen and Amena stepped outside after another gruelling shift in the operating theatre. 'Look at those two,' said Dr Rosen and pointed to Haddad and Nazir sitting under a tree, obviously deep in conversation.

'Thick as thieves, wouldn't you say? The patient appears to be doing well.'

For the first time in days, Dr Rosen didn't feel quite so exhausted, and decided to join them. 'How are you?' she asked, and sat down next to Haddad. Haddad put his hand on Dr Rosen's arm. 'I appear to have a charmed life. Thanks to you and Amena, I live to see another day,' he said, 'and hopefully, finish what I began such a long time ago ... *inshallah.*'

'And what might that be?' asked Dr Rosen.

'It's a long story.'

'We have time ...'

Dr Rosen noticed that Haddad's dressing had been changed and his complexion had greatly improved. Satisfied, she sat back and relaxed. Sensing that Dr Rosen and Haddad wanted to talk, Nazir and Amena excused themselves and left. Privacy was a rare luxury in the camp. Dr Rosen had intentionally stayed away from her patient since the operation, giving him time to recover before asking the obvious questions. Haddad, a sensitive man, realised this and appreciated her tact and obvious concern for his wellbeing. Above all else, Dr Rosen was a healer; the patient always came first.

'Can you hear it?' said Haddad.

'Hear what?'

'The silence.'

Dr Rosen nodded. 'I understand,' she said.

'For the first time in years no bombs; no gunshots; no screams. Especially no screams. The screams were the worst.'

'Where was that?'

'In the prisons. I spent a lot of time in prisons ... horrific places; unspeakable.' Haddad closed his eyes. 'Why do ghosts never leave?' he asked, sounding tired.

'We all have our ghosts,' said Dr Rosen. 'I have mine too. You just have to learn to live with them.'

Haddad opened his eyes and looked at Dr Rosen. 'You're right. But enough of this. You obviously want to know how I survived and where I've been.'

'Yes.'

'I believe it was destiny. Why do I say that? Because I had unfinished business ...'

'Unfinished business?'

'I made a promise. A promise to Marcus after his wife and daughter were killed in that shocking terrorist attack in Luxor.'

'What kind of promise?'

'Let me tell you. Unfortunately, I couldn't make it to the funeral in Sydney. So I sent Marcus a note instead. I still remember what it said, word for word. I have repeated it a thousand times to myself in prison. During the interrogations, the pain ... *That you have lost your family in such barbaric circumstances in my country fills me with deep shame and regret. You have my solemn promise that I will not rest until the perpetrators are brought to justice.* That's what I promised Marcus.'

'But Sheikh Omar was killed,' interjected Dr Rosen.

'Yes, and so was one of his two bodyguards who caused most of the mayhem at Luxor. The other one got away. He was the worst.

146

That's the man I've been trying to hunt down ever since. That's my unfinished business.'

'I saw you being swept away in that dreadful cave in Lalibela just after Habakkuk was sucked under by the current and disappeared in the whirlpool. I didn't think anyone could have survived that.'

'But I did.'

'How?'

'Habakkuk saved me; that's the irony.'

'*He saved you?* How?'

'Habakkuk drowned, but his body saved me.'

'I don't understand.'

'As I was being swept downstream through the cave, I was pushed against a protruding rock. Habakkuk's body was there; wedged into a crevice. I managed to pull myself on top of his body and keep my head above water just before we were both swept away again; together as one. Habakkuk's body became my life raft. I held onto it until we were washed up onto a sandbank near a village. I was barely conscious by then. Fortunately, some women doing their washing in the stream found me.'

'Incredible!'

'But that's the end of the good news, I'm afraid. As you know, that part of Ethiopia was in rebel hands.'

'Yes, of course.'

'I was handed over to the rebels and spent two years in various prisons. I still don't know why I wasn't killed; so many were. Beaten to death. Obviously it just wasn't my time. Unfinished business, you see ...'

'What an amazing story,' said Dr Rosen. 'And then?'

'There's so much more to tell, but let me cut this short for you. One day, as the rebels were being attacked, I managed to escape and made my way to Yemen. By then there was no point trying to return to Egypt; everything had changed there. I too had changed ... there was no turning back. Yemen was in a dreadful mess. Such poverty, despair. Lots of fighting, terrorists everywhere – Al-Qaeda.

'That's where I came across Ibrahim el-Masri, a Lebanese jihadist. A young firebrand. Of course, I didn't know who he was at the time nor do I believe el-Masri was his real name. But then one night, he bragged about having been close to the "Chosen One", the legendary Sheikh Omar. He claimed to have taken part in that spectacular terrorist attack in Luxor where hundreds were killed during an open-air opera performance.'

'The Aida massacre; the whole world was talking about it,' said Dr Rosen.

'Correct. At first no-one believed him, but when I questioned him further about all this, he provided some detailed information that backed up his claim. After the attack he travelled to Mecca with Sheikh Omar and then returned with him to Egypt. That was just before Omar was killed in Luxor. Ibrahim said he was there.'

'Was he?'

'Yes, I believe so. He told me things only someone who was there could possibly have known. He knew that Omar's other bodyguard was killed. He himself was wounded and managed to escape – to Yemen, where I met him. It all made sense.'

'What did you do in Yemen?'

'I joined some of the fighters ...' came the evasive reply. 'I was wounded in an ambush, captured, and once again spent some time in prison. It was an awful time ... daily executions; torture ... But somehow I survived; again.'

'How?'

'Luck, and using my wits, I suppose. But mainly luck.'

'What about Ibrahim?'

'He was there too, but I was biding my time. He was a young, upcoming leader closely linked to al-Qaeda at the top. He knew people. He was street-smart, ambitious, cunning. I wanted to learn more about the organisation and stayed close to him. Don't forget, I was a policeman once, fighting terrorists in Egypt. Intelligence used to be my life. I know how to read people and know how important information can be, especially in that troubled part of the world ... I thought it might come in useful later. I was right.'

For a while Haddad and Dr Rosen sat in silence. 'One day, quite unexpectedly, the prison was liberated and I was free again,' continued Haddad. 'I left Yemen and went to Iraq with some of the liberated fighters ...'

Haddad didn't explain what kind of fighters they were, nor did Dr Rosen ask him to elaborate. 'What about that unfinished business?' she prompted after a while.

'I lost contact with Ibrahim during a skirmish in Iraq. I thought he had been killed or captured. However, I caught up with him again later in Camp Bucca.'

'You were in Bucca – that notorious detention facility run by the US military?'

'That's the one. I was there for several years.'

'Good God!'

'It was the birthplace of IS. I saw it all ... could write a book about it. Perhaps one day I will ...' Haddad waved through the air with his good hand. 'The entire al-Qaeda leadership was there. I met them all,' he said, becoming quite excited. '"The believer", Abu Bakr al-Baghdadi, the future leader of IS was there, and so was Abu Muslim al-Turkmani, his deputy. Mohammed al-Adnani – a most dangerous man, thought to be behind the terrorist attacks in France – was there too with Abu Abdulrahman al-Bilawi, who masterminded the seizure of Mosul.'

'Incredible!'

'Camp Bucca was known as the "Academy". Why? Because it allowed many prominent jihadists and former members of Saddam's military and security services to be incarcerated together – twenty-four thousand of them – effectively providing a "think tank" and talent pool for the creation of IS. The Americans had unwittingly provided what the jihadists couldn't have achieved in their wildest dreams.'

'What's that?'

'Bringing them all together in one place! At a very critical time. But that's another story ...'

'And Ibrahim?'

'He worked with the Americans; under protection. He turned informer. There were rumours that he provided vital information that got a number of key IS leaders killed later. He was an opportunist and became a traitor. He had serious ambitions of his own, but he played a dangerous game. The last I heard, he was taken to the US for questioning, and his own protection I suspect. The whole of IS was baying for his blood. However, he was a master of reinventing himself. Unfortunately, I lost him after that; he slipped through my fingers. Needless to say, I regret that. Very much. I should have acted sooner when I had the chance,' said Haddad, a melancholy look on his face.

'What would you have done, had you known?'

'I would have made sure he got what he deserved.'

'What, killed him?'

'Executed would be more accurate; yes.'

'But that's not you, Naguib,' said Dr Rosen, and reached for Haddad's hand. 'That's not what you believe in, is it? You promised Marcus justice, not a killing.'

'I failed.'

'No, you didn't. If you had killed Ibrahim earlier, many of the IS leaders would still be alive, creating mayhem. Have you thought about that?'

'You're right. I never looked at it that way,' said Haddad, feeling a little less dejected.

'See?'

'Never mind about that now ... I haven't given up just yet.'

'What will you do now?'

'I have a lot of information,' Haddad paused and pointed to his head, 'in here, that could be useful. In the right hands, if you know what I mean. Especially now, with IS on the run.'

'I do.'

'As soon as I'm better, I will make contact with the security services here in Turkey.'

'But before you to that, you should do something else.'

'What?'

'Tell Marcus that you are alive. Only fair, don't you think? Now that I know ...'

'Yes, you're right.'

Dr Rosen reached into her pocket and pulled out her satellite phone. 'We could call him right now, if you like,' she said. 'He's back in Australia. It's about seven in the morning in Sydney now. Perfect time to reach him.'

Haddad looked at Dr Rosen and nodded. 'Let's do that.'

'I'd love to see his face when he hears your voice.'

Dr Rosen selected Marcus Carrington's autodial number and listened to it ring as the connection raced across the globe.

23

Tristan sat on the terrace facing the Canal Grande and watched Venice wake up to another perfect spring day. It was just after sunrise and the first rays of morning sun gave the familiar church steeples and rooftops a pinkish glow, reminding Tristan of iconic paintings by Canaletto he had admired during his studies. There are few cities in the world where it is possible to take in the same scene that had inspired a painter several centuries ago. Yet Venice that morning was just such a place. Tristan looked at the Rialto Bridge a short distance away and tried to imagine what life would have been like in Canaletto's time.

Lorenza walked up to Tristan from behind and ran her fingers playfully through his hair. 'You're up early,' she said, and sat down next to him.

'How could anyone sleep with this outside the window?'

'Spectacular, isn't it? God, how I missed this! It's great to be home.'

'I bet. Especially wearing the *Top Chef Europe* crown and bringing home the trophy. I'm sure the whole of Venice is talking about it.'

'Could be. You know Italians; always a little too exuberant, always a little over the top, always exaggerating just a little—'

'But always full of life and fun,' interrupted Tristan. 'That's exactly what makes them so likeable. And don't forget food. Somehow, it's always about food.'

'Not wrong. Speaking of food, there's virtually nothing in the house.' Lorenza shook her head. 'Dad is hopeless and our housekeeper is almost eighty. See what happens when I'm away? I have to do some shopping, urgently, or our guests will starve and leave in disgust.'

'Fat chance. You won't get rid of us that easily.'

'I'm off to the market. Want to come along?'

'Wouldn't miss it for the world. Is it close? Are we walking?'

'No, of course not. This is Venice; we are going by boat. Come.'

'Wow!' said Tristan. 'What a beauty.' He ran his fingers along the polished timber of the sleek boat moored in what would have been the cellar in a normal house. But in the da Baggio Palazzo, it was a mooring under the house with an iron-studded wooden gate opening straight onto the Canal Grande. 'Garage Venetian style?'

'Something like that. You like the boat?'

'Straight out of a James Bond movie!'

'It was Antonio's,' Lorenza said, the sadness in her voice obvious. 'How he loved this boat! Hard to believe it's almost forty years old. Dad got it for his eighteenth birthday.'

'Stunning! What is it?'

'This, my friend, is a *Riva Aquarama*; a classic. The epitome of luxury and style. It's been in several movies. Pietro Riva was a master yacht builder and founded the company in 1842. The Riva family ran the shipyard until it was sold in 1969,' said Lorenza. 'The hull is sheathed in mahogany and varnished to show off the woodgrain. Only two hundred and eighty-one of this particular model were built.'

'You obviously know a lot about the boat, and I'm sure know how to drive it; let's go!'

Lorenza and Tristan jumped into the boat. 'But the best part is this: listen,' said Lorenza. She inserted the key and pressed the starter button. The two Cadillac engines roared into life, the deep throb of the powerful engines bouncing off the wet stone walls, promising speed and excitement. 'Two hundred and fifty-horsepower per engine,' continued Lorenza over the sound of the motors. 'Top speed forty-five to fifty knots. We can outrun the fastest villains in this; promise. Let me show you.'

'I want one of these,' said Tristan, watching Lorenza expertly manoeuvre the boat out into the canal and then into the busy traffic outside.

'That may be difficult. These boats are much prized and sought after by collectors. They rarely come up for sale. But if you behave yourself, I may teach you how to drive this one and lend it to you – occasionally.'

'Tempting.'

'Hold on; here we go.'

Lorenza pulled out into the middle of the canal, found a gap and put on some speed. The powerful boat roared past barges, gondolas and vaporettos packed with waving tourists.

'What do you think?' asked Lorenza, enjoying the spray hitting her face, her wet cheeks glowing with excitement. After weeks of intense competition, the sudden freedom of the moment was sheer joy.

'Do you always go this fast to do the shopping?' shouted Tristan, exhilarated.

'The best tomatoes go early.'

'Ah.'

With only centimetres to spare, Lorenza steered the boat expertly past lumbering barges, stone steps and bridge pylons.

'Are there no rules or speed limits here?'

'There are, but no-one cares. This is Italy, remember?' said Lorenza, laughing. 'Hold on, we're turning.'

Lorenza made a sharp right-hand turn in front of a water taxi and turned into a narrow side canal. 'Almost there,' she said. 'Duck!' Tristan almost hit his head against a low wooden bridge as the boat slowed down.

The market turned out to be a collection of boats and small barges tied to a wooden pier. The produce, mainly vegetables fresh from fields on the mainland, was displayed on deck in wooden crates and baskets, the eager vendors literally singing the praises of their wares to attract the attention of shoppers strolling past.

'Mainly for the locals,' said Lorenza, and stopped the boat. 'Quiet spot; tourists don't come here. You'll like it. Hold this.' Lorenza handed Tristan a large basket and tied up the boat.

Two young boys on one of the barges spotted Lorenza. 'Lorenza da Baggio, *Top Chef*, over there!' shouted one of them, and pointed in her direction. Within moments, Lorenza was surrounded by an excited crowd, congratulating her on her win and patting her on the back.

'You've been here before,' said Tristan, struggling to keep up.

'Once or twice.'

'Quiet spot, eh?'

'Did you say something?'

'I hope there are some tomatoes left,' shouted Tristan.

'So do I.'

Surrounded by laughing children and smiling faces, Lorenza went slowly from boat to boat with her entourage of admirers and selected her vegetables. But when she tried to pay, none of the stall-keepers would accept her money. Instead, they beamed when Lorenza promised to come back soon for more because she knew their produce was the best. When Lorenza and Tristan finally made it back to their boat, they found a large bunch of flowers on the steering wheel and several crates of fruit behind the seats, all gifts from proud Venetians saluting one of their own.

'So, this is how they treat celebrities in Venice? With food. What did I tell you?'

'I didn't quite expect this.'

'Better get used to it. But please a little slower on the way home, or we'll lose most of this stuff overboard. Tourists being hit by flying tomatoes may quickly tarnish your reputation.'

'Aye aye, sir,' said Lorenza, and started the engines.

Because of all the traffic on the Canal Grande, Lorenza didn't notice that a speedboat was following her. Belmonte turned to the man at the steering wheel. 'Perhaps next time she goes to the market, we make our move,' he said, and lit a small cigar. 'Unless something better comes along. Whatever happens, we have to do it soon.'

24

Cesaria was already at her desk early, working on the report Conti had requested, when her new boss walked into the Squadra Mobile headquarters. As expected, Conti's surprise appointment was viewed with suspicion, but he had the backing of the police commissioner and the chief prosecutor. While there was certainly some resentment, there was also grudging respect. Conti's reputation as a fearless Mafia hunter was legendary, and deep down, many welcomed his appointment. Strong leadership and direction were badly needed in the Squadra Mobile, and had been sadly lacking for some time. That was the main reason morale was low, and discipline lax. Conti had sensed this the moment he met his new team. He had seen it all before, and knew exactly what to do about it.

Conti stopped in front of Cesaria's desk and put down his car keys. 'Let's go; you drive,' he said, and walked out of the room.

'Where are we going?' asked Cesaria, following Conti down the stairs.

'"Fortezza" Gambio.'

Taken aback, Cesaria looked at Conti, but didn't say anything. It was certainly not the destination she had expected.

'Rule number one; get to know your enemy. Today, we are paying Salvatore Gambio a surprise visit,' said Conti.

'Does he know you are coming?' asked Cesaria, apprehension in her voice.

'Of course not. Otherwise it wouldn't be a surprise, would it?'

This will be interesting, thought Cesaria, and looked around for Conti's Fiat in the carpark.

Gambio was in his study making phone calls when his secretary walked in. He looked at her, annoyed. He didn't like to be interrupted.

'I'm sorry to disturb you, but there's someone at the gates asking for you and—' began the secretary.

'We have security guys; let them deal with it,' interrupted Gambio curtly.

'They didn't know what to do ...'

'What are you talking about?' barked Gambio, getting angry.

'It's Chief Superintendent Conti.'

'*What?* He's at the gates?'

'Yes, asking for you.'

'He's got balls, I give him that.'

'What shall I tell security?'

'Let him in, of course. Take him to the library; I'll meet him there. You know the drill.'

The security guard opened the gates and gave Cesaria directions to the house and where to park.

'I'm impressed,' said Cesaria. 'I didn't think he'd let us in. Not without a warrant, or at least an appointment, and not without his lawyer present.'

'I know these guys,' replied Conti. 'I know how they think. You have to learn to think like them. It's the only way. Coming here like this, unannounced, is counterintuitive, I know. Especially for the police. But that's precisely my point. That's the kind of thing they would do. It's what they understand and respect. Audacity will get you admitted here, well before courtesy or convention, every time. Trust me.'

Gambio's secretary, an impeccably dressed young woman in her thirties, waited for them at the stairs leading up to the entrance. Cesaria admired the woman's high heels and designer clothes, and looked at her own faded jeans and leather jacket in disgust.

'Show pony,' whispered Conti, reading Cesaria's thoughts. 'They only win parades, we are here to win the race.'

Feeling better, Cesaria smiled.

'Mr Gambio will meet you in the library,' said the young woman. 'Please follow me. Would you like some coffee?'

'That would be lovely, thank you,' said Conti, and held the door open for Cesaria.

'Impressive!' said Cesaria, looking around the large, wood-panelled room with the beautiful handcrafted floor-to-ceiling mahogany bookcases filled with leather-bound tomes.

'Intended to be,' said Conti. 'I can tell you exactly what will happen next.'

'Oh?'

'He will make us wait; for a while. Not too long, just long enough to give us time to be suitably impressed. Just look at these paintings. Do you really think a man like Gambio gives a damn about paintings, or antiques? Of course not. They are here to impress. He's showing off. Our polite hostess will serve us coffee and pastries and then leave us alone. Gambio will then make his entrance. My guess is from that door over there. He always liked the theatrical.' Conti pointed to a door between two bookcases. 'He will be affable, oozing politeness and cooperation; you watch.'

'How do you know all this?' asked Cesaria.

'I've met him before.'

'*What?* Would he remember you?'

'Oh yes. This guy has a long memory. And so have I. Should be interesting.'

'You are full of surprises,' said Cesaria, and shook her head, 'and audacious ...'

'You have to be if you want to stand a chance against these guys. Any moment now,' said Conti, and put down his coffee cup. 'Watch.'

As if on cue, the door between the bookcases opened, and Gambio swept into the room. 'What a pleasant surprise, Chief Superintendent,' he said, beaming, 'and how courteous of you to pay us a visit so soon after your appointment.'

'What a magnificent home,' said Conti, ignoring the remark, but playing along. 'And what a contrast.'

'Contrast?'

'If I remember correctly, last time we met was in a police cell in Palermo, the day Chief Prosecutor Muti was gunned down.'

If looks could have killed, Conti would have dropped dead on the spot. 'Thank you for reminding me, Chief Superintendent,' said Gambio affably. 'An unfortunate misunderstanding, as I recall it. I was only in there for a few hours ...'

'Yes, until your lawyers arrived ... with the mayor, who got you out.'

'I'm so sorry about your wife,' said Gambio, lowering his voice. *Two can play this game*, he thought, and watched Conti carefully.

Conti had been expecting something like that and was ready for the remark. 'You know what they say about the wounded bull,' he retorted calmly. 'The deeper the wound, the more dangerous he gets.'

'But that's all in the past; it happened years ago,' continued Gambio, waving his hand dismissively. 'I'm sure you didn't come here to talk about history, and give this charming young officer the wrong impression.' Gambio pointed to Cesaria and smiled. 'I am a respected businessman, with extensive interests in property – hotels mainly – and transport. I provide employment for several hundred locals, and contribute considerably to the prosperity of the place. But I'm sure you know all that, Chief Superintendent. Your superiors would have told you ...'

'Yes, I do know all that, and you are right, I didn't come here to talk about history, or just to introduce myself.'

Gambio lit a cigarette and let the smoke drift slowly towards the high ceiling. 'Then please tell me, why did you come?'

'I'm investigating a triple murder.'

'Ah, yes; poor Mario. Very unfortunate. In the middle of town and in the middle of the day, with all those tourists. What is Florence coming to? And to think that his father was right here when it happened ...'

Gambio paused to let this sink in. Inhaling deeply, he looked at Conti. He could see that he had caught his visitor off guard. The expression on Conti's face gave it away.

'Giordano was here?' asked Conti casually, recovering quickly.

'Yes, we were discussing business when he received the call ... very tragic. He was distraught.'

He's telling me something, thought Conti, his mind racing. He had certainly not expected this. *Gambio and Giordano, two bitter rivals, together at the very moment the son is killed,* thought Conti. *Interesting ... this could change everything; perhaps I'm wrong ...* 'That must have been awful,' he said.

'It was. But why are we discussing this?'

'I thought that a well-connected businessman like you may have heard something that could throw some light on this tragedy.'

'Ah. I'm afraid I can't help you, Chief Superintendent. I'm as much in the dark as you obviously appear to be,' said Gambio, the sarcasm in his voice obvious.

Shall I do it, thought Conti, *after what he just told me? Trust your instincts,* Conti answered his own question and decided to press on. 'Well, perhaps not entirely in the dark,' said Conti, and reached into his pocket.

'Do enlighten me, Chief Superintendent.'

Conti pulled a white feather out of his pocket and put it on the marble table in front of him. 'There is this here ... the killer left it behind. Some kind of calling card or message, no doubt.'

'A white feather? How curious.'

'Not this one, of course, the original is in the evidence room, but one just like it.' Conti was watching Gambio carefully. 'Any idea what this could mean?' he asked.

Gambio shrugged. 'No idea,' he said. 'But why are you asking me this?'

'You know exactly why!' said Conti, raising his voice.

'You speak in riddles.'

'Do I? Let's not insult each other.'

Arrogant bastard, thought Gambio, and shot Conti an angry look. He wasn't used to being lectured in his own home.

'Let me help you,' said Conti, leaning forward. 'When we found Chief Prosecutor Muti's bullet-riddled body gunned down in front of his home by the Lombardos, there was a white feather; remember? The whole of Palermo was talking about it. And you know what happened after that, don't you?'

Gambio shook his head.

'War. It was a declaration of war!' said Conti. 'A war you lost. And I think that's exactly what's happening here!'

'Nonsense!' Gambio almost shouted. 'To suggest that a white feather stuck in a corpse's mouth should be a declaration of war is absurd!'

Gambio stubbed out his cigarette and stood up, eyes blazing. 'I think you better leave now, Chief Superintendent, before we say something we may both regret.'

'You are right,' said Conti, smiling. 'But I think that may have already happened.' Gambio had just told him all he needed to know. 'Thank you for the coffee.'

As the secretary showed Conti and Cesaria to the door, Conti stopped and turned around to face Gambio, watching him leave. 'Something bothers me,' said Conti, scratching his head. 'What makes you think the feather was stuck in Muti's mouth? As I recall it, that wasn't the case at all.' Conti turned around again and smiled at the secretary holding the door open for him. 'The feather was found in the lapel of his jacket.' Conti stopped again, and for a moment stood perfectly still. 'The unfortunate Mario, on the other hand, did have a feather stuck in his bloody mouth. But you obviously knew that already,' he said casually, and walked outside.

Gambio clenched his fists in frustration, but didn't reply.

'That was amazing,' said Casaria, as soon as the gates of Fortezza Gambio closed behind them. Cesaria looked at Conti sitting next to her in the car. 'How did you know?' she asked.

Conti tapped his nose. 'Instinct; and luck.'

'He virtually made an admission – unwittingly – and that's the brilliant bit in all this. You trapped him.'

'No, he trapped himself, with arrogance and anger,' said Conti. 'That's what gave him away. He's certainly involved, no doubt about it. There's only one way he could have known about the feather in the mouth. Nothing has been released about that. He probably arranged the hit. I think he's behind it all. I thought that all along. It's classic Mafia and it has Gambio written all over it. Echoes of a bloody past ...'

'What's the significance of the white feather anyway? Do you know?' asked Cesaria.

'I do.'

'Well?'

'In certain Mafia circles it's an accusation of cowardice. You send a white feather to a coward. It's a grave insult. It originated in World War One. White feathers were sent to men who refused to fight.'

'No wonder Gambio got all excited when you mentioned the feather.'

'The hit and the white feather were sending a message, *but to whom? And why?* The fact that Mario's father was with Gambio at the time threw me. For a moment there, I began to have serious doubts.'

'But you followed your gut feeling.'

'I did, and it paid off ... at a price.'

'What do you mean?'

'We humiliated a man who doesn't like to lose. Losing isn't an option for him. I hope you realise that. We made a mortal enemy this morning. And he knows we're onto him.'

'Part of the job.'

'Perhaps so, but this guy is really dangerous, trust me. We have wounded his pride and I can tell you he will stop at nothing to remedy that. From now on, we look over our shoulder at all times. Clear?'

'Sure. But we go after him, right?' said Cesaria, her cheeks glowing with excitement.

'You bet!'

25

It was Tristan's last day in Venice and Lorenza had promised to take him to the Gallerie dell'Accademia to show him some of her favourite Venetian paintings by Canaletto and Carpaccio. Housed in the Scuola della Carità on the south bank of the Canal Grande, it was within easy walking distance of Palazzo da Baggio.

Lorenza pointed to the imposing entry. 'My mother and grandmother used to bring me here after church on Sundays to show me paintings,' she said. 'It started when I was about five, I think. But as I remember it, I was more interested in the gelato on the way home and cooking lunch, of course, but it was a wonderful introduction to art.'

'How lucky,' said Tristan, remembering his own chaotic, poverty-stricken childhood in Sydney. His mother, a Maori psychic, used to read Tarot cards at markets and country fairs to eke out a meagre living. Always on the road; always struggling to make ends meet; always running away from something.

Lorenza knew the girl at the desk, and after a brief chat they were waved through without having to pay.

'I can see why you like living in Venice. Home is a stunning palazzo on the Canal Grande, transport is a vintage motor yacht James Bond would kill for, and then there are the freebies: veggies at the market, presents from strangers, and now free museum entry as well. Not bad. Venice is obviously the place to be, if you're a celebrity that is,' said Tristan, as he followed Lorenza up the stairs and into the first room filled with breathtaking masterpieces.

'You know, it's a funny feeling to look at paintings you first saw as a child. I see different things in these wonderful pictures every time I come here. They tell me different stories, stir up different emotions;

memories,' said Lorenza dreamily. She reached for Tristan's hand and stopped. 'It's a real shame you have to leave tomorrow. These past few days have been magic,' she said. 'I haven't felt this carefree … this happy, since Mum and Antonio died.'

'You've achieved something amazing; you've become a star with a bright future. They would be very proud of you.'

'That's not it. That's not the reason,' whispered Lorenza, tears in her eyes.

'Oh?'

'No; can't you see? *It's you.*' Lorenza put her arms around Tristan's neck and kissed him ever so tenderly on the mouth.

Belmonte turned to the young woman next to him and smiled. They sat on a bench facing the Accademia, and had been watching the entrance since Lorenza and Tristan had gone inside. 'Perfect. We'll try to do it today, when they come out,' Belmonte said, 'but only if they go back the same way they came. Did you notice that little bridge we passed, just around the corner from here?'

'Over that narrow canal? Sure, but isn't that a very public place?'

'That's why I like it. It's still early. See, there's hardly anyone around.'

Belmonte pointed to the entrance. 'The tourist hordes come later.'

'How do you want to do it?'

'We'll use the hearse. I'll ring the guys and get everything ready. You stay here and watch. I'll go back to the bridge and take another look.'

'If you say so, darling,' said the young woman, and kissed Belmonte on the cheek.

'That's my girl,' said Belmonte, and stood up to leave.

Belmonte had been watching the da Baggio Palazzo for days. He had followed Lorenza and Tristan everywhere they went, noting their habits and routine. It was the way he prepared every assignment: waiting for the right opportunity. Every detail counted. Belmonte walked across the wooden bridge and looked under it. *Perfect*, he thought, and reached for his phone. *Deserted and out of view.* Trees and bushes along the narrow side of the canal obscured the view from the houses, most of which were boarded up. Within a few minutes, Belmonte had formulated a plan. By the time he sat down again next to his girlfriend on the bench, he knew exactly what he would do.

'That was truly amazing,' said Tristan, shielding his eyes from the glare as they stepped into the square outside. A few tourists were beginning to arrive, but everything was still very quiet.

'Which was your favourite?' asked Lorenza, linking arms with Tristan.

'Too many ...'

'But surely, there must have been one?'

'Yes, Leonardo da Vinci's *Vitruvian Man* – The Canon of Proportions.'

'We were lucky to see it. It's only displayed on rare occasions.'

'My lucky day then,' Tristan winked at Lorenza, 'in more ways than one. For me, that was the highlight. Do you know what it is?'

'Tell me.'

'Leonardo's iconic drawing is based on the work of a Roman architect; Vitruvius. It shows the ideal proportions of man. Vitruvius believed that the classical principles of architecture were based on the ideal human figure. Inspirational!'

'I can see the Sorbonne has been useful,' teased Lorenza.

'Perhaps just a little. Now, I would like to take you to a really nice place for lunch. Any suggestions?'

'I know just the place, but we have to go home first to get the boat.'

'Wonderful,' said Tristan. 'I do love that boat, you know.'

'I wouldn't have guessed. Perhaps you'll come back soon then. Just for the boat, I mean.'

'Oh, there could be some other attractions ...'

'You mean apart from the boat and the Vitruvian man?' teased Lorenza and squeezed Tristan's arm.

'Perhaps it's time to explore the Vitruvian woman? You know, just to get a feel for the proportions ... What do you think?' asked Tristan, a naughty sparkle in his eyes.

'What a splendid idea! Let's go.'

As Lorenza and Tristan approached the wooden bridge, a woman approached them from behind and asked for directions. Lorenza explained where they were, and pointed to the map in the woman's hand. As the woman thanked them, Tristan felt a sudden chill run up his spine. *Just like Ponte Vecchio*, he thought. *Another warning, how strange.*

Belmonte watched from a distance as his girlfriend went through the prearranged distraction. He could just see the hearse tied up under the bridge and the two men dressed in black hiding in the bushes, waiting for his signal. Belmonte looked around for the last time. Satisfied, he raised his hand and gave the signal. After that, everything happened very quickly.

The two men in black stepped out of the bushes. One hit Tristan over the head from behind with a cosh, and dragged him under the bridge. The other pressed a cloth drenched in chloroform against Lorenza's face. Lorenza collapsed into the woman's arms. The man picked Lorenza up like a doll and carried her down the embankment to the hearse.

The black hearse – a converted, open water taxi – was used for traditional Venetian funerals. It had a coffin strapped to the open deck for all to see. The man opened the coffin and dropped Lorenza inside. The other man made sure Tristan was still unconscious. Satisfied, he left him lying on the embankment and jumped on board.

Belmonte looked at his watch. The entire operation had taken less than three minutes. *Perfect*, he thought, and walked over to his girlfriend waiting at the bridge. 'Well done, darling,' he said and slapped her on the bum as they watched the hearse drift slowly down the canal on its way to the Cimitero di San Michele.

26

Cimitero di San Michele: 28 May

The first thing Lorenza could feel as she drifted slowly towards consciousness was a raging thirst clawing at her parched throat. When she tried to lick her cracked lips they felt like sandpaper, and a pungent, nauseating stench of stale vomit irritated her nose, making her retch. Slowly, the comforting layers of cottonwool-bliss dulling her senses began to peel away. With memory her only friend, she desperately tried to remember what happened, but her brain refused to obey. When Lorenza opened her eyes, fear banished confusion as she realised that she was lying in what looked and felt like a narrow, padded box with its lid open. *A coffin!* she thought, trying to control the wave of panic rushing through her. *Perhaps I am dead?* Lorenza closed her eyes, hoping it was all a bad dream.

'Good; you are awake,' said a voice, sounding distant and strange. At first, Lorenza thought she must have been mistaken. She opened her eyes again and tried to sit up. With her wrists and ankles tied together, it wasn't easy, but gritting her teeth, she ignored the pain caused by the tight rope cutting into her flesh. After several awkward attempts she managed to pull herself up and looked around: two candles spluttering in the corner of a small, dank chamber were the only source of light piercing the darkness like shafts of hope.

For a while, Lorenza's eyes followed crazy shadows sweeping across the moss-covered floor like a dance macabre, up the wet stone walls and then along the low ceiling covered in tree roots before coming to rest on a row of dusty coffins – lids closed – lined up in a row next to her. *I am not dead,* she thought, *but everyone else in here appears to be.* Noticing some movement out of the corner of her eye, she turned her head and gasped. A strange-looking shape was drifting out of the shadows towards her like a ghost.

'Who's there?' croaked Lorenza, staring at the shape coming closer. A hand reached out of a black cloak, and a finger pointed in her direction. Mesmerised, Lorenza watched the finger move slowly upwards until it came to rest against the smiling lips of a golden mask, reminding her of Carnivale.

'Shh,' said a voice behind the mask, 'we don't want to wake the dead, do we?'

'Who are you?' whispered Lorenza, staring at the golden mask's sardonic smile.

'I am your keeper.'

'Where am I?'

The masked figure began to laugh. 'Look around you. Can't you guess? You are in a tomb, suspended between life and death. You can either stay here and join the others, or you can leave and resume your life. It's all up to you and those who care about you.'

'What do you want?'

'A sensible question at last. Let's begin with a number; a phone number. Your father's mobile number.'

'I don't understand,' stammered Lorenza.

'You will; soon. The number, please.'

Do as he asks, thought Lorenza, her mind racing, and called out her father's phone number.

'Excellent, thank you,' said the masked figure, and took a bow. 'In return, I will now untie you. There is water in the jug over there. If you do as I ask, you will have all you need, and please remember, there is no way out of here except through me; trust me. And there is no point in screaming. The dead cannot hear.'

'Where is Tristan?'

'Ah, the young man. Back home by now, I'd say. With a sore head.'

'What do you want from me?' shrieked Lorenza. 'Who are you? Why?'

The finger moved towards the golden lips again. 'Shh,' said the voice, 'all in good time.' Then another hand appeared, holding a knife.

The hand reached slowly into the coffin and cut the rope around Lorenza's ankles. 'Hold up your hands,' said the voice. Lorenza did as she was told, and the hand cut the rope tying her wrists together. 'Better?' Taking another bow, the shape turned around, doffed a tricorne hat and quickly melted into the dark. Moments later, Lorenza heard the scraping of iron against stone, followed by a dull thud and the clanking of chains.

Exhausted, Lorenza fell back into the coffin and began to rub her painful wrists; an eerie, distant laughter echoing through the chamber a sinister reminder that she wasn't dreaming.

Gambio hated waiting. He looked at his watch again and walked over to the window overlooking the manicured rose garden. *He should have called by now*, he thought, tapping the window with his fingertips to calm himself. As a man used to being in control, he loathed uncertainly. He was about to look at his watch again, when the phone vibrated in his shirt pocket.

'Done!' said Belmonte.

'No surprises?' asked Gambio, feeling calm again.

'None. Went like clockwork.'

'Good. You have the number?'

'Yes.'

'I'll take it from here. All under control at your end?'

'Absolutely. You can rely on my boys.'

'I am relying on *you*,' Gambio reminded Belmonte, to make sure he realised that the buck stopped with him.

'Understood.'

'Good. Istanbul tomorrow as planned?'

'Yes.'

'You remember what I told you about Bahadir?'

'I do; leave him to me.'

'We need fresh supplies, urgently. *Ars Moriendi* ...'

'I know. I'll try to arrange it as quickly as I can.'

'You do that. Well done, Luigi! Keep me posted. Now, give me that number.'

Gambio walked over to the wall safe concealed behind the mahogany panels in his study, opened it and took out one of the cheap, disposable phones he kept for important calls. He would use each phone for only one call to make sure it could not be traced. He attached the phone to an electronic encrypting device that distorted his voice and switched on the phone. *Let it begin,* he thought, enjoying a rush of excitement caused by the high stakes of the game.

'Hold still,' said the countess. 'Nasty gash. This will sting a bit.' Tristan winced as the countess continued to disinfect the wound on the back of his head. 'That's better. Now, tell us once again exactly what happened.' The countess looked at da Baggio standing by the window, watching. After Tristan had staggered through the door, covered in blood and, still in a daze, recounted what had happened, da Baggio had hurried back to the bridge with the gardener to search for Lorenza.

'Not much to tell,' said Tristan, the sadness in his voice obvious. 'It all happened so quickly, just as I told you before.'

'Again; please?' pleaded the countess. 'Even the smallest detail could be important.'

'All right. There was this woman asking for directions. She looked like a tourist and had a map in her hand. Lorenza explained where we were. That's the last thing I remember. Next thing, I am lying on a footpath under the bridge. I am covered in blood and my head feels like it's about to explode. I crawl up the embankment and start looking for Lorenza. I call her name. Nothing. The place is deserted. Somehow, I find my way back here. That's it.'

'What do you *think* happened?' asked da Baggio.

'Lorenza has been abducted,' replied Tristan without hesitation. 'I've feared something like this for days. I can't explain it, but I have sensed danger. I've been uneasy ever since the grand finale.'

The countess nodded, remembering her conversation with Tristan: *Her victory will come at a price ...'*

'I don't understand,' said da Baggio, obviously distressed. The countess walked over to him and put her hand on his arm. 'We must call the police, Leo,' she said. '*Now.'*

'You are right.' As da Baggio reached into his pocket to retrieve his phone, it began to ring. Da Baggio answered the call.

'Don't hang up,' said a voice, sounding hollow and speaking quite slowly. 'We have your daughter—'

'Is she all right?' interrupted da Baggio, almost crushing the phone in his hand. The countess looked at him, alarmed.

'Keep calm. She's fine and will remain so as long as you do exactly as I tell you. Now, listen carefully ...'

27

Jack sat in the conservatory at the Kuragin Chateau just outside Paris reviewing his manuscript of *The Forgotten Painting*, when he received a phone call from the countess. Stunned, Jack listened without interrupting as he tried to come to terms with the extraordinary chain of events the countess was telling him about.

'How's Tristan?' he asked at last.

'Shaken, but fine,' replied the countess. 'We are all in shock; especially Leonardo. You can imagine, after that phone call ...'

'Strictly no police; those were the instructions?'

'Yes. Jack, we don't know what to do ... We need you; here.'

'I'll be on the first plane I can get.'

'Thanks, Jack. This is serious.'

'I know.'

'We haven't got much time.'

'I know that too.'

Jack pushed his manuscript aside and kept looking into the garden and across the pond. It was his favourite spot in the chateau, his 'place of inspiration' he called it. A place that helped him think, reflect. He had watched *Top Chef Europe* for weeks, and had cheered on Lorenza during the nail-biting final and saw her win. *How extraordinary*, he thought. *Lorenza, a celebrity, abducted in broad daylight in the middle of Venice. Audacious. Professional job; had to be. And then there are these curious demands ...* Jack felt a strange sense of excitement wash over him, something he hadn't felt since he'd discovered Brother Francis's diary and the paintings hidden in the Imperial Crypt in Vienna two years earlier. He was ready for a new challenge, and what he had just heard had all the hallmarks of just that, and a lot more ...

Working on the Fuchs interview notes was certainly interesting, rewarding even, and kept his publicist happy, but was not all that exciting. Jack hated the tedium of writing and got bored easily. He was a people person and writing is a solitary endeavour. He always struggled to reconcile the two, but enjoyed chasing the story more than writing it and loved nothing more than being in the thick of it all. Jack gravitated towards danger and liked living on the edge. Something new was definitely needed. Experience had taught him that the best stories always seemed to find him when he least expected it. *This is it*, he thought, and closed his notebook. *I'm sure of it.* When he turned around, he noticed François, the countess's butler-cum-chauffeur, standing in the doorway.

'Would you like another cup of tea?' asked François.

'No thanks, but I wouldn't mind a lift to the airport,' replied Jack, smiling, and went to his room to pack.

Marco Polo airport was chaotic as usual. Excited tourists were milling around looking for transport into Venice. Jack collected his duffel bag from the carousel, walked into the arrivals waiting area and began to look for the countess. Tristan saw Jack first. 'There he is,' he said, and began to push through a noisy group of backpackers who had just arrived from Germany. 'Jack!' shouted Tristan, waving. 'Over here.'

Jack turned around and looked at Tristan coming towards him. At first, he didn't recognise him with his head bandaged.

'Taking up kamikaze, mate?' said Jack, and embraced Tristan. 'You look like a Japanese suicide pilot wearing a *hachimaki*.

'What's a *hachimaki*?' asked Tristan.

'A headband, a bandana. The only thing missing is the rising sun and the kanji characters. You're gone for a couple of days without me, and look at you.' The bandage wound around Tristan's head did in fact look a bit like the headband of a kamikaze fighter.

'He's almost as bad as you,' said the countess, kissing Jack on the cheek. 'Never a dull moment with you two around, that's for sure. Thanks for coming so quickly, Jack,' continued the countess, lowering her voice. 'This is serious.'

'Sure,' replied Jack. 'Any news?'

'Nothing further so far, but Leo's in a bad way. He's glued to the phone, waiting for the next call.'

'Understandable.'

'He's waiting at the dock with his boat. It's the quickest way to get home from here.'

'Wait until you see this boat,' said Tristan, and picked up Jack's duffel bag. 'Travelling light?'

'I've got all I need,' said Jack.

The countess raised an eyebrow. 'Bomber jacket and two pairs of socks?' she asked.

'And don't forget the notebook,' interjected Tristan. 'He goes nowhere without it.'

'You know me too well. Let's go, guys.'

Jack had met Leonardo da Baggio before and remembered him as an excellent chess player and jovial raconteur. However, the man waiting for them in the sleek motor yacht in no way resembled the elegant bon vivant Jack remembered. Jack recognised all the signs: deep worry, confusion, despair bordering on depression. As soon as they jumped on board, da Baggio took off.

'What did I tell you?' shouted Tristan.

'See what you mean,' Jack shouted back, enjoying the breathtaking speed of the powerful boat and the sea spray tickling his face.

Boys and their toys, thought the countess, holding on tight in the back.

After an exhilarating ride past some of the icons of Venice, they pulled into the mooring under the palazzo. 'I can't tell you how grateful I am,' said da Baggio, carrying Jack's duffel bag up the slippery stairs. 'Let me show you to your room.'

'Could we talk first?' said Jack. 'Time's precious. The room can wait.'

Da Baggio looked at Jack, relieved. 'Of course. Let's go in here,' he said and opened a tall, polished timber door leading into the grand salon on the first floor.

'Wow!' said Jack. 'I've only seen something like this in the movies.' Two huge identical marble fireplaces – one at each end of the large, opulent room – faced each other like duellers frozen in time, defending their honour. Mirrors above the fireplaces reached all the way up to the tall ceiling decorated with frescoes, making the room look twice the size. Glass double doors in the middle of the room opened onto a balcony overlooking the Canal Grande. The stone floor was covered with Persian rugs, and the walls with paintings, mainly family portraits.

Da Baggio motioned towards a comfortable-looking lounge and chairs in front of one of the fireplaces. 'My late wife's favourite room,' said da Baggio quietly. 'This has been our family home for over four hundred years. Lots of ghosts and sad memories ...'

The countess walked over to da Baggio. 'And a lot of joy and precious links to the past as well,' she said, and sat down next to him. 'Few families today have something like this.'

'Perhaps, but history can be overwhelming. At times I feel the weight of this place pressing down on me like a rock pushing me into the canal.'

The countess watched Jack pull his little notebook out of his pocket and smiled when he took off the rubber band holding it together and kept searching for his pen. She had seen him do this many times before. It was an endearing habit of a special man she adored.

'Can we start at the beginning, please?' said Jack. 'It's been just on twenty-four hours since Lorenza disappeared – right?'

'Yes,' said da Baggio, 'and about twenty-two hours since that phone call.'

Jack looked at Tristan sitting opposite. 'Please tell us what happened yesterday,' he said.

'Not much to tell, really,' said Tristan, and then gave a step-by-step account of the events leading up to the bridge attack.

'And then what happened?' asked Jack.

'Tristan arrived here, injured and covered in blood,' said the countess. 'He told us what had occurred and we were about to call the police, when Leonardo's phone rang.'

175

Jack turned to da Baggio. 'Can you tell me exactly what was said?' he asked.

Da Baggio pulled a piece of paper out of his pocket. 'Katerina asked me to write it all down immediately after the call.'

'Excellent! Please tell us.'

'To begin with, the voice sounded quite strange ...'

'In what way?'

'Difficult to say; distant, like in a chamber with echoes.'

Jack nodded. 'To disguise the voice, no doubt.'

'I was told not to hang up and to just listen. The voice said: "We have your daughter." And then: "She is fine and will remain so as long as you do exactly as I tell you ..."'

'And then?'

'I was told to arrange a million euros, and ...' Da Baggio paused, and looked up at a gap between two paintings on the wall opposite.

The countess reached for da Baggio's hand and squeezed it. 'Tell him,' she said quietly.

Da Baggio stood up, walked across the room to an intricately carved oak chest, opened its heavy lid and lifted out what looked like a large photo album.

'I have to hand over these,' said da Baggio, and placed the portfolio carefully on the table in front of Jack.

'What is this?' asked Jack.

Da Baggio opened the portfolio. 'Original recipes that used to belong to Suleiman the Magnificent.'

'How extraordinary,' said Jack, and looked at the beautifully illustrated parchment crowded with intricate Arabic writing.

'They have been in our family for four hundred years.'

'Are these the recipes Lorenza mentioned during *Top Chef*? The grand final?'

'Yes. The Hunkar Begendi recipe that won her the contest is right here.'

'Incredible. And you were asked to hand these over?'

'Yes; that's the really baffling bit. The instructions were quite specific.'

'And the one million euros represents the prize; the amount she won in the contest,' said Jack. 'You think this is somehow all related to *Top Chef?*'

'It would appear so,' said the countess.

'How weird. The money I can understand, but the recipes ... And you were told *no police?*'

'Yes. He was very emphatic about that. He said if I involve the police, I will never see Lorenza again,' said da Baggio, choking with emotion.

'What else?' asked Jack.

'I was to wait for further instructions, by phone.'

'And so far, nothing?'

'No.'

Jack kept looking at the portfolio. 'Magnificent,' he said. 'So, these are the original recipes brought here by Osman, if I remember correctly, from Constantinople? Lorenza told us the story during the *Top Chef* final.'

'Yes. Osman was Cosimo da Baggio's grandson. He escaped from the Topkapi Palace in Constantinople after his father, Murad III, died.'

'And all his half-brothers were killed; all nineteen of them,' interjected the countess.

'To secure the succession and allow his oldest brother, Mehmed, to become sultan,' said da Baggio. 'All possible rivals were eliminated, except one: Osman.'

'What a story,' said Jack.

'Osman was the son of Cosimo's abducted daughter.' Da Baggio pointed to a small portrait hanging above the chest. 'That's her over there.'

Jack stood up, walked over to the chest and looked at the exquisite little picture.

'It was painted by Marco Vecellio,' said da Baggio.

'Titian's pupil,' said Tristan.

Jack shook his head, momentarily overcome by the living history in the room.

'We had a wonderful portrait of Osman as well,' said da Baggio, and pointed to a gap between the two paintings. 'It was painted when he was much older. He was a famous physician by then right here in Venice. It used to hang over there.'

'A *physician*? What happened to it?' asked Jack, staring at the wall.

'The Nazis took it during the war.'

Good God! thought Jack. *It can't be ... surely.* 'Can you describe it to me?' he asked quietly, sounding hoarse.

'Of course. It showed Osman, an imposing man, examining a patient – a cardinal – lying in bed in the Doge's Palace. Osman is holding a book in his left hand and a—'

'Scalpel in his right?' interrupted Jack.

Da Baggio looked at him, surprised. 'How on earth do you know that?' he asked.

Jack reached into his pocket, pulled out his mobile, selected a photo and handed the phone to da Baggio. 'Because of this,' he said.

For a while, da Baggio kept staring at the screen. 'I don't understand! *How?* What?' he stammered, looking incredulous. Before he could ask more questions, he was interrupted by the phone ringing in his pocket. Da Baggio paled, took a deep breath and answered the phone, the silence in the room paralysing.

'Listen carefully,' said a voice, sounding distant and hollow and speaking quite slowly. 'This is what I want you to do ...'

PART II
ARS MORIENDI

28

Sultan's Table was Istanbul's most famous restaurant, serving authentic Ottoman cuisine. It occupied several floors of an opulent, eighteenth-century merchant's home close to the Hagia Sophia, and reservations had to be made several days, sometimes weeks, in advance. The most prized tables on the roof terrace overlooking the Golden Horn and the Bosporus were reserved for special guests, usually referred to the iconic establishment by the concierges of luxury hotels. International film stars, politicians, even royalty, were frequent diners at the restaurant, and Bahadir – a consummate host – enjoyed meeting his famous guests in person and escorting them to their tables. He also liked to boast about the unique dishes based on secret Ottoman recipes coming straight from the sultan's fabled kitchens in the Topkapi Palace a stone's throw away, which were the hallmark of his restaurant.

Sultan's Table was Bahadir's world. It was the flagship of his restaurant chain and the nerve centre of his culinary empire. His entire reputation rested on the unique, authentic Ottoman dishes exclusively created in his kitchen. As the author of several acclaimed cookbooks and his own TV show, Bahadir was the undisputed authority on Ottoman cuisine in Turkey, if not the world. The only shadow hanging over his reputation was his recent, very public defeat during the *Top Chef Europe* competition. To have been beaten by a twenty-year-old woman using one of his own signature dishes was humiliating in the extreme. But more serious by far, was her claim regarding the original Ottoman recipes that apparently had been in her family for centuries. This seriously undermined Bahadir's authority and he realised that something drastic had be done to discredit and silence the rival, and salvage his reputation as the undisputed king of Ottoman cuisine.

The kitchen on the ground floor was huge and Bahadir ruled it with an iron fist. Recruited from various parts of Turkey, twenty hand-picked chefs created delectable Ottoman specialities only served at the Sultan's Table by an army of well-trained local waiters and waitresses.

Belmonte got out of the taxi and walked up to the doorman greeting the guests in front of the tall, ornate wooden double doors leading into the restaurant.

'You have a reservation, sir?' asked the doorman, sizing up the stocky, broad-shouldered man in the ill-fitting suit with no tie. Compared to the elegant diners arriving by hire car, he definitely looked out of place. But something in his demeanour radiated not only confidence, but authority and danger. The experienced doorman recognised the signs immediately and decided to proceed with caution.

'No, but Mr Bahadir is expecting me,' replied Belmonte. Smiling, he slipped a large banknote discreetly into the doorman's breast pocket, stepped back, and lit a cigarette.

'Who shall I say?' asked the doorman politely.

'*Ars Moriendi*,' replied Belmonte, laughing.

'Very well. Please follow me, sir.'

The doorman escorted Belmonte to the crowded bar on the ground floor lit up by beautiful coloured, ball-shaped lights dangling from the wooden ceiling, giving the bar an inviting, exotic look with whispering echoes of Ali Baba and secret harem tales. 'I will tell Mr Bahadir you have arrived. May I order you a drink?'

'Scotch, please.'

'Coming up.'

Looking a little flustered and obviously annoyed, Bahadir followed the doorman to the bar. 'That's him over there,' said the doorman, and pointed discreetly to Belmonte leaning casually against the bar.

'I didn't expect to see someone so soon,' said Bahadir. He hadn't met Belmonte in person before but had of course heard of him from Gambio. Bahadir pulled up a stool and sat down next to his surprise visitor. 'As I recall it, last time we "saw" each other, you were officiating at a unique ritual and wearing a mask.'

'Correct. *Ars Moriendi*,' replied Belmonte casually, sipping his Scotch. 'And that is precisely what brings me here ...' Belmonte put down his glass and looked at Bahadir.

'Oh?' Bahadir had met men like Belmonte before and was on guard. Judging by what Gambio had told him, Belmonte was a loyal, ruthless killing machine, not to be crossed. At the moment, Belmonte was an extension of Gambio; he *was* Gambio, with all the authority and clout of the capo himself. 'Would you care to elaborate?' said Bahadir, and signalled to the barman to refill Belmonte's glass.

'Sure, but could we go somewhere a little more private?' asked Belmonte, and pointed to the noisy crowd surrounding the bar.

'Of course; follow me.'

Bahadir went to the back of the room, pulled a key out of his pocket and unlocked a door concealed behind a curtain. 'Welcome to my underworld,' said Bahadir, and led the way down some narrow, winding stairs leading into the murky darkness below. 'This is part of the vast Palace of Constantine complex – Roman ruins – buried under the Sultan Ahmed district here,' said Bahadir. 'Just about every shop and restaurant around here is built on top of it. A maze of secret passages criss-cross this area right up to the famous Basilica Cisterns; very handy at times. Most of the underground chambers are filled with rubble, but we excavated this part and use it as storage and other things ... it's very secure.'

'I can see that,' said Belmonte, and looked up at the tall, vaulted ceiling constructed of the small, characteristic bricks used in Roman times.

Bahadir opened a steel door and stepped aside. 'My office,' he said, and pointed into a huge, vaulted chamber. Looking like some command centre, the entire back wall was covered with illuminated CCTV screens showing various parts of the restaurant above.

'Impressive,' said Belmonte.

'From here, we can see every corner of the building, including the entrance and the kitchen.' Bahadir motioned towards a lounge and chairs next to a large desk facing the screens. 'Please, make yourself comfortable,' he said, and walked over to a glass drinks cabinet. He took out a bottle of Scotch and two glasses and put them down on the coffee table in front of Belmonte. 'Help yourself.'

'Salvatore sends his regards. He has kept his part of the bargain,' said Belmonte. Looking totally relaxed, he crossed his legs and leaned back into his comfortable chair.

'What do you mean?'

'Europe's new *Top Chef* is securely entombed on an island in Venice.'

'Entombed?'

'She was abducted two days ago and a ransom demand has been made,' replied Belmonte, sidestepping the question.

'She's alive?'

'Of course, and—'

'The recipes?' interrupted Bahadir. '*You got them?*'

'Negotiations are in progress.'

'What negotiations?'

'Salvatore has the matter in hand; he's running everything personally.'

'No results then?'

'It's only been two days ...'

'So, why are you here? Now?'

'*Ars Moriendi*. The last game was more costly than expected. We have run out of, you know ...'

'And?'

'We urgently need new ones, but the right kind. An important game has been scheduled with some big players arriving from Abu Dhabi.'

'What has that to do with me?' demanded Bahadir, looking nervous.

'Everything. Your side of the bargain ... Surely you remember?' said Belmonte, leaning forward.'

'But—'

'It's urgent,' interrupted Belmonte, his voice steely and threatening.

'I haven't received—'

'You will,' Belmonte cut in. 'There's a lot at stake ...'

'There always is,' said Bahadir, the sarcasm in his voice obvious.

Belmonte recognised the signs of irritation and displeasure and decided to turn up the heat. For him, to walk away from this empty-handed was unthinkable; too much depended on it. And then there was the additional matter – another unexpected emergency Gambio had raised on the phone the day before. This had placed Belmonte under even more pressure.

Belmonte lit another cigarette and, inhaling deeply, looked at Bahadir.

'This isn't all, I'm afraid,' he said quietly. 'There's more ...'

'What do you mean?' snapped Bahadir.

'We've lost our surgeon.'

'I don't understand.'

'The body parts ... You've seen the operation.'

'What do you mean *you've lost the surgeon?*' demanded Bahadir, raising his voice.

'The surgeon is no longer with us,' came the evasive reply. Belmonte waved dismissively. 'And we urgently need a new one. Usually, we recruit doctors who have been struck off for misconduct and find themselves in a desperate situation and are therefore easy to manipulate. I'm sure you get my drift. The problem is, this takes time, and time we haven't got. We have urgent orders to fill; very lucrative ...'

'Why are you telling me this?' asked Bahadir.

Belmonte, a lateral thinker and ruthless pragmatist, saw an opportunity to solve two urgent problems at the same time: sourcing new young combatants for *Ars Moriendi*, and recruiting a much-needed surgeon to extract the body parts. If he pulled this off, his standing as a valuable new member of the *famiglia* was bound to skyrocket. Not only in Gambio's eyes, but also in the eyes of those who had questioned his appointment. Belmonte knew that the recognition he craved so much had to be earned, and the best way to earn it was to deliver results. In this case, resolve a crisis with a lot of money at stake.

'You told us you have contacts in the border camps and have sourced cheap labour for your restaurants from there before.'

'Yes. I have an agent working for me in the camp. As you can imagine, there are many desperate people looking for a way out and are prepared to do almost anything ...'

Belmonte looked at Bahadir and smiled. 'Good,' he said. 'Let's put a surgeon on our shopping list. With so many displaced people, we are bound to find one in the camp looking for a lifeline. What do you think?'

Something in Belmonte's demeanour sent an icy shiver down Bahadir's spine. He had dealt with dangerous men before and recognised all the signs. Contradicting Belmonte, and therefore resisting Gambio, was out of the question. It was time to change direction. 'How much time do we have?' he asked.

Smart guy, thought Belmonte, and smiled. 'A few days,' he said, and refilled his glass.

'We have to travel to Kilis on the Syrian border. It's a long way.'

'The container camps?'

'Yes.'

'When?'

'We leave in the morning.'

29

The countess woke with a start and for a while just stared into the darkness, listening. Orientating herself, she thought she could hear animated voices drifting up from below. Then she turned on the bedside lamp and looked at her watch: it was just after four. As the fog of sleep receded, the turbulent events of the previous day crept into her consciousness: Jack's surprise revelation about the painting and its extraordinary discovery; the chilling phone call and its implications.

Jack, da Baggio and the countess had stayed up until late, discussing the dramatic abduction and working out a plan. Overcome by fatigue, the countess had excused herself just after midnight and had gone to bed, leaving Jack and da Baggio with a half-empty bottle of cognac in front of the fireplace, arguing about whether to involve the police and ask for help.

The countess put on her dressing gown and went downstairs. When she stopped in front of the door leading into the salon, all was quiet. Slowly, she opened the heavy door and peered inside. Jack was alone in the room and stood in front of Vecellio's portrait of Cosimo's abducted daughter. He had a brandy balloon in his hand and was obviously deep in contemplation.

'Do you *ever* sleep?' whispered the countess.

Jack spun around and smiled. 'How can I? Your fault,' he replied. 'Too much going on ...'

'How unusual.'

'Can you believe all this stuff about the painting? The missing pieces falling into place? The unexpected twists and turns, almost as if it was meant to be?'

'Perhaps it was,' ventured the countess.

187

'The hairs on the back of my neck are tingling just thinking about it. Suddenly, everything appears to be coming together; making sense; answering all the questions. Here, right now, in this place.'

'*All* the questions?'

'Perhaps not all, but at least some of the important ones.'

'And posing new ones.'

'Sure.'

'It is rather astonishing,' agreed the countess, and pointed to the exquisite little painting on the wall in front of Jack. 'And to think that this beautiful young woman is the mother of the physician in your mystery picture from the Habsburg crypt.'

'Osman, the prodigal grandson who escaped from the sultan's assassins in the Topkapi Palace and returned to his homeland and his family.'

'And became a physician.'

'Reaching out from the past by holding a copy of Ibn Sina's famous book in his hand—'

'For all to see. Do you think he was trying to tell us something?' asked the countess.

'By showing us *al-Qanun*, the famous book the Nazis were after?' said Jack. 'I'm sure of it. I wonder where it ended up, or if it still exists?'

The countess linked arms with Jack. 'Who knows,' she said, 'but this story has *you* written all over it.'

'You think so?'

'Trust me ...'

'I hope you're right. I need a new challenge.'

The countess looked at Jack and pointed her finger at his chest. 'Be careful what you wish for,' she said.

'Always,' replied Jack, grinning, and lifted his glass.

'Where's Leo?' asked the countess, turning serious.

'Just left. Gone to bed, I think.'

'Did you sort things out? About the police, I mean?'

Jack put down his glass and looked at the countess. 'Yes. He will contact the police first thing in the morning.'

'Good,' said the countess, relieved. 'He was so adamant. How did you manage to persuade him?'

'The latest demand ... the property in Florence. That's what got him over the line.'

'In what way?'

'It's complicated. Sit down and I'll tell you.'

Cesaria knocked on the chief prosecutor's office door and entered. Grimaldi and Conti stood in front of a whiteboard by the window and turned around to face Cesaria. It was just before seven in the morning.

'You wanted to see me, sir?' said Cesaria.

'Yes. There's been a development; a serious one.'

'Oh?'

'For now, not a word of this must leave these four walls; clear?'

'Absolutely, sir,' said Cesaria, a ripple of excitement pulsing through her. To be taken into the chief prosecutor's confidence was rare and therefore special.

'Lives depend on it. I will let Fabio explain,' said Grimaldi, and lit a small cigar.

'It all began with a phone call early this morning,' said Conti. 'A man – Leonardo da Baggio – called Antonio from Venice. Does the name mean anything to you?'

'Da Baggio ... Lorenza, the girl who won *Top Chef* the other day?'

Conti shot Grimaldi a meaningful look and nodded. 'Yes, Leonardo da Baggio is her father. She has been abducted.'

'*What!*' Cesaria almost shouted, her eyes wide with astonishment. 'In Venice?'

'Yes.'

'Then what has this to do with us? Not our jurisdiction ...'

Smart girl, thought Grimaldi. *She put her finger right on it.*

'Everything,' said Grimaldi. 'I'll tell you why.'

During the next few minutes, Grimaldi outlined the circumstances of the motor vehicle accident two years earlier in which Lorenza's mother and brother had been killed, and explained the coroner's finding of accidental death.

'I don't understand,' said Cesaria.

'Leonardo da Baggio approached me after the hearing with an extraordinary claim,' said Grimaldi. 'He knew I was investigating the Mafia here in Florence and came to me for help. He maintained that the crash was no accident and that the car had been deliberately run off the road by a truck owned by – wait for it – Gambio.'

'But why?' asked Cesaria. 'How?'

'It all had to do with a property deal involving Lorenza's grandparents, a prominent family living right here in Florence,' continued Grimaldi. 'Gambio was after a property they own here in Florence to make way for a hotel he wanted to build. They refused to sell and the accident was supposed to be a warning to put pressure on them to make a deal, but it all went terribly wrong. Their daughter and grandson were both killed.'

'Did da Baggio offer any evidence?'

'Only circumstantial. It wasn't enough to reopen the matter. And the coroner ... you know ...' Grimaldi shrugged. 'Well, this is Florence.'

'How awful. But how is this linked to the abduction in Venice?'

'The circumstances are still a little sketchy at the moment,' said Conti, stepping in. 'But one of the demands for Lorenza's release has to do with the same property deal. That's the link. And besides, it looks like a pro job; classic Mafia. We've seen it all before.'

'Gambio?' asked Cesaria, her cheeks flushed with excitement.

'At the top of my list.'

'How brazen.'

'That's Gambio,' said Grimaldi. 'The man is that sure of himself.'

'And that ruthless,' interjected Conti.

'And reckless,' added Grimaldi, slowly grinding the stub of his cigar into the ashtray. 'That's his weakness, and our opportunity.'

'So, what do we do now?' asked Cesaria.

'We step in. You and Fabio go to Venice straight away and talk to da Baggio. But remember this: one of the specific instructions given by the abductors was *strictly no police involvement*. I don't have to tell you how sensitive and potentially explosive a matter this is and how much is at stake here. This is a high-profile case involving an international celebrity. One mistake ... if the slightest thing goes wrong ... da Baggio has been very courageous in coming to us and has placed a lot of trust in me. For the time being, this stays strictly between the three of us. No outsiders; you know why. Let's not disappoint da Baggio. Let's give him our best. After what has happened to this man, he deserves nothing less. That's all.'

30

Haddad looked across to Dr Rosen's container surgery and watched the relentless convoy of injured being delivered to the doorstep of hope. It was just after sunrise. *So much misery,* he thought, and ran his fingertips over the bandage covering his chest and shoulder. The wound was healing well, and thanks to the surgical skills of Amena and Dr Rosen, a full recovery was expected. However, he still felt a little weak and knew he had to be careful.

A man carrying a boy of about ten in his arms came running towards the surgery. The man put the boy down on the ground in front of Haddad. The boy appeared seriously injured. His face was covered in blood, but he was conscious.

'Mortar fire at the border,' said the man. 'Do what you can. I'm going back; there are many more.'

Haddad hurried into the surgery to get help. Nazir and two nurses were getting the operating theatre ready for the morning. 'Where's Dr Rosen?' asked Haddad.

'Next door in recovery; doing her morning rounds with Amena,' said Nazir.

'There's an injured boy outside. It's serious ...'

'I'll have a look,' said Nazir.

'I'll get Dr Rosen,' said Haddad, and walked outside.

As soon as Nazir saw the large wound in the side of the boy's head, he realised the injuries were life-threatening. He picked up the boy, carried him inside and put him on the operating table. When Nazir began to unbutton the boy's blood-soaked shirt, he noticed something hard underneath. The boy opened his eyes, and looked at him. For a moment, their eyes locked. It was a look Nazir would never forget; like staring into infinite sadness. Then he peeled away the boy's shirt, looked down and gasped. *Oh no*! he thought, panic clawing at his heaving chest. 'Everybody out!' shouted Nazir and ran for the door.

Because he was so weak by then, it took the boy a few seconds to activate the detonator in his hand. This gave Nazir enough time to make it to safety before a massive explosion blew the container apart, killing the two nurses and several patients waiting outside.

After the fire crews had put out the blaze, the Turkish authorities in charge of the camp cordoned off the entire area in a desperate attempt to avoid panic. Dr Rosen's surgery had been totally obliterated, and no-one was permitted to go near it.

Dr Rosen stood under a tree close by and watched in silence as a fleet of ambulances began to take away the bodies, some of them disfigured beyond recognition and with entire limbs torn off by the powerful explosion. She put her arm around Amena who stood next to her, sobbing, and tried to comfort her distraught friend who was still in shock.

'I can't believe this has happened,' said Dr Rosen, shaking her head. 'Evil has now reached us even here, on the operating table.'

'How can anyone do such a thing?' asked Amena, still shaking. 'Turn an injured boy into a human bomb? It's inconceivable. What kind of human being ... I can't stay here; I just can't.'

'I understand. At least Nazir was lucky. The way he survived is almost a miracle,' said Dr Rosen, changing the subject. The blast had blown Nazir clear of the collapsing container. Apart from a few scratches and bruises, he was unharmed. 'Where is he? Do you know?'

'He went into the main camp to talk to a friend. Nazir wants to get away from here as soon as he can.'

'Is that what he told you?'

'Yes. Can you blame him?'

Dr Rosen shook her head. 'No,' she said sadly.

'What will you do?' asked Amena.

'I don't know yet. I have to think. But there doesn't seem to be much left for me here either,' said Dr Rosen. 'Everything's gone. All our equipment, the supplies; everything. We can't operate out in the open with our bare hands, can we?'

'No, we can't.'

Haddad sat in front of the tent he shared with Nazir and two others and watched the evening settle on the sorry scenes of the mayhem. Soon the blanket of darkness would hide the reminders of the carnage. Terror was taking a break. However, the injured still kept coming from the border, but now had nowhere to go. Hope too, had been obliterated. The main camp was bursting at the seams and the medical facilities couldn't cope. It was chaos as usual.

Haddad had formed a close bond with Nazir, who was fascinated by the older man and his stories. It was therefore hardly surprising that Nazir should turn to him for advice in a matter of great importance and urgency.

Nazir had just returned from the main camp and had made some tea. He sat down next to Haddad and handed him a cup.

'You look worried,' said Haddad, sipping his tea.

'Remember you told me that life is like a train journey? From time to time, we reach a station along the way and have to make a decision?'

Haddad nodded.

'We have to decide whether to get off and change trains and direction, or stay put and continue the journey,' added Nazir.

'Yes?'

'But there is usually little time to make the decision, and once it has been made, it cannot be reversed because the train has moved on. The opportunity has passed, forever.'

'Correct. It's all about choices. But what has brought this on?' asked Haddad.

'Well, I have to make such a choice.'

'Oh?'

'I can't stay here forever.'

'No, of course not.'

'Something has come up; an opportunity.'

'What kind of opportunity?'

'A chance to get away from here.'

'Care to tell me about it?'

'Two men from Istanbul are in the main camp, recruiting.'

'*Recruiting?*'

'They are looking for young men like me prepared to go to Istanbul to work. I suppose they are looking for cheap labour.'

'Interesting. Tell me more.'

'As you can imagine, there are many willing takers, but the men are very particular. They aren't taking just anyone. They have strict guidelines ... They are only interested in someone young who can speak good English. A friend of mine – Ammar, you've met him – has already been accepted and told me about this. There are only four places, but that's not all.'

'What do you mean?'

'They are also looking for someone with medical qualifications.'

'So?'

'Amena is talking to them right now. She wants to get away.'

'I see ... And you are interested in going?' said Haddad.

'Yes. I've always wanted to go to Istanbul. I've already spoken to one of the men. I think I'm in with a chance,' said Nazir, becoming excited. 'What do you think?'

For reasons he couldn't quite explain, Haddad felt uneasy and the mention of Ammar made him nervous; policeman's instinct. He had only met him briefly, but something about him suggested danger. 'It's all a bit sudden, isn't it?' he said.

'Yes, it is. They need an answer within the hour. They are returning to Istanbul tonight. The train doesn't wait ...'

'You want to go?'

'Yes. I've nothing to lose and I get away from here.' Nazir pointed to the smouldering ruins that only a few hours ago had been a hospital saving lives. 'Just look at this place.'

'I understand. But not everything that glitters is gold.'

'What do you mean?'

'Sometimes what we have is infinitely better than the tempting alternative ...'

'Are you telling me not to go?' asked Nazir, frowning.

'No. I'm telling you to be careful. Decisions like this shouldn't be rushed.'

'There's no time.'

'I know.'

'So, what do you suggest I should do?'

Haddad took his time before replying. He realised that a great deal was at stake for his young friend and he therefore had to tread carefully. 'You must follow your instincts,' he said. 'This must be your decision, and yours alone.'

Nazir nodded and looked anxious.

'It's Dr Rosen, isn't it?' said Haddad.

'Yes, that's the really difficult bit about all this.'

'Then why don't you talk to her? Here she comes now.'

Belmonte walked over to Bahadir standing in front of their car surrounded by curious onlookers. He was talking animatedly to one of the men from the camp who had helped him recruit workers before.

'He wants more commission because he found us a doctor willing to come with us,' said Bahadir, turning to Belmonte.

'Pay him! I am particularly interested in the woman we spoke to. She ticks all—'

'Dr Algafari?' interrupted Bahadir.

'Yes, and that boy ...'

'Nazir?'

'That's the one. He's the best by far. Young, good-looking, smart, eager. And no family, no ties. A loner. And he speaks English; perfect. I hope he—'

'Why don't we ask him?' interrupted Bahadir again and pointed to the wire gate. 'Here he comes now.'

Nazir came running towards Bahadir and Belmonte, his face flushed with excitement.

'Well?' said Bahadir. 'Are you coming with us?'

'Yes!' replied Nazir, catching his breath. 'And so is Dr Algafari,' he added excitedly. 'We worked together at the surgery.'

'Excellent,' said Belmonte, smiling. The pieces were falling into place. 'We leave in an hour. Get your stuff, but remember, one small case only.'

'I'll tell Dr Algafari,' replied Nazir. He waved to his friend Ammar, leaning casually against a Land Rover parked behind Bahadir's car, and hurried back to one of the tents to pack.

'I hate goodbyes,' said Dr Rosen, a sad look clouding her face. 'We'll miss you.' Dr Rosen realised that talking Nazir and Amena out of going would have been wrong, but like Haddad, she too felt uneasy about the rushed decision. Haddad would like to have met the men Amena and Nazir had been talking to, but his injuries prevented him from walking over to the main camp with Nazir. And besides, he didn't want to become too involved.

Nazir put down his little brown suitcase and embraced Dr Rosen. 'I will never forget you,' he said. 'Your kindness saved my life.'

Amena took off her backpack and watched Dr Rosen hug Nazir. Swept along by the relentless tide of fate, she realised she had reached another important fork in the road. Part of her wanted to stay and help Dr Rosen rebuild the surgery, but her past wouldn't allow this. The memories conjured up by the suicide bomb and torn limbs were too painful and had forced her hand. She knew she had to leave, however uncertain or dangerous her future may be. But travelling with Nazir was some comfort and the man in the main camp who had introduced her to his Istanbul contacts had reassured her.

Dr Rosen turned to Amena. 'Remember my door is always open. Call me any time,' she said, tears in her eyes. 'You have my mobile number and my email address?'

Amena nodded, choking with emotion. 'Perhaps one day we'll meet again,' she said. '*Inshallah.*'

'Now go before they leave without you,' said Dr Rosen, and embraced Amena. 'You are a remarkable doctor. You are a *healer*. It's a gift. You can make a real difference; use it wisely.'

Nazir walked over to Haddad. 'You are a wise man; thank you for your friendship,' he said.

'You have a train to catch,' replied Haddad, and ruffled Nazir's curly hair. 'And remember what Dr Rosen told you: if this doesn't work out, call her.'

'What will you do?'

'I have already made contact with the officer in charge of security here. He wants to talk to me.'

Just then a car pulled up behind the row of stretchers blocking the way to the surgery, followed by a black Land Rover, which also stopped. 'We have to leave,' shouted a man through the open passenger window of the car. 'Get in.'

Nazir and Amena hurried over to the car and got into the back seat. Moments later, the car accelerated and disappeared into a cloud of dust.

That voice, thought Haddad, watching the dust settle onto the road. *Where have I heard that voice before?* He asked himself. *I wonder ...* For a while Haddad just stood there, deep in thought, trying in vain to dismiss the troubling echo from the past as a trick of his imagination.

31

Jack met Conti and Cesaria at the Santa Lucia railway station near the western end of the Canal Grande. With backpacks slung casually over their shoulders, they looked like all the other tourists flocking to Venice on that sunny afternoon. Da Baggio was waiting with his boat nearby and took off as soon as they all jumped aboard. He still felt uneasy about his decision to involve the police, but logic told him he had made the right choice. As the countess and Jack had correctly pointed out, to just wait and do nothing wasn't an option supported by reason in the circumstances.

The moment da Baggio met Conti and Cesaria, he felt relieved. In no way did they look, or act, like police officers. They looked more like father and daughter on holidays than members of the notorious Florentine Squadra Mobile hunting the Mafia.

As soon as they arrived at the Palazzo da Baggio, Conti took over. His calm, methodical manner was not only reassuring, but inspired confidence, and put the countess and da Baggio instantly at ease. For the first time since Lorenza's abduction, da Baggio felt calm, and no longer so helpless and alone.

Conti listened to Tristan's account of what had happened, and how, without interrupting. Cesaria took notes, and prepared a detailed timeline. Then it was da Baggio's turn to talk about the two phone calls.

'Good. Very good,' said Conti as soon as da Baggio had finished. He stood up and walked to the large window overlooking the Canal Grande and just stood there with his hands folded behind his back, obviously deep in thought. 'In case you are still wondering,' he began, 'you have definitely made the right decision by coming to us.' As an experienced police officer who had dealt with Mafia abductions before, he knew that a successful outcome could only be achieved with the complete trust and cooperation of everyone involved, especially those close to the victim. Unless everyone worked together as a team and followed instructions, a complicated case like this could quickly turn into a disaster. It all came down to discipline and nerve; especially nerve.

'This has all the classic footprints of the Mafia,' continued Conti. 'There is a clear pattern here and therefore a correct way to approach the situation.'

'What do you mean?' asked da Baggio.

'Mafiosi use intimidation and fear to achieve results. Yes, they are bold and ruthless, but they are also predictable. Surprisingly so. Lorenza is a means to an end. There are definite patterns in their modus operandi, even rules. And so far, this case is displaying all that and we have to respond accordingly. In my experience, as long as they believe they are getting what they are after, Lorenza will be safe. It is only if something goes wrong, usually because someone does something foolish or reckless that—'

'What are you saying?' da Baggio interrupted again.

'What I am saying,' Conti replied calmly, 'is that if you trust us to handle this matter our way, you are giving your daughter the best chance ...'

'*The best chance?*' da Baggio almost shrieked. The countess put her hand reassuringly on da Baggio's arm to calm her anxious friend, but didn't say anything.

Conti looked at da Baggio. 'I cannot give you any guarantees,' he said, 'but I can give you a commitment: my team and I – and that includes Chief Prosecutor Grimaldi – will leave no stone unturned to ensure the safe return of your daughter and bring those responsible for her abduction to justice. We will give you the benefit of our collective experience and put all our resources at your disposal, unconditionally. In short, this has top priority.'

Conti paused, letting this sink in.

Cesaria was carefully watching da Baggio and the countess. Her instincts told her that the matter was hanging in the balance; it was time to step in.

200

'There is something you should know,' she said quietly. 'I hope Chief Superintendent Conti doesn't mind me raising this, but I believe the situation is serious enough to warrant it.'

Everyone in the room looked at Cesaria, surprised.

Cesaria knew she was taking a considerable risk, perhaps even stepping over the line, but decided to follow her instincts and press on regardless. 'Two years ago, Superintendent Conti's wife was brutally murdered by the Mafia in Palermo. He knows, you see ... This may have a bearing on what he is suggesting, and perhaps put his commitment into perspective.'

Instead of being annoyed, Conti looked at Cesaria with renewed respect. She was quickly turning into a formidable partner, instinctively evaluating the situation and not afraid to act. These were rare qualities in someone so young.

'And Cesaria's father, a judge in Rome, was abducted and tortured by the Mafia a few years ago,' said Conti. 'She too, knows ...'

For a while there was complete silence in the room. The countess reached for da Baggio's hand and squeezed it, the signal obvious. Da Baggio looked at her and nodded. Then he stood up and walked slowly over to Conti standing by the window and held out his hand. Conti extended his, and they shook hands.

'What's next?' asked Jack, cutting through the emotional moment before it became awkward.

'We begin at the beginning,' replied Conti. 'We go to the bridge and let Tristan show us exactly where it happened.' Conti paused and ran his fingers through his unkempt hair. 'But only Tristan. You stay here, please. I don't want to attract more attention than necessary.'

It was getting dark by the time Tristan showed Conti and Cesaria the spot where the assault had taken place.

'And where did you wake up?' asked Conti.

Tristan pointed to the bridge. 'Down there,' he said.

'Show us,' said Conti, and followed Tristan down the embankment.

'I was lying right here.'

When Conti looked at the row of houses facing the canal, he noticed a light come on in one of the few windows that were not boarded up. Conti turned to Cesaria. 'Can you see?' he asked.

'What exactly?' replied Cesaria.

'Someone is watching us. From that window over there.' Conti pointed with his chin to the window with the light. 'Worth having a look. Could you please?'

Cesaria nodded and left.

Conti turned to Tristan. 'Keep walking with me,' he said and put his arm around Tristan's shoulder. 'Act naturally; come.'

Cesaria caught up with them a few minutes later.

'Any luck?' asked Conti.

'Perhaps. An old woman lives in there by herself. She sits by the window most of the day and does what old people do: she watches—'

'And?' interrupted Conti impatiently.

'When I questioned her about the day of the abduction, she was very vague. Her concept of time and dates is very confused. But she did notice something unusual the other day ...'

'What?'

'A black funeral boat with a coffin; under the bridge.'

'Anything else?'

'No. Her eyesight isn't good either, but she was adamant about the boat. You know, old people and funerals.'

'Quite. Good work. Let's go back.'

Later that evening, Conti established that there were three undertakers in Venice operating traditional funeral boats. He contacted Forensics in Florence and instructed them to go through their database and check them out, especially for possible links to the Mafia.

'We'll pay the funeral parlours a visit tomorrow,' said Conti. 'First thing in the morning.'

Looking tired, Cesaria nodded.

'Now get some sleep while you can. Being able to stay here is a great help ... excellent cover.'

'It sure is. And what a place!'

'You did very well today,' continued Conti.

'You didn't mind?'

'No. It was the right approach. If we expect others to open up and trust us, we have to be prepared to do the same. And you didn't mind either? About your father, I mean?'

'No. I like them all: da Baggio; the countess; Jack; Tristan. Now, there's an interesting character ...'

'Tristan?'

'Yes. The countess told me some amazing things about him.'

'Oh?'

'He can hear the whisper of angels and glimpse eternity.'

'You don't say,' said Conti, looking bemused.

'I know it sounds weird.'

'Never mind. We make a good team.'

'Thank you.' Cesaria switched off her iPad and stood up.

As she walked to the door, Conti called out after her: 'We may need someone like that.'

Cesaria stopped and turned around. 'Like what?'

'Someone who can hear the whisper of angels.'

'A little divine help, you mean?'

'You never know; could come in handy.'

Cesaria smiled and left the room, leaving Conti sitting by the window as he listened to the bells of Venice announcing midnight.

Tristan recognised the signs: his subconscious was telling him something. *The funeral boat*, he thought, unable to get the idea of a floating hearse out of his mind, and kept turning restlessly in his bed. When he finally drifted into a slumber, a certain image kept haunting him with alarming persistence like a desperate plea for help. He saw Lorenza lying motionless in a coffin on top of a black boat drifting slowly down the canal and then melting silently into the mist like a ghost.

32

Cardinal O'Brien's Residence, Sydney:
30 May

Alexandra got out of the taxi and looked up at the stately Victorian sandstone mansion that had housed princes of the Church for more than a century. When Alexandra had contacted Cardinal O'Brien earlier that day to give him her answer, he indicated he would prefer to discuss the subject in person, and invited her to afternoon tea at his residence.

The cardinal's secretary – a young Jesuit – met Alexandra at the door and escorted her into a wood-panelled drawing room on the ground floor. Furnished with early Australian cedar pieces, the large room radiated comfort and style without being opulent or pretentious. Flowers on the sideboard and an open grand piano – with sheet music covering the piano stool – in front of the tall windows gave the room a personal touch.

'His Eminence will be with you in a moment,' said the young priest. He motioned towards a settee facing a marble fireplace, and withdrew. The walls on either side of the fireplace were crowded with paintings, mainly landscapes dating back to colonial times. Alexandra walked over to them, but before she could take a closer look, one of the doors opened, and the cardinal swept into the room.

'I see the paintings caught your eye,' he said.

'This is better than the Sydney Art Gallery,' replied Alexandra, pointing to the paintings. 'Conrad Martens, Eugene von Guerard and even a Tom Roberts … and a McCubbin. Amazing.'

'The Church has been here since early colonial days. I am only a temporary custodian,' said the cardinal, smiling. 'Thank you for coming over.'

'Well, it certainly wasn't far. It took me less than ten minutes to get here from the institute. We are almost neighbours.'

'Quite. Some tea perhaps?'

'Please.'

The cardinal walked over to the sideboard. 'Mrs Kelly, my housekeeper, made this especially for you,' he said, and pointed to a fruitcake on a silver platter. 'You must have a big slice, or I'll get into trouble. I don't have many visitors, you see, and when I told her you were a Nobel prize winner, she became quite excited.'

'I must thank her.'

'She'll appear any moment,' said the cardinal, lowering his voice, 'but you'll have to speak loudly; she's almost deaf, I'm afraid,' he continued with a shrug. 'I remind her of her grandson. That should give you an idea ...'

Enjoying the casual banter, Alexandra looked at the cardinal. *How extraordinary*, she thought, *I feel like I've known this man all my life.* As if on cue, a door opened and an old lady dressed in black entered carrying a tray with cups and a large teapot with a colourful tea cosy she had knitted herself.

'So, what's the verdict?' asked the cardinal after Alexandra had thanked Mrs Kelly and eaten two slices of her delicious fruitcake.

'The Gordon Institute and I would be honoured to help in any way we can,' replied Alexandra.

'Excellent; thank you,' said the cardinal. It was the answer he had expected. He was watching Alexandra carefully. 'Where to from here?'

'Our top priority will have to be an accurate diagnosis of the disease. Without that, we are in the dark.'

'Of course. And how do you intend to approach that?'

'With genome sequencing.'

'I understand.'

'I would like to begin with sequencing His Holiness's genome.'

The cardinal nodded. 'You appreciate the urgency involved?'

'I do. But do you appreciate the risks, Eminence?'

'Risks?'

'I don't want to create high expectations. There are no guarantees here. A lot of this is new, uncharted territory. We are stepping into the unknown. In many ways, we are feeling our way ...'

'Quite. What will you need to start it all?' he asked.

'A recent blood sample.'

'Professor Montessori will provide that and everything else you may require. The Vatican's entire medical team is at your disposal. The Church has a reliable courier service; fast and discreet. I can have a sample here within a couple of days.'

'Excellent. But all of this is just the easy part, I'm afraid.'

'What do you mean?'

'We need more; a lot more. And that's where things become …complicated.'

'Oh?'

'Allow me to explain: From what I've been able to piece together so far from the information provided by Professor Montessori, we are most likely dealing with a late-onset autoimmune disease.'

'Do we know what could have caused this?' asked the cardinal.

'Yes. It's all about inheritance; genes, I mean. If my interpretation turns out to be correct, then His Holiness's disease would have resulted from inheriting germline mutations in both copies of his LRBA gene. One from his mother and another from his father. All the symptoms support this.'

Alexandra paused and looked at the cardinal sitting opposite. She could see from his expression that the significance of what she had just told him had not been fully appreciated.

'Without going into too much technical detail at this stage,' she continued, 'what this means is …' Alexandra paused again, searching for the best way to explain the complex subject without sounding patronising.

'I think I know where this is heading,' said the cardinal, stepping in.

'You do?'

'You would need to sequence the genomes of the parents for comparison, right?'

Alexandra looked at the cardinal, surprised. 'Spot-on.'

'And to be able to do that, you would need their DNA?'

'Right again.'

'But they are both dead.'

'I suspected that,' said Alexandra. 'And that's our problem, because without that, we cannot ...'

The cardinal stood up and walked over to one of the tall windows overlooking the cathedral. He clasped his arms behind his back and stared at the lofty steeple reaching towards heaven. 'Is it possible to extract useful DNA from someone who's been dead for say, twenty or so years?' he asked.

'Yes, that's possible,' replied Alexandra.

'Have you done something like that before?'

'Yes, but mainly for forensic identification purposes.'

'How was it done?'

'Well, we prepared sequencing libraries for our Illumina X-Ten machine I showed you the other day—'

'How *exactly*?' interrupted the cardinal, and turned around to face Alexandra.

'We used exhumed long bones. In one recent case, the shaft of a femur. Sequencing libraries can be prepared from trace amounts of DNA isolated after grinding slices of bone to a powder. The bone was quite degraded, but we could still use it for short-fragment sequencing used today for genomes.'

'If such a bone were to be made available say, from each dead parent, useful DNA could be extracted to allow genome sequencing?' asked the cardinal. 'For comparison purposes, I mean?'

'Yes, that should be possible, provided certain strict procedures are observed to prevent contamination with DNA from live humans handling the samples.'

'I understand.'

'But surely, this is all purely hypothetical, Eminence?'

'Not necessarily.'

'What do you mean?'

'His Holiness's parents are buried in a family crypt in Venice. In lead-lined coffins. Tradition. If I remember correctly, they died about twenty or so years ago.'

'You are not suggesting?' said Alexandra, looking incredulous.

'A little drastic, I know, but the gravity of the situation demands drastic measures. If this is the only way, then ...'

'Are you seriously suggesting you could arrange something like that?'

'You mean open the coffins and extract a femur from the remains of each parent?'

'Yes.'

'If the life of His Holiness depends on it, I will leave no stone unturned, not even a headstone if necessary.'

'How will you do this?'

'The Church has long arms ...' came the cryptic reply.

'You are full of surprises, Eminence,' said Alexandra, and stood up.

'And so are you, Professor Delacroix. Please leave this to me.'

33

It had rained during the night, and a dense fog hovered over Venice like a shroud, giving the facades of the palazzos along the Canal Grande an ethereal, ghostlike appearance. Conti had barely slept and was in the breakfast room on the first floor making phone calls. He had already briefed Grimaldi, and spoken to Forensics. Out of the three undertakers operating traditional funeral boats, two had been in the same family for over a century. However, one had recently changed hands and was owned by a corporation registered in the Cayman Islands, a tax haven frequently used by the Mafia. It had an office and an embalming room at the Cimitero di San Michele, the main cemetery of Venice.

By the time Cesaria walked into the dining room at seven, Conti had finished his breakfast and was sipping his third cup of coffee.

'Have you slept at all?' she asked, and joined him by the window, the fog outside muffling the sound of the motorboats and bells and casting a melancholy mood across the breakfast table. There was no-one else in the room.

'A little, but time is precious and we haven't much to go on here.'

'Any leads?'

'Could be. We start at the Cimitero di San Michele right here.' Conti pointed to a small island on the map on the table in front of him.

'Any reason?'

'Just a hunch.'

'How do you want to approach this?'

'We speak to the undertaker and make an enquiry about a traditional Venetian funeral with all the whistles and bells.'

'What, honouring Nonna's departure with a final journey along the Canal Grande in a funeral gondola?' asked Cesaria, smiling.

'Something like that. We'll take Jack and Tristan with us, but da Baggio and the countess should stay here. Just in case—'

'There is another phone call?' Cesaria finished his sentence.

Conti nodded. 'And besides, no-one knows us here.'

'Good point. When do you want to leave?'

'As soon as we can.'

Because visibility was poor, progress was slow. The gardener who was driving the boat had to carefully feel his way along the busy waterways crowded with all kinds of vessels. 'Almost there,' he said, dodging a vaparetto packed with morning commuters. As they left the canal and entered the open lagoon, the fog parted to reveal a small island almost completely enclosed by a high wall. A beautiful church with a white Istrian stone facade dominated the water's edge. Designed by Mauro Codussi, a renowned architect in 1469, the church of San Michele in Isola was the first example of Renaissance architecture in Venice.

'San Michele?' asked Conti.

'Yes,' replied the gardener, and put on speed.

'Dedicated to Saint Michael. A most appropriate guardian of the faithful dead,' said Tristan.

Cesaria turned around and looked at Tristan sitting behind her. 'Why?' she asked.

'Because he will hold the scales on Judgement Day.'

'I see. Not only an expert in art, but biblical studies as well?' teased Cesaria.

'It is art that taught me all that. Renaissance paintings are full of biblical scenes and hidden meanings. You can't understand Renaissance art without the religious bits.'

Cesaria nodded. *What an extraordinary young man*, she thought.

Unless there was a funeral, the island was usually deserted that early in the morning. That day, however, several boats, including a police launch, were tied up at the wharf, making it difficult to find a suitable spot to disembark. A young policeman stood on the wharf, watching.

'I wonder what's going on?' asked Conti.

'I'll go and find out,' said Cesaria.'

'Good idea. Give him your best smile. We'll wait here.'

Cesaria returned a few minutes later.

'Well?' said Conti.

'An exhumation is in progress in the church over there.'

'A criminal investigation?' asked Jack.

'No, not exactly. Something to do with the clergy. Apparently, some bigwigs from the Vatican are here overseeing things. The whole area is off limits at the moment.'

'Great,' said Conti, annoyed. 'Did you ask about the undertaker?'

'Yes. He's in the church. You know; helping.'

'Not a good time then.'

'Doesn't look like it. But I did ask the officer to see if we could have a quick word with the undertaker. I told him about Nonna's funeral.' Cesaria winked at Conti. 'He understood.'

'Okay. We wait.'

Cardinal Borromeo stood in the shadows, watching the two workmen operate the portable winch straddling a marble slab in front of a side altar. Chains had been attached to four iron rings set into the slab covering the entrance to the crypt. The crypt had served as the final resting place of the pope's family for three centuries.

Cardinal Borromeo still had serious doubts about the exhumation, but Cardinal O'Brien had been adamant that it was the only way. And besides, His Holiness had given his permission, which had made all the difference. Wheels started turning. Professor Montessori and his assistant were standing by, ready to do what was necessary. Apart from the undertaker and his two workmen, the church was empty and the police had cordoned off the area to make sure they wouldn't be disturbed. To open a grave inside a church was a serious matter, whatever the reason.

Professor Montessori turned to his assistant. 'Remember, the main problem here is contamination,' he said. 'We must follow the protocol to the letter.'

The assistant, a young surgeon, nodded. 'I understand.'

'Once the coffins have been opened, you and I will be the only ones down there. No-one else will handle the remains. Professor Delacroix's instructions are clear.'

As soon as the marble slab had been lifted, exposing the entry to the crypt beneath the altar, Cardinal Borromeo walked over to Professor Montessori. 'Ready?' he asked, and looked down into the crypt, the cold air rising from below sending a shiver down his spine.

'I still don't know how you did it,' said Montessori, shaking his head.

'Persuade His Holiness?'

'Yes. I was certain he would refuse. I know I would have.'

'You forget, I'm a diplomat,' interjected the cardinal, smiling. 'Persuasion is my domain.'

'Ah. That must be it.'

'When faced with a choice between hospital and this ...'

'You took advantage of a sick man,' reprimanded Montessori.

'No, an ambitious one. His Holiness knows if he doesn't get better, the fragile peace process is bound to fail.'

'Remind me never to say *no* to you,' said Montessori, pointing a finger at the cardinal.

'Let's do it,' said the cardinal, changing the subject.

'I feel like a grave robber,' said Montessori. 'You and I should go down first and identify the sarcophagi.'

Cardinal Borromeo nodded and began to climb down the narrow set of stairs leading into the darkness below. 'I know how you feel,' he said, 'but this is better than doing nothing.'

The young police officer walked over to the man in the dark suit standing in front of the church, smoking. 'Are you the undertaker?' he asked.

'I am.'

'Some people over there are looking for you,' said the officer, and pointed to the wharf.

'What do they want?'

'Arranging a funeral. They asked if you had a funeral boat.'

'Tell them to come back another time; I'm busy,' replied the undertaker, annoyed.

The officer shrugged and walked back to the wharf.

They asked about a funeral boat, thought the undertaker, feeling uneasy as he watched the police officer talk to a young woman standing on the wharf. When the woman climbed into the waiting motorboat, the undertaker walked towards the wharf for a closer look. As the boat pulled away, he looked at Tristan sitting in the back with his head still bandaged. *I wonder,* he thought, watching the boat turn in front of him. Just before it accelerated, Tristan turned around and looked in the undertaker's direction. Their eyes locked for an instant, igniting a flash of recognition in the undertaker. *The guy under the bridge?* the undertaker asked himself, remembering the daring abduction from a few days before. Then, shaking his head, he pulled his phone out of his coat pocket and dialled Belmonte's number as the boat disappeared into the morning mist.

34

Belmonte glanced nervously at his watch, again. *He's late*, he thought, and ordered another drink. Belmonte was waiting for Bahadir in the restaurant bar to finalise urgent travel arrangements for the four young men and the doctor they had recruited in the container camp the day before.

Due to an unexpected change of plans by high rollers from Abu Dhabi, the date for the next *Ars Moriendi* session had to be brought forward by two days, making it almost impossible to groom the new combatants and get them ready. To overcome the problem, Gambio had offered to send his private plane to Istanbul to bring everyone back to Florence in time for the big game.

Belmonte, a meticulous planner, hated to work under such unexpected pressure. It undermined his modus operandi and took him out of his comfort zone. He was used to working independently and on his own, and knew from experience that haste was the enemy of caution, and therefore fertile ground for mistakes.

Bad news rarely travels alone. Belmonte was facing another serious problem with potentially disastrous consequences, and it all had to do with a phone call. The long journey back to Istanbul from the container camp had been exhausting. They had driven through the night and covered the twelve-hundred kilometres in record time. The phone call Belmonte had received from one of his men – the undertaker at the Cimitero di San Michele in Venice – had been unnerving. If the man was right about the sighting, the hostage had to be moved; at once. Belmonte didn't believe in coincidences, only danger.

As soon as Belmonte set eyes on Bahadir hurrying towards him, he knew something was wrong. The worried look on Bahadir's face was alarming. 'What's wrong?' asked Belmonte, frowning.

'They're gone! I still can't believe it,' stammered Bahadir.

'What are you talking about? Who's gone?'

'The boys from the camp.'

'What?' Belmonte almost shouted.

'They were all in the kitchen, being shown around by one of the cooks speaking Arabic, when it happened ...'

'What happened?' demanded Belmonte impatiently.

'Three of them slipped out the back door. A car was waiting for them.'

'They got away? Just like that?'

'Yes.'

'What about the fourth one?'

'He was left behind. Apparently, he didn't know anything about this.'

'Which one is it?'

'Nazir.'

'Do you realise what a disaster this is?' fumed Belmonte, 'The consequences?'

'I understand. This was totally unexpected,' lied Bahadir, who had known about this all along. 'We had no idea they had accomplices here in Istanbul and were planning to get away. You met them ...'

Walking the dangerous tightrope of double agent, Bahadir had been playing a dangerous game for years. First, he'd provided safe passage to Istanbul for young suicide bombers sent to Turkey by IS, only to pass information about them to the Americans. They in turn informed the Turkish authorities, who had them arrested and often executed.

'I did. We got it all wrong,' said Belmonte, his mind racing. 'It's funny really. We were duped. Instead of being used, they used us!'

'I'm just as surprised as you are, but they were not prisoners!'

'And the doctor?'

'She's downstairs, with Nazir.'

Belmonte, a pragmatist, didn't believe in wasting time analysing what had gone wrong. He was already thinking about how to fix the problem. *Ars Moriendi* needed two combatants. He had one. Fortunately, the best of the four by far. He needed one more, but time was running out, fast.

'Gambio's plane is due to land in less than two hours. Is Nazir ready?' he asked.

'I think so.'

'You *think* so?'

'Come on. There hasn't been much time to work on him. Get to know him; prepare ...'

'What did you tell him?'

'I told him that an important job was on offer. An opportunity of a lifetime was waiting for him in Italy, and that we thought he was the right man for the job. Something that could set him up for life.'

'Or death ... And he bought that?'

Bahadir shrugged. 'Hope is the friend of desperate men. With the others gone, I suppose he's feeling vulnerable and alone. In a situation like that, any lifeline looks attractive.'

'Did he ask what the job was about?'

'He did, but of course I didn't tell him anything specific. All I said was that he would find out once he got to Italy. By private plane. That impressed him.'

'Good. So, he's willing to come along?'

'Sure. He's got nothing to lose and nowhere else to go.'

'What about the doctor? What did you tell her?'

Bahadir shrugged. 'Something similar, but of course she asked more questions. I told her that she would be working for a wealthy employer in Italy. I hinted at a private job requiring discretion. A job needing surgical skills and experience. That's all I said. She seemed happy about that, at least for now.'

'And she accepted that?'

'This woman has been through a lot. I think she's taking all this one step at a time.'

'Smart woman. Well done.'

'And the fact that she and Nazir know each other and have worked together certainly helped as well. They seem quite close.'

Belmonte managed a crooked smile. 'Can you fix all the formalities here at your end?' he asked. 'Departure documentation, immigration and all that? Quickly? You know they have no passports? They have to leave here without a trace.'

'Yes. Leave that to me.'

'Good. Florence won't be a problem. Once we are in Italy, no-one will know they exist.'

'What will you do? About the others, I mean? You need more than one.'

'I'll think of something.'

Bahadir looked at Belmonte, relieved. He hadn't expected to get off so lightly. 'It will be easier next time; promise.'

'Just make sure we don't lose Nazir as well.'

'We won't.'

Belmonte realised there was no point in blaming Bahadir. As far as Gambio was concerned, he was the one responsible, not Bahadir. It had all been left to him. The abduction in Venice, and the vital recruitment of new blood in Turkey. These were his assignments, and there were now serious problems with both. As a seasoned campaigner, Belmonte knew what was at stake and how the Mafia dealt with failure. The Cosa Nostra was unforgiving and punishment was swift and certain. That's how the organisation survived. Self-preservation at all cost.

Belmonte had nerves of steel and had been in tight spots before. He did his best thinking with his back against the wall, and right now, the pressure on his back was so severe, he could barely move. However, something daring was already taking shape in his mind. What was needed to get out of tight situations was imagination and courage, and Belmonte had both in abundance. And on this occasion, he had an unexpected ace up his sleeve: the doctor.

What if by solving one problem, I solve the other as well? he thought, *definitely worth a shot!*

Feeling calmer, Belmonte turned to Bahadir. 'I could use another drink,' he said, collecting his thoughts. 'After that, we get ready to go to the airport to meet the plane. But first, I want a brief word with Nazir and the doctor.'

'You got it.'

Strapped into a comfortable leather seat next to Amena, Nazir's head was spinning. He had never been in a plane before. Mesmerised, he looked out the window and watched the lights of Istanbul disappear below as the plane circled the city and turned south towards Greece. After the carnage in the camp and all the suffering and death in Dr Rosen's surgery, the opulent, dimly lit cabin of the luxury jet looked almost surreal.

Nazir ran the tips of his fingers along the walnut burr trimmings of his armrest as he remembered his earlier conversation with Belmonte. *What kind of job could possibly warrant all this?* he asked himself, wondering what he would have to do.

Belmonte, a skilled negotiator, had persuaded many a young man to participate in *Ars Moriendi* and risk all. He knew exactly which buttons to press and what kind of picture to paint. He had only spoken in generalities, but had hinted at possibilities he knew would appeal and tempt a young man like Nazir.

Belmonte had a similar conversation with Amena. However, her questions and view of the situation were quite different and far more complex. Belmonte was certain she suspected something wasn't quite above board, but realised she wasn't in a position to ask too many questions, and certainly not in a position to refuse. Ordinary jobs didn't come with private planes. However, Belmonte knew that a promise of something can appear more powerful and persuasive than the delivery. Even to a person of Amena's intellect.

Belmonte looked at the young man sitting behind him and smiled. He knew he had one willing combatant. He was certain of it. It was now time to arrange the second one. 'Feel like something to eat?' he asked, and unbuckled his seatbelt.

Nazir nodded, but didn't say anything.

'Yes, thank you,' said Amena. *He's a dangerous man,* she thought, watching Belmonte get out of his seat. *I wonder what he has in store for us?*

218

I have to be vigilant. He needs me for my medical skills, so much is clear, but what does he want from Nazir? she thought, mulling over the obvious questions with a mixture of fascination and fear.

Belmonte went to the galley in the back and asked the stewardess to prepare a snack. Then he poured himself a Scotch and carefully went over each step of the daring plan. He always looked for flaws before committing himself. Playing devil's advocate was the best way to keep the devil at bay. Finally satisfied, he reached for the on-board satellite phone and called the undertaker.

35

Tension had been growing all day in the Palazzo da Baggio, and it had reached breaking point. Nothing is quite as demoralising as waiting; inaction is the mother of frustration, which leads to speculation and fear. Apart from the phone call on 29 May – the day Jack arrived – there had been no further contact from the abductors. After the aborted visit to the Cimitero, Conti had decided against a return visit, which could only arouse suspicion if he was right about the Mafia connection. It was therefore safer to wait for the next round of instructions before making another move.

It was almost eleven pm when da Baggio's phone rang. Da Baggio took a deep breath, looked at Conti sitting opposite him and answered the phone.

'Listen carefully and pay attention,' said a voice, speaking slowly. 'This is what I want you to do.'

Conti, Jack and Cesaria were seated closest to da Baggio and watched him carefully. Tristan and the countess sat at the other end of the salon and listened. The phone call lasted less than a minute, but by the time da Baggio put down his phone, his forehead was covered in tiny beads of perspiration, and a haunted look on his tired face. He had been instructed by Conti not to interrupt; just listen. For a long, tense moment there was total silence in the room. After a while, the countess stood up, walked over to da Baggio and put her hand on his shoulder. This seemed to calm her distraught friend, who had desperately wanted to ask questions about his daughter, but had been advised not to.

'Tomorrow morning at ten precisely, Tristan is to take the recipes to Caffè Florian in St Mark's Square, sit down at a table, order a coffee and wait for instructions.'

'What? He mentioned Tristan by name?' demanded Conti.

'Yes, he did.'

Conti shot Cesaria a meaningful look. 'Interesting,' he said. 'He is to wait for instructions? Was anything said about how, in what way?'

'Yes, by phone.'

'I don't understand.'

'Tristan is to take his mobile with him and wait for a call.'

'Extraordinary,' said Jack. 'Not only do they know Tristan's name, they obviously know his phone number as well. How can that possibly be?'

Conti turned to Tristan. 'Did you have your wallet and your phone on you when you were mugged?' he asked.

Tristan nodded. What no-one in the room could have known, was that Belmonte had obtained all that information much earlier in the jewellery shop on the Ponte Vecchio in Florence.

'That could explain it,' said Conti. 'Simple really. However, they are sending us a clear message.'

'In what way?' asked the countess.

'Intimidation through information; classic Mafia. They are telling us that they know a great deal about us and can find out everything they need to know and reach us anywhere, anytime.'

'How scary,' said the countess.

'Clever,' interjected Jack. 'Each move has been carefully planned. We are obviously dealing with a formidable opponent ...'

'Yes, and a clever tactician,' said Conti. 'I have no doubt this house is being watched, and they know we are here. However, they probably don't know who we are; yet.' *But it's only a matter of time,* he thought. 'We could be guests or family friends,' continued Conti. 'Another good reason not to go back to the cemetery at the moment.'

'The only way to defeat a clever tactician is—' said Jack.

'By being a smarter one,' interrupted Cesaria.

'Precisely,' Conti agreed. 'I have an idea.'

'What's on your mind?' asked Jack.

'Could I have another look at the recipes?' asked Conti.

'Of course,' da Baggio said. He stood up and walked over to the chest by the window, opened it, took out the folder with the recipes and placed it on the table in front of Conti.

Conti ran his fingertips along the spine of the folder and smiled. 'Yes, that should work,' he said. 'But we have to act quickly.'

'Doing what, exactly?' asked Jack.

'Let me make a phone call first, then I'll tell you.'

Clara Samartini arrived just after four am by water taxi. She had left Florence by car shortly after receiving Conti's call and had covered the distance between Florence and Venice in record time. Conti embraced the young woman at the front door and escorted her into the salon. Apart from the countess, no-one had gone to bed.

'This is Dr Samartini,' said Conti, introducing the new arrival, 'the youngest, and one of the brightest members of our Forensics team. What she is about to suggest, is our best chance by far to make progress in this case.'

Da Baggio looked at the young woman with interest. Petite, in her twenties with mousy-brown hair cut quite short and wearing thick glasses that amplified her eyes and gave her an almost comical appearance, Dr Samartini looked more like an earnest, short-sighted librarian than an electronics expert specialising in cutting-edge surveillance.

'Before we go any further, may I see the portfolio?' she asked. 'We haven't got much time.'

'Certainly,' said da Baggio, and pointed to the table in front of the fireplace. 'That's it right there.'

Dr Samartini examined the spine of the folder just as Conti had done. Then she opened her toolkit – a shiny metal box on wheels, which reminded Jack of expensive designer cabin luggage – and pulled out a small container made of plexiglass. 'In here I have a set of tiny transmitters that allow us to track the movements of objects or people with great accuracy; GPS on steroids,' said Dr Samartini, and turned towards Conti. 'If we decide to go ahead with this, I believe I can insert one of the transmitters into the spine of the folder here. No-one would know it's in there unless they are specifically looking for something and pull the spine apart. Of course, I can only do this with the folder ...'

'Not the contents,' said Jack. 'You can't have transmitters attached to single pages?'

'Correct,' said Dr Samartini.

'So, let's be clear about this,' continued Jack. 'Tristan delivers the bugged folder with the recipes tomorrow as instructed, and we track the folder in the hope it will lead us to Lorenza?'

'It's a start,' said Conti, sidestepping the question.

'Isn't that risky?' said da Baggio.

'Everything we do here has risks. It's a balancing act. We have to weigh it all up. But I'm sure you agree we have to do something! At the moment, I believe this is our best – and safest – option.'

'What happens if they take out the recipes and discard the folder?' asked Jack.

'Sure, that's possible, but unlikely don't you think?'

'Nobody has asked Tristan about tomorrow,' interjected Cesaria. 'We don't know if he's prepared to ...'

Conti turned towards Tristan. 'You are right,' he said, and looked at Tristan without asking the obvious question.

'Of course I'll do it,' said Tristan. 'I agree with Fabio. This is our best chance, and doing nothing isn't an option.'

Da Baggio stood up, walked over to the little portrait of Cosimo's abducted daughter and looked at it in silence. 'There have been many turbulent events in our family's history,' he began, speaking quite softly. Da Baggio turned around and faced the others. 'Let's hope this one has a happy ending. Let's do it.'

Before leaving the palazzo, Tristan consulted his tour guide on Venice to familiarise himself with the caffé:

Caffè Florian, a Venetian icon with a colourful history, has been in continuous operation since 1720. Famous patrons in its early days included such notables as Goethe, the playwright Carlo Goldoni and Casanova, who no doubt frequented the establishment because it was the only coffee house that allowed female patrons. Other famous visitors included Charles Dickens, Marcel Proust and Lord Byron.

Tristan closed the little book. Fascinating, he thought.

By the time he arrived just before ten, the caffé was already crowded with tourists prepared to pay an exorbitant amount for a coffee just to be able to rub shoulders with history. He found an empty table in the gallery outside and sat down.

Standing in the shadows, the undertaker was watching him from across the square. Before Tristan could order a coffee, his phone rang. 'Leave now and go to the western end of the Piazza,' said the undertaker, 'and wait for further instructions.' Then the phone went dead.

Tristan stood up, put the folder wrapped in brown paper under his arm, and left the caffé. As he approached one of the narrow side canals, his phone rang again. 'Can you see the little bridge?' asked the undertaker.

'I can,' replied Tristan.

'Go to the bridge and wait.'

Jack and Conti were watching Tristan from a distance. Surrounded by tourists and flocks of pigeons, they had difficulty keeping up with him.

'What is he doing?' asked Jack, pushing through the throng of tourists blocking his view.

'He's standing on top of a bridge, obviously waiting. Let's stay here and watch.'

Tristan's phone rang again.

'Can you see the boat approaching the bridge now?' asked the undertaker.

'I can.'

'The boat will stop for a moment under the bridge. Go down there now. As soon as it stops, you jump on board; understood?'

'Understood,' said Tristan. He quickly crossed the bridge and then walked down some stairs to the water's edge.

'What's going on?' asked Jack.

'I lost him,' said Conti. 'Come.'

'Jesus! Where is he?' shouted Jack as they hurried towards the bridge.

'Somewhere under the bridge; I can't see him.'

Just then, a noisy group of Japanese tourists came walking towards them. They were following a guide holding up an umbrella with pink ribbons attached. This slowed Jack and Conti down even more. By the time they reached the bridge, they could just see a boat moving slowly down the narrow canal, away from the bridge.

'There he is!' shouted Conti, and pointed to the boat.

Just before the boat disappeared around a corner, Jack could see Tristan standing on deck, alone. 'What do we do now?' he asked.

Conti shook his head. 'Nothing. We wait,' he snapped, clenching his fists in frustration, 'and hope that Clara has done a good job.' Conti hated surprises, but what he hated more was being outmanoeuvred. And that, he had to admit, had just happened. It wasn't what he had expected.

Tristan couldn't see who was driving the boat. He stood behind the cabin as he had been told to do when his phone rang again.

'Now throw your phone into the canal,' said the undertaker, and hung up.

36

Colonel Ali Riza, a senior officer in the *Jandarma* – the Turkish Gendarmerie – a military law enforcement unit responsible for investigating terrorist acts in south-eastern Anatolia, had arrived early in the morning from Ankara and took over the investigation into the bombing of the field hospital at Kilis. Trained in intelligence by the army, Colonel Riza had been involved in several sensitive counterterrorist operations in the area before and was therefore well-qualified for the task.

The security officer who had spoken to Haddad the day before, took the colonel to the bomb site. 'That's the man I told you about,' he said, 'over there.'

Haddad sat in front of his tent staring at the burnt-out ruins of Dr Rosen's container surgery, deep in thought. It was now a crater full of twisted steel, wires, shards of glass and memories of innocent lives, snuffed out by a senseless act of fanaticism. The colonel walked slowly across to the tent and looked at Haddad. *It's definitely him*, he thought. *Amazing!*

'It never stops, does it Naguib?' said the colonel, and lit a cigarette.

Haddad turned around in his canvas chair and looked at the man standing behind him. '*Ali?*' he said, his eyes wide with astonishment. For a while the two men just looked at each other in silence, their thoughts racing back to a time when they used to be inseparable, united by a common cause. Haddad stood up, walked over to his friend and embraced him. 'I thought you were dead,' he said, patting his friend on the back.

'That's what I thought about you, yet here we are.'

'Wasn't my time,' said Haddad.

'Still chasing shadows?'

Haddad clenched his fist. 'Yes; el-Masri. I haven't given up yet. And to think I had him in the palm of my hand. I should have killed that monster when I had the chance.'

'What happened?'

'I lost him. But that's another story. What about you?'

'The last time we saw each other was just before the Americans closed the "Academy" in 2009.'

'Camp Bucca; they were all there, graduating ...'

'Yes, in fanaticism and terror,' said the colonel.

'Camp Bucca; what a place,' said Haddad. 'What did you do after that?'

'Many things,' came the evasive reply. 'You know how it is. Some of them I'm proud of, others not.'

'Sounds just like me.'

'There aren't many of us left, you know.'

'Still alive, you mean?'

'Yes. And having seen it all, but with the fire still burning within. We were right there where it all began,' said the colonel.

'We were. What are you doing now?'

'Intelligence. Counterterrorism.'

Haddad pointed to the crater. 'So, that's why you're here.'

'That's part of it ... This attack is bad; really bad.'

'A cowardly act; completely senseless,' said Haddad, shaking his head.

'Desperate. As IS is pushed out of Mosul, and soon Raqqa, we'll see more of this, I'm afraid. Here, and abroad.'

Haddad and the colonel looked at the ruins in silence.

'Looks a bit like our lives, doesn't it?' suggested Haddad.

'True, but we can still give it some meaning. We can make a difference.'

'That's not easy, but I'm trying.'

'So am I,' said the colonel.

'I can see that. You and I don't know how to give up,' said Haddad, a wan smile creasing the corners of his mouth.

'I hear you wanted to make contact; with intelligence, I mean,' said the colonel, changing the subject.

'News travels fast. I only mentioned this yesterday to the officer in charge here.'

'He reported it to me, and when he mentioned your name, I couldn't believe it. I had to see for myself.'

'Well, here I am.'

'I could use someone like you.'

Haddad pointed to his bandaged shoulder. 'A wreck like me?' he asked and raised an eyebrow.

'No, someone I can trust. Interested?'

'Absolutely.'

'When do you want to start?'

'How about right now?' said Haddad, a sparkle in his eyes.

The colonel extended his hand. 'Welcome to the *Jandarma*,' he said.

'What rank?'

'Trusted friend.'

'That will do.'

Sitting in the back of his chauffeur-driven car, the colonel began to relax. He had left one of his officers in charge of the investigation and was on his way back to Ankara with Haddad.

'The suicide bomb wasn't the real reason I came to the camp,' said the colonel, turning to Haddad sitting next to him.

'Oh?'

'Apart from wanting to meet you, the real reason was this ...' The colonel reached into his briefcase, pulled out a photograph and handed it to Haddad. It had been taken the day before and showed Amena and Nazir getting into a car.'

'I don't understand. What's your interest in this?'

The colonel handed Haddad another photograph. 'This man here.' It was a close-up of a man talking to Nazir in front of Dr Rosen's surgery.

'Who's he?'

'Someone we've been watching for some time. He runs a famous restaurant in Istanbul. He's a high-profile celebrity chef with a murky past and lots of dubious contacts, internationally. His name is Kemal Bahadir.'

'Never heard of him.'

'He's been coming to the camp regularly to "recruit" young men to work in his restaurant.'

'So?'

'We've suspected for some time that this is just a cover.'

'A cover? For what?'

'Transporting jihadists to Istanbul. Quite ingenious, don't you think?'

'Clever.'

'On this occasion, he "recruited" four young men and one woman, a doctor. One of the young men and the doctor you know.'

'Yes. Dr Algafari, and Nazir al-Kafri in the photo here. They both worked in the surgery.'

'The other three are IS suspects.'

'I met one of them – Ammar – I had my suspicions,' said Haddad. 'Something about him ...'

'You and I can spot them. And your suspicions have already been confirmed.'

'How?'

'As soon as they arrived in Istanbul, they were picked up by members of a cell we've had under observation for some time. I think the three are suicide bombers on a mission. Needless to say, we are watching them carefully.'

'What about Nazir and the doctor?'

'That's the really interesting bit in all this.'

'In what way?'

'They don't fit, especially the doctor. Bahadir is using an agent in the camp. He's one of our informers. This time, Bahadir was specifically looking for a doctor; a surgeon to be precise. Don't you think that's odd?'

'Perhaps,' said Haddad. 'And I can tell you for certain that Nazir is not an IS sympathiser. He lost his whole family because of IS. He's not a terrorist. Neither is Dr Algafari.'

'I agree with you.'

'So?'

'There's more,' said the colonel, and reached into his briefcase again. 'This was taken yesterday at the airport in Istanbul,' he said, and handed Haddad another photograph. It showed Nazir and Amena boarding a small jet.'

'Now, that is interesting,' said Haddad. 'Did Bahadir go with them?'

'No, but this man did.' The colonel showed Haddad another photo. It was a close-up of Belmonte standing next to the jet.

Haddad pointed to the photograph. 'I've seen him before,' he said. 'He was right here, sitting in the car. Do you know who he is?'

'No, but you are right. He and Bahadir came here together. According to our informer, he was the one interested in the surgeon. He offered our man a big commission to procure one. It was obviously very important. The question is, *why*?'

'What do you know about the plane? Looks like an expensive private jet.'

The colonel smiled. 'It's good to have you on board, my friend, asking the right questions. The jet is owned by an Italian corporation linked to a notorious businessman.'

'Do we know who?'

'Yes; Salvatore Gambio. He lives in Florence. And in Florence, Gambio stands for only one thing.'

'What?'

'Mafia.'

'Human trafficking, you think?'

'Could be. I don't think this has anything to do with terrorism. The Mafia is not interested in causes, only money.'

'So, your Mr Bahadir has his fingers in many pies?'

'Just as you would expect from a masterchef, right?'

'Where did to plane go?' asked Haddad.

'To Florence, of course.' The colonel lit a cigarette and looked at Haddad. 'And that's where you're going, my friend,' he said.

37

Alexandra returned to her lab after an early morning briefing with her team and was about to open her mail when the phone rang.

'You have an interesting visitor, Professor Delacroix,' said the receptionist, the tone of her voice conspiratorial.

'Oh? I'm not expecting anyone. Certainly not this early. Who is it?'

'A priest ... he says it's urgent,' added the receptionist, lowering her voice.

Alexandra sat up as if poked with a hot needle.

'Father Connor?' was all she managed to say.

'You *know* him?'

'He's Cardinal O'Brien's secretary.'

'Oh. You are full of surprises, Professor.'

'I'll come down.'

It begins, thought Alexandra as she hurried to the lift, a rush of excitement making her heart beat a little faster.

Father Connor was waiting in reception with a small parcel under his arm. Alexandra walked over to him and gave him her best smile. 'We meet again, Father,' she said, and pointed to an empty conference room. 'Please; let's go in here.'

'I apologise for calling on you so early and without an appointment, but His Eminence insisted that you should receive this as soon as possible. Every hour counts ...'

'No problem.'

Father Connor placed the parcel carefully on the conference table in front of Alexandra. 'This arrived from the Vatican early this morning by special courier; diplomatic pouch,' he said, his melodious, sing-song Irish brogue bringing a smile to Alexandra's face. 'Very precious; I'm sure you know what it is.'

Alexandra nodded and tried to stay calm. As she looked at the parcel in front of her, she noticed the Coat of Arms of the Vatican with the crossed keys of St Peter on top. *It's really happening*, she thought, a lump in her throat.

'Please thank His Eminence and tell him we will do everything in our power to ...'

Obviously eager to get away, Father Connor stood up and looked at Alexandra. 'It is impossible to put into words what is riding on this, Professor Delacroix.'

'I know.'

Father Connor bowed, walked to the door and opened it. Then he turned to Alexandra and said, 'There is a lock. The combination is yesterday's date: 1 6 2016. God be with you.' With that, he left the room.

Alexandra hurried back to her lab. She closed the door, placed the parcel on her workbench and for a long, tense moment just stared at it. *If this contains everything I asked for, then we are about to make history*, she thought, and began to peel away the tight plastic skin covering a shiny metal box inside. The custom-made container looked familiar and was just like the ones she had used many times before for transporting sensitive medical supplies. The only difference was the combination lock on the side of the lid. *So far, so good*, she thought. Alexandra put on a pair of plastic gloves and carefully began to punch in the numbers, her fingers shaking.

It's all here, just as I asked, she thought, after she had carefully examined the contents of the three separate compartments. *Amazing. Montessori has done an excellent job and obviously followed protocol, just as I asked. Let's begin.*

Alexandra picked up the house phone and called her two post-doc assistants she had briefed earlier that morning, and asked them to come to her lab. They were by far the two brightest young researchers she had worked with in years. She trusted them completely and knew she could rely on them not only for their professionalism, but also for their discretion.

Due to the sensitive nature of the matter, it had been decided that apart from the CEO of the Gordon, the chairman of the board and Alexandra in charge, they would be the only research scientists in the institute who would know all the facts and the true nature of the extraordinary project they were about to embark upon. This had been gratefully accepted by the cardinal.

As the project had potentially serious bioethical implications, it was agreed that the institute would treat the entire matter purely as a research project without any clinical application. All clinical aspects would be conducted by Professor Montessori at the Vatican, and therefore be subject to Vatican City State law. As a sacerdotal-monarchical state, the Vatican is ruled by the Bishop of Rome – the pope.

Over five hundred scientists from more than thirty-five countries worked at the Gordon. It was therefore a totally international organisation bringing together the brightest and the most gifted from every corner of the globe. It was this aspect of the Gordon that had persuaded Alexandra to stay at the institute after receiving the Nobel prize, and continue Professor K's work.

Ayah Gamal from Oman was the first to arrive. Wearing a smart *hijab* – a headscarf that covered her head and neck, but left her pretty face open to the world – she was a gifted young Muslim woman specialising in genomics. And she adored Alexandra.

Vimal Singh from Bangalore swept into the room next. Tall, good-looking and wearing a blue Sikh *dastaar,* or turban, to cover his long, uncut hair and sporting a dashing moustache, he looked more like a movie star from Bollywood than a groundbreaking immunologist with several articles published in *Nature.* Both still in their twenties, they were the very best the Gordon had to offer.

'Sit down and listen,' said Alexandra. She pushed the open metal container slowly across her workbench towards her protégées. 'This is where we start.'

'What's that?' asked Ayah.

'What does it look like? Look, but don't touch.'

234

Ayah pointed to a tube in one of the compartments. 'A blood sample?'

Alexandra nodded. 'What else?'

'Two bones,' ventured Vimal. 'How curious.'

'Remember what I told you this morning? This just arrived from the Vatican.'

Ayah and Vimal looked at each other and smiled.

'The HH Project? No way!' said Ayah, bending over the container.

'It is. Exactly as I told you. If we succeed, this could turn out to be the most important research project of your professional lives. Treat it as such. We cannot afford any mistakes here; the stakes are too high. And remember, apart from anything else, this is a race against time. For that reason, we'll divide up the tasks. Ayah, you will prepare the blood sample for DNA sequencing as soon as possible. That's our starting point.'

Alexandra turned to Vimal. 'You will be in charge of preparing Illumina sequencing libraries from trace amounts of DNA you will extract from the bones here. As you can see, they have been clearly marked. HHP is part of a femur belonging to HH's father – padre, the other femur marked HHM belongs to his mother. I don't have to tell you that avoiding any kind of contamination is of the utmost importance.'

Vimal nodded.

'You know the procedure. We discussed it this morning. You will grind slices of the bones into a fine powder and then isolate the DNA for sequencing. Any questions, you come to me. From now on, we'll refer to our subject as HH—'

'HH, for His Holiness?' interrupted Ayah.

'Exactly. And one more thing ... we work around the clock; understood?'

Ayah and Vimal looked at Alexandra and nodded, their faces flushed with excitement.

'Good,' said Alexandra, and ran her fingers through her red hair. 'Now get cracking, guys! I have some serious thinking to do.'

38

Instead of going home after another gruelling day, Grimaldi had spent the entire night in his office, worrying. He was trying to come to terms with the disastrous news from Venice. Tristan's daring abduction had taken them all by surprise. Somehow, it just didn't fit, which made Grimaldi even more anxious. *Another kidnapping*, he thought, *right under our noses! Damn! Someone is toying with us ...*

Felt pen in hand, Grimaldi stared at the whiteboard behind his desk as he tried to unravel the puzzle. He had no doubt the Mafia was behind it all. The latest demand clearly pointed the finger at Gambio. He was the only one who would benefit from the property deal. However, the other demands were bizarre and made no sense, and proving it all and implicating Gambio was a different matter altogether. *A set of old Ottoman recipes; why?* he thought, tapping the whiteboard with the tip of his pen. *What is it I cannot see here? At least the tracking device is working; it's our only lead. We can always rely on good old Clara.*

Grimaldi listened to the familiar church bells greeting the new day. They never chimed on time, but he knew them all. First came the majestic bells of the Duomo followed by the sonorous voices of Santo Stefano al Ponte, followed by Orsanmichele and then Santa Croce, his favourite. From his office in the centre of Florence, he could hear them all distinctly that early in the morning before they drowned in traffic noise and the monotonous hum of the tourist invasion.

Grimaldi walked across to the window and opened it. Sucking in the cool, fresh air, he looked down into the familiar street melting out of the darkness. Feeling very tired and hungry, he watched the baker open the shutters of his favourite little café. *A latte, fresh pastries and a cigar*, he thought, smiling. He reached for his coat and hurried to the lift.

The security guard sitting at the desk in the foyer waved as Grimaldi stepped out of the lift. 'I didn't know you were in, sir,' he said. 'There's someone here to see you.'

Grimaldi looked at the guard, surprised. 'At this hour?' he asked.

The guard shrugged and pointed to a man sitting on a bench at the far end of the foyer. 'He's been here for a while.'

Slowly, Grimaldi walked over to the visitor. The man had his eyes closed and appeared to be asleep. 'You wanted to see me?' asked Grimaldi.

The man opened his eyes and looked at him. 'Chief Prosecutor Grimaldi?' he asked, and stood up.

Grimaldi nodded, sizing up the little man in the crumpled suit.

'Chief Inspector Haddad,' said the man, extending his hand. 'I believe you are expecting me.'

'Ah, yes. Colonel Riza called me and said you were on your way. I just didn't expect you so soon.' Grimaldi and Colonel Riza had collaborated on a number of high-profile cases in the past and knew each other well. 'You are from the Jandarma?' asked Grimaldi.

Haddad spread his fingers. 'It's complicated,' he said, 'but urgent.'

Grimaldi nodded. 'Always is. I think you and I can both do with some coffee,' he said, extending his hand. 'Come.'

Grimaldi headed straight for his usual table at the back of the café and ordered two lattes and a plate of cornetti; delicious and still warm. Then he turned to Haddad. 'What can I do for you, Chief Inspector?' he said. 'As I understand it, Colonel Riza is now in counterterrorism. Not exactly my field.'

'But this may be,' said Haddad. He reached into his briefcase, pulled out two photographs taken at the refugee camp and placed them on the table in front of Grimaldi.

'Who are these men?' asked Grimaldi.

'This is Kemal Bahadir,' replied Haddad, and pointed to a man standing next to a car in the photo. 'A shady character.'

'The celebrity chef? He was here just recently, on *Top Chef Europe*.'

'That's him.'

'What's your interest in him?'

'He's associated with a terrorist cell in Istanbul.' Sipping his coffee, Haddad briefly described the 'recruiting' encounter at the refugee camp and then pointed to the second photo. 'Bahadir came to the camp with this man here. Do you recognise him?'

Grimaldi looked at the photo showing a grinning Belmonte standing next to a woman, and shook his head. 'No. And this is relevant because?' he asked, sounding a little impatient.

Haddad reached into his briefcase and pulled out another photograph. ''Because of this,' he said calmly, and handed the photo to Grimaldi. 'Recognise the plane?'

Grimaldi nodded. 'Yes; this is the *Furioso;* Salvatore Gambio's private jet.'

'Two days ago, this plane took off from Istanbul; destination Florence. On board were the man I just showed you, the woman standing next to him, and a young man. The woman and the young man came straight from the camp. She is an experienced surgeon, and the young man was working with her in a field hospital at the camp before it was destroyed by a suicide bomber. Both are refugees from Syria. Bahadir and his associate were quite specific in what they were looking for at the camp: they were looking for a surgeon. In fact, they offered a huge commission to one of our informers to help them find one.'

'Interesting ...' said Grimaldi. 'What are you suggesting?'

'Not sure yet. But there's definitely a connection between Bahadir – a suspected terrorist – and Gambio, the notorious Mafioso.'

'Terrorist activities?'

'Unlikely; that's the really interesting bit here.'

'Why do you say that?'

'Because both the woman and the young man do not fit the profile. Quite the opposite, in fact. I met them both at the camp. Terrorism killed their families. They are most unlikely candidates.'

'They went willingly?' said Grimaldi.

'It looks that way. But what were they promised?'

'Or threatened with, more likely,' interjected Grimaldi. He lit a small cigar and sat back in his chair. 'A surgeon, and a young man ... *why?*' he speculated, watching the smoke curl towards the ceiling. 'Why does Gambio need a surgeon smuggled into the country?'

Haddad shrugged. 'You don't send a private plane just to help two desperate refugees without papers slip unnoticed out of Turkey. Not without a good reason.'

'No; especially not someone like Gambio.'

Just then, the phone in Grimaldi's pocket began to vibrate, signalling an incoming call. Grimaldi excused himself and answered the phone. It was Conti.

'They are on the move,' said Conti, sounding excited.

'What do you mean?'

'We have a good signal. According to Clara, they are moving south along the freeway towards Florence. Well, at least the tracking device is—'

'Where are you?' interrupted Grimaldi.

'In the car; not that far behind them.'

'Excellent! You know what to do. Keep me informed.'

'Will do.'

Grimaldi turned to Haddad. 'It's urgent. I have to go,' he said, and stood up to leave.

Haddad nodded.

'Do you have somewhere to stay, Chief Inspector?'

'Not yet.'

'I'll ask my secretary to arrange something close by. She will also arrange some office space.'

'Thank you. I would appreciate that.'

Grimaldi liked the unassuming, quietly spoken man and instantly recognised in him qualities he valued. He also understood why Colonel Riza had referred to him as a man who could be trusted, unconditionally. Men like Haddad were rare.

'Do you mind if I ask you a personal question?' said Grimaldi, holding the door open for Haddad.

'Please, go ahead.'

'Why did you turn to me, rather than go to the anti-terrorist boys?'

Haddad stopped, looked at Grimaldi and took his time before answering. 'Because of your reputation ...' he said quietly.

'What reputation?'

'May I quote Colonel Riza?'

'Of course.'

'He said you are a fearless crusader for truth and justice who cannot be bought and always has the Mafia in his sights.'

Grimaldi looked embarrassed. It wasn't the answer he had expected. 'Isn't that a little melodramatic?' he asked, trying to brush the compliment aside.

'A little old fashioned, perhaps; melodramatic, no.'

'Dinner tonight?' asked Grimaldi.

'That would be lovely, thank you.'

The back of the delivery van driven by the undertaker was full of expensive designer coffins. Handcrafted, traditional coffins were in great demand, especially by the wealthy living in Tuscany. Some of them cost more than a society wedding.

Tristan tried to move his aching ankles. He had been lying in the narrow coffin for hours, and each time the van lurched from side to side, the rope cut into his chafed wrists and ankles. A wooden, window-like flap at the top of the coffin designed to allow mourners to catch a last farewell-glimpse of the deceased's embalmed face had been left open, making breathing possible. Otherwise, the coffin was closed, encasing Tristan like an iron lung.

I hope it's working, thought Tristan. He was trying to move his bruised ankles to feel the bulge in his sock and smiled as he remembered how he had removed the tracking device from the portfolio. Just before the motorboat came to a halt near a concealed mooring at the end of a deserted canal, Tristan had sensed that something bad was about to happen. He had quickly removed the tracking device from the portfolio he was carrying and slipped it into his sock before he was overpowered by two men jumping on board.

The back of the van was divided into two separate compartments, each containing new coffins destined for Florence. Unbeknown to Tristan, Lorenza was lying in a coffin just centimetres away in the compartment next to him. Feeling numb and exhausted, Lorenza was desperately trying to keep focused. The day of her abduction seemed an eternity away, and having spent most of her time in total silence and virtual darkness only intensified her disorientation.

The way Lorenza kept fear and panic at bay was to remember her favourite recipes; line by line; ingredient by ingredient. She would then transport herself into her mother's kitchen and begin to cook. So powerful was her imagination that soon she could smell the cooking and taste the dish. This helped to keep her calm – and sane.

Clara kept her eyes glued to the GPS tracking device on her lap. *So far so good*, she thought, watching the beeping dot move along the screen of her monitor. 'They're about fifty kilometres ahead of us,' she said, and looked at Cesaria sitting next to her in the backseat. 'Travelling at a steady speed.'

Jack turned towards Conti, who was driving. 'So, what's the plan?' he asked.

'We keep our distance, watch and wait.'

'Makes sense.'

'We have to find out where they're heading. It's all we have,' said Conti. 'I don't have to tell you what would happen if they got wind of what we're doing.'

'And we still don't know where Lorenza and Tristan are being held, or what has happened to them,' said Jack, running his hand nervously through his hair. 'The silence is the worst; the waiting, the uncertainty. And now Tristan ...'

'I know,' agreed Conti, 'but we've got to keep our nerve and stay focused.'

'And hope?'

'That too,' said Cesaria.

Since the handover of the recipes and Tristan's unexpected disappearance, there had been no further contact with the abductors.

Conti had decided to leave Leonardo and the countess in Venice. They would stand-by and wait for further instructions. The countess was the only one who could console Leonardo and keep him calm. His cooperation was vital.

'Does any of this fit a certain pattern?' asked Jack.

'No, it doesn't,' said Conti. 'Not anymore, and that's what worries me. Usually, they would ask for the money first; not so here. They told Leonardo to get it ready. That's all. Weird.'

'And the property deal?' asked Jack.

'Nothing yet.'

'They are taking their time; why? What do you think is going on here?'

'Don't know. But I can tell you, these guys don't do anything without a reason.'

'So, anything could happen?'

Conti shrugged without taking his eyes off the road.

39

Grimaldi sat in his office and looked at his watch, again. *They should have been here by now,* he thought, and lit another cigar. The ashtray brimming with stubs on his desk reminded him he had smoked far too much that day, but he didn't care. He was deeply concerned about the da Baggio abduction case and the unexpected turn it had taken. He was also concerned about the return of his entire team to Florence. What if the tracking device was flawed, or failed? While he admired Clara's technical abilities, he felt uneasy about allowing the whole investigation to rely on only one lead. Grimaldi preferred more traditional policing methods. Perhaps the team should have remained in Venice, he speculated, drumming his fingers nervously against the arm of his chair.

Grimaldi reached for his phone and was about to call Conti again, when he heard voices in the corridor outside. Moments later, Conti swept into the room, followed by Clara and Cesaria, and a man he didn't know.

'At last,' said Grimaldi, and stood up. Conti introduced Jack and explained who he was and why he was involved.

'Ah, the famous author who singlehandedly brought down the British government and then wrote a book about it?'

Grimaldi was surprised, but decided this was not the time to question Conti further about Jack Rogan.

'That's him,' said Conti and walked over to the large map of Florence and its environs hanging on the wall behind Grimaldi's desk. 'We managed to follow the tracking device to this point here,' he continued, stabbing his finger at the map. It's a rural area just outside the city, not far from here. The bug was moving at a steady pace until it reached this point. Then it stopped; well, almost.'

243

'What do you mean, *almost?*' asked Grimaldi.

'Clara will explain.'

Clara stood up, put her monitor on the floor and walked over to the map.

'After coming to a sudden stop – right here – suggesting that the intended destination had been reached, we had movement again, but in a very different way.'

'What do you mean?' asked Grimaldi.

'The entire afternoon, the signal was moving along the freeway at a steady pace. This new movement, however, was entirely restricted to this spot.' Clara pointed to the map.

'Suggesting?'

'That someone was walking around with it in a confined area.'

'Say, carrying the portfolio from room to room, for instance?'

'Yes, could be. But I think this is unlikely.'

'Why?'

'Because this has been going on for some time now, mostly covering the same space; pacing up and down. So, I have to ask myself, why would someone carry the portfolio around like this; for the past hour and a half?'

'Conclusion?' asked Grimaldi.

'The most likely interpretation,' said Clara, warming to her subject, 'is that the bug, as we like to call it, has been transferred to a person who is walking around with it.'

'Do we know what this place is?' asked Grimaldi, pointing to the map.

Conti looked at him and smiled. 'We do. It's a rural property owned by ...'

'Yes?' urged Grimaldi.

'An entity controlled by the Gambio family.'

For a while, no-one said anything.

'A surveillance team is already on its way to keep it under observation,' said Conti, breaking the silence. 'Needless to say, we won't go in until we have further information ...'

Grimaldi nodded, feeling better. 'So, where to from here?' he asked.

'May I make a suggestion?' said Jack. He was leaning against a bookcase in the background and had listened carefully to what had been said.

'Please, go ahead.'

'So far, thanks to Clara, we've followed the only solid lead we have in the case: the tracking device concealed in the portfolio. This has now brought us here. What we still don't know is where Lorenza and Tristan are being held, or what happened to them. On the way here, Clara told me something that may be of help in that regard.'

'Go on,' said Conti.

'Clara, you spoke of a friend who works in a top-secret government agency gathering information; collecting all kinds of data. Phone calls, internet traffic, stuff like that. All very hush-hush, using cutting-edge technology and involving other agencies worldwide, mainly for combating terrorism.'

Clara nodded. 'Yes, that's right,' she said. 'As I understand it, it all goes through Pine Gap in Australia, one of the most sophisticated listening and data gathering installations on the planet. Operated by Australia and the US.'

'Yes?' said Grimaldi, wondering where this was going.

'Apparently, this technology is so advanced,' continued Jack, 'that it can track phone signals with absolute accuracy faster than anything else being used by the police at the moment. It can pinpoint the location of the caller and tell us not only the content of the calls, but where the calls are being made from ... The US military is using this technology right now to identify targets in real time – mainly IS leaders on the most-wanted list – and for directing airstrikes, apparently with deadly accuracy. The program is called PRISM. You may have heard if it?'

'I have,' said Grimaldi. 'It was in the news not that long ago ... Killer drones and the Snowden affair. WikiLeaks ...'

'That's it,' said Jack. 'It's all about global surveillance on an unprecedented scale, and the US drone program.'

'You seem to know a lot about this …'

Jack shrugged. 'I did a series of articles about PRISM and the killer drones …'

'What's on your mind?' asked Conti.

'What if we could do the same?'

'What do you mean?'

'Supposing, next time the abductor calls, we ask Lorenza's father to insist that he be allowed to speak to his daughter to make sure that she's all right before he agrees to the next round of demands, especially the money. Risky, I know, but not unreasonable in the circumstances.'

'Interesting …' said Grimaldi. Now that he was convinced that the Mafia was behind the abduction – Gambio, most likely – he was more inclined to entertain what Jack was suggesting, and take the risk. Gambio would expect such a request, and perhaps grant it. And what Grimaldi had learned about a possible terrorist link between Bahadir in Istanbul, and Gambio in Florence, could provide the right angle for an approach.

Grimaldi turned to Clara. 'Could we find out which agency your friend is working for?'

'Sure.'

'What do you think, Fabio?' said Grimaldi, addressing Conti.

'Definitely worth a try.'

'Good. 'Let's talk to the commissioner about this and see what he can do,' said Grimaldi, warming to the idea. 'But we have to act quickly.' Grimaldi looked at Jack. 'Excellent suggestion, Mr Rogan. I could use someone like you on our team.'

'He already is,' said Conti, laughing.

'I suppose we have to be careful or we'll end up in his novel.'

'You have nothing to fear,' said Jack, a sparkle in his eyes. 'I only use colourful characters.'

'Ah. I feel better already,' said Grimaldi and turned to Cesaria. 'Why don't you look after Mr Rogan, and perhaps you can introduce him to some colourful characters? I'm sure we have a few lurking

246

around here somewhere. In the meantime, I'll call the commissioner. Let's regroup in an hour. We work around the clock.'

'Understood,' said Conti, and headed for the door.

Clara was about to follow when Grimaldi held up his hand. 'Could you stay for a moment, Clara?' he said. 'Please tell me more about this surveillance facility – Pine Gap and PRISM – and how it all works. If I'm to persuade the commissioner to step in and help us here, we must go in with the right information, don't you think?'

'Yes, sir.'

40

Fortezza Gambio, Florence: 3 June

Gambio called Belmonte late in the afternoon and requested an urgent meeting. The curt nature of the call immediately set off alarm bells in Belmonte. Something was up. Not surprisingly, he approached the meeting with some trepidation because he had hoped to report to his boss once everything was ready and in place and not before. He hated to be caught on the back foot. So much had happened in the last few days, and not all of it had gone according to plan. He wasn't used to improvising and making decisions on the run. Changing circumstances required flexibility in a situation where so much was fluid and unpredictable, results were all that mattered, and failure was unthinkable.

Since his arrival in Florence on Gambio's jet the day before, Belmonte had intentionally avoided Gambio and had spent his entire time at the farm, the *'fattoria'*, as Gambio liked to call it, frantically making preparations for *Ars Moriendi*. Belmonte hated loose ends. But more than anything else, he hated failure.

Gambio had made it clear that *Ars Moriendi* had top priority and time was of the essence because so much was riding on it. Amena and Nazir had been taken from the airport under guard straight to the fattoria, effectively as prisoners. Preparing Nazir for *Ars Moriendi* had already begun. Belmonte had his best team working on him – using drugs mainly, and other tried and tested methods of persuasion. As expected, dealing with Amena required a different, more subtle approach, and Belmonte had assigned this critically important task to himself. Her cooperation was vital. Without her surgical skills, harvesting the lucrative body parts was impossible because finding a replacement surgeon would take too long and freshly harvested organs couldn't wait.

248

Thankfully, the last few pieces of the complex puzzle had fallen into place that afternoon. Just in time. The undertaker had arrived in Florence with his precious cargo: Lorenza and Tristan, neatly encased in designer coffins. A nice touch, thought Belmonte. However, he realised that by transferring the two hostages from Venice to the fattoria just outside Florence without consulting Gambio, he had taken a considerable risk. But if *Ars Moriendi* was to be ready to go in a few days' time, it had to be done.

Belmonte also realised that his biggest challenge would be something entirely different: explaining it all to Gambio and justifying his decisions and the actions he had taken. Because Gambio knew nothing of all this, nor had he been told about Tristan's abduction and the reasons behind it, Belmonte realised he would need all his powers of persuasion to explain himself. All Gambio knew was that the recipes had been handed over, and that Belmonte had returned from Istanbul on his private jet.

It was already dark by the time Belmonte arrived at the compound. Gambio was waiting for him in his study as usual. 'Have you been avoiding me?' he asked, the irritation in his voice obvious. 'You arrived yesterday, yet not a word ... I have to ask myself, *why*?'

Belmonte had been expecting something like that and was ready. 'The answer is quite simple: I didn't think there was any point in bringing you up to date before everything was ready.'

He's got balls, thought Gambio. Because he obviously liked the answer, his face began to relax a little. 'All right,' he said, 'let's hear it: are we ready? Time is running out faster than we thought. Scotch?'

Belmonte nodded. 'You told me that *Ars Moriendi* was our top priority.'

'It is.'

'I acted accordingly. It wasn't easy, but I think we can do it. *Ars Moriendi* is on track.'

'Excellent. Run me through it.'

'Okay. Let's start at the beginning. We needed a new reliable source of combatants, urgently. Bahadir told us he could provide this

249

through his contacts in the Turkish refugee camps. That sounded very promising. In return, apart from the money you promised him, he wanted these original Ottoman recipes, which would allow him to repair the damage to his reputation.'

Gambio chuckled as he remembered the expression of humiliation on Bahadir's stunned face during the *Top Chef* final.

'Lorenza da Baggio was abducted in Venice last week as planned. You made the ransom demands yourself, and the original recipes were handed over a couple of days ago.'

Belmonte pointed to the package on the couch next to him. 'Here they are,' he said. 'First step completed.'

Belmonte paused and reached for his glass, to allow this to sink in.

'Very good,' said Gambio, obviously pleased.

'Next, I contacted Bahadir in Istanbul and we travelled to a refugee camp on the Syrian border,' continued Belmonte. 'With the help of his contacts, we recruited four young men I thought would make good candidates for *Ars Moriendi*. Unfortunately—'

'What do you mean?' interrupted Gambio, raising his voice.

'Three of them turned out to be terrorists. They ran off as soon as we arrived back in Istanbul; with outside help.'

'And Bahadir didn't know about this?'

'He claims not to, but I think he did. The three young men were introduced to us by his agent. I don't completely trust Bahadir,' added Belmonte, lowering his voice. 'He has his own agenda – and he certainly wasn't too pleased to see me when I arrived unannounced. There was a certain reluctance ...'

'Hmm ... And the fourth?'

'He came to us separately and was added to the group later, just before we left. I spoke to him and thought he would make an excellent combatant.'

'What happened to him?'

'He's here.'

'So, we have one?'

'We have more than that.'

Gambio looked at Belmonte, surprised. 'We do?'

'Yes. But first let me tell you about the surgeon.' Belmonte was beginning to relax. The worst was on the table. It was time to play his trump card.

'You managed to find one?' interjected Gambio, becoming excited.

'Yes, in the camp. And I think she will be ideal for the task.'

'She?'

'Yes, a woman. A Syrian refugee who recently lost her family in an air strike in Aleppo. Desperate and alone, with nowhere to go; perfect.'

'Where is she?'

'At the fattoria.'

Gambio looked at Belmonte with renewed respect. *There's more to this guy*, he thought, pleased that his instincts to bring Belmonte into the famiglia had been vindicated. '*Ars Moriendi* requires at least two combatants,' he said.

'I know. We have two.'

'Explain.'

Belmonte took another sip of Scotch. It was time to introduce Tristan. He took Gambio step-by-step through Lorenza's abduction and explained the part played in it by Tristan, paying particular attention to the relationship between them. A lot was riding on that, and to some extent that was the key to what he had in mind. It would be the way to ensure Tristan's complete cooperation when it came to playing his part in *Ars Moriendi* ... A combatant had to be both desperate and willing, and Belmonte knew exactly how to manipulate the players and impose his will. The important thing was to explain this to Gambio and make him see how it would all come together, and work.

Gambio listened in silence as Belmonte explained each part of his bold plan, and how he intended to cover his tracks and make sure there were no loose ends. From the expression on Gambio's face, it was impossible to tell what he was thinking. However, Belmonte had instinctively chosen the right approach. What he was suggesting appealed to the gambler in Gambio. It also appealed to his ruthless nature. Not only did he like Belmonte's plan, he loved it, and his admiration for his new protégée rose by the minute.

Satisfied that he had explained everything in sufficient detail, Belmonte sat back and reached for his glass. After a long moment of complete silence, which sent Belmonte's stomach into a spin, Gambio began to clap, the gesture obvious. Then he walked over to his visitor and embraced him. It was the way things were done in the famiglia.

'Now let me tell you what happened while you were in Istanbul chasing new blood,' said Gambio, enjoying himself. 'It's quite a story and it fits perfectly into what you are suggesting. It's all about a fabulously rich Arab prince with dark desires, a new heart, and lots of money. Interested?'

'You bet! Sounds like our kind of guy.'

'We'll make a lot of dough out of this.' Gambio reached for his glass. 'To *Ars Moriendi*,' he said. 'Salute!'

41

Prince Khalid and his entourage arrived by private plane just before sunset and were met by a fleet of black limousines waiting at the airport. The prince, a frequent visitor to Florence, was driven straight to his favourite luxury hotel where the two top floors had been reserved for him.

The hotel manager and his assistant greeted the prince at the entrance and escorted him to the lift. Excitement rippled through the hotel lobby as the prince, surrounded by his bodyguards and wearing a traditional white flowing *kandoorah* and black *agal* to keep his *ghurtah* – headscarf – in place, made an impressive entrance.

He's here, thought Gambio, enjoying the familiar rush of anticipation. It was a similar feeling to watching the ball rolling around the inside of the slowing roulette wheel, or the dealer placing the next card on the gaming table. The hotel manager had kept Gambio informed of the prince's every move. It was time to arrange the welcome present for the high roller. Gambio had discussed the arrangements with Belmonte the night before and knew that everything would be ready. All that remained to be done was to let Belmonte know.

Gambio reached for his phone and called Belmonte. 'It's on,' he said. 'Tonight. I just spoke to the hotel manager. The prince will have dinner in his suite at eight pm. You are to present yourself to his secretary on the fifth floor at ten sharp. Clear?'

'Absolutely.'

'Use the back entrance where the deliveries are made. The manager will meet you there. There's a lift only the staff use. The manager will show you. And for God's sake be discreet. I hear the prince is very temperamental – and demanding. We can't afford any mistakes here. Absolutely nothing must go wrong; nothing!'

'Don't worry. I've taken care of everything myself, personally.'
Gambio chuckled. 'What's the present like?'

'Stunning.'

'Good.'

'Ten thousand euros buys a lot of present.'

'I hope so. You did explain?'

'Of course.'

'Good luck! Keep me informed.'

'Will do.'

At five minutes to ten, Belmonte pulled up at the rear entrance of the hotel. He got out of the car and opened the back door. Two tall, elegantly dressed young women got out and smiled at the manager, who was looking a little anxious. He escorted them to the lift and pressed the button. 'Fifth floor. The prince's secretary will meet you there,' he said.

'All right, ladies; you know what to do,' said Belmonte on the way up. 'Whatever the prince wants, he gets. Do we understand each other?'

'Don't fret,' said one of the women, laughing. 'We've done this before, you know.'

'I bet.'

Prince Khalid's secretary – a quietly spoken, middle-aged man – met them at the lift and ushered them inside the Imperial Suite occupying the entire floor.

'Mr Belmonte, Your Excellency,' said the secretary, and withdrew. The prince, a handsome man in his early forties with a finely chiselled face dominated by a prominent nose and thin, closely trimmed black beard, sat on a lounge near the window, a glass of champagne in his hand. Casually dressed in a pair of grey slacks, white shirt and loafers, he looked relaxed and at ease. 'Good evening, ladies,' he said in perfect English, his accent hinting at an Oxford education, and stood up. 'Champagne?'

'Mr Gambio sends his regards, Your Excellency,' said Belmonte after he had introduced the two young women. 'He is very much looking forward to meeting you.'

'Please thank him for his hospitality.'

'I certainly will,' replied Belmonte, and turned towards the door. It was obvious he was about to leave.

'Please don't go, Mr Belmonte,' said the prince. 'Not yet. Let's have some champagne first; Arab hospitality.'

Belmonte watched the prince with interest as he reached for the champagne bottle without taking his eyes off the two women sitting opposite.

'The game,' asked the prince, filling the champagne flute in front of Belmonte, 'when will it be?'

'The day after tomorrow, Your Excellency.'

'I've heard a lot about it from my uncle. He said he hadn't seen anything quite like it; a "life-changing experience", he called it,' said the prince, laughing. 'I can't wait.'

'You could call it that. Your uncle has been to one of our ...?' asked Belmonte, surprised.

'Oh yes. He hasn't stopped talking about it for weeks.'

The prince turned to the young woman sitting on his right. 'Please take off your clothes,' he said casually, and took a sip of champagne, 'but not the shoes.'

'Here? Right now?' asked the woman.

'Yes please.'

The woman giggled, looked at her friend and shrugged. Then she stood up and began to undress. The prince watched her without saying a word. It took the young woman only a few moments to take off her clothes. Then she placed her hands on her hips and gave the prince a coquettish look. 'What now?' she asked.

'Please sit down,' said the prince quietly and turned to her friend. 'Your turn,' he said.

A few moments later, the other woman was naked too, her tanned body glowing in the subdued light like silk near an open fire.

'Now, Mr Belmonte, if you were looking for a life-changing experience, which one would you choose?'

'Why not both?' suggested Belmonte.

'A good answer, but if it had to be just one ...'

'It's a difficult choice, Your Excellency. Such beauty and perfection demand a more experienced eye than mine.'

Prince Khalid smiled. He liked the way Belmonte had diplomatically sidestepped the question and passed it back to him. 'Very well,' he said and put his hand on the knee of the woman who had undressed first and squeezed it; hard. For a while he just left it there, his cold touch making her feel vulnerable and sending a shiver of fear racing to her empty stomach. Then he reached into his shirt pocket with his other hand, pulled out a beautiful pearl and handed it to her. 'Please get dressed. Mr Belmonte will drive you home now.'

Grimaldi was a light sleeper. He lived by himself in an apartment overlooking the river near his office, and woke with a start when his phone rang. Instantly awake, he reached for his mobile on the bedside table and looked at the screen. *Conti at three in the morning; must be important*, he thought, and answered the call.

'Apologies for calling at this hour,' said Conti, 'but I thought you should see this.'

Grimaldi turned on the light. 'What's up?'

'A badly mutilated body of a young woman. Dumped in a rubbish bin. A waiter found her and called us.'

'Where are you?'

'Not far from you.' Conti gave Grimaldi an address.

'I'm on my way.'

'Right. I mean *badly* mutilated ... you know, in ...'

'Jesus! On top of everything else, we certainly don't need something like this right now.'

'No. We're stretched as it is—'

'Is Cesaria with you?' interrupted Grimaldi.

'She's coming. The entire Squadra has been mobilised.'

'Can be confronting ...'

'She's a big girl.'

'Still ...'

'I hear you,' said Conti, and hung up.

42

Grimaldi turned into the dark back lane littered with rubbish and parked his car behind a pack of stray dogs fighting over a chicken carcass. Then he followed the flashing lights of the police cars ahead, showing him the way to the crime scene. Despite having attended countless crime scenes before, a sense of sadness and foreboding descended on the chief prosecutor as he walked towards the bright lights.

Conti met Grimaldi at the cordon. 'You won't believe this,' he said, looking agitated.

'What are you talking about?'

'She's alive.'

'What?'

'When the pathologist arrived and we lifted her out of the bin over there, he detected signs of life.'

'Where is she?'

'On her way to hospital; emergency.'

'Will she live?'

Conti shrugged. 'She's in a bad way.'

'Anything I should see here?'

'The Forensics guys are already well into it, but you could have a look at the bin. It's one of these big ones full of restaurant kitchen rubbish and broken bottles. Glass everywhere. She was lying on top. Only been there for a short while ... Lucky the waiter found her when he did.'

'Anything else?'

'As a matter of fact, yes.'

'Oh?'

'We know who she is and where she lives.'

'That was quick.'

'Cesaria is at her place right now, speaking to a flatmate. Apparently, she has quite a story to tell about last night.'

'What kind of story?'

'I think in the circumstances, you should hear this from her direct. If only half of what she is telling us is true, we have a sensational case on our hands.'

Grimaldi looked at Conti and raised an eyebrow. 'Serious?'

'Absolutely.'

'Sounds like trouble. Let's go.'

Cesaria and a young woman in a dressing gown were sitting in the tiny kitchen of a modest flat on the outskirts of Florence, an area popular with students. The young woman had been crying, smudged mascara running down her beautiful face like war paint on a Sioux brave. Cesaria was taking her statement.

'Don't mind us,' said Conti, standing by the door. 'Please continue.'

'After that, he gave me this,' said the young woman. She reached into her purse and took out a beautiful pearl.

'And then what happened?' asked Cesaria.

'I got dressed, and the man who took us there drove me home.'

'And Francesca?'

The young woman began to sob. Cesaria stood up and put her arm around her to calm her. 'Take your time,' she said.

'She stayed behind ... with the prince,' whispered the young woman, barely able to speak.

'What prince?' said Grimaldi.

The young woman looked at him with teary eyes. 'An Arab. I don't know his name.'

'Where was that?' asked Conti.

'In his hotel suite.'

'Which hotel?'

'The Medici Grande by the river.'

Grimaldi looked at Conti. 'Gambio,' he whispered.

Conti and Grimaldi went from the flat straight to the hospital. Cesaria stayed behind to complete the young woman's statement.

The victim, Francesca Ottoboni, was in intensive care, hanging on by a thread so thin it surprised the surgeon in charge that she was still alive. Grimaldi and Conti were waiting for him in the corridor.

'She's a fighter,' said the surgeon, who knew Grimaldi well. They had crossed paths on numerous cases before. 'It's a miracle she's alive.'

'Will she live?' asked Grimaldi.

The surgeon shrugged. 'Touch and go. She's in a deep coma. If they had brought her in fifteen minutes later, she would have been dead on arrival.'

'So, what can you tell us about her injuries?' asked Conti.

'To begin with, she's been badly beaten, especially around the face. There's bruising all over the body, suggesting she had several falls. But no broken bones. Then there are deep cuts in her wrists and ankles.'

'Suggesting what?' said Grimaldi.

'I would say she's been tied up and struggled. This would explain the cuts.'

'What else?' asked Grimaldi, expecting the worst.

'Vaginal and anal mutilation.'

'What kind of mutilation?'

'Sharp objects, thrust deep – some of the worst I've seen.'

Grimaldi held up his hand. He didn't have to hear any more.

'While extremely painful, none of this would have killed her,' said the surgeon. 'Most serious by far, was the strangulation. The marks around her throat make this clear. I would say she was repeatedly strangled to within an inch of her life and then somehow revived.'

'Until the last time, when it all went too far,' suggested Conti, 'and she appeared lifeless and slipped into a coma.'

The surgeon nodded. 'Quite possibly; that fits,' he said.

'And then dumped and left for dead,' interjected Grimaldi.

'Any evidence of intercourse? Semen, body fluids?' asked Conti.

'Strangely, no,' said the surgeon. 'I couldn't find any. Only evidence of extreme violence.'

'Any drugs?'

'Don't know yet. I'm waiting for the toxicology report.'

'If she regains consciousness, please let us know,' said Grimaldi. 'I'll arrange for a guard, around the clock. Needless to say, we have to talk to her.'

'That may take a while,' said the surgeon, 'if it happens at all,' he added, the sadness in his voice obvious.

Grimaldi nodded and headed for the exit. 'Let's go back to my office,' he said to Conti. 'I could kill for a cigar.'

Grimaldi walked into his office, headed straight to the whiteboard behind his desk and picked up a cloth. It was just after six am. 'Something bothers me,' he said, and began to wipe the board clean.

'What?' asked Conti.

'It's all a little too obvious; too pat, don't you think?'

'That bothers me too,' replied Conti, and lit a cigarette.

'How many cases have you seen where everything fits together so neatly? No attempt appears to have been made to conceal anything. Even her handbag with her ID and credit cards has been left in the bin, for Christ sake. We've been handed this on a plate. I don't get it.'

'Crimes of passion can be like that,' suggested Conti.

'Involving a high-profile foreign dignitary, an Arab prince? Risking an international incident? Come on; I think we were supposed to find everything exactly as we did, and quickly. An all-too-obvious trail has been left behind for us to follow. Think of the flatmate. She was there for Christ's sake! And it all leads to this man: the prince.'

Grimaldi wrote down Arab prince in the middle of the board, and then surrounded it with bullet points of information they had pieced together so far. 'Just look at it,' he said. 'It's either reckless stupidity, or something more sinister, and possibly very clever ... a strategy.' Grimaldi tapped the board with his felt pen. 'But I think there's one thing no-one anticipated.'

'What?'

'Her survival. I don't think anyone saw this coming. It's the fly in this odious ointment, and that, my friend, could be the wild card that will buy us a seat at the table. It could be our way into this bizarre game.'

'So, where to from here?' asked Conti.

'Simple. Let's find out if we're on the right track.'

'How?'

'We talk to the man who can answer that question and see what he has to say. Fancy meeting an Arab prince before breakfast? Let's go.'

'God, I love this job,' said Conti, grinding his cigarette into the ashtray on Grimaldi's desk. 'Never a dull moment!'

43

The liveried doorman doffed his hat and showed Conti and Grimaldi to the hotel manager's office.

'What can I do for you, gentlemen?' asked the manager affably, but looking concerned. To have the chief prosecutor and the head of the Squadra Mobile call at six-thirty in the morning didn't happen without a good reason.

'We are here to see one of your hotel guests,' said Conti, watching the manager carefully. Conti was aware of the role the manager had played the night before in taking the two young women to meet the prince. Francesca's flatmate had been quite specific about that.

'And who might that be?'

'Prince Khalid,' said Grimaldi.

The manager paled and stared at the expensive pen on his desk.

'May I ask what this is all about?' he asked.

'A confidential matter,' said Conti, assessing the manager's reaction, 'of the utmost importance.' *He's obviously nervous*, he thought. *To be expected.*

'We may have some questions for you after we've seen the prince,' added Grimaldi, putting more pressure on the manager.

'Certainly. I'll contact his secretary and tell him you want to speak to His Excellency. You can wait in here if you like.'

'Please tell him it's urgent,' said Grimaldi.

The manager nodded, excused himself and hurried to the door.

He returned a few minutes later. 'His Excellency cannot see you right now, I'm afraid,' he said, looking quite flustered.

'Is His Excellency still asleep?' asked Conti, unable to keep the sarcasm out of his voice.

'No; he has just finished his morning prayers and will be with you in half an hour.'

Touché, thought Grimaldi, smiling.

'He has asked if you would care to join him for breakfast in his suite,' added the manager, looking more confident.

'Thank His Excellency and tell him we are looking forward to it.'

'Gentlemen, you can wait in the lobby. It's more comfortable. May I offer you some coffee while you wait?'

'That would be excellent, thank you,' said Grimaldi, and stood up.

'Over there,' said the manager, and pointed to Grimaldi and Conti sitting under palm trees by the fountain in the centre of the opulent lobby. The prince's secretary nodded and walked over to them.

'His Excellency is looking forward to making your acquaintance, gentlemen,' he said, his English a little stilted, and bowed. 'Please follow me.'

Impeccably dressed in a dark navy pin-striped suit that whispered Savile Row, white shirt, and silk tie, Prince Khalid stood facing the open doors leading out onto the balcony. He was looking across the rooftops of Florence towards the green hills surrounding the city.

'Chief Prosecutor Grimaldi and Chief Superintendent Conti to see you, Your Excellency,' said the secretary, and withdrew.

'Good morning, gentlemen,' said the prince, and turned around. 'I never tire of this view. What a splendid city. My apologies for making you wait. Please allow me to make it up to you. In a small way at least.' The prince pointed to a table set for three. 'The world looks better after breakfast. Shall we?'

As a man who had studied human behaviour all his professional life, Grimaldi was impressed. *He's good,* he thought, admiring the prince's easy-going manner, exuding confidence and control. At the same time, he was searching for the right way to approach the delicate subject he was about to raise. *If he's indeed our man, we must tread carefully.* Grimaldi decided to begin with polite small talk. 'What brings you to Florence, Excellency?' he asked, sipping his coffee. 'Pleasure?'

'Business; official business. Tourism and trade. My family owns an airline and I am here to negotiate landing rights. Here in Florence and

Milan. Our ladies love to shop in Italy. Handbags and shoes mainly, but fashion too, of course. And you have such outstanding jewellers. So many temptations ...'

Conti was watching the prince's elegant, almost feminine hands and perfectly manicured fingernails as he buttered his roll. *Could these hands have inflicted those horrendous injuries?* he wondered as he remembered the bloody face of the young woman found lying in the rubbish bin, and the surgeon's graphic description of the mutilations ... *Is a monster lurking under this urbane, sophisticated facade? Let's find out.*

'You must be wondering why we're here, Excellency,' he said, and reached for another croissant in the silver breadbasket. The prince looked at him, but didn't say anything. 'We understand you entertained two young ladies here in your suite last night,' said Conti.

The prince picked up his serviette and carefully wiped his mouth. 'That's correct,' he said. 'And what, may I ask, is your interest in this?'

'One of the women was found in a rubbish bin early this morning not far from here, with injuries too horrible to mention at breakfast. They would make the world look decidedly ghastly,' replied Conti.

Grimaldi thought he could detect a flash of anger narrow the prince's eyes. It only lasted for an instant, but Grimaldi was satisfied he had chosen the right approach. He decided to press his advantage, however small, and come straight to the point.

'You may have been one of the last people to see her before she was dumped,' he said, watching the prince carefully. 'The other young woman made it home safely after you gave her that beautiful pearl,' added Grimaldi casually, to see if he could get a reaction.

'You are well informed, Mr Grimaldi.'

'My job.'

'Of course.'

'It is also my job to find out why the other woman didn't.'

'Perhaps this will help. For the record, I can tell you that I know absolutely nothing of what you've just told me. The young lady was well and in good spirits when she left here,' said the prince, raising his voice just a little.

264

Grimaldi just looked at him without saying a word, the doubt on his face obvious.

'You have your answer, gentlemen, are we done?' asked the prince and pushed his chair back, making it obvious that he was about to get up.

Arrogant bastard, thought Conti. 'No, we are not,' he said calmly. 'In many ways, this is just the beginning.'

'The beginning? What do you mean?'

'This entire suite will have to be examined by our Forensics team, and everyone – and that includes you, of course, Your Excellency – who had any contact whatsoever with the woman will have to be interviewed. Statements will be taken. This is all part of our investigation. Routine. I don't know how you conduct these matters in your country, but this is the way we do things here.'

The prince looked at his watch. *Any time now*, he thought, smiling.

'In a moment, Chief Superintendent, you will receive a phone call. May I suggest you take it?'

Conti looked at the prince, surprised. 'And why should I do that?' he asked.

'Because in my country we do things differently.'

As if on cue, Conti's phone began to vibrate in his coat pocket. He reached for the phone and answered it. It was the police commissioner. The conversation was brief and to the point. Conti was ordered to stop his enquiries and leave at once. *Diplomatic immunity*. Conti nodded and slipped the phone back into his pocket.

'Are we done now, gentlemen?' asked the prince, and stood up.

'Yes, your Excellency; for now,' said Conti, and stood up too. Grimaldi looked at him, amazed, but didn't say anything.

Conti stopped at the door, turned around and looked at the prince. It was time to play his trump card. 'There was one more thing, Your Excellency, I forgot to tell you ... How silly of me.'

'Oh?'

'Against all odds, the young woman survived and is under police guard in hospital. We are hoping to interview her as soon as she comes out of the coma.' Conti just stood there for a while to let this sink in. 'Sorry, I should have told you earlier.'

'And of course we don't control the press, Your Excellency. Not in this country. A media briefing is scheduled for later this morning,' said Grimaldi, 'with all the facts as we know them so far. Out of courtesy, we wanted to speak to you first before that happens.'

The prince, an experienced tactician and negotiator, kept staring at the two men standing at the door, his mind racing. *Is he bluffing?* he asked himself. *Unlikely.* What he had just heard changed everything. It was time to introduce a sacrificial lamb. And from what he knew about the chief prosecutor, he would be unable to resist the tempting offer. 'Mr Grimaldi, may I have a word? *In private?*' he said, just as Grimaldi turned to leave.

Grimaldi looked at Conti and nodded. Conti bowed, left the room and closed the door.

Grimaldi turned around and walked back to the breakfast table. 'Yes, Your Excellency?' he said, and looked intently at the prince. The prince held his gaze, his face expressionless.

'Please take a seat, Mr Grimaldi,' he said. 'I have some information for you I know you will find interesting ... I also have a proposal.'

44

Grimaldi looked decidedly agitated as he hurried over to Conti waiting for him in the hotel lobby. 'Let's go back to my office,' he snapped, and hurried to the exit.

Conti unlocked his car parked in front of the hotel and glanced at his friend. *He looks like he's seen a ghost,* he thought.

Grimaldi got into the car, lit one of his small cigars and kept looking out the window without saying a word.

'Are you going to tell me what happened, or do I have to die of curiosity first?' asked Conti.

'Let's call Cesaria and ask her to meet us in my office. I'll tell you when we're all together.'

'That important – eh?'

'What has just been put to me is without question the most extraordinary proposal I've heard in my entire career,' said Grimaldi, enjoying the nicotine rush. 'I still find it difficult to get my head around it all. At first I thought he must be having me on.'

'Are you serious?'

'Deadly. If what he just told me is true, then we are faced with one of the most sinister and evil criminal enterprises imaginable. But we have to act fast; very fast!'

Conti looked at his friend sitting next to him. 'Are you all right?' he said.

'Don't worry, I haven't lost my marbles. Just when I thought we must have seen it all, along comes this. This dark prince makes Machiavelli look like a schoolboy.'

'Do you mind if I put on the siren?' joked Conti. 'It may get us back to your office a little faster.'

'Don't bother, we're almost there.'

Cesaria had arrived first and was waiting in Grimaldi's office. She stood up as Grimaldi stormed in, followed by Conti.

'Close the door,' he said, 'and sit down. What I'm about to tell you is absolutely confidential and must remain strictly between us. Not a word of this must get out. Lives depend on it. You'll see in a moment why.'

Cesaria looked at Grimaldi, her face flushed with excitement. Conti sat down and lit a cigarette. Grimaldi pointed to the whiteboard behind his desk with all the notes about the prince he had made earlier.

'There is absolutely no doubt in my mind,' he said, tapping the board, 'that Prince Khalid is responsible for what happened to Francesca. Everything we know so far clearly points in that direction. He virtually admitted it all, except for almost killing her. In a roundabout way, he's even admitting that. However, what we need is proof and that may be difficult, if not impossible, to obtain. Why? Because the prince is claiming diplomatic immunity. The commissioner has instructed Fabio accordingly; orders from above. The prince has friends in high places. As of now, our investigation stops right here. Officially at least. It's hands off the prince.'

'That's not right!' exclaimed Cesaria. 'Sorry, sir,' she added, embarrassed by her outburst.

'That's what I think too,' said Grimaldi. 'The prince may be beyond the reach of the law, but he's not beyond the reach of the press and scandal, and he knows it.' Grimaldi turned to Conti. 'Remember when we threatened him with a press briefing later this morning? I think that's what did it. His Excellency is terrified of the press and scandal. Even if only a whiff of this would find its way into the public domain, any hope of negotiating landing rights for his airline would be dead in the water, and his name and reputation not only here, but back home in his country would be severely damaged, perhaps beyond repair.'

Grimaldi looked at Conti and Cesaria. 'So, what does all this mean to us?' Grimaldi paused, letting the tension grow. 'What it means is this: a *deal*.'

'What kind of deal?' asked Conti.

'The prince is handing us Gambio in return for immunity, and more importantly, for keeping his name out of the press. It's quite clever really when you think of it. He obviously knows how we feel about the Mafia.'

'What do you mean *handing us Gambio*? How?' Conti asked, becoming excited.

'Do the words "*Ars Moriendi*" mean anything to you?' Conti and Cesaria looked at each other and shook their heads. 'I didn't think so. *Ars Moriendi* – the art of dying – is a term used for a most deadly and evil game imaginable. It's a life and death gamble involving real people and it is taking place right here just outside Florence in a day or so. It's all about gambling for the highest stakes possible: *life.*'

'I don't follow,' said Conti, shaking his head. 'How—'

'You will in a moment,' interrupted Grimaldi. 'But for this to work, we need the cooperation of others … We can't do this alone.' He lit one of his small cigars and let the smoke drift towards the whiteboard like incense in a chapel. 'I have an idea,' he continued, lowering his voice, 'but it's daring and dangerous. But if we pull this off …'

Conti looked at Grimaldi and raised an eyebrow, but didn't say anything.

'Cesaria, could you please ask Chief Inspector Haddad to join us?' said Grimaldi.

'Right away, sir,' replied Cesaria, and left the room.

Grimaldi walked slowly over to Conti standing near the window. 'We've been friends for a long time, haven't we, Fabio?' he said, and placed his hands on Conti's shoulders.

'Yes, and both of us have several war wounds to prove it.'

Grimaldi nodded.

'You must promise me one thing, right now,' he said.

Conti looked at Grimaldi, surprised. 'Sounds serious.'

'It is. What I'm about to suggest may be one of the craziest things we've ever done. You could even call it desperate. But if it means bringing down a monster like Gambio, I'm prepared to do it. However, you must form your own view of this. If you think I'm going too far, or the risks are too high, you must say so and you cannot – no – you must not, allow our friendship to get in the way and cloud your judgement. Will you promise me that?'

For a long moment, Conti just stared at his friend, concerned and somewhat perplexed by this unexpected and uncharacteristic outburst.

'Sure, but I can't help wondering what brought this on.'

'You'll find out as soon as Cesaria and Chief Inspector Haddad get here.'

'I'm intrigued. What has he to do with all this?'

Grimaldi smiled. 'He's the main player in this game. We can't do this without him; you'll like the guy. If anyone can pull this off, he can.'

'Please, take a seat,' said Grimaldi after he had introduced Conti to Haddad. 'Cesaria, may we assume that you have briefed the chief inspector about the latest developments in the da Baggio abduction case and the Prince Khalid matter?'

'I have – I also told him about PRISM.'

Grimaldi turned to Haddad, sitting closest to him. 'I have good news,' he said. 'The da Baggio telephone intercept has been approved. And it's all thanks to you.'

'How come?' asked Haddad. 'Cesaria told me it was Jack Rogan's idea.'

'True, but what got us over the line was this: Apparently, Turkish intelligence are not the only ones interested in Mr Bahadir and his activities here in Florence. The Americans have been watching him for some time as well and are suspecting terrorist links, in Turkey, and right here involving the Mafia. They are particularly interested in Gambio and his business activities in Europe, the US and the Middle East. Arms deals mainly, but also people smuggling and false papers. If we are right about Gambio's involvement in the da Baggio case, well ...'

'Does this mean the phone intercept can go ahead?' asked Conti.

'Yes. I know it's a long shot, but it could just give us the breakthrough we so desperately need. Cesaria has already spoken to da Baggio in Venice and alerted him to this. He's ready and knows what to do.'

'That was quick.'

'Don't forget, as far as the Americans are concerned, this is part of their war. As Clara so correctly pointed out, some amazing, top-secret intelligence gathering technology is involved in all this; military grade. These guys can do things we couldn't even dream of. For it to work it has to be both fast, and accurate. Drone strikes depend on it. The commissioner was certainly impressed. I still don't know how we've pulled this off, but we seem to have done it. And it's all thanks to the information you provided about Gambio and his possible links to terrorism.'

'Glad to be of help,' said Haddad, smiling.

Grimaldi walked over to his whiteboard and looked at it for a while without saying anything. 'It would appear that all the threads in our two most urgent cases lead to this man here: Gambio. He's the spider sitting in the middle of this deadly web.' Grimaldi stabbed his finger at the centre of the whiteboard. 'He's involved; no doubt about it. Exactly how and to what extent, we don't know; *yet*. But we are about to find out! And what I'm about to tell you will shock you.'

'Shock us?' asked Conti and lit another cigarette. 'How exactly?'

'I'll tell you in a moment. Cesaria, is Jack Rogan in the building?'

'Yes.'

'Could you please ask him to join us?'

'*Jack Rogan is in the building*?' said Haddad, looking incredulous.

'Yes.'

'*The* Jack Rogan, the writer, who suggested the telephone intercept?'

'Yes. Do you know him?'

'We go back a long way ...'

'Grimaldi shook his head. 'You are full of surprises, Chief Inspector,' he said.

'Story of my life.'

Jack followed Cesaria into the room and walked over to Grimaldi leaning against his desk. 'That's great!' he said, 'Cesaria just told me. If Clara's right and the Yanks get their act together, well ...'

For a while no-one spoke. 'Something wrong?' asked Jack, looking around.

Haddad stood in the background near a window and was watching his friend. 'Hello Jack,' he said, breaking the silence and walked slowly towards Jack. 'It's been a long time. I've lost count of the years ...'

Jack spun around and looked at Haddad. At first, he didn't recognise him, but as Haddad came closer, recognition lit up Jack's face. 'Naguib?' he whispered, his eyes misting over.

'It's me, Jack,' said Haddad, raising his arms. The two men embraced and for a long moment held each other tight, lost in memories and the relentless passage of time.

'When Marcus called me a few days ago and told me you were alive, I didn't believe him at first,' began Jack. 'Then I spoke to Bettany at the camp and she told me all about you. How you just turned up at her surgery – on a stretcher. What a story! Let me have a look at you,' stammered Jack, trying to compose himself. 'What are you doing here? I was told you were in Turkey; intelligence ... I still can't believe this is happening.'

Jack looked at Grimaldi watching him. 'This is a moment of destiny,' he said, trying to explain what was happening.

Grimaldi nodded and smiled. 'Fabio and I know all about moments of destiny, don't we, Fabio?'

'Sure do.'

'I think all of us here are heading towards just such a moment,' said Grimaldi, turning serious. 'But there isn't much time, and destiny doesn't wait. You have to go and meet it.'

'How exactly?' asked Conti.

Grimaldi turned towards his whiteboard, picked up a rag and wiped the board clean. Then he reached for a felt pen on his desk and said, 'Here, let me show you,' and began to write.

45

Gambio slammed down the phone, fuming. *How the fuck could this have happened? What a disaster!* The hotel manager had just called, telling him the news about the surprise visit by the chief prosecutor and the head of the Squadra Mobile. Gambio was about to call Belmonte when his phone rang. It was Prince Khalid's secretary, whom he had met before.

Gambio listened to what the secretary had to say without interrupting, his eyes wide with astonishment. 'Please tell His Excellency I will do my best,' was all he managed to utter at the end of the extraordinary call. *This changes everything,* he thought, walking slowly to the window overlooking the garden and staring at the roses greeting the morning sun. He often did his best thinking that way. Then he reached for his mobile and called Belmonte.

Belmonte arrived half an hour later. 'We have a problem,' said Gambio curtly.

'What problem?'

'You won't believe what happened at the hotel last night after you left and went back to the farm.'

'Oh?'

'Our prince has been a naughty boy.'

'In what way?'

'He beat the crap out of the girl, mutilated her, you know in ... and then had her dumped in a rubbish bin by his bodyguard and his valet early in the morning.'

'Jesus! Nice guy. They should have called me, and perhaps we could have done,' said Belmonte, assuming the girl was dead.

'I agree, but we can't undo what's done. In fact, as things are playing out, it's better you didn't.'

'I don't get it,' said Belmonte, looking perplexed.

'You will in a minute; bear with me.'

'I'm all ears.'

'The police are already onto it. They left the hotel a short while ago.'

'What a mess,' said Belmonte, his mind racing. He was in the middle of finalising arrangements for the big 'game' at the 'farm' and realised at once that this could be a game changer.

'What about *Ars Moriendi*? Most of the big punters are already in town staying at our hotel. We've collected a lot of money. We can't just ...'

Gambio turned to Belmonte and smiled. 'It's not all bad news, buddy; calm down.'

'Isn't it?'

'The good prince has caused this mess, and the prince will clean it up.'

'How?'

'I spent most of the morning on the phone, preparing the way.'

'The way for what?'

'*Immunity*. His Excellency will be claiming diplomatic immunity. I spoke to my contacts in Rome and here in Florence, right at the top. It's all fixed. He doesn't deny that the girl was with him last night and that they had a little 'rough fun' together. All consensual, of course. However, he claims that she was perfectly well when his bodyguard drove her home—'

'And ended up in a rubbish bin, beaten to a pulp?' interrupted Belmonte. 'Come on; how does he explain that?'

'He told the police that on the way home she spotted someone she knew, and asked the driver to let her out. He did, and that was the last time he saw her.'

'And the police are buying this?'

'I'm sure they don't like it and have their doubts, but they have no choice. Orders from above. That's the real beauty in all this; immunity.'

Belmonte was not convinced.

'There's one more thing that's working in our favour.'

'What?'

'I just found out that the girl is alive. She's in a coma, under guard in hospital.'

'And this is helpful?'

'It is.'

'Why?'

'Because the immunity will only work if she survives. If she dies, we've got a murder investigation on our hands. Dealing with an assault is one thing, murder is something quite different. Prostitutes get assaulted all the time, but murder?'

'So where to from here?'

'If all goes well, the prince will return home later today; urgent family business. Hopefully, the girl will survive until then. He won't be detained if she does. At least that gets him out of the country and away from any investigation.'

'There goes our high roller,' interjected Belmonte.

'Not quite.'

'What do you mean?'

'The prince is leaving, but his whole entourage has to stay. They are helping the police with their enquiries. And there's another reason why they are staying behind ... You'll be happy to hear this.'

'I can do with some good news.'

'The prince is sending us another player who will take his place with even bigger stakes, and take delivery of you know what.'

'Who?'

'His uncle. He will arrive tonight.'

'How did you manage to persuade him to do that?'

'That's the price for our silence and our cooperation. The price for cleaning up his mess. You have no idea how many strings I had to pull and palms to grease for this immunity to work. But it will only hold if the girl survives.'

Belmonte looked impressed. It was all classic Gambio. 'What if she talks?' he asked.

'Too late. Immunity. The prince is gone. Case closed. And besides, the prince will look after the girl, generously, to make sure she keeps her mouth shut, or at least has selective memory. We can help him there ...'

'What about the hotel?'

'Come on ... we own it! And the escort agency as well. People will do, and say, as they are told. The entire hotel suite has already been cleaned from top to bottom. The police will find nothing by the time they get their act together. The manager has taken care of that.'

'What about the other girl?'

'She wasn't there when it happened. The prince is admitting everything, except hurting the girl. She too will be looked after. Clever, right?'

'Not bad.'

'The police won't like it, especially Chief Prosecutor Grimaldi and his cocky buddy Conti from the Squadra Mobile, but who gives a stuff! Arrogant bastards,' Gambio burst out laughing. He was beginning to enjoy himself. 'Now tell me about *Ars Moriendi*. Is everything ready?'

'Almost.'

'Good.'

'And what about our *Top Chef* and her friend?'

'Under lock and key at the farm. They have no idea where they are.'

'And will whatshisname play ball?'

'Tristan? Just leave him to me. I think I know how to get to him. He'll make an excellent combatant by the time I'm finished with him.'

'And the other guy, the one from the camp?'

'No problem. He'll be ready too.'

'Good. And what about the doctor? We really need her. The heart ...'

'She could be a bit of a problem,' said Belmonte, lowering his voice, 'but I'm working on it. Leave her to me. But I don't think we can use her in the long run.'

'I don't care. As long as she performs for us this time, all is well. We must have the heart. You know that. So much depends on it!'

'How are things going in Venice?'

'All right, so far. I just made another call to the father. He's arranging the money right now and standing-by for further instructions. He could barely speak. The stress is getting to him.'

'Hardly surprising.'

'But he did insist on one thing ...'

'What?'

'He wants to talk to his daughter before he hands over the money ...'

'What did you tell him?'

'We expected something like that – remember?'

'So?'

'Just do it. Make the call and tell her what to say. You won't have to say anything. As long as they exchange a few words ... Make it short. One call, then you dispose of the phone; usual stuff. I don't see a problem. He'll know she's okay and hand over the dough; done. He's played ball so far, right?'

For reasons he couldn't quite explain, Belmonte felt uneasy about this, but realised he had no choice. 'So, do you now agree that bringing them here was a good idea?' he asked.

Gambio looked at Belmonte and nodded. 'In hindsight, yes. But it's still risky and nothing, absolutely nothing, must go wrong! You understand that, don't you? You know what's at stake here. Not only a shitload of money, but a lot more ...'

'I do.'

'Now go back to the farm, make the call and leave the rest to me. You do your bit, and I'll do mine. The game's on. With all the trimmings!' Gambio slapped Belmonte on the back. 'We'll make a fortune out of this – you'll see.'

Belmonte beamed.

'Welcome to the famiglia,' said Gambio. 'I'm proud of you.'

46

Belmonte was on a high. Gambio's praise and trust had made him lightheaded. What he craved more than anything was within reach: recognition and a more prominent place in the famiglia, next to Gambio. However, he knew this was not the time to be complacent. *Ars Moriendi* was locked in for the next day and there was still a lot to be done. Gambio would not be disappointed; he would make sure of that. Nothing would go wrong.

Before making the phone call to da Baggio, Belmonte decided it was the right moment to bring Tristan and Lorenza together, face-to-face. He was certain that would be the key. It would ensure that Tristan would do his bidding when the time came to play his part. Lorenza of course knew nothing of Tristan's abduction, nor was Tristan aware that she was being held in the underground chamber next to his. Belmonte, a master manipulator and meticulous planner, knew how to use fear and hope, despair and gratitude to bend even the most stubborn personality to his will. All he needed was a little more time – but time was running out.

The cellar of the remote fattoria had been modified to provide secure "accommodation" for the combatants as they were called, while they were being groomed for the game. It was also a safe and practical location for the mobile surgery unit used to harvest the precious organs. The valuable cargo could be transferred to Florence airport and be on a plane within the hour.

Belmonte was satisfied that Nazir was ready. A cocktail of drugs, intimidation, outrageous promises and fear had done its usual job. However, it was the drugs that had worked so well in this case, but it didn't really matter because Nazir was going to be liquidated as part of the climax of *Ars Moriendi* that everyone expected. He would be dramatically killed during the game, but not before huge amounts of money had been wagered, and lost, to pay for the ultimate thrill. Belmonte would see to that. He knew exactly how to rig the game and when to introduce the fatal shot. It was all about anticipation, excitement and timing.

Nazir was the perfect victim. No-one knew he was in the country, no-one would miss him or come looking for him. No-one even seemed to know he existed. And besides, he was young and healthy, with a strong heart that would fetch a small fortune on the black market. The heart had been promised to Prince Khalid to save a prominent member of his family. In return, he would wager huge amounts and attract other high rollers eager to participate in *the* game, accessible only to the privileged super-rich always on the lookout for the next exciting excess. In short, an excellent fit.

Tristan, on the other hand, was a different case altogether, and Belmonte knew he had to proceed with caution. It was vital to keep Tristan alive and release him and Lorenza unharmed when the time was right. To make them disappear would blow the case wide open and propel it into the spotlight, resulting in a major police operation and international media frenzy. It was also essential that Tristan play his part as a serious combatant convincingly. The success of the entire venture depended on that.

The only possible sticking point was the doctor. So far, nothing appeared to have worked to get her to cooperate. As a courageous, intelligent and principled woman, Amena had been exceedingly difficult to deal with. Belmonte could also foresee problems when Amena was faced with a dead Nazir on the operating table and be expected to remove his heart, which only moments before had been alive and beating. Despite all this, Belmonte wasn't too concerned. He would force her, at gunpoint if necessary, to perform the operation. After that, he had already decided to eliminate her as well. A loose cannon like her couldn't be allowed to stay around. Belmonte couldn't take the risk. She would join the other body parts in the acid vats used to dissolve the damning evidence. She too, wouldn't be missed by anyone and would therefore vanish without a trace. Problem solved. It all came down to meticulous planning and never losing one's nerve.

Belmonte put on his mask, tricorne hat and black cloak, unlocked the door to Lorenza's cell and stepped inside. Lorenza sat on the edge of the narrow bunk and looked up, unable to suppress the shiver of fear making the fine hairs on her neck tingle every time she faced the strange man behind the golden mask.

'There is someone here who wants to see you,' said the man, speaking softly, his voice sounding distant and faint. Then he turned slowly around and pointed to the open door. 'Send him in,' he said, raising his voice ever so slightly. Lorenza kept staring at the door. Suddenly, a shape materialised out of the shadows. 'Tristan?' she whispered, not trusting her eyes, and stood up, her legs shaking. Tristan came towards her and embraced her without saying a word. Lorenza began to sob uncontrollably – hot tears running down her wan cheeks – as the floodgates opened, letting her pent-up emotions run free. Tristan just held her in his arms and pressed her to his chest, letting his presence do the talking.

'This is the prize I mentioned,' said the man behind the golden mask. 'You know what you have to do if you want to see her again. If you fail ...' The man paused, letting the threat find its mark. 'It's in your hands. Don't disappoint me, Tristan. Take him away!'

Two men also wearing masks, hats and black cloaks stepped into the room.

'Stay strong. This will soon be over; promise,' whispered Tristan, brushing his lips against Lorenza's burning forehead before the men pulled him roughly away and dragged him outside.

'There is one more thing we have to do before I go,' said the man. He reached into his cloak, pulled out a mobile phone and handed it to Lorenza. Lorenza wiped the tears from her cheeks and looked at him, the question on her worried face obvious. 'Call your father; now,' said the man. 'He will ask you how you are, and you will tell him that you are unharmed and well. He may ask about Tristan. If he does, you will tell him that he is here with you and that he too is well. That's all. Nothing else. Clear?'

Lorenza nodded.

'Now dial the number – and don't disappoint me.'

Lorenza punched in the number and listened to it ring as the connection raced towards Venice. What she couldn't have known was that some of the most sophisticated military monitoring devices were listening too.

Clara stared at her computer screen, a jubilant smile spreading across her face. It was quite late but the entire Squadra Mobile was standing by. '*Yes!*' she called out and took off her earphones. Then she scribbled down the coordinates on her screen and hurried to Conti's office on the floor above.

'It worked! We got it,' she said, holding up a piece of paper. 'Lorenza's father has done an excellent job. He asked all the right questions, took his time, and didn't lose his cool.'

'Where is she?' asked Conti, taking a deep breath. The moment of reckoning had arrived.

Clara walked over to the map of Florence hanging on the wall. 'Right here, sir,' she said, 'at the country property we have under surveillance ... And there is more good news.'

'Oh?'

'Tristan appears to be with her. Here's a transcript of the conversation.'

This is too good to be true, thought Conti. All his instincts told him to be extremely careful. Too often, when something was too good to be true, unexpected disaster was never far away.

'Well done, Clara,' said Conti, heading for the door. 'Let's join the chief prosecutor and the others and put them out of their misery.'

The mood in Grimaldi's office was electric. At first, the news was greeted with a mixture of subdued incredulity and scepticism, but when Clara calmly explained the details of the intelligence report, the room erupted.

Grimaldi held up his hand, trying to silence his exuberant team and bring everyone back down to earth. 'Jack, we must congratulate you. This was your idea,' said Grimaldi, 'and we must also congratulate Clara for pulling it all together. Excellent work! But we mustn't lose sight of the fact that in many ways this is just the beginning. We have valuable information, yes, but how we now use it is critical. I don't have to tell you that we cannot afford any mistakes here. Too much is at stake, and there will be no second chances. Let's take stock and see where we're at.' Grimaldi looked at Conti. As the head of the Squadra Mobile, it was now up to him to take charge. 'Fabio, please take us through the next steps.'

Conti stood up and walked over to the whiteboard. Then he turned around and faced the others. 'As you know, Prince Khalid left this morning on his private jet. He was allowed to return home, effectively shutting down our investigation into the brutal assault on the young prostitute. Because the young woman is alive and likely to recover, his immunity is legal and working. There is nothing we can do about that. But as you know, this isn't the end of the matter. In many ways, it's just the beginning, and the most important missing link has just been handed to us. We must use it wisely.

'This brings me to the – let's call it an "understanding" – between the prince and the chief prosecutor and what this means to us right now. It's all about one man: Gambio, and his evil empire that is corrupting this city. It's time we put a stop to it, and I believe we can do just that. All of you here have a critical part to play in this, and we will only succeed if we work together as a team.'

Grimaldi looked at his friend, impressed. He saw in him a passion and confidence he thought had been buried in tragedy and grief a long time ago. It was obvious that the others in the room were equally inspired by Conti's words.

'Naguib and Cesaria, it begins with you,' continued Conti. 'It's almost time for you to go. Prince Khalid's jet is on its return journey right now and is due to land in less than two hours. The prince's secretary will meet you at the airport with his driver. You know what to do.'

Haddad looked at Cesaria and nodded.

'Naguib, we are all indebted to you for taking this on,' said Grimaldi. 'We couldn't do this without you.'

'Tomorrow will be all about timing and a great deal of improvisation,' continued Conti. 'We have commandos in place and air support is standing by. No-one can go in or out of the fattoria without us knowing about it. We'll have all the resources we need. However, we'll have to meticulously synchronise everything and make decisions on the run. We have no choice but to go in blind and feel our way, and you all know what that means ...'

'Thanks, Fabio. That's probably as far as we can take this tonight,' said Grimaldi. 'Now go home, all of you, and get some sleep. We'll regroup in Fabio's office at six am sharp. *Ars Moriendi* is scheduled for tomorrow night. As you know, everything will have to work around that.'

Conti held up his hand. 'Before you go, there's one more thing,' he said quietly. 'When my wife was murdered by the Mafia two years ago, I made a promise,' said Conti, his eyes misting over. 'Please, help me keep it.'

'May I say something?' asked Cesaria.

Conti nodded.

'When my father was abducted and tortured by the Mafia, and later died a broken man, I too made a promise ...' Cesaria paused and looked straight ahead at something only she could see. 'I thought you should know this,' she added quietly, and stood up to leave.

47

The tiny office set aside for Haddad and Cesaria belonged to the airport police. Conti had made sure they wouldn't be disturbed. Haddad stood by the window and stared at the empty runway. It was well after midnight. *It should have arrived two hours ago*, he thought, trying to stay calm. *What if they changed their mind?* Haddad knew that Grimaldi's daring plan was like a house of cards. If only one card fell, the entire structure would come crashing down. The arrival of the plane was critical.

Cesaria was on the phone speaking to the control tower again. She put down her mobile and looked at Haddad. 'Prince Khalid's jet has changed its flight path and taken a detour to skirt around a sandstorm blowing in from North Africa, but is now en route and should arrive shortly,' she reported, relieved.

'I hope so. If it doesn't ...'

'I know. The entire operation depends on this. Without it ...'

Then a bright light appeared at the end of the runway and moments later, the jet landed, the welcome roar of the engines cutting through the tension in the room.

'It's here!' said Haddad. 'Let's get ready.'

He reached for the neatly folded *kandoorah* on the back of the chair and put it on. Next came the *ghurtah*, the head scarf, followed by the black *agal* to keep it in place. Finally, Haddad put on a pair of dark glasses and turned to Cesaria. 'How do I look?' he asked.

'Like an Arab prince, Your Excellency. Let's go.'

Instead of meeting the plane, the black limousine driven by Prince Khalid's bodyguard pulled up in front of the customs building at the end of the runway. The prince's secretary got out and opened the back door. Haddad and Cesaria got in quickly. The limousine then turned around, left the airport and headed back to the hotel. Haddad reached for Cesaria's hand and squeezed it. 'So far so good,' he whispered. Apart from that, no-one spoke a word until they reached the Medici Grande.

The hotel manager was waiting at the entrance with the liveried doorman to welcome the distinguished guest they had been expecting for hours. *Gambio will be pleased*, thought the manager as he opened the back door of the car. Haddad got out, spoke a few words in Arabic to the secretary and, ignoring the manager, followed the secretary to the lifts with Cesaria walking demurely a few steps behind him.

This was all part of the elaborate "arrangement" proposed by Prince Khalid. It had been agreed that Haddad would take the place of the prince's uncle, who hadn't left his country. This would provide the police with a valuable opportunity to infiltrate *Ars Moriendi* and, it was hoped, expose Gambio and his deadly game. In return, the prince's entourage would be allowed to leave and return home on the private jet and the entire assault matter would be buried and kept away from the media. The prince's staff had been briefed accordingly and were all part of this ingenious charade. In the prince's household, his word was law, and to question it was unthinkable.

Gambio was on a high. He had just received the call from his hotel manager he had been waiting for. Prince Khalid's uncle – the high roller – had arrived, *Ars Moriendi* was on track and could now go ahead as planned. The additional monies promised by the prince had been deposited, and all the other players had also arrived and were looking forward to the "game" with anticipation. Everything was ready to go. It was time to tell Belmonte the good news.

Gambio took another sip of cognac, reached for his encrypted Blackberry and called Belmonte. 'How's everything at your end?' he asked, leaning back in his chair.

'We are ready.'

'What about the doctor?'

'Under control.'

285

Gambio knew this was the weak link. 'How did you manage that?' he asked.

'I told her that *Ars Moriendi* is a play, part of a unique charity performance for well-heeled socialites and that we are expecting large donations for Médecins Sans Frontières – your favourite charity.'

'*She bought that?*' said Gambio, unable to keep the scepticism out of his voice.

'Not at first, but when I showed her our mobile operating theatre, she became quite excited. I told her that if the "fundraising" reaches a certain target, the operating rig will be donated as well and made available for use in the refugee camp she came from. I also told her that this was the reason she and the young man had been brought here in the first place. To help us make sure the theatre is fully equipped and has the necessary supplies to do the job at the frontline. I think that did it.'

Ingenious, thought Gambio, impressed. 'And the boy?' he asked.

I told him the same thing. If he plays his part convincingly and the "fundraising" is a success, the mobile operating theatre will be sent to the camp in Turkey. I think they both want to believe this—'

'And the game? What about that?' interrupted Gambio again.

'Blanks. We've assured him the gun can't go off because it will have blanks. After all, as far as he's concerned, this is a game; a performance; make-believe. And don't forget, he's on drugs. Serious stuff, like all the others before him.'

'What about the heart, the operation?'

'I'll cross that bridge when we come to it,' came the somewhat evasive reply.

'It's important.'

'I know.'

Amazing, thought Gambio. *He's pulled it off!* 'And the arrangements for tonight?' he asked.

'All in place. Our cars are standing by to pick up the punters exactly as planned. After that ... well, you know the drill. The main thing is, we hold the money. I'll take care of the rest.'

'And you will cover your tracks?'

'Trust me, I will.'

'Excellent! Well done, Luigi. Pity men like you are so rare.'

'You are not coming to the game?'

'No. I think it's better I stay away this time.'

'Understood.'

'Good luck!'

'It's not luck we need, but balls,' said Belmonte, laughing. 'You told me so yourself.'

'I'll drink to that; salute!'

48

'They're in!' said Conti. 'It worked. "Prince" Naguib and his girlfriend can now relax in the Imperial Suite before the fireworks begin.' He slipped the phone back into his pocket and looked at Grimaldi. 'Haddad's just been told *Ars Moriendi* is definitely on tonight.'

'Do we know where?' asked Grimaldi, and lit another cigar.

'Not yet. Gambio is sending a car to pick them up. I can't see it being very far out of town, do you?'

'I agree. They'll use one of Gambio's properties, for sure.'

'Makes sense.' Conti paused and looked at his friend. 'That's why you brought me back, didn't you? For a moment just like this?'

'Would you want it any other way? After all that's happened?'

'No.'

'We have unfinished business, you and I.'

Conti nodded. 'Do you think this could put it all to rest?' he asked quietly. 'Once and for all?'

'Perhaps. It's as good a chance as we'll get. That's why it's worth the risk.'

'*Ars Moriendi*; the art of dying. Ironic, isn't it?' said Conti. 'After all the death and mayhem we've seen, it should come down to something like this.'

Grimaldi nodded and watched the cigar smoke curl towards the ceiling. 'How do you want to run this?' he asked.

'We form two teams. One for the fattoria, and one for *Ars Moriendi* – wherever it may be held. The tricky thing will be to synchronise the raids. We must go in at the same time in both places. That's absolutely critical. If we stuff that up ...' Conti shook his head. 'Unthinkable! It would be a disaster. The commandos are standing by. Seasoned pros under the command of someone reliable we both know well and can trust, absolutely.'

288

'Aren't you worried about the hostages, Lorenza and Tristan?'

'What do you think? Of course I am. But can you see a better way? We've both made mistakes before, and it was all about waiting too long – remember?'

'True. What about Rogan?' asked Grimaldi. 'Will you involve him in the raids?'

'Yes. Amazing guy. I want him at the fattoria. He knows both Lorenza and Tristan. To have him there could be useful. I'll be there too. The hostages ... top priority.'

'I understand. As Haddad and Cesaria are both putting their necks on the line with *Ars Moriendi*, I think I should too ...'

'Good. I was hoping you'd say that.'

'It's all settled then?' asked Grimaldi.

'It is.'

'A little sleep? Big day ahead.'

'We should.'

'What did Rogan call it? A moment of destiny?'

'He did,' replied Conti. 'You'd expect something like that from a writer. But do you know what?'

'What?'

'I think he's right. Come here; give me a hug.'

Grimaldi put his cigar into the ashtray, walked over to his friend and embraced him.

'Thanks for bringing me back,' said Conti.

'Back from where?'

'The brink.'

Haddad and Cesaria were picked up from their hotel at eleven pm. As soon as they arrived at the property hidden behind tall hedges and wrought-iron gates twenty minutes later, they were handed their mandatory masks, cloaks and tricorne hats to put on. Several other guests had already arrived and were drinking champagne in a marquee, the chapel ruins lit up with laser lights in the distance forming a spectacular backdrop, suggesting mystery and danger.

Cesaria checked her gun and slipped on the cloak, which was a little too big for her. Haddad did the same, and made sure his radio transmitter was within easy reach. It would be up to him to give the signal for the raid to begin. He still had his doubts about *Ars Moriendi*. What he had been told about the event so far sounded almost too fanciful to be true. Looking around, it was difficult to believe that all the people laughing and chatting casually with each other and enjoying the freedom of anonymity behind their identical masks, had come to witness the tantalising possibility of brutal death and wager on its outcome.

'Let's go and mingle,' said Haddad, his voice sounding strange behind the golden mask. 'Stay close to me at all times.'

'I'm number four,' said Cesaria, pointing to the number pinned to her cloak.

'I'm three,' said Haddad. 'Come.'

Cesaria took a glass of champagne from one of the waiters in front of the marquee and walked inside.

Haddad was chatting to a man with a heavy Slavic accent, when the lights abruptly went out, the music stopped and a clock began to chime somewhere in the distance. Everyone fell silent and an uneasy hush descended on the marquee as the clock announced the midnight hour. Then, a shaft of blue light pierced the darkness and a tall shape dressed in the same costume as all the guests but wearing a red mask, materialised out of the shadows. As the shape came closer, the music returned – stirring organ music this time – suggesting piety and prayer and conjuring up images of kneeling altar boys, statues of bleeding saints, and holy relics in glass coffins.

Belmonte, the consummate performer, doffed his tricorne and took a bow.

'Ladies and gentlemen, welcome to the enchanting world of *Ars Moriendi*, where everything is possible and limited only by your imagination.' Belmonte paused and slowly turned towards the ruins behind him. 'Come, follow me,' he said, and pointed to a stone arch leading into the chapel. 'Let the journey begin.'

Cesaria felt a shiver of fear race down her neck as she followed Haddad into the chapel illuminated by flickering torches and dozens of tall candles, sending crazy shadows dancing across the marble floor worn smooth and shiny by the footsteps of worshippers long gone.

After all the guests had taken their seats on the wooden church pews facing the stone altar, Belmonte explained the extraordinary rules of the deadly game.

Haddad turned to Cesaria sitting next to him in the back row. 'Can you believe this?' he whispered. She squeezed his arm in silent reply, mesmerised by what was happening around her.

An excited hush descended on the spellbound spectators when Belmonte announced it was time to meet the combatants. Belmonte turned around with a flourish and pointed to a gap in the wall behind the altar like a magician introducing his next act. Two young men wearing only loincloths, their faces covered in heavy, almost theatrical make-up, moved slowly into the circle of light in front of the altar, the beads of sweat covering their pale bodies glistening in the candlelight like the tears of weeping angels.

Cesaria gasped and squeezed Haddad's arm so hard, he almost cried out. '*Tristan!*' she whispered, barely able to speak.

Haddad looked at her, surprised. 'What are you saying?' he hissed.

'It's him; *Tristan*. The tall one ...'

'Are you sure?'

'Absolutely.'

Good God, thought Haddad, his mind racing. *This changes everything!* Then he reached under his cloak and put his hand on his gun, the reassuring touch of cold steel helping him think.

Conti reached for his binoculars and looked at the fattoria lit up by moonlight down in the valley below. All appeared quiet. The entire farm was surrounded by commandos waiting for his signal to enter and secure the buildings. Everyone realised that in a hostage situation, extra care had to be taken; timing was everything.

Grimaldi and his team were also ready to go.

Conti's men had followed Haddad's car to the remote property and had pinpointed the chapel ruins where *Ars Moriendi* was about to take place. After assessing the terrain, it had been decided that the most effective way to execute the raid on the chapel was from the air. There was sufficient space for the helicopters to land, and the element of surprise and speed could only enhance the chances of success of the delicate operation.

Grimaldi and the Squadra Mobile were standing by and waiting for the signal to enter the property. They would secure the area once the helicopters had landed.

Conti looked at his radio and took a deep breath. It was now all up to Haddad and Cesaria.

49

Belmonte held up his hand to silence his spellbound audience like a conductor about to begin a performance, paused for effect, and then turned around to face Tristan standing behind him. 'Remember what I told you,' he whispered. 'His gun isn't loaded. Only yours will be; when I decide. Now go and play your part, and don't disappoint me ...' Nazir stood on the other side of the altar, glassy-eyed like a zombie and pumped full of drugs. Belmonte knew he would do exactly as he had been told.

Ars Moriendi needed a loser; everyone was expecting it and all the betting depended on it. Someone had to die, but it couldn't be Tristan. The kidnapping strategy needed him; alive. To ensure that Tristan remained unharmed and survived the evening, Belmonte had come up with an ingenious way to rig the game.

He had two identical .357 magnum Colt Python revolvers. One was loaded, the other – which he kept concealed in a pocket inside his cloak – wasn't. After going through the ritual with the bullets, loading the gun and the drama of spinning the drum for effect, Belmonte would exchange the guns as he turned around to face the combatants. This was quite easy-to-do and wouldn't be noticed in the heat of the moment when everyone was filled with excitement and anticipation. It was a simple, but effective trick that not only made sure Tristan wouldn't be the one to be killed, but would have a significant impact on the betting, as Belmonte controlled the outcome and could decide when it was time to hand the fully loaded gun to Tristan for the kill.

Belmonte turned around again and held up the loaded gun for all to see. 'Remember, ladies and gentlemen, we start with one bullet. I give you ten to one if the gun goes off. One bullet in a drum of six. These are good odds. Please place your bets. Call out your number and the amount you would like to wager. We will begin with number one. Your bet, please.'

Haddad knew it was almost time. He couldn't risk waiting much longer. He had to make his move before the first round of the potentially fatal exchange began.

Haddad turned to Cesaria. 'Ready?' he whispered.

'Yes.'

Haddad waited until number two had placed a bet and it was his turn. *'Now!'* he said and pressed the button on his radio transmitter, which sent the prearranged signal to Conti. Then he reached for his throat, stood up and began to tear furiously at his collar. Crying out and gasping for air, he ripped the mask off his face and began to stagger about before collapsing on the ground.

Cesaria jumped up and knelt down beside him. 'Heart attack!' she shouted. 'Help, someone!'

'CPR,' said someone in the first row. 'He needs CPR!'

Shit! It's the prince, thought Belmonte, as he watched Cesaria pump Haddad's chest and apply CPR. Everyone stood up as well and gathered around Haddad and Cesaria, forming a morbid circle of curiosity. Belmonte realised *Ars Moriendi* was over and he had to move quickly into damage control. But how? Calling an ambulance was out of the question. He had to somehow get the prince to a hospital without one.

Belmonte was desperately looking around the chapel to find one of his men, when he heard the roar of an approaching helicopter. As the chapel had no roof and was open to the sky, the noise was deafening. Suddenly, a bright searchlight illuminated the inside of the chapel as the helicopter hovered above and a voice called out through a loudspeaker: *'Stay where you are and put your hands up.'*

Belmonte realised at once what was happening and knew he had to get away; fast. He turned around and headed for the gap in the wall. As he rushed past Tristan standing at the altar, Tristan tackled him from behind and put his arm around his neck. 'You are not going anywhere!' he shouted as they both fell to the ground. Belmonte reacted quickly. He rolled to his side, trying to shake off his assailant, but Tristan wouldn't let go. Belmonte still had the gun in his hand and realised that time was running out. He raised his hand, pressed the gun against Tristan's chest and pulled the trigger. As he pushed Tristan away with both hands he dropped the gun. Moments later, desperate and covered in blood, he ran through a gap in the wall and disappeared into the dark.

When Cesaria heard the gunshot, she stood up and pulled out her gun. Shouting, 'Police! Stand back!' she ran towards the altar. Haddad got up as well and hurried after her just as the commandos stormed into the chapel with Grimaldi following close behind.

As soon as Haddad saw Tristan lying on the ground – convulsing and bleeding profusely out of a large chest wound – he knew instantly the injury was life-threatening. He pulled out his radio and called Conti.

The fattoria raid had gone off like clockwork. The commandos had entered from three sides at once. The surprised guards had been drinking, and offered no resistance. The place was secured within minutes without a shot being fired.

'How bad is he?' asked Conti.

'Bad.'

'I'll call an ambulance.'

'No time.' said Haddad.

'Jesus! Wait! There's some kind of mobile surgery truck in one of the sheds here. Amena was locked inside it.'

'Amena is with you?' asked Haddad, surprised.

'Yes.'

'Where are you?'

'Close.'

'How close?'

'Very. Minutes ...'

'This could work! Amena has treated more gunshot wounds than an entire college of surgeons combined. If anyone can keep him alive, she can.'

'Get him over here! Find Grimaldi, he knows the way. Hurry!'
'Done! What about Lorenza?'
'Still searching. This is a rabbit warren ...'
'Say a prayer.'
'I will.'
'Me too.'

The police car turned into the long driveway leading to the fattoria and pulled up in front of the big barn. The barn doors were wide open and the inside was lit up with lights so bright, they were blinding like a landing site of an alien spaceship. Jack and Conti hurried over to the car and opened the back door. Haddad sat in the back, holding Tristan. He was pressing a towel against the large chest wound, trying desperately to stem the flow of blood. Cesaria sat next to him, cradling Tristan's head in her lap.

Wearing a surgical gown, face mask and gloves, Amena ran out of the barn and helped Jack lift Tristan out of the car. 'Careful,' she said, and looked at Haddad. 'You do turn up in unexpected ways,' she said. 'Good to see you; Fabio told me. You can assist me; there's no-one else. I'm sure you've seen more of this than I ... Come, I'll tell you what to do. Quickly!'

Haddad, Jack and Amena carried Tristan into the barn and then up the ramp and placed him on the narrow operating table inside the semi-trailer.

'I'll take it from here,' said Amena. 'Naguib, scrub your hands, put on the gown over there and the gloves. Essential supplies and equipment are missing here. We have to make do with what we have and improvise until the ambulance gets here.'

A police officer walked up to Conti. 'We found something, sir,' he said. 'In the cellar ... You should come.' Conti looked at Jack, concern on his face. Things were going from bad to worse. 'You stay here,' he said, and hurried after the officer. Jack nodded without taking his eyes off the operating table.

'Let's have a look,' said Amena, slowly peeling away the blood-soaked towel. She always felt a pang of dread every time she was faced with a situation like this. The next few seconds would reveal if the patient had a chance, or not. Life and death, hanging in the balance. Haddad too, realised what was happening and was watching intently as Amena put aside the towel and began to gently probe the deep wound. Jack held his breath, Haddad did too.

After a moment that seemed an eternity, Amena straightened up. 'He's one lucky young man,' she said. 'Somehow, the bullet missed the vital organs and main arteries and went cleanly through his side, leaving a huge exit wound; right here. What kind of bullet was this? Judging from the size of the wound, it could have killed an elephant.'

'Point 357 magnum,' said Haddad, 'fired point-blank.'

'Ouch! A little to the right and he would have been killed instantly. The main problem we have now is catastrophic blood loss. We have to stem the flow.'

For the next fifteen minutes, Amena worked feverishly to limit the blood loss and stabilise her patient until the ambulance team arrived. It was all about skill, improvisation, hope and luck. Especially luck.

'Stay with me,' she said, pressing the wound and blood vessels together with her fingers. Then a smile lit up her face as she heard the distant siren of the approaching ambulance. *Not long now,* she thought. *The guys will have everything we need.*

The ambulance raced through the open barn door and came to a sudden halt behind the semi-trailer. Two paramedics jumped out and looked around. Amena was shouting instructions from inside. One of the paramedics opened the back of the ambulance and climbed inside to get some equipment. The other ran up the ramp with his kit.

During the next twenty minutes it was touch and go. After that, the drugs kicked in and the crisis appeared to be over, for now. 'He's young and a fighter,' said Amena, and stepped back. 'He'll live.'

'I haven't seen anything like this, ever,' said one of the paramedics, shaking his head in disbelief. He looked at Amena with amazement. 'I don't know how you did it,' he said.

'Never mind,' said Amena, a hesitant smile creasing the corners of her mouth. She pointed to the operating table behind her. 'Lucky we had all this,' she said. 'Couldn't have done it without it. Let's get him to a proper hospital, give him some blood and sew him up. I'm coming with you.'

'Me too,' said Haddad, and took off his blood-splattered gown.

Jack walked over to Amena and embraced her, tears in his eyes.

'Thank you,' he said, overcome with emotion. 'You are one very special human being.'

'From what I've heard from Dr Rosen, you're not too bad yourself,' replied Amena, and hurried to the ambulance.

50

Conti followed the commando down the stone stairs leading into the cellar.

'There,' said the officer, and pointed to a steel door at the end of a damp, dimly lit corridor. 'This was hidden behind a movable wooden partition we broke down earlier.'

'Can't you open it?'

'Solid steel with an electronic digital lock; there. We would need heavy equipment; lots of noise. If there's someone in there ...'

'Good point. Go and lean on one of the security guards. Someone must know the combination. Do what you must; quickly!'

'Pleasure, sir.'

Conti hurried back upstairs to get Jack, who was still in the barn. 'How is he?' he asked.

'The ambulance just left. Dr Algafari saved him. It was incredible. She went with them to the hospital. All going well, Tristan should be all right.'

'That's a relief!'

'Sure is. No trace of Lorenza?'

'Not yet.'

'But she was here when the call was made!'

'I know.'

'And you said ...'

'Yes, we had the place under surveillance. No-one could have left here without us knowing about it. That's what worries me.'

The officer returned a few minutes later, grinning broadly. 'Got it,' he said, rubbing his knuckles.

'Let's see what's behind that door,' said Conti, and followed the officer downstairs.

Taking his time, the officer punched in the numbers. A green light began to flash as the door clicked open, revealing another dark corridor behind it, the wet, vaulted ceiling covered in clumps of moss, glistening like green eyes of ghouls watching from above. Jack's stomach began to churn as he followed the officer inside.

Conti too, felt uneasy. 'What does this look like to you?' he asked.

'A medieval prison,' said Jack, unable to suppress a feeling of dread, the silence, rusty chains and dank smell conjuring up images of torture, torn flesh, even death.

'You never get used to it, do you?' said Conti. 'The uncertainty is the worst, not knowing what to expect.'

The commando in front of them turned on his powerful torch, adjusted his machine gun and began to methodically search the corridor. Several rusty iron doors were set into the wall on their left, like cell doors in a dungeon. The commando opened the first door and looked inside. 'Empty,' he said, and moved along. The tiny, dark cell behind the second door was empty too. By now, they had reached the end of the corridor and there was only one door left.

The commando looked at Conti.

'Doesn't make sense,' said Conti. 'Why have a state-of-the-art security door to protect this junk? Go on ...'

The commando opened the door and looked inside, the beam of the torchlight creeping along the stone floor like an accusing finger of a ghost.

'There!' said the commando. Jack pushed past him, stepped into the room and gasped.

Lorenza was lying curled up in a foetal position on a narrow bunk, with her back turned towards the door. It was impossible to tell if she was dead or alive. Jack walked slowly towards the bunk. 'It's me; Jack,' he said quietly, resisting the temptation to lean forward and touch her. At first, there was no movement, then Lorenza began to turn around to face the light.

'Jack?' she said, shielding her eyes from the glare of the torchlight with her hand.

'Yes!' said Jack. He sat down on the edge of the bed and embraced Lorenza, who by now was shaking uncontrollably like a brittle leaf in a stiff autumn breeze.

Lorenza was taken by the police to her grandparents' villa. A medical officer examined her there and pronounced her unharmed, at least physically. After that, she was questioned by Conti and Cesaria.

Da Baggio and the countess arrived by car from Venice four hours later. The kidnapping crisis appeared to be over. The only cloud hovering over the joy and relief of finding Lorenza alive, was Tristan and his brush with death.

The countess walked into the hospital ward, looking for Tristan's room. The policeman at the door checked her ID, and it was only after he had spoken to Conti on the phone that she was allowed to enter.

Jack sat in a chair facing the bed, asleep. Tristan was lying propped up in bed with all kinds of tubes and monitoring devices attached to his arms and chest. He turned his head towards the door as the countess entered.

Putting on a brave face, she walked over to the bed. 'Is there any part of you I can touch without causing more damage?' she said, her eyes misting over.

'Earlobes might be the safest,' replied Tristan, a hint of a smile creeping across his ashen face. 'Great to see you.'

'I told you, taking up gambling can be dangerous,' continued the countess, going along with the banter and finding it reassuring. Tristan appeared alert and in good spirits despite his serious injuries.

Jack opened his eyes and looked at the countess. 'I told him the same thing,' he said. 'At least now he knows to stay away from Russian roulette!'

The countess turned around. 'I don't know about you two,' she said, pretending to be cross. 'Every time you do something together, it ends ...' The countess threw her hands up in the air, 'like – like this!'

'Here we go,' said Jack.

The countess walked over to Jack and put her hand on his shoulder. 'Wonderful news about Lorenza,' she said, turning serious. 'You should have seen Leonardo and the grandparents ... Words can't describe how grateful they are for what you two have done.'

'See? We're back in the good books already, mate,' said Jack, pointing a finger at Tristan.

The countess shook her head. 'So, where to from here?' she asked. She pulled up a chair and sat down next to Jack.

'Conti is bringing Gambio in later this morning for questioning. That should be interesting. He's a slippery customer; unpredictable and dangerous. There's no doubt he's involved in all this; the abduction, *Ars Moriendi* and a recent triple murder right here in town.'

'What about you?'

'For me, it's back to *The Forgotten Painting* ... Can't wait.'

'Your manuscript?'

'Yes. What happened at the palazzo a few days ago changes everything. Now that we know who that mystery man is in the picture, a whole new chapter has opened up ... new possibilities; fascinating.'

'It's all about that book – *al-Qanun*,' said Tristan. 'He wants to find it; for Alexandra. You watch.'

Jack turned to the countess. 'Almost back to the old Tristan. A mere bullet can't stop this guy.'

'He's right though, isn't he?'

Jack shrugged. 'More questions than answers,' he said, sidestepping the question, 'but exciting stuff, don't you think?'

The countess nodded, smiling. 'Sure. Have you spoken to Leonardo about all this?'

'Only briefly. Lorenza's abduction and Tristan here have overshadowed everything. It didn't seem important at the time. But he did mention one thing ...'

'What?'

'A family chronicle—'

'Here we go. What did I tell you?' interrupted Tristan.

'Interesting. Have you told Alexandra about Osman da Baggio, the mystery physician in the picture?' asked the countess. 'I'm sure she'd love to know.'

'Not yet. As Tristan here isn't going anywhere for a while, I was thinking of going to Sydney for a few days. I'll tell her then. Surprise visit ... Haven't been home for ages.'

'Will do you good, after all that's happened.'

'Leonardo is taking Lorenza back to Venice as soon as she's finished with the police. He wants to get her away from here. I'm going with them to pick up my stuff—'

'And have a peek at that chronicle, I bet,' interrupted Tristan, 'before you go to Sydney and talk to Alexandra.'

Jack just looked at Tristan, but didn't reply.

'Lucky the money wasn't paid over,' said the countess.

'Lucky all right. At least now, Lorenza can get on with her restaurant plans.'

'The whole thing is so weird,' said the countess. 'Like a bad dream. The abductions, handing over the recipes; everything. None of it makes any sense. Crazy.'

'What about you?' asked Jack, changing direction.

'I'm staying here with Tristan.'

'I thought you might. I told Conti I want to stay on the case until we nail the bastard who did this to Tristan.'

'The guy got away, didn't he?'

'We'll find him.'

'And this is okay with Conti and the Squadra? You staying "on the case" as you put it?' asked the countess, a sparkle in her eyes.

Jack shrugged. 'Italians are different. They understand stuff like this.'

'I don't know what you mean.'

'Passion.'

'Ah. Is that what this is? Nothing to do with an exciting new story for another book, perhaps?'

Jack looked at the countess and smiled. 'It could have something to do with it, I suppose,' he conceded. 'And besides, incorrigible rascals never change. You told me so many times yourself.'

'Hear, hear,' said Tristan, grinning cheerfully from plastic tube to bandaged ear.

'You stay out of this, mate, and concentrate on your recovery. I'll be back in a week.'

'To see how Conti and the Squadra Mobile are doing?' asked Tristan. 'Keep an eye on things?'

'No, to keep an eye on you!'

'I give up,' said the countess. 'I can see the staff here will have their hands full, dealing with this patient and his mate.'

'You think so?'

51

Gambio slammed down the phone, stunned. *Porca miseria!* he fumed, carefully going over the telephone conversation with Belmonte for a second time. *Outwitted by Conti and an Arab prince; a bloody Muslim! Unthinkable! After I arranged immunity for that scum!* He had to admit that switching the wealthy uncle for a policeman and turning *Ars Moriendi* into a humiliating fiasco in return for getting Prince Khalid out of the country, had been a stroke of genius.

Gambio realised if what Belmonte had just told him was true, a visit from the police was only a matter of time. Chief Prosecutor Grimaldi and Chief Superintendent Conti would see to that. It was time to fight back.

Gambio reached for his phone and called his lawyer. He had been in situations like this before and knew the next few hours were critical. He also knew exactly what had to be done. His lawyer would contact all the right people in all the right places and alert them to what was about to happen. For various reasons, they would do what was necessary to make sure that Gambio stayed well out of the reach of the law and remained untouched. It was time to call in favours and apply pressure where needed. Quickly.

Alfonso Giuliani had been Gambio's trusted lawyer for years. With offices in Florence, Rome, London and New York, his firm was well-positioned to look after his notorious client and his many shady business interests. A ruthless, master tactician who knew how to exploit every legal loophole, make evidence disappear or witnesses change their minds, and seize every opportunity to obstruct and delay by bribing or intimidating those in power, he had been able to successfully navigate the treacherous waters of the law for years to keep his client out of trouble.

Giuliani arrived just after four in the morning. Over the next few hours, lawyer and client locked themselves into Gambio's study to work out the best way to deal with the situation. An arrogant man of irrepressible confidence, Gambio didn't believe in defence, only attack. By the time he received a visit from the Squadra Mobile later that morning asking him to help them with their enquiries – a euphemism for being brought in for questioning – he was ready.

Conti had received clear instructions from the commissioner to play everything strictly 'by the book'. Grimaldi had warned him about Giuliani and his fearsome reputation. He had also warned him that despite everything that had happened that morning, evidence obtained so far to link Gambio to the crimes was questionable – tenuous at best. More was needed; much more …

The men who had been arrested at the fattoria and questioned about the abduction were unimportant foot soldiers who knew little and kept their mouths shut, as expected by the Cosa Nostra code of silence. They would accept whatever was coming without question, knowing that they would be looked after. They also knew what would happen if they didn't. The man in charge who had shot Tristan and could perhaps implicate Gambio, had slipped through the net and was on the run.

However, the biggest problem was something else: the high rollers arrested in the chapel ruins during the raid. Grimaldi was stunned when he found out who was among them and realised at once that he had to tread carefully. He had already received pressure from above to be circumspect, discreet and proceed with caution to avoid possible scandal and embarrassment in high places. Grimaldi was furious; it had all the hallmarks of another cover-up.

Conti decided to question Gambio only about the fattoria and stay away from *Ars Moriendi* altogether for the time being. He knew that would unsettle a man like Gambio, who would have expected *Ars Moriendi* to dominate the interview.

'We meet again, Chief Superintendent,' said Gambio affably as he and Giuliani were shown into Conti's office. 'And so soon. What can I do for you?'

He's good, thought Conti. He lit a cigarette and for a while just looked at Gambio. Then he stood up and walked over to the map of Florence hanging on the wall.

'Early this morning, a raid was carried out by the Squadra Mobile … here,' said Conti and pointed to the fattoria. 'I understand you own this property?'

'That's right,' said Gambio. 'Do you mind if I smoke?'

'Go right ahead.'

Gambio lit a cigarette, sat back and smiled at Conti.

Conti then took Gambio and his lawyer step-by-step through the fattoria raid. He calmly described what had taken place and what had been found, especially in the cellar under the old farmhouse. However, he didn't mention Lorenza by name, and was intentionally vague about the abduction.

'Any comment?' asked Conti, carefully watching Gambio.

'How extraordinary,' replied Gambio, smiling infuriatingly. 'And all this, you say, has taken place right here just outside town?'

'Yes; on *your* property,' Conti shot back.

Gambio turned to Giuliani and whispered something in his ear.

'I'm sure you are well aware, Chief Superintendent,' said Giuliani, 'that my client has extensive property interests throughout Italy and that this property is but one of many owned by him. The property you are referring to was leased some time ago … My client is shocked and surprised by what you have just told us, but has no knowledge whatsoever of the matters you've raised. We can produce the leases—'

'We can also put you in touch with my estate agent,' interrupted Gambio, 'and it goes without saying, we'll cooperate with the police in every way we can. In fact,' continued Gambio, enjoying himself, 'the police must be congratulated on their efforts here. An abduction involving a young woman; how terrible! We can all feel a little safer now …'

Giuliani tried to stop his client from going any further by raising his hand, but Gambio ignored the obvious gesture and continued undeterred. 'And that is a good thing for Florence, especially after all the publicity the city has recently received during the *Top Chef Europe* finale …'

He's toying with me, thought Conti. *The arrogant prick is sending me a message … Lorenza! He knows that I know he knows and there's nothing I can do about it.* It took all of Conti's self-control to stay calm and not show his rising anger and frustration. And the best way to do that was to turn up the heat. It was time to play his trump card.

Conti opened the folder in front of him, took out a large photograph and pushed it across his desk towards Gambio. 'This was taken a few days ago in Istanbul,' he said quietly, changing the subject. The photo showed Belmonte, Nazir and Amena boarding a plane. Gambio looked briefly at the photo, shrugged and then handed it to Giuliani. If he was in any way surprised or concerned, he certainly didn't show it.

'Do you recognise the plane?' asked Conti.

'Of course. It's my jet, the *Furioso*.'

'What about the people? Do you recognise them?'

Gambio held up the photo and pointed to Belmonte. 'Only this man,' he said.

'And he is?'

'Luigi Belmonte. A business associate of mine. He's also the lessee of the farm …'

'What about the other two?'

'Never seen them before.'

'I can tell you that the woman is Dr Amena Algafari, a Syrian refugee. We found her locked inside this vehicle here … also found on your property. She's being interviewed downstairs right now.'

Conti handed Gambio another photo showing a semi-trailer parked inside a large barn. 'I understand this vehicle is owned by your transport company and is part of the fleet. Is that correct?'

'It is,' said Gambio cheerfully.

'But it's no ordinary vehicle, is it?'

'No. It's a mobile operating theatre. I had it custom built recently and fitted out with the latest equipment …' Gambio paused, letting this sink in.

'Why?'

'I will let my lawyer answer this. He knows the subject much better than I. He was instrumental in—'

Giuliani leaned forward and looked at Conti. 'Have you heard of the Gambio Foundation, Chief Superintendent?'

Conti shook his head.

'I didn't think so. My client set up the Foundation after his father was killed. Something to remember him by. The Foundation supports many charities, especially Médecins Sans Frontières. Several hundred-thousand euros are donated each year to worthy causes.'

'Very commendable,' said Conti, 'but how is this relevant?'

'The mobile operating theatre is owned by the Foundation,' continued Giuliani, 'and is about to be donated to MSF. There is a desperate need for something like this in the refugee camps in Turkey—'

'You may have heard about that terrible suicide bomb attack,' interjected Gambio. 'It only happened recently. A field hospital in one of the camps on the Syrian border was completely destroyed; many were killed …'

Conti was wondering where this was going, but didn't interrupt.

'Dr Algafari was one of the surgeons working there when it happened. My client sent his private plane to Istanbul to bring her and her assistant back here,' said Giuliani, and sat back.

'Why?'

'To help us make sure that the operating theatre we intend to send to the camp is adequately equipped and has everything that's needed. That's why she's here.'

'I see. And what is Mr Belmonte's role in all this?'

'As I mentioned before,' said Gambio, 'he's a business associate. Well-connected in Istanbul. He went there to assist. He offered …'

'What about the young woman we found locked in the cellar?' asked Conti, changing the subject again.

'My client cannot help you there. As we stated before, he has no knowledge of those matters. I suggest you ask Mr Belmonte. He is the one leasing the property.'

Conti closed the folder on his desk and stood up. 'Thank you, gentlemen; you may go,' he said, 'for now.'

Gambio gave his lawyer a meaningful look, the question on his face obvious. Giuliani shook his head and stood up too. Gambio didn't understand why Conti was terminating the interview so abruptly. Too many questions had been left on the table, unanswered. And when he didn't understand something, Gambio became concerned.

'You will be talking to Mr Belmonte, I presume?' he asked, pushing back his chair.

'How do you know we haven't already?'

Gambio shrugged and followed Giuliani to the door.

'And by the way, congratulations,' continued Conti casually.

Gambio stopped and turned around. 'Congratulations? What for?'

'Your recent property deal; quite a coup. I hear you've just secured a building you've been after for quite some time. Right next to the Medici Grande. How fortuitous. Hotel expansion? An upgrade for Prince Khalid's next visit perhaps?'

A flash of anger raced across Gambio's face. He didn't like being made fun of. 'Is this a police matter?' he snapped.

Two can play this game, thought Conti. It felt good having the upper hand for once. 'Not yet,' he said, 'and please don't leave town for the time being without letting us know. We may wish to talk to you again – soon.'

Conti sat in his office, alone, and listened to the church bells. He realised that Gambio and his lawyer were playing a clever game: explaining what couldn't be denied, and denying what couldn't be proved. *They are pointing the finger at Belmonte,* thought Conti. *They must be pretty confident we won't be able to find him. It all comes down to that. Perhaps he's dead already.*

Conti reached for the photograph showing Belmonte, Amena and Nazir in front of Gambio's plane in Istanbul, and held it up. *Who is this man?* he wondered. *Is he the man behind the golden mask Lorenza*

310

mentioned in her statement? And is he also the man behind the red mask who officiated at the Ars Moriendi ritual and shot Tristan? Are they both one and the same? Is it Luigi Belmonte?

Conti was about to slip the photograph back into its envelope, when Cesaria burst into his office, breathless and excited.

'You won't believe this,' she said, holding up a piece of paper.

Conti smiled. Cesaria's enthusiasm was infectious. 'What is it?

'Forensics just finished examining the gun …'

'The one the shooter dropped?'

'Yes, after shooting Tristan. As expected, there were excellent prints all over it,' said Cesaria.

'And?'

'Of course, Forensics went straight to the database—'

'You *are* drawing this out for a reason?' interrupted Conti, becoming a little impatient.

'You won't believe this,' Cesaria said again.

'Try me.'

'The prints belong to … Raffaele Bangarella,' announced Cesaria, beaming.

For a long, tense moment, there was complete silence in the room as Conti kept staring at Cesaria, stunned.

'What did you say?' he asked after a while.

'Raffaele Bangarella. You know, the notorious killer who disappeared—'

'The Archangel of Palermo. I know who he is,' interrupted Conti, 'are you sure?'

'No doubt about it; perfect match. Here, have a look.'

Cesaria handed Conti the Forensics report.

Good God! thought Conti, feeling dizzy. He reached for his tie and loosened it.

'Are you all right?' asked Cesaria.

'Do you believe in destiny?'

'I suppose so. Why do you ask?'

'Raffaele Bangarella was the most-wanted man in Palermo when I was there; Mafia, of course. He was an executioner working for the mob. Known as the Archangel – the angel of death. We were hunting him for years. No-one really knew what he looked like, but we had his prints from one of the murder weapons. He also had a signature …'

'What kind of signature?'

'He only killed on Tuesdays.'

'How weird; why?'

'It's complicated. It has to do with an early Judaic system of seven archangels. Michael is Sunday; Gabriel, Monday; Raphael, Tuesday – see?'

'Incredible! And that became his signature?'

'Yes. And then we were getting close,' continued Conti. 'One of his associates was in jail and wanted to make a deal … he was going to hand us the Archangel in return for a shorter sentence. That's when it happened …' Conti paused and covered his face with his hands.

Cesaria walked over to him and put her hand on his shoulder. 'What happened?' she asked quietly.

'My wife was killed,' whispered Conti, 'on Tuesday, the seventh of January 2014. I was the target, but the shooter missed and shot her instead.'

'I'm so sorry,' said Cesaria. 'But …' She looked at Conti, withdrew her hand and stepped back. 'Surely you are not suggesting …?'

'It was widely rumoured that the assassin was Bangarella, the Archangel. After that, he just disappeared without a trace.' Conti sat up and looked at Cesaria, his eyes misting over. 'Until now!'

PART III
MEDICUS

"There are no incurable diseases –
Only the lack of will.
There are no worthless herbs –
Only the lack of knowledge."
Avicenna

52

Feeling drained and exhausted, Alexandra caught the lift up to the top floor of her apartment block on the harbour. Another long day at the Gordon had taken its toll. Too tired to think about dinner, she stopped in front of the door, opened her handbag and began looking for the keys. *A bath and cheese on toast, again,* she thought, and opened the glass door to the penthouse. *How pathetically boring.*

As soon as she stepped into the lobby, she knew something was wrong: the lights were on, and she could smell garlic. *There's someone in the kitchen,* she thought, *cooking? Impossible!* A shiver of fear washed over her as she remembered a dreadful incident in the very same apartment five years before. As she tiptoed down the hall towards the kitchen, she could hear music and someone humming along with it.

The kitchen door was ajar. Taking a deep breath, Alexandra peered inside – and gasped. Jack was standing in front of the stove with his back towards the door, a glass of wine in his left hand and a wooden spoon in his right.

'Jack? I don't believe it!' Alexandra cried out, dropping her handbag and bursting into the kitchen.

Jack spun around, grinning. 'Perfect timing,' he said. 'Almost ready. Spaghetti marinara; your favourite.'

Alexandra threw her arms around Jack and covered his face with kisses.

'Wow!' said Jack, trying not to spill the wine, 'I must cook dinner more often.'

'When did you get in?'

'This afternoon.'

'Why didn't you tell me you were coming?'

'Spur of the moment decision after we found Lorenza.'

'How's Tristan?'

'Recovering.'

'You could have called.'

'I wanted to surprise you.'

'You sure did that!'

Jack pointed with his spoon to a small table set for two by the window. 'Food first, talk later,' he said. 'Light the candle, pour the wine, and leave the rest to me.'

'Yes, chef. Apron suits you, by the way.'

'This was seriously good,' said Alexandra. She pushed her empty plate aside and reached for her glass. 'It's great to see you.'

'I'm impressed. Two bloke-sized serves that would have stopped a starving truckie in his tracks, and half a loaf of bread. Either my cooking is irresistible, or you haven't eaten in a week.'

Alexandra lifted her glass. 'Both,' she said.

'Ah. And I rather naively thought it was just my cooking. Let's go out onto the terrace; come.'

Alexandra followed Jack outside. The roof terrace overlooking the Harbour Bridge and the Opera House was huge and one of the main reasons Jack had bought the stunning apartment.

'It feels good to be back home,' he said, watching the evening traffic crawl across the bridge towards Sydney's North Shore. ·

'How long are you staying?'

'A few days.'

'Is that all? You flew halfway around the world just to be here for a few days?'

Jack shrugged. 'You know me; rolling stone.'

Jack had offered his apartment to Alexandra as a place to stay when she first arrived in Sydney to take up her position at the Gordon after Professor K's death. That was five years ago. What had begun as a temporary arrangement of convenience had turned into a permanent home for Alexandra, and somewhere for Jack to stay when he was in the country, which wasn't often. When he wasn't travelling the world promoting his books, Jack spent most of his time in Europe or New York with his publishers. But Sydney was still home.

'Come on, Jack, I know you too well. Why did you come?'

'The painting ...'

'The mystery Venetian physician? What of it?'

'I know who he is ...'

Alexandra turned to face Jack and looked at him, surprised. 'You do?'

'Yes. He's Osman da Baggio, a fascinating character. But that's not all.' Jack paused, trying to create a little more anticipation. 'I also know a lot *about* him, which you of all people will find most interesting.'

'Is that why you came? Just to tell me that? Or did you miss me desperately and just couldn't stay away any longer?' teased Alexandra, a mischievous sparkle in her eyes.

'There's more,' continued Jack, ignoring the bait.

'Oh?'

'What you really want to know is if the book he's holding in his hand still exists.'

'Yes, of course. That's what the Nazis were after, and Professor K was so keen to—'

Jack looked at Alexandra and smiled.

'No way!' she said. 'It *does* exist! I know that triumphant grin. *Do you know where it is?*'

'Not yet.'

'What do you mean "not yet"?'

'I haven't found it, but I know where to look.'

'You speak in riddles; tell me.'

Jack reached into his pocket, pulled out a bundle of papers and held it up.

'What's that?'

'A copy.'

'Of what?'

'The da Baggio family chronicles that could help us find Osman's book.'

'His *al-Qanun* with annotations? That's incredible! How on earth did you come across all this?'

Jack put down his empty glass. 'I'll get another bottle and tell you.'

It was well past midnight by the time Jack had told Alexandra how he'd discovered the da Baggio connection and how it all fitted together. It was all classic Jack and it was obvious that Alexandra thought so too.

'That's quite a story,' said Alexandra, 'but hardly surprising.'

'What do you mean?'

'Somehow, you are always in the right place at the right time. Stuff just seems to fall into your lap. You sure have the knack. I could use someone like you in my research team.'

'I guess I'm just a lucky bloke. Tristan calls it destiny.'

'Oh, does he now?'

'You know Tristan ...'

'Have you studied the chronicles?'

Jack pointed to the bundle on the table in front of him. 'There's a little problem ...'

'Oh?'

'It's all in Latin,' he said. 'Not exactly my forte. I'm a boy from the bush, remember?'

'You need someone to translate it for you? Someone fluent in Latin? Someone discreet?'

Jack nodded. 'Exactly.'

'I may be able to help.'

'Latin? Another one of your hidden talents?'

'It's not me, but I may know someone ...'

'You do?'

'Maybe.' Alexandra held up her empty glass. 'You are not the only one with a good story. I'll tell you about mine, but only if you fill up my glass.'

'Deal.'

Alexandra paused for a while, collecting her thoughts and then told Jack how she had been approached by Cardinal O'Brien with an extraordinary request. She told him about the pope's mystery illness, the part she and the Gordon were playing in coming up with a diagnosis and, if possible, a cure – or at least a way to manage the devastating disease. She also told him about the confidential nature of 'Project HH' and what was riding on its outcome.

Jack listened without interrupting, growing more excited with each extraordinary revelation.

'So, what do you think about all this?' asked Alexandra, looking dreamily across the harbour and watching the last ferries pull into Circular Quay below.

'Wow! I'm gobsmacked! I could write a whole book about this.'

'Don't even *think* about it,' said Alexandra. 'I've told you all this in strictest confidence – remember?'

'Only kidding.'

'I hope so.'

'This is truly amazing.'

'It is, in more ways than you can imagine.'

'Oh?'

'Remember how my Exceptional Responders and CRISPR projects stalled and almost came to a standstill because of bioethical issues? Especially trialling CRISPR on humans.'

'I know. Very frustrating. Isis was very disappointed, especially after she sponsored your Chair at the Gordon.'

'Tell me about it. How do you think I feel? But all that could change.'

'How?'

'Cardinal O'Brien offered to help.'

'Oh, I see.'

'If we can help His Holiness and do something about this dreadful disease, the cardinal hinted that the bioethical issues could be resolved. He's completely on side.'

'That's marvellous! I'm obviously not the only lucky one here.'

Alexandra turned towards Jack and pointed a finger at him. 'And you could be playing an important part in all this ...'

'Me? How?'

'I believe Professor K was onto something important that could have a direct bearing on the pope's illness. As you can imagine, I've been studying his papers in great depth and what do you think keeps coming up?'

'Tell me.'

'*Al-Qanun*. What the Nazis were after.'

'And you think Osman da Baggio and his annotated copy of the book could help here?'

'More than that. It could perhaps not only point us in the right direction; it could hold the key.'

'You really believe that?'

'I do.'

'Then we better go and find it, don't you think?'

'Exactly. And we should start right now,' said Alexandra.

'What's on your mind?'

'Translating the family chronicles. Surely that's the first step.'

'Obviously.'

'And I know just the man who will help us do that.'

'Who?'

'The cardinal.'

'Are you sure?'

'Aha. After a little convincing from you.'

'You want me to meet him?' asked Jack, surprised.

'Yes. You two will get on famously. As it turns out, I'm due to meet His Eminence for an urgent progress report. His Holiness had another bad episode ... the pressure's on. You could come with me.'

'When?'

Alexandra glanced at her watch and sighed; almost one am. '*This* morning at ten.'

'You don't waste time, do you?'

Alexandra put down her glass and gave Jack a coquettish look. 'Speaking of wasting time ... are you going to take me to bed, or was the cooking your only show of prowess tonight?'

'Is this a challenge?' asked Jack, rolling his eyes.

'Take it any way you like, buster.'

Jack stood up and turned towards the open bedroom door facing the terrace. 'Race you,' he said and began to unbutton his shirt.

'You're on!'

53

Alexandra had barely slept at all, but felt energised and refreshed. Jack's surprise visit had come at just the right time. She couldn't get Osman da Baggio out of her mind and kept going back to Professor K's notes over and over. She could sense a breakthrough. Jack was still blissfully asleep when she left the apartment. He would join her later in the morning and come with her to meet the cardinal.

Instead of taking a taxi, Alexandra decided to walk to work. She found strolling through the Royal Botanic Gardens early in the morning was not only a great way to start the day; it helped her organise her thoughts and focus on the challenges ahead. Alexandra did some of her best thinking that way.

The pope's latest decline had put her team under enormous pressure. However, it had also given her an important clue of how best to navigate the uncharted waters of this complex, groundbreaking project full of uncertainties. Like Professor K before her, Alexandra thrived on exploring the unknown. By the time she arrived at the Gordon at seven am sharp, she had a clear idea of how to approach the next stage.

Her assistants, Ayah Gamal and Vimal Singh, were already at their desks, waiting.

'This is crunch time, guys,' said Alexandra. 'Let's take stock. As you know, HH's condition is rapidly deteriorating. Knowing what we do about the disease so far, this is hardly surprising. However, I have to brief His Eminence later this morning and give him an update of where we're at, and where we're heading. So, let's see what we've got. Ayah, why don't you begin?'

Ayah had been expecting this and was ready. Alexandra had made sure they always worked as a team: every opinion was given a voice and was entitled to be heard.

'I have successfully sequenced HH's genome. Vimal has done the same with the parents.'

'Vimal, a quick snapshot please,' said Alexandra.

'As expected, the bones were quite degraded,' began Vimal. 'However, I was able to prepare sequencing libraries from a trace amount of DNA I isolated after grinding the bones to a powder, ensuring there was no contamination, of course. The powder was suitable for short-fragment sequencing of the parents' genomes, which was successfully completed using Illumina X-Ten procedures. But for this to work, we had to come up with something new and groundbreaking—'

'Deep Sequencing,' interjected Ayah. 'I then carried out a supercomputer analysis of billions of DNA letters and tens of thousands of DNA differences and matched these up with the worldwide database of known disease-causing DNA differences.'

Alexandra nodded and stepped in. 'This in turn allowed me to review the top-ranking DNA differences from the supercomputer results,' she said, becoming quite animated, 'and match them up with the body of published research material in immunology and genetics and with HH's clinical findings provided by Professor Montessori.' Alexandra paused and ran her fingers through her red hair. 'And of course, you both know what we have to do next, don't you?'

'Engineer a mouse avatar,' said Ayah, 'to help us with the diagnosis.'

'Already well underway,' added Vimal, smiling.

'Excellent. I want you to drop everything and get onto this right now. Pull out all stops. We can't really take the next step without this. I don't have to remind you of the urgency. Well done, team!'

Alexandra and Jack arrived at Cardinal O'Brien's residence at ten and were shown to the drawing room by Father Connor. Alexandra had spoken to the cardinal earlier and had explained why she wanted to bring Jack along and make him part of the team. She had also assured him that Jack could be trusted completely.

'I'm sure we'll be offered one of Mrs Kelly's famous cakes for morning tea,' said Alexandra. 'Don't forget to have at least two pieces ... and lots of praise, please.'

'Culinary Church protocol?' asked Jack, a mischievous smile creasing the corners of his mouth. 'Who's Mrs Kelly?'

'The housekeeper. Apparently, every cardinal has one.'

'Fascinating. I've never met a cardinal before.'

'You're about to; here he comes.'

'Mr Rogan?' said the cardinal, extending his hand. 'Good of you to come. I'm a fan.'

'Oh?'

'I've read most of your books. I found your quest for the Ark of the Covenant particularly intriguing.'

Taken a little aback, Jack looked at the cardinal. In no way did he resemble what he had expected. 'You surprise me, Eminence. I didn't think princes of the Church would be interested in my little literary adventures.'

'Don't underestimate yourself, Mr Rogan. I enjoy reading thrillers. They take my mind off Church business and politics, which can be very tedious.'

I knew it, thought Alexandra. *Getting on like a house on fire already!*

The cardinal paused and looked at Alexandra. 'As you know, His Holiness's condition is rapidly deteriorating,' he said, turning serious. 'He has now developed a chronic inflammation of his lungs and his bowels. The bowel inflammation has resulted in chronic diarrhoea and severe weight loss. All public appearances had to be cancelled. His medical team is most concerned.'

'Yes, I know. Professor Montessori has kept me informed.'

Just then, Mrs Kelly entered carrying a large tray, which she placed on the sideboard.

'Ah. Here comes morning tea,' said the cardinal cheerfully and pointed to his housekeeper. Jack smiled as he watched the little woman place three large slices of teacake on a silver platter.

'Looks delicious,' said Jack. He shot Alexandra a meaningful look. 'I didn't have time for breakfast ...' Without saying a word, Mrs Kelly cut another slice of cake, added it to one of the plates obviously intended for Jack, and withdrew.

Amazing, thought Alexandra, *I don't know how he does it. He hasn't even met the woman!*

'Bearing in mind the obvious urgency of the matter,' continued the cardinal after he had poured some tea for everyone, 'can you please tell me what you have established so far?' The cardinal handed Alexandra and Jack a plate with cake each, making sure that Jack's was the one with two slices.

'All right; this is where we're at,' said Alexandra, taking a deep breath. 'As Your Eminence would remember from our previous discussions, we have recently had some success at the Gordon with childhood immune diseases involving germline mutations. Germline mutations are inherited genetic mutations that occur in the germ cells.'

The cardinal nodded. 'Sperm and eggs.'

'Correct. But what we are dealing with here is an immune disease of *adulthood* involving somatic mutations.'

'What exactly are somatic mutations?' asked the cardinal.

'Genetic alterations – often caused by environmental factors.'

'What kind of factors?'

'Exposure to certain chemicals or ultraviolet radiation would be good examples. These genetic alterations can be passed on by a mutated cell to its progeny.'

'Would these mutations affect all cells descended from a mutated cell?'

'Yes.'

'And this can cause serious diseases?'

'Yes, like cancer. In childhood autoimmune diseases involving germline mutations, the DNA differences are present in every cell of the blood. By sequencing the genome of children and their parents using the Illumina X-Ten sequencer and Seave bioinformatics pipeline at the Gordon, we've been able to successfully identify these DNA differences and then use these findings to pinpoint how the DNA differences cause immune system cells to go "rogue". We have also found ways to correct these abnormalities.'

'By identifying clinical interventions that may be available to address these abnormalities?' asked the cardinal. 'Like already existing drugs, for example?'

Alexandra looked impressed. 'Spot-on,' she said. 'Your Eminence is very well informed on this complex subject.'

The cardinal smiled, acknowledging the compliment.

'Unfortunately, this doesn't work in the same way in adults,' continued Alexandra. 'Somatic mutations present a problem.'

'Oh?'

'Because DNA differences causing the immune disease in adulthood are likely to have arisen later in life, these differences are only present in a few "rogue" blood cells, and to find these is the real challenge here. The proverbial needle in a haystack; a very big one.'

'I understand.'

'I hope I'm not being too technical here,' said Alexandra, taking a sip of tea.

'Not at all,' said the cardinal. 'On the contrary, you are explaining this perfectly.'

Speak for yourself, thought Jack, but didn't make a comment. Instead, he was happily munching on his second slice of Mrs Kelly's delicious teacake.

'In order to find this rogue cell, another quantum leap in sequencing technology development is needed—'

'Deep Sequencing?' interrupted the cardinal.

'Correct again. And the good news is that my team at the Gordon has recently developed the necessary lab chemistry required for Deep Sequencing. We have also been able to develop the complex algorithms to spot the DNA differences only present in a fraction of cells causing the disease.'

'Amazing!' said the cardinal, obviously impressed.

Alexandra smiled. 'This is all very new, cutting-edge stuff, a real team effort,' she said.

'Any conclusions?'

'It's a little too early for that,' said Alexandra, sidestepping the question. 'More is needed.'

'What exactly?'

'As Your Eminence knows, we've been able to successfully sequence His Holiness's genome and that of both his dead parents.'

'Yes, you told me,' said the cardinal.

Alexandra noticed the drumming of his fingertips against the armrests – a sign of his growing impatience.

'In order to be in a position to confirm what I suspect to be the cause of the onset of His Holiness's autoimmune disease, we need to create a mouse avatar.'

'I see. And what do you suspect that cause may be?'

'I hate to speculate, Your Eminence ... especially in a matter of such great importance.'

'I completely understand.'

'And what exactly would be the function of such a mouse avatar?'

'We can reproduce the mutations in His Holiness's genome in the avatar and then breed a colony of mouse avatars we can use to pinpoint how the DNA difference causes immune system cells to go rogue, and how these abnormalities could be corrected. Once we understand this, we can then take the necessary steps to hopefully find a cure.'

'How long would that take?'

'We are working around the clock.'

The cardinal realised it would be pointless to press Alexandra further for answers at this stage and decided instead to back off.

'You and your team must be congratulated, Professor Delacroix. You have made remarkable progress in such a short time. The Church is indebted to you.'

'Thank you, Your Eminence. However, there is one more ...'

'Ah, the matter involving Mr Rogan you raised on the phone this morning before you came.'

'Precisely. But I must tell you that at this stage at least, this matter is merely based on a hunch.'

'What kind of hunch?'

'Something I have discovered in the late Professor Kozakievicz's papers,' said Alexandra.

'And this could be helpful here?'

'It could.'

'In what way?'

'Professor K, as I like to call my former mentor and friend, was a remarkable man. In his extraordinary mind, logic, intuition and genius merged into one. He saw the world through different eyes. In essence, he believed that the answers to all our medical questions and challenges can be found in our genome, because millions of years of evolution had already solved all the problems we are faced with today and all we had to do is find the code to "unlock" the secrets.'

'An extraordinary idea,' said the cardinal.

'It is.'

'And do you believe that too, Professor Delacroix?'

Alexandra looked pensively at the cup in her hand, and took her time before answering. 'Yes, I do,' she said quietly.

'That's quite something, coming from a Nobel laureate. And where does this Osman da Baggio fit into all this?'

'Not sure yet, but this could hold the key.' Alexandra reached into her handbag, pulled out a bundle of papers and put them on the coffee table in front of her.

'Intriguing,' said the cardinal. 'What is this?'

Alexandra turned to Jack. 'Would you like to take it from here?'

'Sure. These are copies of the da Baggio family chronicles I recently discovered in Venice. But in order to appreciate the full significance of what this could mean and what it could reveal, we have to travel back thirty years to where it all began: a remote mission in outback Australia, a German missionary with a Nazi past, and a diary.'

'Sounds very much like one of your books, Mr Rogan,' said the cardinal, smiling.

'It's a case of fact being stranger than fiction, Your Eminence,' retorted Jack, and then provided a brief history of the forgotten painting and its extraordinary discovery.

'And this is where the da Baggio chronicles fit into the story.' Jack paused and pointed to the bundle of papers on the coffee table.

'There's definitely a connection between *al-Qanun* – Avicenna's famous Canon of Medicine – and what Professor K was working on at the time he died,' said Alexandra. 'He was on the verge of a major breakthrough. His papers made that quite clear.'

'And that could have a bearing on His Holiness's illness and what we are trying to achieve here?' asked the cardinal.

'It could. The discovery of Professor K's hidden gene – the KALM 30 gene – and the drug Demexilyn, came about in similar ways—'

'And resulted in a Nobel Prize,' interrupted Jack.

'I see,' said the cardinal, looking at the papers in front of him. 'And you think this could lead to something similar? A breakthrough, I mean?'

'It could,' replied Alexandra.

'But there's a problem,' said Jack.

'What kind of problem?'

'It's written in Latin.'

The cardinal laughed. 'That's not a problem. Certainly not here, Mr Rogan. You need some help with translation?'

'Yes.'

'Well. You've come to the right place. In fact, Father Connor, my secretary, is a biblical scholar and an expert on Church history. He's fluent in ancient Greek, Hebrew and, of course, Latin. I'm sure he would be delighted to help.' The cardinal stood up. 'Come, let me introduce you.'

54

Belmonte walked up to the doorman who was greeting guests in front of the *Sultan's Table* and slipped a large banknote into his pocket. 'Tell Mr Bahadir I'm waiting in the bar,' he said and walked straight past him into the crowded restaurant. Bahadir joined him a few minutes later.

'Do you think this is a good idea?' hissed Bahadir, obviously agitated.

'What do you mean?' asked Belmonte, calmly sipping his Scotch.

'Coming here. After the raid ...'

'We had a small setback, that's all.'

'Is that what you call it? That's not what I heard,' Bahadir shot back.

Gambio had called Bahadir after the *Ars Moriendi* disaster and told him what happened. He assured him it would all blow over soon and it would be business as usual before long. However, he didn't mention that Belmonte was on the run and had to disappear for a while.

Belmonte shrugged. 'Setbacks make us stronger.'

'And the money?'

'Least of our problems. We had to refund it all.'

'Great. What next?'

'We wait a while and regroup. Should give us some time to put our supply chain in place.'

'What happened to the doctor and the boy?' asked Bahadir.

'Not your concern.'

'I disagree. They left from here.'

'They are both fine.'

Bahadir wasn't convinced. 'It was all for nothing then?' he asked.

'Not entirely.'

'What do you mean?'

Belmonte reached for his backpack on the bar next to him. 'I have something for you.'

'Oh?'

Belmonte unzipped the backpack, pulled out a folder and handed it to Bahadir. 'We always keep our side of the bargain,' he said.

Bahadir opened the folder and stared at something inside. It was one of the stunning Ottoman recipes he had coveted for so long.

'Magnificent,' he stammered, his hands shaking. 'What happened to Lorenza?'

'She's back home, reunited with her loved ones, unharmed.'

'And the ransom money?'

'Didn't come off.'

'So, this is all we have to show for the entire—'

'These are the risks we take,' interrupted Belmonte, becoming impatient. He didn't like the direction the conversation was taking. 'Better luck next time.'

'What next time?'

'*Ars Moriendi*, of course. As soon as the dust settles, we set up another game. Somewhere else.'

'And if I'm not interested?'

Belmonte began to laugh. 'You know better than that. Once in ... Salvatore would be very disappointed.' Belmonte leaned forward and slapped Bahadir gently on the cheek, as if he were reprimanding a naughty child. 'And you know what happens if Salvatore is disappointed, don't you?'

Bahadir realised this was not the time to play games, and certainly not the time to provoke someone like Belmonte. Especially after the fiasco in Florence a few days ago. He had obviously lost face, and losing face was the worst that could happen to a man like him. 'So, what are you doing here?' asked Bahadir.

'I have to lie low for a while; you understand, don't you?'

Bahadir nodded. He knew at once where this was heading. 'You want to stay here?'

'A good place to lie low, don't you think? And in the meantime, we can plan ...'

Bahadir didn't reply, his mind racing.

'Salvatore would really appreciate it,' said Belmonte and signalled to the barman to refill his glass. 'And so would I.'

Bahadir, an experienced pragmatist, stood up, recognising an opportunity. Helping a man like Belmonte when he was in a tight spot, as was obviously the case, could come in useful and would certainly strengthen his relationship with Gambio. 'All right. Follow me,' he said. 'You can live in my underworld for a while, literally. We have a whole network of tunnels down there. You can disappear and come and go without being seen.'

'Perfect,' said Belmonte and drained his glass. 'Just what I need. I knew we could count on you,' he added, smiling, and followed Bahadir to the back of the restaurant.

A man standing in the shadows, watching, walked over to the bar, picked up Belmonte's empty glass and quickly slipped it into his pocket. He was the same man who had earlier taken photographs of Belmonte entering the restaurant. Then he headed for the door and left.

Colonel Riza looked intently at the two photographs on the desk in front of him, and frowned. One had been taken at the airport in Istanbul on 1 June, showing two men and a woman boarding Gambio's plane; the other showed a man entering the Sultan's Table earlier that day. *Definitely the same man*, he thought, *no doubt about it*. Then he reached for the fingerprint report, read it and smiled. *The Americans and the Italians will be very interested in this*, he thought, *and so will Haddad*. Then he picked up his phone and called Chief Prosecutor Grimaldi in Florence.

55

Conti walked into Grimaldi's office, closed the door and lit a cigarette. 'You said it was urgent.'

'Don't look so glum,' said Grimaldi.

'Why shouldn't I? We aren't exactly making progress, are we?'

'I just had a phone call from Istanbul: Colonel Riza.'

'Complaining, no doubt, that we let the big fish slip through our fingers when we almost had him in the net, and can't seem to nail Gambio? We are becoming the laughing-stock of European law enforcement.'

'That's a little harsh.'

'You think so?'

'I do. In fact, the colonel thanked us for an important lead ...' said Grimaldi, trying to placate his friend. He knew just how dejected Conti had been since he'd discovered that the man who got away after shooting Tristan was none other than Raffaele Bangarella, the notorious Archangel of Palermo who had once again outwitted everyone. Despite all efforts by the authorities to find him, the man seemed to have disappeared into thin air.

And Gambio's arrogant self-confidence during the recent interview hadn't helped either. One explanation was that Bangarella had already been killed by Gambio and his body disposed of, never to be found, which would explain Gambio's cocky behaviour. Deep down, Conti was hoping it wasn't so. He desperately wanted to get his hands on Bangarella and expose him as his wife's killer.

However, with pressure from above to go easy on the *Ars Moriendi* 'players', and Prince Khalid having left the country with his entourage, protected by diplomatic immunity, the entire investigation seemed to have stalled. Once again, the bad guys appeared to be winning.

'What lead?' demanded Conti, inhaling deeply.

'The call was all about one man.'

'Who?'

'I'll tell you as soon as Haddad and Cesaria get here. I asked them to join us.'

'Oh. That important, is it?'

'Wait and see.'

As if on cue, Haddad and Cesaria entered the room and looked expectantly at Grimaldi.

'You had a call from Colonel Riza?' said Haddad.

'Yes, about this ...' Grimaldi pushed the photograph – showing Belmonte, Amena and Nazir boarding Gambio's plane in Istanbul – across his desk towards his curious visitors.

'You said earlier it was all about one man,' interjected Conti, becoming impatient.

'Correct; this one,' said Grimaldi and pointed to Belmonte in the photo.

'Belmonte?' said Conti, surprised. 'What about him?'

'Not Belmonte; *Bangarella*.'

'I don't understand,' said Conti, looking perplexed.

'The man here in the picture is Raffaele Bangarella, currently going by the name of Belmonte, the man behind the red *Ars Moriendi* mask, who shot Tristan and got away.'

There was silence as everyone stared at the photograph.

'What are you talking about?' demanded Conti, his voice shrill.

'Belmonte *is* Bangarella; absolutely no doubt about it, and he's with Bahadir in Istanbul right now.'

Conti looked at Grimaldi. 'Are you sure?' he almost shouted.

'Absolutely. Just been confirmed,' replied Grimaldi. 'Fingerprints.' He then calmly gave a step-by-step account of what Colonel Riza had just told him about the extraordinary events in Istanbul earlier that day.

For a while, Conti gazed at the photograph without saying anything, the cigarette between his fingers turning to a column of ash. 'Good God,' he said at last, 'can you believe this?'

'Once you look at it closely, without all the emotional stuff getting in the way, it all begins to make sense,' said Grimaldi and then lit one of his small cigars. 'The real question now is this: what are we going to do about it?'

'I will have to return to Istanbul at once,' said Haddad, 'and talk to Riza. His jurisdiction; his country. As you know, there's a much bigger picture to all this, involving the Americans and counterterrorism. It seems to me that Bahadir and Gambio are in this up to their necks. But I'm sure they are pulling the strings here, not Belmonte.'

'I agree,' said Grimaldi, turning to Haddad. 'And I have some interesting news for you, Naguib, that may have a bearing on all this.'

'Oh?'

'Where are Amena and Nazir right now?' asked Grimaldi.

'Lorenza's grandparents have kindly taken them in,' said Cesaria. 'They are staying at their villa right here. But they are desperate to get back to Turkey. I think Amena wants to return to the camp to work, and so does Nazir.'

'Not surprising after all that's happened,' interjected Conti.

'Well, the opportunity to do that may just have presented itself in unexpected ways,' said Grimaldi, obviously enjoying himself. 'And they may not have to go back empty-handed ...'

'Care to elaborate?' said Conti.

'I will. And you are all in for a big surprise. I just received a call from Gambio's lawyer.'

'Rarely good news,' observed Conti.

'This may be an exception ...'

'Let's hear it.'

After the meeting with Grimaldi, Cesaria drove Haddad straight to the villa above the Boboli Gardens on the other side of the river. Tristan had been discharged from hospital the day before. He was recovering at the villa under the watchful eye of the countess, and being fussed over by Lorenza's grateful grandparents. Amena and Nazir were there too, waiting for their future to be decided. The countess knew that

Amena had saved Tristan's life. She had promised to do everything she could to help Amena and Nazir get back to Turkey. Jack had suggested she turn to Haddad to somehow make this possible.

The countess greeted Haddad and Cesaria in the entrance foyer and took them straight to Tristan's room on the first floor.

'How's the patient?' asked Haddad.

'Holding court; come and see.'

Tristan was lying in a huge four-poster bed facing a dormer window overlooking the gardens. Amena sat on one side of the bed. She was holding Tristan's hand and taking his pulse. The grandmother sat on the other side and was rearranging Tristan's pillow to make him more comfortable. Nazir and the grandfather stood at the foot of the bed, listening to Tristan telling a story.

'And then, I was told to go to this bridge, see, and ...' Tristan paused as Haddad and Cesaria entered the room. 'Great to see you!' he said and tried to sit up, just to be gently pushed back down again by the grandmother.

'I can see you are in good hands,' said Haddad, smiling, 'and in much better shape than the last time I saw you in hospital.'

'I may never leave here,' replied Tristan cheerfully, watching Haddad out of the corner of his eye. 'Not because I can't, but because I may not want to.'

'Hardly surprising,' said Cesaria.

For a while, Tristan just looked at Haddad intently without saying anything, the sudden silence turning the mood in the room quite tense. 'You didn't come here just to pay me a visit, did you?' asked Tristan quietly.

Extraordinary. How does he know? thought Cesaria, watching Tristan.

'You are right. I come with some news and it concerns Amena and Nazir,' said Haddad.

Amena looked at Haddad, her heart skipping a beat as fear narrowed her eyes.

'What kind of news?' asked the countess.

'Good news. Jack would call it news with echoes of destiny.'

'How intriguing,' said the countess.

'We can all do with some good news,' said the grandmother and stood up.

'Amena, when I brought Tristan to you after he had been shot, I thought he would die.'

Amena nodded, wondering where Haddad was going with this.

Haddad turned to face Tristan. 'I was surprised you were still alive when I held you in the police car. You had lost so much blood. But despite all that, Amena kept you alive until the ambulance arrived. How she did this was truly remarkable. Only a gifted healer could possibly have done so. Amena, do you remember what you said as we put Tristan into the ambulance? It would not have been possible without...'

'Yes, the operating theatre, of course,' interrupted Amena. 'Without that, Tristan wouldn't be here today.'

'Exactly. And what I'm about to tell you has to do with that operating theatre.'

'In what way?' asked the countess.

'Gambio's lawyer called Chief Prosecutor Grimaldi this morning. Cesaria and I were there. He told Grimaldi that the mobile operating theatre had been donated to Médecins Sans Frontières and instructed him to hand the rig over to the organisation as soon as Forensics had finished with it.'

'How extraordinary,' said the countess. 'And when is that likely to happen?'

'It's about to be released,' said Cesaria. 'They didn't find anything incriminating. The rig was clean ...'

'Wait, there is more,' continued Haddad. 'I have to return to Istanbul straight away – urgent police business – and Grimaldi suggested that—'

'That you drive the rig to Istanbul and take Amena and Nazir with you,' interrupted Tristan calmly.

Everyone looked at Tristan, surprised.

'Exactly,' said Haddad after a while.

Amena stood up, walked over to Haddad and embraced him, tears streaming down her wan cheeks. 'We'll take it back to the camp, you and I, and present it to Dr Rosen. It will save many lives. Is that what you have in mind?' she whispered.

'Yes. You and Dr Rosen saved *my* life. It's the least I can do in return.'

'More echoes of destiny?'

'Sounds like it, don't you think?'

'When are we leaving?'

'First thing tomorrow.'

56

Jack and Father Connor were working late. Facing each other at opposite ends of a massive Victorian partner's desk by the dormer window, they were painstakingly going through the da Baggio family chronicle-maze. Smelling of stale cigar smoke and leather, the large, wood-panelled library with its floor-to-ceiling bookcases was the cardinal's favourite room in the residence, where he had welcomed not only Church dignitaries, but many heads of state and even royalty from every corner of the globe.

It was almost midnight and if it hadn't been for Mrs Kelly's supply of sandwiches, cakes and numerous cups of tea, the two scholars wouldn't have eaten anything all day. The task of deciphering the many diverse entries was all-absorbing and required total concentration, leaving no time or inclination to have meal breaks or any kind of interruption.

Many of the entries were almost illegible, making the text often impossible to read with any degree of confidence or accuracy. This in turn led to speculation and deduction in order to piece together some kind of meaning that made sense. This was further complicated by the fact there were multiple authors and therefore many changes in handwriting and style over the years, often leaving frustrating gaps between entries. Moreover, many entries had obviously been made years after the events, therefore lacking detail, context and continuity.

However, the most reliable signposts were of course the dates that helped to put some structure around the laborious exercise and work out a loose chronology. Because there was no family tree, names and relationships were also problematic and difficult to establish.

Just before the grandfather clock in the corner began to chime, announcing midnight, the door opened and the cardinal entered the room.

'I saw the light was still on,' he said. 'Must be interesting … you've been cooped up in here since early this morning like two conspirators plotting. You don't mind the intrusion?'

'Of course not, Eminence.' Jack took off his reading glasses and began to rub the back of his neck. 'It's more than interesting, Eminence, it's fascinating. We have a small window here into an extraordinary family saga spanning more than four hundred years; amazing stuff.'

'Anything useful?'

'Oh yes.'

His curiosity aroused, the cardinal walked over to Father Connor and looked over his shoulder. 'Can you tell me what you've found out so far?'

'Certainly, Eminence. Needless to say, we've been trying to focus on Osman da Baggio and his annotated copy of the book. This hasn't been easy from the start and it took us most of the day to find something concrete about him.'

'How come?'

'Because as we've just found out, he's referred to as *Medicus,* the healer.'

'Interesting … an important clue, you think?'

'Absolutely. Osman da Baggio is mentioned only once by name,' said Jack, 'in a brief entry dated 1597. All we are told about him is that he was a young man of eighteen, that he escaped from Constantinople and that the sultan's men were looking for him. That's all.'

'What, nothing else?' asked the cardinal, surprised.

Jack reached for his notes. 'Not for quite a while,' he said. 'For almost twenty years, there's no mention of him in here at all, which is curious to say the least.'

'However, he reappears in 1617. Only by now, he's referred to as Medicus,' said Father Connor. 'He is married and has two sons.'

'What makes you think it's the same man?'

'Because of what we are told about him,' answered Jack, 'here …'

'Oh?'

'He was born in Constantinople, returned to Venice as a young man, took over the family business from his ailing grandfather and became a healer. Apparently, an outstanding one with quite a reputation ...'

'What kind of reputation?' asked the cardinal.

'His healing powers were thought to be almost miraculous.'

'How fascinating.'

'And dangerous,' added Jack. 'Medical ideas and remedies coming out of the heathen East must have caused quite a stir in certain circles at the time, especially within the Church. Progressive, enlightened ideas were often viewed with suspicion ...'

'Oh?'

'Ibn Sina – Avicenna as he's called in the chronicles – and his famous book, *al-Qanun* – The Canon of Medicine – are specifically mentioned by name. Apparently, the healer always had this book with him when he saw patients and prescribed remedies.'

'Medicus was in great demand,' said Father Connor. 'Especially by the rich and the powerful who could afford his services. And that, of course, included the clergy. There are two events in his life that stand out and are dealt with in some detail.'

'What kind of events?' asked the cardinal.

'The first took place in 1620. By now, Medicus was in his early forties, a mature man. He was treating a cardinal in Venice who was close to death. All the physicians had given up, expecting him to die, but Medicus managed to cure him. This was seen by some as a miracle, others called it witchcraft. The grateful cardinal whom he saved, later became pope,' Father Connor said.

'Incredible.'

'Here, I have something to show you, Eminence,' said Jack, becoming excited. 'The past is reaching out to us.' He opened his iPad and retrieved the photo of the restored painting showing Osman da Baggio and his patient.

The cardinal looked at the painting for a while without saying anything. 'Are you suggesting this is ...?' he asked quietly.

341

'Yes. Leonardo da Baggio confirmed it. The painting used to hang in the family palazzo in Venice, until it was stolen by the Nazis during the war. They were looking for the book Osman is holding in the picture—'

'The one we want to find?' interrupted the cardinal.

'Yes,' said Jack.

'Extraordinary! You are full of surprises, Mr Rogan,' said the cardinal, shaking his head.

'There is more,' said Father Connor. 'And what I'm about to tell you, Eminence, is truly remarkable and has to do with the second event in the healer's life that I mentioned.'

'Go on.'

'The healer Osman da Baggio – Medicus – befriended Galileo around that time. Perhaps he even treated him for some ailment. One can imagine that two great, enlightened minds had a lot in common. Galileo's life is, of course, well documented and we know that he promoted the heliocentric theory of Copernicus – *De revolutionibus orbium coelestium* – which was published in 1543,' Father Connor prattled on, as people who know a lot about a subject often do. 'We also know that in 1616, the Inquisition declared heliocentrism to be heretical. All books dealing with the subject were formally banned by the Catholic Church, which still adhered to the geocentric philosophical ideas of Aristotle and Ptolemy. Galileo was ordered to refrain from holding heliocentric ideas. But he ignored the ban and went on to publish his most famous work – *Dialogue Concerning the two Chief World Systems* – that not only defended, but promoted heliocentrism, which he argued was based on observation.'

'Because the book was hugely popular and obviously at odds with the teaching of the Church at the time, it couldn't be ignored,' said Jack, pointing to the pages in front of him. 'And Galileo was put on trial by the Roman Inquisition in 1633 and found guilty of being "vehemently suspect of heresy". He was sentenced to indefinite imprisonment and kept under house arrest until his death in 1642.'

The cardinal held up his hand. 'Gentlemen ... please ... we know all this,' he said, sounding a little impatient. 'Pray tell me what this has to do with our Medicus?'

'As it turns out, everything,' replied Father Connor.

'How come?'

'Because it would appear the same thing happened to Osman da Baggio.'

'Are you serious?' asked the cardinal after a while. 'Are you suggesting he was put on trial by the Inquisition for being a *healer*?'

'The text supports it,' said Father Connor.

'Incredible!'

'But unfortunately, that's the end of the story as far as the chronicles are concerned,' said Jack.

'What do you mean?'

'The last entry about all this is dated 1634, the year after Galileo went to trial and it states, I quote: "Medicus was summonsed to Rome and put on trial by the Roman Inquisition. He was found guilty of heresy and sent to prison".'

'Extraordinary!' said the cardinal. 'No mention about *al-Qanun*, the book?'

'No, but—' began Father Connor.

'If there was in fact such a trial, Eminence,' interrupted Jack, there would have to be records. And one would expect that the book—'

'Would have been an important part of the trial,' said the cardinal. 'Crucial evidence, just as Galileo's book was part of his.'

'Exactly. And if those records still exist, they would most likely be …'

The cardinal looked at Jack, put his hand on his shoulder and smiled. 'In Rome. In the Vatican archives,' he said. 'Excellent work, gentlemen.'

57

The heavy semi-trailer reached the outskirts of Istanbul just before sunset. They had covered the two thousand kilometres between Florence and Istanbul in record time, stopping only at roadhouses along the busy highway to eat something and catch a few hours' sleep in the back of the vehicle.

Conti had arranged for the urgent release of the rig from Forensics and had cut through all the frustrating red tape to facilitate the smooth transfer of the vehicle to Médecins Sans Frontières, as instructed by Gambio's lawyer. He even provided a young Italian police officer to take care of all the formalities along the way and do most of the driving. However, Haddad and the officer took turns at the wheel, which made the long trip much faster and less arduous.

Haddad was anxious to reach Istanbul as soon as possible to continue the Bahadir investigation. As an experienced detective, he knew that time was always a major issue in matters involving ruthless, unpredictable players with a great deal at stake.

Amena and Nazir were keen to get back to Turkey as well, but for different reasons. For the first time since the suicide bombing carnage that had destroyed Dr Rosen's container surgery, they felt cheerful and relaxed, and couldn't wait to get back to the camp with the big surprise in tow; literally. They hadn't been in contact with Dr Rosen since leaving the camp, and she therefore had no idea what was coming.

Colonel Riza was waiting for Haddad at the headquarters of the Istanbul Gendarmerie General Command team. Conti and Cesaria had flown in earlier that day and had already been briefed in the Bahadir–Belmonte matter. An officer met Haddad and Cesaria at the

344

entrance and took them straight to the colonel. The others were taken to a separate room in the building, given refreshments and told to wait.

The colonel embraced Haddad and patted him on the back. 'You are a man of many talents, I hear,' he said. 'Convincingly impersonating an Arab prince?'

'It was nothing,' replied Haddad and waved dismissively. 'I was hiding behind dark glasses, a headscarf and flowing robes.'

'Undercover work?'

'Something like that.'

'He did more than that,' interjected Cesaria, laughing. 'The Chief Inspector was very believable and played his part to perfection. Fooled everyone.'

'And so did you,' retorted Haddad.

Conti walked over to Haddad and shook his hand. 'You got here fast. We didn't expect you until the morning.'

'We drove around the clock.'

'I can see that,' said Conti. 'Just as well.'

'What do you mean?'

'Colonel Riza will explain.'

Haddad turned towards the colonel and looked expectantly at his friend.

'There have been certain developments ...' said Colonel Riza, turning serious.

'Oh?' Haddad lit a cigarette. 'What kind of developments?'

'Serious ones, with far-reaching consequences.'

'What do you mean?'

'You'll see in a moment. When we briefed the Americans on the latest developments involving Bahadir and Belmonte, it became clear there had to be a close connection between Bahadir and the Mafia in Florence. Once this link had been established, the Americans became very interested and for the first time shared with us some classified information about Bahadir. Explosive stuff you will find difficult to believe.'

'Oh?'

'But before I tell you about that, there are a few things you should know about Bahadir and his clandestine operation in his restaurant complex here in Istanbul.'

'I'm intrigued,' said Haddad, inhaling deeply.

'For several years now, Bahadir's been working for us and the Americans.'

'In what way?'

'For some reason, which I didn't quite understand until now,' said the colonel, 'Bahadir is very well-connected to the IS leadership at the very top, and has been helping them bring terrorists to Istanbul from the Syrian border.'

'How?'

'Well, you've actually seen him do it. He regularly "recruits" young men in the camps and offers them employment in his restaurant. Only the young men are not chosen at random; they are trained terrorists – mainly suicide bombers on a mission – who have crossed the border into Turkey posing as refugees and need safe passage to Istanbul and a place to hide until they are moved on to their destination, which could be anywhere in Europe. There is a sophisticated terrorist network involved here that takes care of all this.'

'And?'

'Bahadir tells us who they are, when they are leaving, where they are heading and so on. He even provides us with photographs and other forms of ID. We can then keep them under surveillance, monitor their movements and hopefully, stop them before they can carry out their deadly missions.'

'And this has worked?' asked Haddad, looking incredulous. 'Here? Under the very noses of ...'

'Yes it has; so far. In fact, this arrangement has been hugely successful, resulting in numerous arrests. We have uncovered sleeper cells in various countries, arrested bomb makers and foiled many carefully planned attacks that could have been catastrophic.'

'Extraordinary.' Haddad shook his head. 'Something puzzles me ...'

'What?'

'What's in it for Bahadir? Why play this dangerous game? Why is a highly successful businessman with an international reputation doing this? Taking this kind of risk? I don't understand.'

'You will in a moment. Until now, Bahadir's been one of our most valuable intelligence assets, providing information for us and the Americans, who've even carried out successful drone strikes on IS leaders on the most-wanted list, based on intelligence provided by Bahadir. Many were killed.'

'You said *until now*. What's changed?'

'You always ask the right questions, Naguib,' said the colonel. 'You have to understand that the Americans groomed Bahadir in the US for years. He's their man. His handlers are in the States and we get all our information from them direct.'

'Interesting … I wonder how they got their hands on him in the first place?'

'No idea, but when the Americans found out that Bahadir now had links to the Mafia in Florence – Gambio to be precise – they became concerned. Apparently, Bahadir had helped them with the Mafia before – in Chicago – with Gambio's shady enterprises. That was before Gambio returned to Florence and took over his father's business after he was assassinated. However, all this was well before Bahadir came to Istanbul "as a new man" and became a celebrity.'

'So, the Americans are worried?'

'Yes, and it all started with Dr Algafari and Nazir, and that plane trip to Florence you know about. But what seems to have pushed them over the edge is something else …'

'What?'

'I think Chief Superintendent Conti can explain this much better than I,' said the colonel, turning to Conti.

'As you know, the Americans helped us with that telephone intercept that led us to Lorenza,' began Conti.

Haddad nodded. 'They cooperated because of only one reason: suspected terrorist links in Florence,' he said, 'involving Bahadir and his Italian associates.'

'Correct. But their help came at a price.'

'What kind of price?' asked Haddad.

'Information. About Gambio and Belmonte. When we had that breakthrough about Belmonte's true identity a few days ago – the fingerprints—' Conti paused and looked at Cesaria.

'That made it clear beyond doubt that Belmonte was in fact Raffaele Bangarella, the notorious Mafia hit man ...' interjected Cesaria.

'And when the Americans found out that he was being harboured right now, right here in Istanbul – by none other than Bahadir, *their* man – they decided to act.' the colonel completed the sentence.

'Act in what way?' asked Haddad.

'The Americans are shutting down the operation here and taking him back to the States.'

'I don't understand,' said Haddad. 'Why?'

'To avoid embarrassment.'

'Embarrassment about *what?*' said Haddad, raising his voice.

'Bahadir's true identity,' replied Colonel Riza quietly. 'He's their man, remember? Doing business with a ruthless, fanatical terrorist – a corrupt traitor – isn't a good look and certainly wouldn't go down well in the States. If that were to get out, well ... red faces in high places ...'

'Care to elaborate?'

The colonel walked over to Haddad and put his hand on his shoulder. 'This is dirty business,' he said.

Haddad looked at him, the question on his face obvious.

'This will come as a shock ...'

'Takes a lot to shock me.'

'This will; trust me.'

'Go on then.'

'Bahadir is ...'

'Yes?'

'El-Masri,' said the colonel quietly.

Haddad looked shocked. He ran his fingers through his sparse hair and gazed into space. 'Impossible. I spent months with el-Masri.

I've been hunting him for years. I'd recognise him anywhere. Bahadir doesn't look anything like him. I know he was taken to the States by the Americans and then just disappeared, but—'

'He had extensive facial surgery in the States a few years ago,' interrupted the colonel.

'Why?'

'To change his appearance, of course. Hide his true identity, wipe the dirty slate clean before he reappeared.'

Haddad shook his head. 'The Americans are having you on. Playing games,' he said. 'As usual.'

'Not this time.'

'I don't believe it. They can't be trusted; *you know that.*'

The colonel walked over to his desk, opened a file and took out a photograph. 'This is a picture of Bahadir before the operation. Taken at a clinic in Washington,' he said, and held up the photo. Haddad kept staring at the picture and began to walk slowly towards the colonel. With each step, the image became clearer, until there was no doubt left in Haddad's mind that the man in the photo was in fact his old foe. 'This is el-Masri all right,' he said, 'but it doesn't prove anything.'

'His extraordinary inside knowledge about IS and its leaders, Camp Bucca and what was going on in there, and the detail and accuracy of the intelligence he has been able to provide over the years says otherwise.'

'No way! Bahadir isn't el-Masri,' Haddad almost shouted.

'Assume for a moment that he is. Think, Naguib, think! The facts fit the man.'

For a long moment, Haddad kept looking at his friend as something in the back of his mind began to take shape: a memory. It was a memory of a voice he had heard recently in front of Dr Rosen's container surgery. In that instant, doubts began to claw at the certainty he had felt so confidently about Bahadir's identity only moments before.

58

Jack turned off his phone, deep in thought, and walked out onto the terrace to watch the sunrise. It was his favourite time of the day, but instead of enjoying the moment, he tried to come to terms with the disturbing news he had just received from Istanbul.

Alexandra walked up to Jack from behind and gave him a hug. 'You're up early,' she said, kissing him on the neck. 'Why so serious?'

'Haddad just called ...'

'What about?'

'Something out of the past that will rock Marcus.'

'Are you going to tell me?'

'Sure. I'll make some coffee first.'

'That serious – eh?'

'Judge for yourself.'

After the early morning phone call from Istanbul, Jack headed straight for the fish market to do some shopping, and some thinking. He needed a little time and space to digest the extraordinary news, and work out what to do about Haddad's urgent request for assistance. Jack decided the best way to address this was to invite to dinner the people who could help him, and that included Marcus Carrington, Jana Gonski, and of course, Alexandra.

He had managed to catch Marcus just before he was due to go into court that morning. Fortunately, Jana, who worked for the Federal Police, was free that evening, and Alexandra promised to come home early.

Jack was in his element. He loved cooking – especially seafood – and enjoyed nothing more than pottering around in his kitchen with a glass of wine in his hand. Surrounded by his favourite cookbooks, he was preparing dinner for his friends in his apartment. *Fresh oysters, prawns, and snapper fillets 'meunière',* he thought. *Can't go wrong.* Everything was ready. All the necessary ingredients were lined up on the kitchen bench with military precision, waiting for the show to begin. Jack looked at his watch. *Not long now,* he thought. *Time to open the wine and take the canapés out of the fridge.*

Jana and Marcus were the first to arrive. 'What a wonderful surprise, Jack,' said Jana, giving Jack a big hug. 'We had no idea you were in town.'

'You know what I'm like ...'

'A little impulsive perhaps? Now and then?'

'What gave you that idea?' asked Jack, continuing the banter.

'Good to see you, mate,' said Marcus, and handed a bottle of champagne to the host.

Just as they stepped out onto the terrace and before Jack could pass the canapés around, Alexandra burst into the apartment. 'Made it!' she shouted from the door and threw her handbag on the hall table. 'Don't start without me!'

Alexandra hadn't seen Jana for several weeks. As a senior police officer, Jana travelled a lot, and Marcus, who had returned to the Sydney bar, was inundated with cases – many of them complex and high-profile – which kept him incredibly busy. As a former judge on the War Crimes Tribunal at The Hague, he was in great demand.

'All right, Jack,' said Marcus, after the obligatory small talk. 'You didn't bring us all together at such short notice just for a friendly chat and a glass of wine ...'

Jack looked at his friend and smiled. 'You know me too well,' he said and reached for the champagne bottle. 'Haddad called this morning from Istanbul with some extraordinary news.'

'What kind of news?' asked Jana.

'A blast from the past you'll find difficult to believe. I'm still struggling. And it's all about a promise involving you, Marcus.'

Alexandra turned to Jana sitting next to her. 'The storyteller is at it again,' she whispered.

'Loves the dramatic,' said Jana.

'I heard that,' said Jack, pointing an accusing finger at Alexandra. 'Perhaps so,' he continued, turning serious, 'but this story is something else.'

'Are you going to tell us about it,' asked Marcus, smiling, 'or are we going to drown in suspense and champagne?'

'All right,' began Jack, collecting his thoughts. He took a sip of champagne and for a moment looked pensively down into the harbour below. 'I understand Haddad called you a couple of weeks ago from Dr Rosen's container surgery in Turkey.'

'That's right,' said Marcus. 'I couldn't believe he was alive; still find it difficult ...'

'He told you how he survived, and where he had been all these years?'

'He did. Spent years in various prisons. In Yemen, Iraq and then Camp Bucca – that dreadful place.' Marcus paused. 'The birthplace of IS,' he added quietly.

'And then turned up, wounded and close to death, at Bettany's surgery in Turkey.' Jack shook his head. 'Can you believe it? Just like that?'

'Apparently, Bettany saved his life,' interjected Jana. 'Marcus told me.'

'She did. And then he turned up again in Florence, where I met him working for the Turkish Gendarmerie; intelligence,' continued Jack. 'He and Dr Algafari – a Syrian refugee – saved Tristan's life. That was less than two weeks ago.'

Because he had heard it all before, Marcus was wondering where Jack was going with this, but decided not to interrupt.

'And then came the bombshell this morning,' continued Jack, running his fingers through his hair. He turned towards Marcus and looked at him intently. 'After the Luxor massacre, Haddad made a promise – right?'

'Yes, he did,' replied Marcus. 'He sent me a note. He promised to bring the perpetrators to justice, whatever it took.'

'And he honoured that promise,' added Jana, surprised that Jack was opening old wounds. Marcus had lost his wife and daughter in the attack. 'Sheikh Omar and his bodyguard were both killed at Luxor. That was years ago.'

'Quite so. But there were *two* bodyguards, remember? One got away – the worst one, responsible for most of the Aida killings – and Haddad's been trying to hunt him down ever since.' Jack paused to let this sink in. 'A proud man, honouring his promise ...'

'I understand,' said Marcus, 'but *eight years?*'

'For some, a promise has no expiration date,' replied Jack.

'Hm ... so?'

'While he was doing time in Camp Bucca, Haddad caught up with the second bodyguard.'

What! Marcus exclaimed. 'After all these years?'

'Yes. Haddad discovered the man's identity and his name.'

'Sure about this?'

'Haddad seems to be. He's an experienced policeman.'

'Okay.'

'Apparently, Ibrahim el-Masri – that was the man's name – turned informer and began to work for the Americans. That too, was several years ago. Camp Bucca was closed in 2009.'

'What happened to him; do you know?'

'Before Haddad could take action – somehow confront the man, or – he lost him.'

'How?' asked Jana.

'Just before the camp was closed, the Americans took el-Masri to the US for protection, I suppose, and future use. With that, he just disappeared.'

'All right, Jack. Put us out of our misery and cut to the chase,' said Marcus, becoming a little impatient. 'There's obviously more to all this. Tell us about the phone call.'

'After Camp Bucca was closed, Haddad stayed in Syria, fighting with the rebels. He had given up finding el-Masri again, until now ...'

'What do you mean?' asked Marcus.

'He found him again.'

'*Where? How?*'

'In Istanbul.'

'When?'

'Yesterday.'

For a while there was stunned silence, as the implications of what Jack had just said began to sink in.

'Can you tell us more?' asked Jana.

Jack stood up and headed for the kitchen. 'I can,' he said, 'but if we don't have dinner now, my cooking will be ruined.'

Jack, the storyteller, couldn't help himself. He had left his guests with a cliff-hanger. However, he had done that quite deliberately to give everyone an opportunity to digest what he had just told them and have a discussion about it while he was preparing the meal.

'That was amazing, Jack,' said Jana. 'You certainly haven't lost your touch.'

'Hear, hear,' said Marcus. He wiped his mouth with a serviette, sat back and looked expectantly at Jack.

'To cut a long story short,' began Jack, 'Haddad found out that el-Masri is running a famous restaurant in Istanbul – Sultan's Table – as a highly successful celebrity chef with his own restaurant chain and TV show. He even featured recently on *Top Chef Europe*. He goes under the name Kemal Bahadir.'

'Are you sure? How can that be?' asked Marcus.

'Haddad seemed quite certain, but there are complications ... and that's where we come in.'

'What kind of complications?' asked Jana.

'It's all about espionage, intelligence gathering, terrorism and IS. The Americans have reinvented el-Masri, and have set him up in Istanbul to work for them. "Recreated" would be a better way to put it.'

Marcus shook his head. 'I don't understand,' he said.

'They took el-Masri back to the US after Bucca was closed. Apparently, he had valuable information about IS and their operations, and access to the leadership at the highest level ... the Americans used him. They not only reinvented him, but recreated him.'

'What do you mean, *recreated?*' asked Jana.

'They changed his appearance.'

'How?' asked Alexandra.

'They not only gave him a new identity, but a new face as well.'

'Jesus!' said Marcus. 'After all these years? Why?'

'They sent him back to Istanbul after grooming him for years in the States, and with the help of the Turkish intelligence agency, set him up as a celebrity chef. He's an American master spy with direct access to IS. He is running a highly successful operation, smuggling terrorists from the camps on the Syrian border to Istanbul. He puts them up and gives them employment in his restaurant until they can be deployed.'

'And?' said Marcus.

'He keeps the Americans informed about all this, and they share this intelligence with their Turkish colleagues. Apparently, this arrangement has been highly successful, resulting in many arrests.'

'Something tells me there's a *but*,' said Marcus.

'Spot-on. The details are still a little sketchy, but apparently, something's gone terribly wrong and the Americans are about to shut him down and take him back to the States. That's how Haddad found out about el-Masri and his new identity in the first place. Just now.'

'You said he asked for your help,' Jana cut in. 'Help him do what?'

'Keep his promise.'

Marcus shook his head. 'I don't understand.'

'Isn't it obvious? He wants to hunt down and expose the last surviving terrorist who carried out the atrocities at Luxor; the Aida massacre that killed your wife and daughter.'

'If el-Masri – Bahadir – is in Istanbul and Haddad knows where he is, then why wait?' asked Marcus, becoming emotional.

'It's complicated,' replied Jack. 'Not only is Bahadir under the protection of the Turkish authorities and the Americans, he's in the middle of an important operation involving a planned terrorist attack in Paris – huge. Apparently, a number of suicide bombers are in transit through Istanbul right now. Bahadir is too important to be touched. Haddad's hands are tied. However, he has a plan ...'

'What kind of plan?' asked Jana.

'He didn't say. All he said was it's too risky to discuss over the phone.'

'Then how can we possibly help him?' asked Marcus.

'Haddad has an unusual request.' Jack turned to face Jana and Alexandra. 'And that's where you two come in.'

'What kind of request?' asked Alexandra, looking puzzled.

'The question is this: is it possible to reconstruct a face using DNA?'

Jana looked at Jack, surprised. 'Yes, it is,' she said. 'The whole thing is still in its infancy. Early days. But the Belgians have successfully used this method in several criminal investigations, and secured convictions. I've read papers on this and heard about it in seminars – quite recently.'

Jack looked at Alexandra. 'Have you come across this over here?' he asked.

'I have. In fact, we are working on something just like this right now. I have a talented young post-doc from Belgium on my team, would you believe, who's quite a whizkid in this area. You are right; the Belgians have stolen the march on this. They are quite advanced ...'

'How does it work?' asked Jack.

'First, you sequence the DNA of the suspect.'

'You can get the DNA from saliva, a drop of blood, or even a hair,' Jana cut in. 'Basic crime scene forensics.'

Alexandra nodded. 'Correct,' she said. 'But then comes the ingenious bit. We have identified specific genes that determine certain facial features. Hair and eye colour, for instance, and of course, a lot more. In fact, it is now possible to reconstruct a human face with thirty-four per cent accuracy, which is surprisingly effective. When you see the reconstruction next to an actual photograph of the subject, the similarities are striking.'

'Enough to convince a jury,' Jana cut in again, 'beyond reasonable doubt. Facial recognition has come a long way. Just think of the electronic passport controls at the airport, using facial recognition from your passport photo.'

'Wow!' said Jack.

'So, why is Haddad so interested in this?' asked Marcus.

'He wants to reconstruct Bahadir's face.'

'To show what it looked like before the surgical alteration?' asked Alexandra.

'Yes, because—'

'Why?' interrupted Marcus, becoming impatient.

'Apparently, to make sure he has the right man. He doesn't trust the Americans. The reconstructed face would tell him if Bahadir is in fact el-Masri. Haddad spent several months with him in prison. He knows what he looked like. Etched into his memory, he said.'

'And then?'

'He has a plan – to keep the promise he made, Marcus.'

'How, exactly?'

'He didn't say.'

'So, where to from here?' asked Jana.

'Alexandra, if you were given say, a blood sample belonging to Bahadir, could you sequence his DNA and then carry out a facial reconstruction at the Gordon?' asked Jack.

'Yes, I believe we could.'

'Excellent! I promised Haddad I'd call him tonight about this.'

'Then what?' asked Alexandra.

'I'm flying to Istanbul. To help him.'

'I thought you were working on the da Baggio chronicles?' said Alexandra, frowning. 'The cardinal?'

'I am. But this ...'

'When are you leaving?'

'I'm trying to get on a flight to Istanbul tomorrow night. Via Abu Dhabi.'

'Then you'll have time to come to the Gordon in the morning – yes?'

'Oh?'

'Don't look so surprised. The avatar mouse demonstration – remember? The cardinal asked me specifically if you would be there.'

'Of course I will. Definitely. We can't disappoint His Eminence, can we?'

Jana shook her head and turned to Alexandra. 'This is all classic Jack. I don't know how he does it,' she said, laughing, 'and gets away with it.'

'Tell me about it,' said Alexandra and lifted her glass. 'Never a boring moment with this guy! Cheers.'

59

Alexandra was waiting for the cardinal in the foyer, preparing herself for what she knew would be a difficult meeting. It was coming up to nine am as she looked at her watch again, frowning. *He'll be here any moment*, she thought, just as the cardinal's car pulled up outside. As soon as His Eminence opened the car door and their eyes locked, she knew instantly something was wrong. After a brief greeting, Alexandra escorted her illustrious visitor to a conference room on the first floor.

'You look troubled, Eminence,' said Alexandra when they were alone in the lift.

'I am. I just had a call from Professor Montessori.'

'Oh?'

'His Holiness almost died a few hours ago. Another turn – a bad one.'

'I'm so sorry.'

'You don't seem surprised.'

'I'm not. If our preliminary diagnosis is correct, well …'

'Could we go over this again? Right now, I mean. I *need* to know.'

'Certainly. Still no hospital?' asked Alexandra.

The cardinal shook his head. 'His Holiness believes in faith, not science,' he said sadly, shaking his head. 'Much to the exasperation of his medical team.'

'Faith can be important.'

'The whole Vatican is praying for him.'

'Do you mind if Jack, Mr Rogan …'

'Not at all,' said the cardinal. 'I invited him to come along – remember?' The more he knows about this, the better. Especially the great urgency and what is at stake here, and the part I believe he's about to play in all this.'

'I understand, Eminence. Please come and meet my team.'

Jack, Ayah and Vimal stood up as the cardinal entered the room. Alexandra introduced her two assistants and then walked straight to the whiteboard by the window. *They are so young,* thought the cardinal as he shook hands with Ayah and Vimal, *but they are the future.*

'I understand you are leaving today?' asked the cardinal, turning to Jack.

'I am, Eminence. Something urgent has come up in Istanbul.'

'And the chronicles? Rome?'

'As soon as I can.'

The cardinal nodded and sat down.

Alexandra stood in front of the whiteboard, trying to focus. She decided it would be best to approach this delicate subject as a team and with great tact. 'His Holiness is deteriorating,' she began quietly, choosing her words carefully. 'Before we talk about the avatar mice and their function in all this, His Eminence has asked me to go over our preliminary findings.'

'I would appreciate that,' said the cardinal. 'I must know what you – that is *all* of you – think we are dealing with here and what the chances are to … I realise of course that a lot more work has to be done before there can be any semblance of an accurate diagnosis. But time is running out.'

'We understand,' said Alexandra. 'So, this is what we've come up with so far. However, much of this is still speculation and conjecture, requiring further research and investigation.'

The cardinal nodded.

'Vimal, would you like to begin?' said Alexandra.

Vimal looked at her, surprised, and stood up. He hadn't quite expected to be singled out like that. 'As Your Eminence knows, we have successfully sequenced His Holiness's genome, and that of his dead parents,' he said. 'This has been our starting point, and the beginning of our investigation—'

'Yes, Professor Delacroix has already told me about that,' interrupted the cardinal, the impatience in his voice obvious.

'What we have found,' continued Vimal, undeterred, 'appears to suggest that the late onset of His Holiness's autoimmune disease has resulted from inheriting germline mutations in both copies of his LRBA gene: one from his father and another from his mother.'

'What does this mean, exactly?' asked the cardinal.

Alexandra pointed to Ayah. 'Please explain,' she said.

Ayah turned to face the cardinal. 'Because of these germline mutations, all the cells in His Holiness's body lack LRBA,' she said quietly. 'The importance of LRBA is this: LRBA is needed to protect the CTLA-4 protein from being degraded in T cells. For this reason, since birth, His Holiness's T cells have had much less CTLA-4 than normal ...'

The cardinal held up his hand. 'Please, you are losing me,' he said. 'You are forgetting I am a man of the cloth, not the lab,' he added, smiling. Everyone in the room smiled too, and began to relax.

Alexandra decided to step in. 'You must forgive the zeal of the young, Eminence,' she said, further diffusing the tension. 'CTLA-4 is a critical brake on the immune system. It works like this: it blocks and degrades one of the key "go" signals for T cells, called CD86. We have recently done some groundbreaking work here at the Gordon involving immune diseases of childhood using avatar mice, just as we are planning to do now with His Holiness ... both of my assistants have been closely involved in this research. Vimal, could you please tell His Eminence what we discovered?'

'Yes, of course. Loss of CTLA-4 was the primary defect in the young patients' avatar mice, preceding any overt dysregulations of immunity and autoimmune disease.'

'If I understand you correctly, that was all about immune diseases of childhood,' said the cardinal. 'But this is not what we are dealing with here, right?'

'Correct,' said Alexandra. 'We are dealing with an immune disease of adulthood.'

'Then, is all this relevant?' asked the cardinal. She noticed the tips of his fingers dancing on the armrests – the tell-tale sign he was growing impatient.

'It is,' said Alexandra, slightly raising her voice. 'Based on our research so far, we have found evidence that in certain cases another, complementary brake on the immune system is working overtime to compensate for the broken CTLA-4 brake. We believe that these backup brakes may explain why some people with inherited LRBA deficiencies – like His Holiness – only develop autoimmunity after many years. The immune system only goes off the rails when the backup brake "wears out".'

'And you think this is what has happened to His Holiness?' asked the cardinal, looking intently at Alexandra.

Alexandra held his gaze and then nodded. 'Yes, I do,' she said quietly, 'but a lot more work needs to be done with the avatar mice to confirm all this.'

'I see. And how long would this take?'

'We have started the process,' interjected Ayah. 'It's quite complex. Twenty days after the oviduct transfer, a litter of newborn mice are born. These become old enough to be weaned from their mother after another twenty days. Once weaned, a tiny skin biopsy is obtained from each young mouse and tested for the desired change in its genome, corresponding to the change in the patient's genome sequence.'

'And then what happens?' asked the cardinal.

'The mice with the mutation are then bred with one another to propagate a colony of mouse avatars—'

'In other words,' the cardinal cut in, 'these avatar mice would then have the same mutations – the same *disease* that is – as His Holiness?'

'Correct. This not only gives us a better understanding of the disease, but it allows us to look for ways to manage it.'

'About forty days from now, you say?' said the cardinal.

Alexandra nodded. 'If we are lucky, and all goes well,' she said, 'but it could take longer.'

The cardinal shook his head. 'Unfortunately, I don't believe we have that much time,' he said, the sadness in his voice a clear reflection of his deep concern. 'So, where to from here?'

Alexandra turned towards the whiteboard, tossed back her red hair and wrote the words *interleukin 10 (IL-10)* on the board. 'This could be the answer,' she said, and pointed to the board.

'What's interleukin 10?' asked the cardinal.

'Ayah, could you please tell us about interleukin 10?' said Alexandra.

'And please keep it simple,' said Jack, 'I am a man of the pen, not the pipette,' said Jack, trying to keep a little levity going.

Everybody laughed.

'Interleukin 10 is an independent and *complementary* brake on the immune system,' began Ayah, giving Jack her best smile. 'It is a cytokine, a small protein hormone secreted by the same regulatory T cells that make CTLA-4.'

'My team here at the Gordon have shown that IL-10 also degrades the CD86 "go" signal I mentioned before,' interjected Alexandra. 'It does that through an independent mechanism from CTLA-4. We are therefore now dealing with two parallel brakes on the immune system: the CTLA-4 brake, and the IL-10 brake.'

'And this is significant because?' asked Jack.

'You must understand that at this early stage we are to some extent merely "feeling" our way here. Relying on instinct; gut feeling,' said Alexandra, sidestepping the question.

We are quickly running out of options, thought the cardinal, his mind racing. As an experienced negotiator and tactician, he realised that some kind of breakthrough was needed if the pontiff was to be kept alive. With some of the best brains in the country, if not the world, working on this problem around the clock, the cardinal had no doubt that Alexandra knew a lot more about the pontiff's illness and how to treat it, but was obviously reluctant to embark on further speculation at this stage without more scientific evidence. And that would take some time – time the pope didn't have.

Slowly, the cardinal stood up and turned to face Alexandra. 'First-ly, Professor Delacroix, I would like to thank you and your team for the extraordinary work you have done here in advancing this difficult matter in such a short time and with such dedication and tact. The Church is indebted to you, and so am I. But what is at stake here is much more than a human life, albeit the life of His Holiness, the pon-tiff. What we are dealing with here is a moment of history, and moments of history often require extraordinary actions and courageous decisions.'

The cardinal paused to let this sink in. Jack was carefully watching him, impressed by the way he was taking charge of the situation, but wondering where he was heading with all this.

'I understand that science requires proof and cannot, no, *must not* rely on gut feeling and speculation alone,' continued the cardinal. 'However, progress and real breakthroughs often depend on instinct and gut feeling to ignite a train of thought that can reach into the unknown and illuminate the darkness. Instinct and gut feeling are genius fuel ...'

Alexandra listened to the cardinal's words, mesmerised. *Extraordinary. He sounds just like Professor K,* she thought, remembering many a conversation with her mentor and friend about this very subject.

'Would you mind if I ask you a personal question, Professor Delacroix?' said the cardinal.

'Please go ahead,' said Alexandra, a little taken aback.

'Would I be right in assuming that you have formed a view – albeit a preliminary one – about His Holiness's illness and its likely cause, but are perhaps somewhat reluctant to discuss it at this early stage without further investigation and proof?'

How does he know? Alexandra asked herself, her heart beating like a drum. Was he merely guessing, or could he look into her soul – just like Professor K used to? *Does he know me that well? Scary!*

'If you do not wish to answer this,' continued the cardinal, lowering his voice, 'I completely understand.' *Give her a way out,* he thought.

Very clever. Another moment of destiny, thought Jack, wondering how Alexandra would respond.

'You are very perceptive, Eminence,' began Alexandra, sounding hoarse. 'Yes, I have formed a view ...'

Wow! She is going to tell him, thought Jack, admiring Alexandra's courage and resolve. *She's following her instincts.*

'I believe His Holiness's autoimmune disease did not develop in childhood because he was protected by inheriting another mutation from his mother.'

'Did you find such a mutation?' asked the cardinal.

'Yes, we did. Vimal, would you please tell us what you discovered?'

'The protective mutation was a *gain-of-function* mutation in the IL-10R gene, making the IL-10 brake overactive. What this means is His Holiness's mutation is opposite to that of children who inherit the loss-of-function IL-10R mutations that can cause serious, life-threatening inflammatory bowel disease. This mutation has protected His Holiness against developing this dreadful bowel problem and autoimmunity, despite the broken CTLA-4 brake … *until now*.'

There was silence while the cardinal and Jack digested Vimal's explanation.

'Can you please tell us what all this means?' asked Jack after a while.

'As we age, somatic mutations accumulate in the stem cells that replenish our blood,' said Alexandra, warming to the subject. 'Several years before his autoimmune disease crisis, one of His Holiness's stem cells acquired a somatic loss-of-function mutation in his overactive copy of the IL-10R gene.'

'And this resulted in …?' asked the cardinal, hanging on Alexandra's every word.

'The mutant stem cell went on to divide, copying itself to regenerate more stem cells and produce large numbers of blood cell progeny, including immune system cells. All of the cellular progeny of the mutant stem cell had lost the protective gene.' Alexandra paused, looked at Ayah and nodded.

'Instead of having an *over*active brake, these cells were now less re-sponsive to IL-10,' said Ayah, stepping in. 'Effectively, the compensating brake had worn out in these cells because of a somatic mutation.'

'With both brakes now broken in these immune cells,' said Alexandra, taking over once again, 'what is happening at the moment is this: the CD86 "go" signal is unfettered and is driving His Holiness's autoimmunity. This is destroying his red blood cells and platelets, and is also destroying the lining of his large intestine.'

Alexandra paused, and looked at the cardinal. 'I believe that's where we're at right now,' she added quietly.

'And if this continues unchecked?' asked the cardinal, his voice barely audible.

'His Holiness will die,' said Alexandra.

'When?'

'Soon.'

The cardinal sat down and closed his eyes, obviously deep in thought. 'This brings me to my final question,' he said. He opened his eyes and looked at Alexandra. 'Can you think of *anything* we could do to prevent this?'

Alexandra took her time before answering. 'Yes, I believe I can,' she said, tears glistening in her eyes. 'But I would like to give this more thought before we talk about it ...'

'I completely understand,' said the cardinal. Having achieved his most pressing objective, he knew it was time to step back and give Alexandra and her team some space.

Alexandra looked at him gratefully.

'And could Professor K's ideas and this elusive copy of Osman da Baggio's annotated book have a bearing on all this?' asked the cardinal, changing direction.

'Possibly. Professor K was investigating this very same subject just before he died; his papers are quite clear about this.'

'And could this book – *al-Qanun* – perhaps give us some clues or answers?'

'Professor K certainly seemed to think so.'

The cardinal turned to Jack. 'Then we better find it, don't you think?' he said, reaching into his pocket. He pulled out an envelope and handed it to Jack.

'What's this, Eminence?' asked Jack.

'A letter of introduction addressed to Cardinal Borromeo in Rome. He's the Dean of the College of Cardinals. It will open all the necessary doors, especially the doors leading into the Vatican archives ...'

Jack smiled and slipped the envelope into his pocket. 'Thank you, Eminence. Then I better get cracking,' he said.

'I was hoping you would say that,' replied the cardinal, and stood up to leave.

60

Istanbul: 19 June

Haddad met Jack at Istanbul's Kemal Ataturk Airport and took him straight to the Four Seasons Hotel in the famous Sultanahmet district. Jack had carefully chosen this particular hotel, one of his favourites, for a number of reasons. Not only was it close to the Topkapi Palace, the Blue Mosque and the Basilica Cistern, it was also within easy walking distance of Bahadir's Sultan's Table. The luxury hotel, a prime example of Turkish neoclassical architecture, had once been a notorious jail, the Sultanahmet Prison. Many political prisoners waiting for their trials to begin in the city courthouse had spent months languishing in the prison located next door. This unique history gave the beautifully restored hotel a certain charm and appeal. It was therefore the perfect choice for an international writer like Jack.

Instead of checking into his room, Jack left his duffel bag at reception and took Haddad and Cesaria straight to the cosy bar on the ground floor, which he seemed to know well.

'I love this place,' he said, feeling instantly relaxed and at home.

'You come here often?' asked Cesaria, surprised.

'I've been here once or twice; research. I adore Istanbul. It's difficult to imagine that this place was once a prison,' continued Jack, the tone of his voice conspiratorial. 'The rooms are converted prison cells, you know. The walls whisper ...'

'You don't say,' commented Cesaria, raising an eyebrow.

Haddad shook his head and smiled. 'I did as you asked,' he said, leaning back in his comfortable wicker chair. 'A table for two has been reserved in your name at the Sultan's Table tonight. It wasn't easy, I can tell you. But when we told them who you were and where you were staying ... well, the doors opened. Sultan's Table loves celebrities.'

'Excellent, thanks. Did you check if Bahadir will be there?'

'Yes. He'll be there tonight. I told them you wanted to meet him, one famous author wanting to meet another,' teased Haddad. 'Flattery. Works every time.'

'And the cookbook?' said Jack.

'All arranged.'

'Good. We have no time to waste.'

'I agree. So, what's the plan?'

Jack turned to Cesaria sitting next to him. 'Would you care to join me for dinner this evening?' he asked casually.

'With pleasure.'

'I must warn you, this invitation comes at a price,' continued Jack, a sparkle in his eyes.

'Should I be concerned?'

'Only if you are afraid of blood.'

'Are you planning to stab someone, or worse?'

'Close. We need someone's blood; urgently!'

'Who's blood?'

'Bahadir's.'

'You are joking, surely,' said Haddad, frowning.

'Far from it. I'm deadly serious. If you want your face reconstruction based on DNA, we need a sample of Bahadir's blood. *Now!*'

'And how, pray tell me, are you going to obtain that?'

'With the help of this charming young lady here,' said Jack, winking at Cesaria.

'I have a strange feeling about this,' said Cesaria. 'Vampire bait?'

Jack burst out laughing. 'I like that,' he said. 'Nothing quite so dramatic, I'm afraid.'

'Seriously, Jack,' said Haddad, 'what are you planning to do?'

'I'll tell you later, but first let's have a drink,' replied Jack and waved to the waiter at the bar, who seemed to know him. 'Champagne?'

Jack arrived with Cesaria at the crowded restaurant a few minutes before eight. At Jack's request, the hotel concierge had contacted the restaurant earlier to indicate that Jack Rogan – the famous international author – wanted to meet Mr Bahadir if possible. Sniffing a big tip, the maître d' assured his colleague that this could be arranged. The Four Seasons was a lucrative source of well-heeled patrons.

A generous tip, discreetly slipped into the maître d's pocket, made sure he was onside before they were even seated. Jack knew how to oil the wheels of hospitality-cooperation. Cesaria looked stunning in a simple black dress. Heads turned as they were shown to their table, prominently positioned next to the bar and in full view of the large room. With her hair pulled back, Cesaria's striking Mediterranean features were accentuated, giving her prominent cheekbones and large eyes an alluring, exotic look.

'What a stunning place,' said Cesaria. She put Bahadir's cookbook that she had brought with her on the table and looked at Jack. 'Are you sure about this?'

'I am. Are you ready?'

'I think so.'

'Just act naturally. Keep it simple. The rest will follow; trust me.'

Jack had carefully gone over every step of the plan with Cesaria before they came. They had even rehearsed certain aspects of it. However, talking about it in the hotel had seemed straightforward, but now, in the busy restaurant full of people, the plan appeared somewhat daunting to Cesaria. Jack sensed her unease and signalled to the waiter.

'Let's have a drink; martini?'

Cesaria gave Jack a coquettish look. 'Shaken, not stirred?'

'Oh?'

'What we are about to do is straight out of a James Bond movie, wouldn't you agree?' said Cesaria, beginning to relax.

'You certainly look the part,' said Jack, and ordered two martinis. Jack had chosen martinis on purpose because of the distinctive shape of the martini glass.

'What an exciting life you lead.'

'Look who's talking. So, *Ars Moriendi* was just a routine Squadra Mobile assignment then?'

'I've spoken with Tristan. He told me a lot about you ...'

'Ah. You can't believe everything he says. He tends to exaggerate.'

'Why is it I don't believe you?'

Jack waved dismissively.

'And your books?'

Before Jack could reply, the waiter arrived with the two martinis. 'Mr Bahadir will be with you in a moment,' he said and withdrew.

Jack looked at Cesaria. 'We make a good team.' He reached for his glass and held it up. 'Here he comes now,' he added, lowering his voice. 'Ready?'

Cesaria held up her own glass in reply and took a sip. 'Salute.'

Bahadir was in his element. Meeting famous guests and being seen with them in his restaurant was always the highlight of his evening. He liked to bask in the aura of other's people's fame. When his maître d' had told him earlier about Jack Rogan and his request, he had looked him up on the Net. What he found filled him with excitement and anticipation. As he walked up to Jack's table and set eyes on Cesaria, he knew he wouldn't be disappointed. *A stunning young woman and a famous author*, he thought. *How delightful!*

'Mr Rogan, what a pleasure,' said Bahadir, extending his hand, 'I have heard such a lot about you,' he lied. 'Welcome to Sultan's Table.'

'Please, call me Jack.'

They shook hands like old friends and Jack introduced Cesaria.

'Enchanted,' said Bahadir and gallantly kissed Cesaria's hand, aware that many eyes were on him.

'Cesaria is a fan,' continued Jack, coming straight to the point. 'She was hoping you would sign your book for her.'

'With pleasure,' replied Bahadir, obviously pleased to have been asked, and pulled a pen out of his jacket pocket. Cesaria opened the book in front of her and sat back as Bahadir bent down to sign his name. Jack looked at Cesaria and nodded. The critical moment had

371

arrived. Just before Bahadir finished signing his name with a flourish, Cesaria tipped over the high-stemmed martini glass, making it appear that it had been caught in Bahadir's sleeve. The glass shattered on the marble tabletop, spilling the contents over the book.

'I'm so sorry!' Bahadir cried out, mortified, staring at the mess in front of him. Jack quickly reached across, picked up two large shards of glass and began wiping the table with his serviette.

'No! Allow me,' said Bahadir, instinctively reaching for the other pieces of broken glass on the table. As he was about to pick up the long, jagged stem of the glass in front of Cesaria, Jack nicked Bahadir's hand with a piece of glass. At once, the small cut began to bleed profusely, dripping blood over the signature.

'You've cut yourself,' said Cesaria and stood up. Looking concerned, she picked up her serviette and pressed it against Bahadir's bleeding hand to stem the flow. 'Here, let me.'

'It's nothing,' said Bahadir. 'Just a nick. I'm so sorry.'

'Please, it's just an accident,' said Jack. He reached into his pocket, pulled out his handkerchief and stood up as well.

Then the waiters came running and Bahadir barked some orders. In the confusion, Cesaria withdrew her bloodstained serviette and handed it to Jack who quickly slipped it into his pocket, before handing his handkerchief to Cesaria. Still holding Bahadir's arm, Cesaria wound Jack's handkerchief around Bahadir's bleeding hand. 'This should do it,' she said, and let go.

Enjoying the attention, Bahadir smiled at her gratefully. 'Please follow the waiter. He will take you to another table, and please leave the rest to us. Enjoy your evening.' With that, Bahadir took a bow and quickly walked away.

'I told you there was nothing to worry about,' said Jack, enjoying his second martini. 'You're a natural. This couldn't have gone better; cheers.'

'We got lucky, that's all. The marble tabletop was fortuitous and made it easy.'

'You make your own luck.'

'Not always possible. He behaved like a true gentleman.'

'He did, but don't be fooled,' said Jack, sensing where Cesaria was heading. 'In case you're having second thoughts, then let me tell you this: if Bahadir is the man we think he is, he has the blood of hundreds on his hands – brutally murdered in a savage terror attack in Egypt eight years ago. I was there and witnessed it all. And so was Haddad. Close friends of mine were butchered, most horribly. Countless lives snuffed out.'

'The Aida massacre at Luxor. I understand,' said Cesaria. She reached across the table and placed her hand on Jack's arm as a gesture of reassurance. 'It's just ...'

'I know. Look at it this way. We are doing this to make sure, that's all. If Haddad's mistaken, then this'll make that clear beyond doubt. If not, then Bahadir's a monster. Monsters can appear to be civil and charming. I'm sure you've seen it many times and so have I. That's one of the reasons they are so dangerous.'

'Do you think we have enough?' asked Cesaria and opened the cookbook in front of her. A large bloodstain had partially covered Bahadir's signature.

'Sure. Ironic, don't you think? Signed in blood.'

Cesaria felt a chill race down her spine as she looked at the signature and the implications of what it could mean began to sink in. 'And the serviette?' she asked.

Jack patted his pocket. 'Perfect,' he said. 'The book's a bonus. The serviette alone should do it. We have more than enough.'

'Excellent. Ah, here comes the food now. I'm starving.'

When Jack asked for the bill at the end of the evening, he was told there wasn't one. The meal was on the house said the maître d', and handed Cesaria another signed copy of Bahadir's book to replace the one that had been damaged earlier. But when Jack asked to see Bahadir to thank him, he was told politely that unfortunately he wasn't available.

'How odd,' said Jack as they stepped outside. 'At first, he's all over us and then just disappears.'

'Perhaps he's embarrassed?' suggested Cesaria.

'Don't know. It's a little strange whichever way you look at it. Shall we walk back to my hotel for a nightcap and you can catch a taxi from there?'

'You're on,' said Cesaria, who was staying with Haddad and Conti close to the Gendarmerie General Command Centre, and linked arms with Jack. 'As you seem to know this place so well, why don't you tell me a little about it?'

'With pleasure; come ... That huge building over there is the Hagia Sophia, the church of holy wisdom, one of the world's greatest architectural achievements and one of my favourite buildings on the planet. It's stupendous. If you have time while you're here, you must go inside.'

'Couldn't you take me?'

'Love to, but I'm leaving in the morning.'

'Oh? Where are you going?'

'Rome.'

61

Jack got out of the taxi and for a brief moment stood quietly in the shadow of one of Bernini's gigantic columns. The familiar structure formed part of the famous four-row colonnade, extending an open-armed welcome to the faithful flocking to the Vatican. Shielding his eyes from the glare of the morning sun, he looked up at the majestic dome of St Peter's and marvelled at the splendour of Michelangelo's masterpiece, as he remembered the Hagia Sophia he had admired only the night before. *The power of faith,* he thought, *bringing out the best and the worst in mankind. Nothing's changed.*

After going through security, Jack crossed St Peter's Square and went to one of the side entrances he had been directed to. The Swiss Guard at the gate looked at him with undisguised suspicion when he asked to see Cardinal Borromeo. People didn't just walk in off the street asking to see the Dean of the College of Cardinals. But when Jack produced the letter of introduction signed by Cardinal O'Brien, the guard's demeanour changed and Jack was told to wait.

A few minutes later, an elderly monsignor working in the diplomatic service of the Holy See came down a wide set of marble stairs and walked over to Jack waiting in the opulent foyer. 'Mr Rogan? We have been expecting you,' he said in perfect English. 'Please come with me.'

Jack followed the little man through a maze of corridors and up another flight of stairs until he stopped in front of an imposing double door and knocked. Jack could hear a voice call out *"entro"* from inside. The little man opened the door and looked encouragingly at Jack. 'Cardinal Borromeo is waiting for you,' he said and stood aside.

Almost blinded by the bright sunlight flooding into the large room crowded with paintings, Jack looked at the tall man standing by the open window. He was holding Cardinal O'Brien's letter in his right hand as he looked pensively down into St Peter's Square below.

'I never tire of this view,' said the cardinal. 'These days it's the only thing that appears to be constant. We live in troubled times, Mr Rogan. Cardinal O'Brien speaks very highly of you.' The cardinal held up the letter, turned towards Jack and looked at him with penetrating, ice-blue eyes that seemed to belong to a much younger man. Jack held his gaze and smiled, but didn't say anything. 'His Holiness is dying, and according to Cardinal O'Brien you seem to be his last hope. What would you call that, Mr Rogan?'

'I would call it destiny, Eminence,' replied Jack, a little taken aback by the cardinal's curious remark. The cardinal nodded, walked slowly towards Jack and extended his hand. 'So would I. And that is exactly what His Holiness has been telling us all these troubled months: *Trust in faith and believe in your destiny.* Thank you for coming.'

'It's a privilege to be here, Eminence. Thank you for seeing me,' said Jack and bowed his head slightly.

'This is all about destiny, Mr Rogan,' continued the cardinal. 'His Holiness believes it is his destiny to reach out to Islam and broker peace in the troubled Middle East, where thousands are dying every day. He also believes that one of the ways he can achieve this is to address the United Nations in New York and the US Congress in Washington. He's an inspirational speaker with great presence. These historic events were arranged months ago and are due to take place soon – very soon. The eyes of the world will be on the pontiff.'

The cardinal paused to let this sink in.

'In his present state, His Holiness is too ill to travel. Unless there's a dramatic improvement in his health, everything will have to be cancelled. The consequences would be, well ...' The cardinal didn't complete his sentence. He didn't believe in failure, only solutions. Instead, he turned towards Jack, looking worried. 'His Holiness may not even be ... I would like to ask you a question, Mr Rogan, and you must give me a straight answer.'

'Certainly, Eminence.'

'Do you seriously believe that a sixteenth-century medical text, with origins reaching back to much earlier times still, could contain answers that may have a bearing on this situation? Could Osman da Baggio's annotated copy of *al-Qanun* contain information important enough to influence the latest, cutting-edge medical research and the way we look at and treat, certain life-threatening diseases?'

Jack took his time before replying. He realised that everything was hanging in the balance and may well depend on how he answered. He had to choose his words carefully.

'Yes, I do.'

'Why?'

'Because I've seen it happen before, Eminence. An ancient Aztec codex and a Mexican jungle plant were instrumental in facilitating a stunning medical breakthrough that resulted in the discovery of a certain gene, and a drug that has been a game changer. In fact, Professor Delacroix has recently been awarded the Nobel Prize for that discovery.'

'The KALM 30 gene and Demexilyn,' interjected the cardinal.

'Your Eminence is very well informed,' said Jack, surprised.

'Cardinal O'Brien has been very thorough with his briefings.'

Suppressing a smile, Jack continued.

'I can tell your Eminence that Professor Delacroix believes something similar may be happening here, right now, with Osman da Baggio's copy of *al-Qanun*. That's why I've agreed to become involved and that's why I'm here, searching for his annotated book.'

The cardinal nodded, obviously deep in thought, and for a long, tense moment he didn't say anything.

'In that case, Mr Rogan, I will do everything in my power to help you find it,' he said quietly.

Relieved, Jack took a deep breath. 'Thank you, Eminence.'

'In fact, the search has already begun,' continued the cardinal, 'by someone I believe you know. He's waiting for you in the archives right now.'

The cardinal reached for the bell button on his desk and pressed it. 'My secretary will take you to him. God be with you, Mr Rogan. We are all instruments of fate.'

Cardinal Borromeo's secretary, a young Jesuit from Spain, escorted Jack to the labyrinthine, fortress-like Vatican archives. After several security checks, a pass was issued to Jack and he was finally allowed to enter where only a privileged few were given access to – the fiercely guarded literary treasures and secrets of the Catholic Church.

The Church had realised long ago that the word was much more powerful than the sword and had skilfully used censorship for centuries to protect its interests against ideas and teachings that could threaten its power and influence. One of the most effective ways to do this was to use the accusation of heresy as a convenient justification, and the ruthless Inquisition as a devastating weapon to silence critics and inconvenient dissenters. For centuries, the Church had protected itself in that way.

However, rather than destroying the offending material, meticulous records were kept of all proceedings, interrogations and trials, and the heretical "evidence" was carefully studied and stored in the Vatican archives. This had resulted in one of the unique and most valuable collections of ideas and historical records on the planet.

Jack's Jesuit guide pointed to the pass Jack had just been given that he was now wearing in a plastic sleeve around his neck. 'I've never seen one of these before,' he said, surprised. 'Only certain cardinals are allowed this kind of unrestricted access. You can virtually ask for and view anything you like in here.' The young Jesuit shook his head. 'Unheard of.'

'Where are we going?' asked Jack.

'To a research room. The archives are strictly temperature and humidity controlled. All work in here is carried out in separate, air-conditioned rooms, specially designed for that purpose. Here we are.'

The young Jesuit pointed to a small, brightly lit, glass cage-like room at the end of a corridor filled with all kinds of books and records. As he opened the door to let Jack enter, a man sitting hunched over a small desk and wearing white gloves turned around, looked at Jack and smiled.

'You?' said Jack, surprised. 'When did you get here?'

'Last night,' said Father Connor, and stood up. 'Cardinal O'Brien sends his regards. You will be pleased to hear I've already made a good head start.'

'Great. I was wondering how I would manage in here all by myself.'

'No need to worry. The Vatican's most experienced archivists are at our disposal,' said Father Connor, lowering his voice. 'Eminent scholars one and all. Around the clock. Cardinal Borromeo made sure we have everything we could possibly need. The stuff in here is amazing. Wait till you see what I've found so far. Here, put on these gloves. You are not allowed to touch anything without them.'

Jack took off his jacket, put on the gloves and sat down facing Father Connor. 'Just like Sydney,' he said, smiling.

'But without Mrs Kelly's cakes.'

'Bummer! Now, tell me, what have you discovered?'

Father Connor held up one of the pages of the da Baggio chronicles he had been working on and pointed to a sentence he had highlighted. 'This was the important clue: one entry. It was difficult to find because it appeared years after the event.'

'What is it?'

'A date.'

'What kind of date?'

'A trial date.'

'Wow!'

'And the date led me to this.' Father Connor pointed to an open, leather-bound tome on the desk in front of him.

'What's that?'

'This, my friend, is a transcript of a trial. Do you want to know whose trial?'

'Tell me.'

'The trial of Osman da Baggio of Venice, also known as "Medicus", accused of heresy by the Inquisition right here in Rome, because of dubious medical practices.'

'Amazing! What does it say?'

'Don't know yet. Just started.'

Jack leaned forward and slapped Father Connor good-naturedly on the back. Then he pulled his beloved notebook held together by a rubber band out of his coat pocket and placed it on the desk in front of him. 'What are we waiting for? Let's get stuck into it!' he said and reached for his pen.

62

For Haddad, Conti and Cesaria, Istanbul had quickly turned into a frustrating waiting game. Colonel Riza had given orders that no action was to be taken until the Paris suicide bombers – who were in transit from Syria, according to reliable intelligence – had arrived in Istanbul and were arrested. After that, the Americans would take Bahadir back to the States and shut down his operation in Istanbul. Until then, nothing must be allowed to occur that could in any way jeopardise the operation. However, after that, Riza would have a free hand. And that included moving against Belmonte who, it was thought, was still holed up somewhere in Bahadir's Sultan's Table complex.

For Haddad, allowing el-Masri to slip through his fingers a second time was unthinkable. But because of Colonel Riza's strict orders, his hands were tied, and a man like Haddad wouldn't dream of disappointing a friend and colleague who had so generously held out his hand and placed such trust in him.

As a battle-hardened police officer with many years of frontline experience in the turbulent world of terror, Haddad knew exactly how the IS leadership operated and who its important leaders were. Familiar with their mentality, he also knew how they strategised, and what they considered to be important. Punishing traitors was a priority because without discipline and obedience, IS couldn't operate. El-Masri was still on top of IS's most-wanted list and Haddad was going to use this festering sore to somehow get to Bahadir before he was once again taken back to the US and therefore out of reach. But first, Haddad had to be certain that Bahadir *was in fact* el- Masri.

At Haddad's request, Colonel Riza had couriered Bahadir's blood sample to Alexandra at the Gordon. Until the facial reconstruction – which was still in doubt – was completed, Haddad wouldn't act. He had to be sure, and for what he had in mind, he needed proof.

To make waiting easier and use his time productively, Haddad decided to accompany Nazir and Amena – who were desperate to get back to the camp and surprise Dr Rosen – to Kilis Oncupinar and help them deliver the operating theatre rig. However, there was another, more important reason behind this: Haddad wanted to be near the Syrian border when the facial reconstruction results came back from the Gordon. In case the results confirmed what Haddad suspected, he would act immediately before it was too late. He knew that every hour counted. He also knew what he had to do.

Muddy and covered in dust, the rig pulled into the camp just after sunrise. Taking turns at the wheel with the driver provided by Colonel Riza, Haddad had made sure they covered the long distance in record time.

Tired, but elated, Amena and Nazir went looking for Dr Rosen. They found her already at work in the main camp, doing her rounds in the overcrowded field hospital.

'Looks like you could do with some help here,' said Amena, walking up to Dr Rosen from behind and putting an arm around her shoulders. Dr Rosen started and looked at Amena. '*You? Here?*' she said, surprised, and embraced Amena. 'Is everything all right? You haven't called.'

'Everything's fine – now. Look, there's someone else who wants to help.'

Amena pointed to Nazir standing in the open doorway, grinning broadly. Dr Rosen held out her arms and he came running towards her, tears in his eyes.

'Come, tell me what you've been up to,' said Dr Rosen, a lump in her throat.

'We will,' said Amena, 'but first you have to come with us. We have something to show you.' Amena took Dr Rosen by the hand and pulled her towards the door.

'What about the patients?'

'This won't take long. They can wait, this time,' replied Amena, laughing.

Haddad was leaning against the bonnet of the rig, smoking. Dr Rosen saw him first and waved. Haddad waved back and came walking towards her.

'Another injury needing attention?' asked Dr Rosen, holding out her hand.

'No, thank you, Bettany. The old one will do just fine for a while, I think.'

'All of you back here? So soon? How come?' asked Dr Rosen.

'We've brought you something,' said Amena, no longer able to contain her excitement.

'Oh? What?'

Amena pointed to the rig. 'This.'

'*A semi-trailer?*'

'Ah. But this is much more than a semi-trailer,' said Haddad, laughing.

'In what way?' asked Dr Rosen.

'Here, let me show you. Nazir, would you please open the back doors?'

'With pleasure,' said Nazir and hurried to the back of the rig.

Amena took off her headscarf and turned towards Dr Rosen. 'Here, allow me,' she said. She covered Dr Rosen's eyes with the scarf, pulled it gently and then tied it at the back of her head. Haddad and Amena each took one of Dr Rosen's hands and guided her to the back of the rig.

'We have a surprise for you,' said Amena. 'Ready, Nazir?'

Nazir nodded.

Amena untied the scarf. 'Here, this is for you.'

Dr Rosen opened her eyes and looked straight into the back of the rig, her eyes wide with astonishment. 'My God! Is that what I think it is?' she asked.

'Aha,' said Amena, smiling. 'Fully equipped and ready to go.'

'I-I don't know what to say,' stammered Dr Rosen, feeling a little dizzy. 'How? Where from?'

'It's a long story,' said Haddad. 'We could do with some breakfast, and then we'll tell you all about it.'

'You're on. Come!'

Amena and Nazir went straight to work with Dr Rosen, and Haddad went to see the camp commander to talk about the new mobile operating theatre. They met again at the end of the day for dinner. By then, Amena and Nazir had told Dr Rosen all about their adventures in Istanbul and Florence and how the mobile operating theatre ended up with them.

'I think it's all your fault,' said Dr Rosen, turning to Haddad. 'You are as bad as Jack.'

'In what way?'

'Do I have to spell it out for you?' said Dr Rosen, putting a second helping of chicken curry on Haddad's empty plate.

Haddad shrugged. 'I guess not,' he said and began to attack the plate with gusto.

Exhausted, Amena and Nazir went to bed early. Haddad and Dr Rosen stayed behind, enjoying the cool breeze and being alone.

'I understand why Amena and Nazir came back, but you?' began Dr Rosen.

'Very perceptive of you, as usual,' said Haddad and lit another cigarette.

'So, why are you here?'

'I believe I've found el-Masri ...'

Dr Rosen looked at Haddad in surprise and disbelief. 'Are you serious?' she said.

'I am,' said Haddad, and then he told Dr Rosen all about Bahadir and his transformation in America, and the pending genomic face-reconstruction arranged by Jack in Sydney.

Dr Rosen shook her head. 'I've seen a lot in my days, but *this*? Extraordinary!'

'Sure is.'

'What are you going to do?'

'I'm waiting for the results from Professor Delacroix.'

'How long will that take?'

'She knows it's urgent.'

'And then?'

Haddad shrugged.

'You obviously have a plan.'

Haddad nodded.

'Care to tell me about it?'

'No obedience in sin, but rather obedience to what is right.'

'Says who?'

'The Prophet.'

'Meaning?'

'If, as I believe, the results prove that it's el-Masri, then I will disobey my friend, Colonel Riza.'

'In what way?'

'I will not stay away from el-Masri and allow the Americans to take him back to the US – again.'

'Because?'

'Justice demands otherwise. And I made a promise ...'

'You're going to—'

'Kill him?' interrupted Haddad. 'No. I will *expose* him. Expose him for what he is.'

'And how are you going to do that?'

'I'm going back into Syria, to see someone.'

'Who?'

'Someone high up in IS who has been sending suicide bombers through here to Bahadir in Istanbul.'

'You know who that is?'

'I do.'

'And he will see you?'

'He will, when I let him know that I have information about el-Masri.'

'I see.'

'And who he is and, more importantly, where he will see me is significant and meaningful in a rather special way.'

'Oh?' said Dr Rosen, her interest aroused.

'The man I will go to see lives in a small village called Dabiq, not far from here.'

'And this village is important because?'

'You may remember, IS fought a fierce battle to capture this village back in 2014.'

'I do remember.'

'But do you know why?'

'Not really.'

'It's all about an apocalyptic Sunni End-Time Prophesy talking about the Day of Judgement and a final battle, the Grand Battle, to be fought between Muslims and the infidels. Many of the fighters who have flocked to IS believe the time has come ... apocalyptic notions have been a great recruiting drawcard for IS. And do you know where that final battle is to take place?'

'Tell me.'

'According to the Prophet, the Day of Judgement will come after the Muslims defeat the infidels at – wait for it – *Dabiq*. This is the famous Dabiq Prophesy quoted by Abu Umar al-Baghdadi, IS's first commander of the faithful, a few years ago. The prophesy, however, dates back to the early eighth-century.'

'Extraordinary.'

'Sure is.'

'And you believe the man you are going to see will do something about el-Masri?'

'I'm sure of it.'

'What do you think he'll do?'

'He will punish him for his treachery.'

'In what way?'

'In a way that fits the crime.'

'And going to see this man—'

'They call him Al-Gharib, "the Stranger",' interrupted Haddad.

'Will that not be dangerous?'

'Quite possibly.'

'And that doesn't worry you?'

Haddad ran his fingers through his sparse hair. 'No. I am very tired, Bettany, and I am ready—'

'Ready for what?'

'Whatever the stars have in mind.' Haddad paused and looked up at the stars blazing in the clear night sky above. 'I may not come back, but I will fulfil my promise to Marcus. It's my destiny ...'

Dr Rosen reached across to Haddad and put her hand on his. 'I understand,' she said quietly.

63

Grimaldi kept staring at the two photographs on his desk. It was just after sunrise and the chiming of the familiar church bells drifting through the open office windows helped him focus. *Belmonte is Bangarella,* he thought. *That's the key to all this, the connection.* The news from Istanbul had just confirmed it. Grimaldi picked up one of the two photographs and held it up. It was a snapshot of a man sitting at a restaurant table behind Mario Giordano ten minutes before Mario was shot. An enlargement of the image extracted from one of the security street cameras next to the restaurant showed the face of the man looking directly at the lens.

It's him, thought Grimaldi. Bangarella, the notorious hitman, was working for Gambio. Grimaldi didn't believe in coincidences, only logic and facts. Bangarella killed Mario Giordano, no doubt about it. The question was why, and on whose orders? Grimaldi lit one of his small cigars and watched the smoke curl towards the open window. *At the time of the killing, Mario's father was meeting with Gambio at his home. Gambio told me so himself. It doesn't make sense! ... Or does it?* Grimaldi asked himself.

He picked up the second photograph on the desk in front of him and smiled. It showed Belmonte, Nazir and Amena boarding Gambio's plane in Istanbul, reinforcing the Gambio–Bangarella connection. But then there was the white feather. It seemed to point to the Lombardos. This had bothered Grimaldi from the beginning. It was just too obvious. And when something was too obvious, Grimaldi became suspicious. The killer – Bangarella – had placed a white feather into Mario's mouth, deliberately implicating the Lombardos; why?

Increasing pressure from above regarding *Ars Moriendi* had made it clear to Grimaldi that it would be almost impossible to successfully pursue Gambio about his involvement in the deadly, bizarre gambling extravaganza and link him to Lorenza's abduction unless Conti was able to hunt down Belmonte in Istanbul. Even then, it was highly unlikely that Belmonte would talk, and without Belmonte pointing the finger at Gambio, trying to implicate him appeared futile and Gambio knew it.

Grimaldi realised he had to find another way. To let Gambio slip away would not only be humiliating in the extreme and embarrass the Squadra Mobile; it would open the floodgates to even more outrageous crimes and further strengthen Gambio's grip on the Florence underworld. However, Grimaldi was well aware that he mustn't allow frustration and disappointment to cloud his judgement. Experience had taught him that the best way to avoid this was to take a step back, apply some lateral thinking, and start from the beginning.

As Grimaldi reached for his ashtray, his eyes fell on a note his secretary had handed to him the day before. Riccardo Giordano, Mario's father, had called again asking when his son's body would be released for burial. It had now been a month since the killing, but for abundant caution, Grimaldi had instructed Forensics not to release the body just yet.

That's it! thought Grimaldi and smiled. *Of course. If you can't go through the front door, try the one at the back.* He placed the note next to the two photographs and called Giordano's number. He realised that the early morning phone call would unsettle Giordano and underscore the importance of what he was about to say.

One of Giordano's bodyguards answered the phone. Grimaldi asked to speak to his boss and said it was urgent. Moments later, Giordano came on the phone.

'What can I do for you, Chief Prosecutor?' said Giordano, sounding irritated.

'I have some important news regarding your son's murder.'

'What kind of news?'

'The kind of news one shouldn't talk about over the phone ...'

'Your office?'

PROFESSOR K: THE FINAL QUEST

'That would be best.'

'When?'

'Say, in an hour?'

'I'll be there.'

Giordano arrived early. He was nervously pacing up and down in front of the reception desk on the ground floor, waiting. He had sent his bodyguard outside and told him to wait in the car. To meet the chief prosecutor with a bodyguard standing next to you wasn't a good look. But without him, Giordano – who never went anywhere without a guard – felt strangely vulnerable. The violent death of his son had hit him hard, and he could barely wait to hear what information Grimaldi had regarding the killing. It had to be important because to be summoned to the chief prosecutor's office just like that was almost unheard of.

'Chief Prosecutor Grimaldi will see you now,' said Grimaldi's secretary. 'Please follow me.'

Giordano stubbed out his cigarette and adjusted his uncomfortable tie. He owned many, but rarely wore them because they chafed against his stubble. Standing up, he followed the secretary up the stairs.

'You have some news about my son?' asked Giordano, coming straight to the point after the secretary had closed the door behind her.

'Please take a seat,' said Grimaldi calmly and pointed to a chair facing his desk.

'Do you mind if I smoke?' asked Giordano, unable to hide his obvious anxiety and unease.

He's definitely out of his comfort zone, thought Grimaldi.

'Go right ahead.'

For a while, Grimaldi just watched his notorious visitor without saying anything. Recognising the importance of what he was about to say, and the far-reaching consequences that would be inevitable once he said it, he was deliberately taking his time. Every word counted. If his superiors would not allow him to use the law to do his job then he would find other ways, because to do nothing wasn't an option for a man like Grimaldi.

In this case, he would use a father's grief and anger to hold those responsible for the killing accountable and bring them to justice. While this began to look more and more like retribution rather than justice, Grimaldi wasn't a man to let this bother him too much. He knew he had to fight fire with fire. Too often it was the only way, and what had occurred in Florence during the past few weeks definitely warranted such a radical approach. However, he also knew he had to tread carefully, because letting a man like Giordano loose could easily ignite the very war in Florence he was so desperately trying to prevent.

'I believe I know who killed your son,' began Grimaldi, 'but unfortunately, I can't prove it.'

Inhaling deeply, Giordano stared at Grimaldi, the question on his troubled face obvious.

'You brought me here to tell me *this*?' said Giordano, breaking the awkward silence.

'No. I asked you to come here so I can show you what I've found out.'

'Why?'

'On my watch, everyone's entitled to answers – especially a grieving family.'

Giordano nodded. Obviously satisfied with Grimaldi's answer, he began to relax. It was completely in line with the chief prosecutor's reputation as a fearless straight shooter who tolerated no nonsense and wasn't intimidated by those in authority, or anybody else.

'Understood,' said Giordano, his interest aroused.

'This was taken a few days ago,' said Grimaldi and pushed the photograph showing Belmonte, Nazir and Amena boarding Gambio's plane across his desk towards Giordano.

Giordano picked up the photo. 'What am I looking at?' he asked.

'I believe the man in the photo is your son's killer, and he was hired to do the killing by the man who owns the plane.'

For a few long, tense seconds, the church bells chiming outside were the only sound.

'This is Gambio's plane.'

'It is.'

'Are you suggesting that ...?' Giordano stopped mid-sentence and kept staring at the photograph. 'Impossible! This is nonsense!'

'Is it?' Grimaldi leaned forward and pointed a finger at Belmonte in the photo. 'Would you like to know who this is?'

Giordano nodded.

'He goes under the name of Luigi Belmonte. But that's not his real name ...' Grimaldi paused to let the tension grow.

'Oh?'

'No doubt you've heard of Raffaele Bangarella?'

'Who hasn't?'

'I can tell you with absolute certainty that the man here in the photo is none other than Raffaele Bangarella.' Grimaldi held up a bundle of papers. 'Fingerprint evidence; impossible to refute.'

'You are joking, surely! Bangarella disappeared years ago. He was wanted in Palermo.'

'I know. But he's back, working for Gambio.'

Giordano shook his head. 'Even if what you say is true, this doesn't link him to my son's killing.'

Grimaldi had been expecting this. 'But *this* does,' he said and pushed the photograph showing Belmonte/Bangarella sitting at the table behind Mario and his girlfriend in the restaurant ten minutes before Mario was shot.

For a while, Giordano stared at the photograph with the camera time and date stamp in the corner and didn't say anything, his face ashen.

Watching him carefully, Grimaldi realised it was time to present the final piece of evidence that would remove any doubt that may still be lingering in the grieving father's mind. Slowly, he pushed another photograph across his desk. It was taken fifteen minutes after the photo he had just shown Giordano. It showed Mario's girlfriend sitting at the table, alone. Bangarella's table was empty, Mario was gone and his bodyguard was nowhere to be seen.

'This was taken at approximately the time your son and his bodyguard were gunned down in the restaurant toilet,' Grimaldi said quietly and sat back.

'B-but why?' stammered Giordano, shaking his head in disbelief. '*Gambio?*'

'I thought you could answer that much better than I. As I understand it, you were with Gambio at his home when all this happened.'

Grimaldi paused to let this sink in.

Alleanza, thought Giordano, turning pale. *This is all about the fucking Alleanza!*

'Too much of a coincidence, don't you think?' continued Grimaldi, speaking softly. 'I have no idea what the meeting was all about, but common sense and reason suggest that the killing must have had a bearing on it. And then, there was the feather.'

'What of it?' barked Giordano, unable to suppress a toxic anger welling up from somewhere deep inside him as it dawned on him that he may have been manipulated by Gambio in a devastatingly cruel way.

'A little too obvious for me,' said Grimaldi.

'What do you mean?'

'The white feather was left behind to point the finger at Lombardo, yet I don't think he had anything to do with it,' said Grimaldi and pointed to the photographs on the desk in front of him. 'All the evidence supports this,' he added quietly and looked intently at Giordano. 'I don't believe I can take this matter much further with what I have … but you can.'

'How?' Giordano almost shrieked.

'That's one question you will have to answer for yourself, in good time.'

Grimaldi stood up, making it obvious the meeting was over. 'Your son's body will be released tomorrow morning,' he said quietly. 'I am sorry for your loss.'

Giordano stood up as well. 'And Bangarella?'

'I'll take care of him. You have my word.'

Giordano held out his hand. 'You are a good man, Chief Prosecutor Grimaldi. I will certainly think carefully about what you've just said.'

'From time to time, I'll turn a blind eye to things, but there's one thing I will not tolerate,' said Grimaldi, opening the door.

'What's that?'

'A turf war in Florence.'

'Understood,' said Giordano and quickly left the office.

PART IV
POMAX 16

"Only by understanding the wisdom of natural foods and their effects on the body, shall we obtain mastery of diseases and pain, which shall enable us to relieve the burden of mankind."
William Harvey

64

Father Connor rang Alexandra from the airport as soon as his plane landed and asked if he could come straight over. Expecting his call, Alexandra told him that she and her team were working late and would be waiting for him.

Father Connor arrived just after nine pm. Vimal greeted him at the entrance and helped him with his luggage – a modest black bag – and took him straight to a conference room on the first floor.

'Welcome home,' said Alexandra, extending her hand. 'I understand you and Jack had an interesting time in Rome ...'

'Interesting time? More like an adventure, I would call it,' said Father Connor and placed his briefcase on the table in front of him. 'I had no idea that working for Cardinal O'Brien could be that exciting. And Jack ... well, that's another matter altogether.'

Alexandra nodded, a knowing smile spreading across her face. '"A pair of archive-detectives beavering away in the Vatican under the watchful eyes of zealous guardians protecting the secrets of the Church." I think those were Jack's words when he called me the other day.'

'That's pretty accurate, actually,' said Father Connor, laughing. He opened his briefcase. 'Well, here it is.' He pulled out a bundle of papers and placed them carefully on the table next to his briefcase. Alexandra, Vimal and Ayah kept staring at the bundle. The moment they had been waiting for had arrived, the anticipation in the room palpable.

Father Connor pointed to the papers. 'It may not look much, but this is a copy of Osman da Baggio's annotated *al-Qanun,* which was presented as evidence by the Inquisition during his trial in Rome. We located the original in the Vatican archives with the help of those zealous guardians Jack mentioned. Couldn't have done it without them. The book was the main reason Osman was convicted of heresy. Ironically, the only reason he wasn't condemned to death was due to the intervention of the pope himself, whose life he had saved some years before in Venice.'

'What happened to Osman?' asked Ayah.

'He was placed under house arrest and forbidden to practise medicine. He spent the rest of his life in the family palazzo in Venice. He didn't practise, but he did a lot of teaching.'

'That fits,' said Alexandra. 'Several medical texts used by his pupils and, later, physicians who used this knowledge, survived in various libraries, especially in monasteries. Many refer to Osman da Baggio and his teachings and contain passages from *al-Qanun*. That's where Professor K came across all this material and began looking for Osman's copy of the book you've just found – the same book the Germans were after. His papers are quite clear about this.'

'Amazing,' said Ayah. 'Under house arrest for the rest of his life.'

'Just like Galileo,' said Vimal, his face aglow with excitement.

'Did you have an opportunity to look for the passage I sent you?' asked Alexandra, turning to Father Connor.

Father Connor placed his hand on top of the papers. 'The long flight back from Rome was very productive,' he said. 'Amazing what you can do strapped into a seat for twenty-six hours.'

'And?' prompted Alexandra. After Jack had called her to let her know that he had found the book, Alexandra had emailed him two pages of Professor K's handwritten notes. The pages were annotated extracts from passages of Avicenna's *Canon of Medicine*, as *al-Qanun* was known at the time, dealing with the very subject Alexandra and her team were investigating. Professor K's notes were littered with complex comments and references to this text, and full of often-confusing questions, which Alexandra was desperately hoping Osman's annotations would answer.

Father Connor reached across to the bundle of papers on the table, picked up a few loose pages with handwritten notes scribbled all over them, and held them up. 'I believe this is it,' he said. 'By the way, Jack says hello.'

'I know you've just had a long flight, Father, but would you mind if we were to start working on this together, right now? We cannot do this without you.'

Father Connor put down the papers and smiled. 'I already told the cardinal I would be here, most likely for most of the night,' he said. 'A strong coffee would help.'

'Coming up,' said Ayah and hurried out of the room.

Cardinal O'Brien called Alexandra at five am the next morning. 'Still at it, I see. How's it going?' he asked.

'It's been a long night, Eminence.'

'Productive?'

'I believe so ...'

'Fancy some breakfast? Mrs Kelly's scrambled eggs with sautéed mushrooms and bacon are legendary – I promise.'

'Ah, a little temptation perhaps, to come over to see you?'

'Something like that.'

'We'll be there in half an hour.'

'I'll tell Mrs Kelly to put the kettle on.'

'Thank you, Eminence, we are starving.'

'I thought you might be. No army can march on an empty stomach; even scientists have to eat.'

'Quite.'

'On a more serious note,' said the cardinal, lowering his voice, 'I just had a long call from the Vatican; Cardinal Borromeo. His Holiness is in a bad way ...'

'Oh?'

'He's fading away, quite literally. Chronic diarrhoea, extreme weight loss. The bowel inflammation is killing him.'

'I understand, Eminence,' said Alexandra quietly. She realised at once where this was heading. The moment she had been dreading for some time now, had finally arrived.

'I thought you should know. I'll send my car over.'

''Thank you, Eminence,' said Alexandra and hung up.

The first thing Alexandra noticed when she and her team walked with Father Connor into the dining room of Cardinal O'Brien's residence, was the mouth-watering aroma of frying bacon. Everyone was exhausted, but elated by the progress made during the night. Passage by passage, entry by entry, they had begun to unravel the vision and inspired ideas of an extraordinary man. The intellectual challenge had stretched them to the limit, as Professor K's notes were not only difficult to follow, but often cryptic and full of supposition and leaps of genius, which thanks to Osman da Baggio's annotations in the book, were slowly beginning to come together and make sense. Professor K's brain had always been in a hurry; restless and full of curiosity, but always guided by logic and purpose.

Father Connor's contribution had been invaluable. Not only did he know how to navigate the difficult text, but his instant and accurate translation of complex Latin terms and phrases made sure they didn't get bogged down, or lose their way altogether and fall into error.

After everyone had finished breakfast – with seconds, and in one case, third helpings, to Mrs Kelly's delight – the cardinal suggested they go to the library.

'I cannot tell you how grateful I am for what you are doing. It is more, much, much more, than I could have expected, but I'm afraid this has now turned into a race against time. As I discussed with Professor Montessori on the phone earlier, His Holiness hasn't much longer to live, unless we – that is *you* – can come up with something ...'

The cardinal paused and looked sternly at Alexandra. 'I must therefore ask you this: Is there anything, anything at all you can think of – however far-fetched or speculative it may be – that could buy His Holiness a little more time? We are dealing with more than just a man's life here. We are dealing with – and I don't say this lightly – *history*, Professor Delacroix.'

This is it, thought Alexandra. She ran her fingers through her hair and looked at the cardinal. 'Where to begin?' she said and took a deep breath. 'All right, this is where we're at: Your Eminence will remember, on the last occasion we spoke about the CD86 "go" signal being unfettered and driving His Holiness's autoimmunity ...'

The cardinal nodded.

'And this was because both brakes are now broken due to somatic loss-of-function mutations in His Holiness's overactive copy of the IL-10R gene.'

Alexandra looked at the cardinal again, hoping she hadn't lost him. His expression told her she didn't have to worry. Encouraged, she pressed on.

'As I recall it, that's where we left our discussion last time we spoke about this—'

'And we then touched on Professor K's ideas and Osman da Baggio's annotated book,' interrupted the cardinal, 'and its possible relevance.'

'Correct.'

'And I then asked you if you could think of anything, anything at all that could help His Holiness ... Do you remember what your answer was?' asked the cardinal, watching Alexandra carefully.

'I do. I answered in the affirmative, but I also said that I needed to give the matter more thought before taking it further.'

'Yes, and did you?'

Alexandra looked first at Vimal, then at Ayah and took her time before replying. 'Yes, I have,' she said quietly.

'Any conclusions?' asked the cardinal, breaking the growing tension in the room.

'Yes, but first let's take a closer look: one inherited broken brake – fortunately offset by a second overactive brake that eventually wears out – can be addressed in a number of ways. In fact, Professor K touched on this in his papers and was exploring this very subject when he died. He believed that the missing brake – CTLA-4 on the outside of T cells – is the very mechanism that will underpin the greatest breakthrough in cancer treatment this century. And it's all do to with the immune system.'

'And you believe that too?' asked the cardinal.

'Yes, I do. In fact, many significant breakthroughs have already occurred since Professor K died. One in particular, is the discovery of a drug called Yervoy, or anti-CTLA-4, which has just recently been approved in Australia and around the world to reactivate immune system reactions against melanoma, lung cancer and other tumours.'

'How does it work?' asked the cardinal.

'Yervoy is the first in a class of new cancer drugs called "checkpoint inhibitors". It's an antibody that binds to CTLA-4 and prevents it from working as a brake on the immune system. In a subset of cancer patients, when the brake was broken with Yervoy, it released a T cell response that destroyed the cancer cells throughout the body in a lasting way.'

'But His Holiness's brakes are already broken – both of them?'

'Correct. And his problem is different, but the mechanism – CTLA-4 on the outside of T cells – is the same, only with different consequences. However, the patients treated with Yervoy had one quite devastating thing in common with His Holiness ...'

'What?'

'A potentially life-threatening side effect of Yervoy is that patients often develop autoimmune diseases and acute bowel inflammation.'

'Ah. The same thing His Holiness is suffering from?'

'Yes.'

'Are you suggesting, if this could in some way be treated ...'

'It could revolutionise and improve ways we treat cancer. *Generally*,' Alexandra said, becoming excited.

'Extraordinary!'

'It is. And that is exactly what Professor K was looking into, and that's why he was so interested in autoimmune disease and Osman da Baggio's copy of the book.'

'Any suggestions?' asked the cardinal again, steering the conversation back to the subject that interested him most: a possible answer to the pope's predicament.

'I believe we have several treatment possibilities that could work here ...'

The cardinal looked up, like someone close to drowning who had just been thrown a lifeline. 'What kind of possibilities?' he asked, unable to hide his deep concern.

'One possibility would be to give His Holiness a stem cell transplant. More than a million people worldwide have already received a haematopoietic stem cell transplant – the transplanted stem cells harvested either from bone marrow, peripheral blood or umbilical cord blood. But without going into too much detail, this is not a realistic option here because the risks are too great due to tissue compatibility and other related factors.'

The cardinal nodded.

'This brings me to something new and very exciting: CRISPR. Your Eminence will recall, we talked about this before.'

The cardinal nodded again.

'This revolutionary new technology would allow genome-editing to correct His Holiness's defective LRBA gene in his own stem cells. The problem here is this: This somatic cell editing has only been done in mice, but not as yet in human blood stem cells. It will happen, I'm sure of it, but it will take time. Time His Holiness hasn't got. However, if we could somehow keep him alive, this could become part of a long-term solution to his problem. As your Eminence knows, I am very passionate about this subject and we are doing a lot of work at the moment at the Gordon in this area and hoping to do more. Unfortunately, the bioethical issues are presently holding us back,' Alexandra added, reminding the cardinal of their earlier conversation about this very controversial issue.

'If I understand you correctly, for various reasons none of these options would work for His Holiness.'

'Correct.'

'Is that it then?' asked the cardinal quietly, the dejection in his voice and demeanour obvious.

'Not entirely. We have one more possibility. It's a long shot for sure, but definitely worth pursuing. Professor K has shown us what long shots can do ...'

'What kind of long shot?'

'Vimal, could you please take us through what we found the other day when we had another close look at His Holiness's genome?' asked Alexandra.

Vimal cleared his throat and faced the cardinal. 'We believe we've discovered another new gene that has specific relevance here.'

'In what way?' asked the cardinal.

Alexandra couldn't help herself and decided to step in. 'We believe – and please I must stress this is very early days – that the somatic mutation that precipitated His Holiness's autoimmunity has activated one copy of a previously unknown gene, a gene related to Professor K's KALM 30 gene.'

Alexandra paused to let this sink in.

'Another *hidden* gene?' asked the cardinal, frowning.

'Yes, Eminence,' said Vimal.

'We even gave it a name,' interjected Ayah. 'We called it POMAX 16.'

The cardinal smiled. 'POMAX 16? How curious,' he said. 'I think I can guess why.'

'Your Eminence can?' said Alexandra, surprised.

'Something to do with *Pontifex Maximus*, perhaps, discovered in 2016?'

Nonplussed, Alexandra shook her head. 'Why go to confession, if Your Eminence already knows ...'

'And it would appear that this gene blocked the action of the IL-10 brake system,' continued Vimal, 'allowing the "go signal" CD86 to stimulate autoimmunity that is the underlying cause of the present problem.'

The cardinal interrupted again. 'And this is helpful?' he asked.

'We believe so,' said Alexandra, smiling, 'and it all has to do with something Jack and Father Connor discovered in the Vatican archives the other day.'

'Osman da Baggio's annotated book?'

'No, something related to it.'

'Care to elaborate?'

Alexandra turned to Father Connor sitting next to her. 'Could you please, Father?'

'Not only did we find Osman da Baggio's copy of the book everyone had been looking for, but we found something else that turned out to be very significant: a transcript of his trial,' said Father Connor.

'Significant in what way?'

'Actually, it was Jack Rogan who decided to have a closer look at the transcript. That's when we found it.'

'Found what?' asked the cardinal impatiently.

'Osman was rigorously questioned by the Inquisition about his medical practices. They wanted to know how he had managed to cure so many when traditional, accepted methods in use at the time had failed. It was his answer to this question that provided the vital clue. He said that all of his treatments were based on three interrelated elements: food, diet and herbal medicines originating in the East.'

The cardinal looked stunned.

'Osman da Baggio was arguably one of the first serious naturopaths; well ahead of his time. Unfortunately for him, the Inquisition thought it was witchcraft and he was convicted of heresy,' said Alexandra. 'And that's what makes him so fascinating, and so tragic. He even referred to the *doctrine of signatures* in his notes and used it in his defence during his trial as a theological justification for what he was doing. A very clever argument.'

The cardinal frowned. 'He used the doctrine of signatures?'

'Your Eminence is familiar with the concept?' asked Alexandra, surprised. 'The ideas of Dioscorides and Galen?'

'Yes. As I understand it, it's all about using herbs that resemble various parts of the body to treat diseases affecting those body parts.'

'Correct. These ideas were developed further by Paracelsus in the sixteenth-century and then expanded by Giambattista della Porta in his famous *Phytognomonica*. Professor K refers to these works extensively in his papers and examines the *doctrine of signatures* in great detail. I believe he became interested in Osman da Baggio's notations in the book because of this. That's also the reason the Germans were after it.'

The cardinal nodded.

'It was Jakob Boehme's work *The Signature of All Things*, published in 1621 I think, that gave the ancient doctrine its name,' continued Alexandra.

'Please give me one moment,' said the cardinal and stood up. 'I have something in my study that you will find interesting ...'

The cardinal returned moments later with a small book in his hand. 'This is a facsimile of the botanist William Coles' famous book *The Art of Simpling and Adam in Eden,'* he said, and held up the book. 'It was Coles who made the *doctrine of signatures* widely known in the seventeenth-century, especially in theological circles. Coles believed that objects were marked by the Creator with a sign, or "signature" for their purpose. Plants resembling certain body parts were believed to be useful in treating ailments affecting those parts and so on. This amounted to a well-reasoned theological justification of the ancient doctrine reaching back to Galen in the second-century.'

'And surprisingly, Osman used this very argument in his defence during the trial,' added Father Connor.

'Unfortunately, it didn't help him,' said Alexandra. 'When asked to explain his cryptic entries, symbols and notes in his copy of the book, Osman took his interrogators through them, step-by-step. Many of the entries were what we would call case histories and studies about specific illnesses he had treated. This alone is interesting enough, but what is more intriguing by far, are his notes about the various treatments he prescribed.'

'What kind of treatments?' asked the cardinal.

'Food mainly. He prescribed specific diets to be followed and apparently provided detailed recipes for his patients.'

'Incredible!'

'The Inquisition viewed this with great suspicion because his copy of the book, which was under consideration, did not contain any recipes. Instead, there were strange symbols next to the case notes, like this one here,' said Father Connor and held up a page. 'This is part of the transcript. The symbols are all shown right here. Osman was questioned about them in some detail and asked to produce the recipes. He said he couldn't because all the recipes were in his head, and the symbols simply helped him remember which recipe was to be used in the case at hand. The Inquisition didn't believe him and he was convicted.'

'This is fascinating, Father Connor,' said the cardinal, 'but please tell me how all this is relevant?'

'It is possible that expression of this new gene we found could be switched off by epigenetic modification of the genome,' said Alexandra, stepping in again.

'How? Layman's speak, please.'

'Through *food*. A specific diet.'

'Are you serious?'

'Absolutely. Specific foods could be the answer here. Professor K certainly thought so. One of Osman's case notes describes the chronic bowel inflammation in surprisingly accurate detail and claims that it can be cured through diet. That's what made Professor K so interested in all this because he, too, was thinking along similar lines. I don't believe that a stem cell transfer would correct His Holiness's LRBA deficiency in the lining of his intestines, where LRBA may have additional functions to suppress autoimmunity. But, like Professor K, I *do* believe this could be achieved through diet: food based on a specific recipe outlining exact ingredients to be used. A recipe that was known to, and successfully used by, Osman.'

'Haven't we reached a dead-end here?'

'How come?' asked Alexandra.

'Father Connor just told us there were no recipes in Osman's book because they were all *in his head*. Osman's long gone ...'

'True,' said Father Connor, 'but we found the same symbols shown in the trial transcript, noted in the margins of Osman's copy of the book, right next to the case histories.'

'So?'

'We believe – and it was Jack who first came up with this,' said Alexandra, 'that the symbols refer to actual ancient recipes that do in fact exist.'

'Come on,' said the cardinal. 'How can he possibly know this?'

'Because he has actually seen them, quite recently.'

'Where?'

'In the Palazzo da Baggio in Venice.' Alexandra paused to let this sink in. 'But that's where the good news ends.'

'Why?'

'Because the original recipes are no longer available.'

'I don't understand.'

'It's a long story ...'

'I have time.'

65

Haddad sat next to the fax machine with the built-in colour printer in Dr Rosen's surgery, waiting. It was the only colour printer in the camp and used mainly for medical business. Jana and Alexandra had called Haddad earlier on his satellite phone to tell him that the face reconstruction based on Bahadir's genome had been successful. The only issue was how to get an accurate image of the face to Haddad in the remote camp with its poor reception.

Haddad sat up as the printer clicked into life again. He had spent several hours hovering over the fax machine during the night, trying desperately to make it work. The first two attempts had been unsuccessful, with images too blurred to make sense. This time, however, the image appeared to be a lot clearer. Haddad held his breath as the facial features began to take shape and the page emerged slowly out of the slot and then fell to the floor.

For a while, Haddad just stared at the piece of paper at his feet. He knew the moment of reckoning had finally arrived. Taking a deep breath, he bent down, picked up the paper and held it up, his stomach churning.

'It's him,' he whispered, staring at the face in front of him. 'Unbelievable!' The clear colour image removed any doubt that may have lingered that Bahadir was in fact el-Masri, as the face on the page merged with Haddad's memory of it, to create a perfect fit.

Dr Rosen had been watching Haddad for a while. Realising the importance of the moment, she had kept away, working instead at her desk.

'Success at last?' she called out from the other side of the room.

Haddad nodded, his face ashen.

Dr Rosen walked over to him and looked at the image. 'It's him, isn't it?'

409

'Yes, no doubt about it. I really don't know how they did this, but it's an uncanny likeness.'

'So, what now?'

'I'm going to Dabiq to meet Al-Gharib, "the Stranger". It's all arranged.'

'When?'

'At first light.'

'Then I may not see you before you leave. I really must get some sleep before surgery starts again in the morning.'

Haddad turned around and looked at Dr Rosen. 'You are an extraordinary woman, Bettany. It's been a privilege to know you.'

'And you, Naguib, have been a true friend. I know what Marcus and Jack think of you. Thanks for everything ...'

'Let's hope I won't disappoint them with this.' Haddad pointed to the image on the table.

'I doubt it.'

'Tell Marcus ...' Haddad paused, an unsettled look on his face. 'No, don't tell him anything,' he continued. 'If I succeed, circumstances will speak for themselves.'

'What do you mean?'

'If I manage to see Al-Gharib and persuade him that Bahadir and el-Masri are one and the same, then ...'

'Then what?'

'The whole world will know that I've succeeded, *inshallah*.'

It was a strange answer, but Dr Rosen knew better than to ask for clarification. Instead, she embraced Haddad and for a moment held him tight, realising they were saying goodbye.

'Good luck, Naguib,' she said and let go, tears in her eyes.

'God be with you,' whispered Haddad.

'And with you.'

Since his arrival at the camp three days before, Haddad had used his time wisely. Using his old IS contacts, he had established a line of communication with Al-Gharib. This hadn't been easy, and his approach was viewed with obvious suspicion. It was only after he had provided some compelling information about el-Masri and the time he had spent with him in Camp Bucca, hinting that he may have intelligence about el-Masri's present whereabouts that Al-Gharib agreed to a meeting. But with strict conditions. Haddad was to cross the border into Syria on foot and wait at a designated intersection some five kilometres from the border.

Haddad set off at sunrise with only his phone, wallet and a bottle of water in his backpack. It took him just over an hour to reach the intersection, already choking with refugees heading for the Turkish border. He didn't have to wait long. A battered Toyota pickup – the type popular with IS fighters – appeared out of a cloud of dust and stopped in front of Haddad.

'Naguib Haddad?' asked one of the armed men sitting in the back.

Haddad nodded.

'Put down your pack and empty your pockets.'

Haddad did as he was told.

The man climbed down and carefully frisked Haddad, before examining his backpack. Obviously satisfied, he handed it back to Haddad but kept his phone, which he switched off. Then he told him to get into the car.

It didn't take them long to reach Dabiq, which was close to the border. As they approached the village, without saying anything the man sitting next to Haddad pulled a black hood over Haddad's head. Instead of driving into the village, the car turned off the dirt road and headed away from the border.

A cautious man, Al-Gharib didn't stay in the same location for more than a few days. On that occasion, he and five of his men were camping in a small cave just outside Dabiq. Still wearing the hood, Haddad was led into the cave by one of the men. 'Wait here,' said the man and left.

For a while, Haddad stood in silence and listened. He could smell smoke, but couldn't hear anything.

'You can take it off now, Chief Inspector,' said a voice, sounding quite close. Haddad pulled off the hood and looked around. As his eyes became accustomed to the gloom, he could see someone sitting, legs crossed, on the ground by a small fire.

'Come, sit,' said the man and pointed to a frayed carpet on the rough stone floor in front of him. Haddad walked over to the man and sat down. 'Tea?'

Haddad nodded and looked at the small, bearded man sitting opposite. Wearing a turban and dressed in baggy trousers, a loose shirt with no collar, and a vest, the man looked like any one of the many IS fighters roaming the country, only older. The grey streaks in his beard suggested a man of about fifty and his accent told Haddad he was most likely Egyptian, like himself. However, his most striking feature was his glasses: very thick and perfectly round, they gave him an almost comical look, like a storyteller sitting in the bazaar entertaining the children. But Haddad, an experienced man when it came to sizing up notorious characters, realised he was looking at one of the most dangerous, clever and ruthless men still alive in the IS leadership.

Al-Gharib, "the Stranger", was at the very top of the US's most-wanted list.

Al-Gharib poured some tea into a small glass, leaned forward and handed it to Haddad. 'Egypt, Ethiopia, Yemen, Iran, Syria, Turkey, and now Dabiq. You've certainly been around, Chief Inspector. You are a survivor, just like me.'

A clever opening remark, thought Haddad. *He's telling me he's done his homework and knows a lot about me. Good.*

'Have you come here for the final showdown and to join the many others waiting for the Big Battle to begin?' continued Al-Gharib. 'Do you believe in the Dabiq Prophesy, Chief Inspector?'

'I am not a pious man like you,' replied Haddad, sidestepping the question and choosing his words carefully, 'but a practical one. My battles are more about justice. I am sure both of us believe in justice.' Haddad realised that to patronise or deceive an obviously well-educated man like

Al-Gharib would be a huge mistake.

Al-Gharib nodded, but it was impossible to tell from his expression or body language if he liked the answer, or not.

'And is that what brings you here?'

'It is.'

'I am always interested in justice. Please tell me why you've come all this way to see me.'

Collecting his thoughts, Haddad took another sip of tea and looked at his host. 'It's all about one man: Ibrahim el-Masri, going under the name of Kemal Bahadir. I understand you've had a long association with him?'

'With Bahadir, yes, but el-Masri ...' Al-Gharib didn't complete his sentence. Instead he kept looking at Haddad through his thick glasses, like a curious fish in a glass bowl staring at freedom. 'What's your interest in this man?'

'Justice, and a promise.'

'A promise, you say? How intriguing.'

'El-Masri was one of the men responsible for the violent death of many in my care, especially the family of a friend. That was years ago. I made a promise at the time to bring him to justice and have been trying to do that ever since.'

Al-Gharib nodded. 'And you believe you've now found him and the time has come for justice? You believe that Kemal Bahadir is Ibrahim el-Masri?'

'I do.'

'Chief Inspector, you of all men will understand that I cannot just take your word for this extraordinary assertion. But I'm sure you didn't come here empty-handed. Can you offer some proof?'

Haddad had, of course, been expecting something like this and was ready. 'I can,' he said and reached into the inside pocket of his jacket.

Al-Gharib was watching Haddad with interest as he pulled a few papers out of his pocket and carefully spread them out on the carpet in front of him.

'As you would no doubt be aware, the Americans took el-Masri back to the US after Camp Bucca was closed. Why? Because he supplied them with important information about IS.'

Al-Gharib nodded.

Haddad leaned forward and picked up a photograph in front of him, held it up and then handed it to Al-Gharib.

'This was taken a few years ago in a clinic in Washington,' said Haddad quietly. 'The date is here in the corner. It shows el-Masri on the operating table before his face operation—'

'What face operation?' interrupted Al-Gharib, raising his voice ever so slightly.

'The Americans didn't just give el-Masri sanctuary, a new identity and a new home – obviously in return for valuable information – but they reinvented him altogether and even gave him a new face ... this one.'

Haddad held up another photograph and then passed it across to Al- Gharib. It was a close-up showing a face a few days after the operation. Facial scars were still visible and so was some swelling, but the new features were unmistakable.

'Enter Kemal Bahadir,' said Haddad. 'As you know, I work for the Gendarmerie in Turkey at the moment. When I came across this information quite recently, all became clear,' continued Haddad. 'Kemal Bahadir is a double agent working for the Americans. I know he appears to be working for IS, but in fact he is working for the Americans, who share some of their intelligence with Turkey. That's how I found out about all this.'

For a while there was complete silence in the cave, as both men gazed into the flames, each reflecting on what had just been said. If Al-Gharib was in any way shocked or surprised by what he had just heard, he certainly didn't show it.

'But I still wasn't convinced that Bahadir was in fact el-Masri, the man I spent several months with in Camp Bucca and have been trying to track down ever since,' continued Haddad, breaking the silence. 'I needed more.

'What finally convinced me beyond any doubt was this: it arrived yesterday from Australia and is the main reason I'm here.' Haddad handed Al-Gharib the fax he had received from the Gordon the night before, and then gave a brief account of the DNA-based, facial reconstruction procedure and how it had been done, but kept his fingers crossed that Al-Gharib would understand what he was telling him and not dismiss it as contrived nonsense and fantasy.

For the first time, a hint of a smile began to spread across Al-Gharib's face.

'You are a very lucky man,' he said after Haddad had finished. 'In my previous life I was a surgeon in Cairo. I have heard about this latest forensic tool; I just didn't know it had progressed so far.'

Haddad looked at Al-Gharib, relieved. The most difficult hurdle had been overcome. Al-Gharib had understood and appreciated the significance of what he had been telling him. There should now be little doubt left in his mind that Bahadir was in fact el-Masri – the traitor responsible for so many lives lost – the man IS had been desperately trying to hunt down for years. And rubbing salt into that festering wound, it had now become clear that el-Masri had returned to continue his treachery under the guise of Kemal Bahadir, the successful restaurateur and masterchef in Istanbul.

However, Haddad had one more piece of evidence up his sleeve that he was certain would shock Al-Gharib even more: irrefutable proof that Bahadir was working for the Americans.

'For years now, as we both know, Bahadir has been assisting IS to smuggle operatives into Turkey through Kilis Oncupinar by providing them with safe shelter and employment in his restaurant in Istanbul before they are moved on to carry out their missions in various parts of Europe.'

Al-Gharib nodded and took a sip of tea, wondering where Haddad was going with this.

'The line of communication is simple and effective: a phone number. This one.' Haddad held up a piece of paper. 'All IS operatives have to do is ring this number on their satellite phone, provide their identification code, and signal the arrival of IS fighters in Kilis Oncupinar. Bahadir and his agents then take care of the rest; no questions asked – right?'

'Correct.'

'But at the same time, Bahadir has another, quite different arrangement in place ...'

Haddad paused, looked at his host and took another sip of tea to let the tension grow.

'Paid informers on the ground working for Bahadir call in with information about potential targets: troop movements, whereabouts of wanted IS men, and other items of interest to the US military.'

Haddad took his time before delivering the punchline.

'And the number these informers call, is this one here.'

Haddad held up another slip of paper and then handed both pieces to Al-Gharib.

'As you will see,' said Haddad, savouring the moment, 'the two numbers are the same.'

Al-Gharib stared at the papers in his hand. 'Your point?' he asked, sounding hoarse.

'Obvious, isn't it? Bahadir is playing both sides. The information provided on this number is recorded and immediately passed on to his handlers in the States, processed, and then passed on again for action. Air strikes mainly. Usually deadly and quite accurate as you know.'

Al-Gharib took off his glasses and began to polish them with a handkerchief. 'Something puzzles me, Chief Inspector,' he said, squinting in Haddad's direction.

'Oh?'

Al-Gharib finished polishing and put his glasses back on, as if to take a fresh look at what he had just been told. 'Why are you telling me all this? If everything is as you say, then why don't you just—'

'Kill him? Because I can't.'

'Why not?'

'Because my hands are tied.'

'I don't understand.'

'As you know, I am working for the Turkish Gendarmerie. Bahadir is not to be touched under any circumstances. As soon as your suicide bombers for the Paris attack arrive in Istanbul and—'

416

'*You know about Paris?*' interrupted Al-Gharib, obviously surprised.

'Yes, and so do the Americans and the French. As soon as the bombers arrive and have been arrested, Bahadir's operation will be closed down and he will be taken back to the US. Turkey will allow him to leave, no questions asked.'

'To hell with the Gendarmerie and Turkey!' Al-Gharib almost shouted. 'If this is as important to you as you say, then why not just ...?'

'Can't you see? Because just executing the man wouldn't be enough,' replied Haddad, raising his voice for the first time. 'His punishment demands more – much more. He has to be exposed and his monstrous treachery made public, and I can't do that. If I walk up to the man and shoot him, I would be silenced at once and most likely disappear, and the whole matter would be covered up by the authorities as if it never happened. What is at play here is politics, not justice.'

Al-Gharib nodded as he began to understand what Haddad was telling him. He looked at Haddad with new respect. What Haddad was doing was very clever. He wanted IS to do what he couldn't and the evidence he had just presented, if true, would make sure it happened.

'Let's have some more tea,' said Al-Gharib. 'I understand what you are trying to do, and why. I respect your convictions and admire your courage. However, I must ask you this ...'

'Yes?'

'Are you prepared to become a martyr for the sake of justice?'

Haddad smiled. 'I wouldn't be here otherwise.'

Al-Gharib nodded again. It was the answer he had been hoping to hear.

'In that case, Chief Inspector, Dabiq may well turn into your Great Battle.'

'I am ready.'

Al-Gharib realised there was one sure way to put everything Haddad had told him to the ultimate test. 'So be it,' he said. 'But I must ask you to accompany the suicide bombers you mentioned earlier to the border. They will leave this afternoon.'

'Very well.'

'If they cross the border and reach Kilis Oncupinar, Bahadir will go unpunished. If they don't make it, justice will be swift and terrible. You have my promise. I'm sure you know what all of this means ...'

'I do.'

Al-Gharib stood up and held out his hand. 'We could do with a man like you in our ranks,' he said.

Smiling, Haddad stood up as well. 'We may not be on the same side, but we believe in the same things,' he replied and shook Al-Gharib's hand.

Bahadir received two phone calls that morning. One from an informer in Syria telling him that the notorious Al-Gharib, "the Stranger", would be in a convoy of three cars travelling from Dabiq towards the Turkish border just before sunset that day. He even provided coordinates identifying the remote dirt road.

The second call came from a man who identified himself as one of Bahadir's IS contacts, telling him that the three Paris suicide bombers were on their way to the camp, and to make arrangements to have them taken to Istanbul as a matter of urgency. The calls were recorded in the usual way and immediately passed on to Bahadir's handlers in the US, who in turn passed the intelligence to the Creech Air Force Base in Nevada for checking and action. What Bahadir didn't know was that both calls had been made by Al-Gharib's men, using the phone number and identification codes provided by Haddad.

The three Toyotas left Dabiq in the late afternoon. Longing for martyrdom, the young suicide bombers driving the vehicles were in high spirits and well aware of what was likely to happen. Al-Gharib, their hero and mentor, had briefed them earlier that day and told them about the importance of their mission. The Paris attack – now compromised – had to be called off. However, Al-Gharib assured them they were the chosen vanguard of fighters heralding the beginning of the Big Battle between Muslims and infidels foretold by the apocalyptic prophesy that held such fascination for IS fighters, especially the young. To die on the battlefield of the Dabiq Prophesy was a great honour and would ensure their rightful place in paradise forever.

Should the convoy be attacked, as Al-Gharib strongly suspected it would be, everyone, including Haddad, would certainly be killed. If there was no attack by the time they reached the Turkish border, Haddad was to be executed, his body left behind and the would-be martyrs were to return to Dabiq.

A US reconnaissance drone spotted the convoy in the designated area just before sunset and conveyed the relevant data to the Incirlik Air Base in southern Turkey. This was seen as corroboration of the Al-Gharib intelligence received earlier that day from Bahadir, which had caused much excitement among the generals, and an attack was authorised. Five-thousand US airmen were stationed at the Turkish base at the time, using state-of-the-art military hardware to fight IS.

A fully armed fighter jet was standing by and took to the air almost immediately. Because the target was quite close, the jet reached the convoy a few minutes later. As the jet screamed past overhead, the pilot had a clear view of the vehicles on his instrument panel. Satisfied, he locked in the target, and fired. Moments later, the laser-guided missile slammed into the convoy, obliterating the three vehicles and everyone inside.

66

Chiesa di San Marco, Florence: 25 June

Italian funerals were always elaborate affairs, but when one of the most powerful families was farewelling a beloved son murdered in tragic circumstances, a funeral could quickly turn into a memorable event. As the head of the family, Riccardo Giordano was determined to make sure that his son's send-off would be a spectacle etched into the history books of Florence, never to be forgotten.

The venue, Chiesa di San Marco next to the famous convent, which had once been the home of notorious Dominican Girolamo Savonarola, who raged against the loose morals of his fellow Florentines and their ostentatious obsession with luxury, was an obvious choice for the funeral.

The Giordano family lived nearby and had worshipped in the church for generations. Mario was baptised there, and Riccardo and his wife had exchanged their wedding vows in front of the very altar where their son's coffin would stand during the service.

Grimaldi had been following the funeral preparations with interest since the release of Mario's body three days before. The whole of Florence was talking about the funeral, and huge crowds were expected near the church and especially around the popular Piazza di San Marco directly in front of it.

The funeral was scheduled for eleven o'clock. The police had decided to close the square and only allow vehicular access for mourners and the funeral procession, to avoid traffic congestion in a busy area frequented by tourists flocking to the convent museum.

Grimaldi arrived at his office early that morning as usual and decided to go straight to his favourite trattoria across the road for his morning latte. Feeling tired and irritable – he had barely slept a wink – he looked again at the handwritten note that had kept him awake most of the night. The note had been delivered to his office the day before by one of Giordano's bodyguards. In essence, the note was a personal invitation written by Giordano himself to attend the funeral. It was courteous and to the point. However, there was one sentence that troubled Grimaldi: *I have given your question a lot of thought and have found the answer staring at me from the rooftops; true justice always comes from above.* Grimaldi realised that Giordano was telling him something, but what? *What have rooftops to do with funerals and justice?* he thought, tucking into his second delicious crostini.

Jack walked in moments later. He had arrived from Rome by train the day before to visit Tristan and had spoken with Grimaldi about the funeral everybody was talking about. Grimaldi had asked him to come to his office the next morning for an update.

'Your secretary told me I would find you here,' said Jack and ordered a latte.

'How's Tristan?' asked Grimaldi.

'He's a tough little bugger. Almost well enough to go to Venice.'

'To stay with the da Baggios?'

'Lorenza ...'

'Ah.'

'From what I hear, this funeral will be something else,' said Jack. 'Invitation only, I hear.'

'Not surprising when you think of it. The entire underworld of Florence will be there. More security than the White House.' Grimaldi pointed to a plate in front of him. 'Have one of these.'

Jack helped himself to a crostini. 'No outsiders, eh? Pity ...'

'What do you make of this?' Grimaldi held up the note he had received from Grimaldi and translated the sentence that had kept him awake the night before.

'"Justice always comes from above"?' said Jack. 'How weird.'

'That's what I thought. What do you think he meant by that?'

Jack shrugged. 'One way to find out ...'

'The funeral?'

'What else.'

'Would you like to come with me?'
'I thought you'd never ask.'

Gambio, a pathologically cautious man where his personal safety was concerned, was angry with himself. He should have anticipated something like this. However, the sudden, almost feverish Giordano funeral arrangements had taken him by surprise, and he certainly hadn't expected such a public spectacle. Attending Mario's funeral was an essential part of his plan. A show of solidarity with Giordano during a time of personal tragedy was absolutely essential; it would send another powerful signal to the Lombardos about the newly-formed *Alleanza*, and make it clear that the new boy on the block meant business and was on the rise.

Gambio's chief bodyguard – a former marine from the US – had serious reservations about attending the funeral. It had all the classic hallmarks of dangers to be avoided. A crowded, exposed public place; predetermined timing; predictable, regimented arrival and departure arrangements – all obvious no-go signals to a man used to dealing with danger in the open. When he mentioned all this to Gambio, his boss made it clear that not turning up wasn't an option.

Normally, Gambio wouldn't have dreamt of attending an occasion like this, but ego and self-interest got the better of him, drowning out the voices of caution and common sense. Throwing both to the wind, Gambio was determined to make an appearance, come what may. Although, he did listen to his bodyguard's advice to keep his attendance at the church to a minimum. This meant being one of the last to arrive and one of the first to leave as soon as circumstances would allow.

Gambio would arrive in his armoured car. Wearing a bullet-proof vest, he would get out of the back seat as close to the church as possible and quickly walk up to the entrance, surrounded by three of his bodyguards. However, only one would go into the church with him. To do otherwise would have been inappropriate, or worse still, cause offence.

Dragan M as he was known in certain Mafia circles, had arrived from Belgrade the day before. He always worked alone and insisted on making all the preparations for the hit himself. As a sought after assassin with years of paramilitary combat experience under his belt, he knew that meticulous planning and split-second timing were the key to staying alive and out of jail. But on this occasion, Giordano's bodyguards had already done most of the obvious groundwork, making it easy for Dragan to do the rest.

The target venue was excellent with several safe getaway options and the line of sight perfect, but most important of all was the suggested gun location for the hit: the rooftop terrace of a building owned by Giordano, facing the square and almost directly opposite the church. As the intended target had to come out of the church, positioning the gun was also straightforward. After spending an hour in the square to orientate himself, Dragan was satisfied that all was in good order. The powerful, untraceable motorbike he had requested for the getaway was waiting at his lodgings. Everything else that was needed, he would supply himself.

The first of the mourners began to arrive at half past ten. To console his distraught wife, a pious woman, Giordano had arranged a requiem mass – Mozart's Requiem in D minor – complete with chamber orchestra, soloists, and a mixed choir positioned in one of the side chapels. Mario would be sent off in style. Presided over by a bishop, the mass would begin as the coffin was being carried into the church by the pallbearers.

Wearing a dark suit, dark glasses and black tie, Grimaldi stood in the shadows close to the entrance and watched the procession of cars inch across the Piazza towards the church.

Grimaldi turned to Jack standing next to him. 'I wonder if Gambio has the balls to attend,' he said, as Florence's Mafia-glitterati and their associates got out of their chauffeur-driven limousines and filed into the church.

'Stay away and miss all this? Come on ...'

Moments before the black, horse-drawn hearse with the coffin turned into the square, Gambio's armoured car pulled up in front of the church. Three of his bodyguards jumped out and one of them opened the back door. Gambio got out of the car, kept his head down and quickly walked into the church.

Dragan watched him through his scope, and smiled. Identifying the target was always a critically important task, especially in a crowded, public venue. But now, after he had clearly seen the man's face, he felt better. Apart from the photograph next to him, specific identification arrangements had been made, and the hit would only go ahead if all was in place and went according to plan. Dragan put down his custom-made, high-powered rifle he had assembled earlier and began to relax. The funeral service was expected to take more than an hour.

Grimaldi took off his glasses and followed Jack into the church just as the coffin was being lifted out of the hearse by the pallbearers.

A spine-chilling silence rippled through the crowded pews as the pallbearers entered, their footsteps the only sound, before the first notes of Mozart's solemn requiem banished the silence and the soprano soloist accompanied by the choir began to sing the *Introitus*: '*Requiem aeternam dona eis, Domine*' – 'Eternal rest give unto them, O Lord', moving many in the congregation to tears.

Dragan knew the service must be nearly over when the hearse moved into position in front of the church. Slowly, he lifted the rifle to his chin and lined up the scope just as the church doors opened and the bishop stepped outside, followed by the pallbearers. It was time to begin the breathing exercises to slow down his heartbeat. Dragan did this before every hit to calm himself and steady his sweating hands. What was required during the next few minutes was nerve and total concentration.

Holding his wife's arm to steady her, Giordano followed his son's coffin out of the church. He stopped at the open door, stood next to the bishop and watched stone-faced as the coffin was being carefully lifted into the back of the hearse. As the organ boomed a last farewell, the hearse rolled slowly forward and left the square.

The bodyguards had made sure that Gambio's car was at the front of the long queue of limousines waiting to enter the square after the hearse had departed and the mourners began to leave. In line with tradition, the mourners would file first past the bishop, and then past Giordano and his wife, to express their condolences.

Gambio, who had been sitting at the back, was one of the first to leave. As he inched closer to Giordano, who was shaking hands with some, embracing others, his stomach began to churn. He hadn't seen Giordano since that fateful day at Fortezza Gambio.

Giordano saw Gambio approaching and reached for the white feather in his pocket. Now, Gambio stood in front of him and their eyes locked. The look in Giordano's eyes told Gambio something was wrong. Then Giordano leaned forward, put one arm around Gambio's shoulders and whispered into his ear: 'I have something for you,' before slipping the feather into Gambio's hand. Gambio looked at it, and paled.

Breathing steadily, Dragan was watching from above. So far everything had gone exactly to plan. All that he needed now, was the signal. Giordano let go of Gambio and placed his right hand on Gambio's left cheek. To some this may have appeared a gesture of affection, but it was in fact a prearranged signal. 'Rot in *hell*, Salvatore,' whispered Giordano and stepped back.

Gripped by panic, Gambio turned away, desperately searching for his bodyguards who were waiting for him next to the car a few metres away. Gambio almost stumbled as he dashed towards the safety of the armoured car. One of the bodyguards saw him coming and opened the back door.

Keep calm, Dragan told himself as he followed Gambio's bobbing head with the scope, *the moment will come.* Another one of Gambio's bodyguards gripped his boss's arm from behind to prevent him from falling as he staggered past. For an instant, Gambio stood still. 'Now,' whispered Dragan as the hairs in his scope crossed Gambio's forehead, and he pulled the trigger. It was a perfect shot. The bullet entered Gambio's head between the eyes and blew away the back of

425

his skull. The stunned bodyguard watched his boss collapse against the open car door, blood and brains splattering in all directions. The other bodyguards came running. Realising what had happened, they bundled Gambio into the back seat and jumped into the car just before it accelerated and sped away.

Standing behind Giordano, Jack and Grimaldi had seen it all. Somehow, Grimaldi wasn't surprised. The sentence that had troubled him so, now made perfect sense. Ignoring the screams and commotion erupting all around him, he turned to Giordano. 'That's some justice from above,' he said, shaking his head. 'I suppose this is one of those occasions I should turn a blind eye?'

'That would be greatly appreciated, Chief Prosecutor,' replied Giordano, hugging his sobbing wife. 'Thank you for coming.'

67

As soon as Al-Gharib received confirmation that a deadly US air attack had wiped out the convoy near the Turkish border, he knew the time for retribution had arrived. Everything Haddad had told him was true and he had backed his word with his life. Al-Gharib would make sure it wasn't in vain.

Three of his most trusted men – all part of an IS death squad – were standing by and waiting for his orders. They would take the place of the three Paris suicide bombers who had just become martyrs. They were to travel to Kilis Oncupinar, make contact with Bahadir's agents in the camp, and then make their way to Istanbul as soon as possible to carry out their deadly mission.

Al-Gharib had used the awesome power of the internet – especially social media – many times, and to great effect. He was a master when it came to manipulating public opinion to further the influence and reach of IS and capture the hearts and minds of the impressionable young. He would use the botched US air attack as a potent signal to tell the world that the Big Battle foretold in the Dabiq Prophesy was about to begin, and he would hold up Bahadir as an example of how IS dealt with traitors who were prepared to do the bidding of the Great Satan, America. And he was going to do that in a way Haddad could not have imagined in his wildest dreams; the world would hold its breath, sit up and take notice.

Three unassuming, quietly spoken bearded men arrived at the Sultan's Table just after closing time and were ushered into Bahadir's restaurant complex through an inconspicuous side entrance, usually used only for deliveries and by kitchen staff.

One of Colonel Riza's agents watching the complex reported their arrival and notified the other men on duty nearby. The arrival of the

427

bombers had been expected for days and was the signal for a large-scale operation with the Americans to begin.

Bahadir was in his office making a call when one of his security men, who was also his personal bodyguard, knocked and entered. 'The men you've been expecting have arrived,' he said, 'and would like to see you.'

This was unusual as Bahadir rarely, if ever, met the new arrivals personally, and would leave all arrangements concerning them and their movements to IS operatives working undercover in his restaurant. Bahadir only concerned himself with intelligence communications – usually with his handlers in the States – which he always attended to personally in the privacy of his fort-like underground office.

'Oh? Did they say what it was about?' he asked, obviously annoyed.

'Yes; an important message ...'

'All right. Give me a minute and then show them in. But you stay in here while I see them, understood?'

The first thing Bahadir noticed about the three men who came to see him was their age. They were much older than most of the men who had passed through his restaurant complex before. One of the men appeared to be well in his forties.

The second thing Bahadir noticed was less obvious. At first, it was just a feeling. Something about the men made him uneasy. The way they moved, their body language, the look in their eyes, all radiated authority and danger. Bahadir looked at his armed Albanian bodyguard standing near the door and smiled. He always found the huge man's presence and unquestioning loyalty reassuring.

'You wanted to see me?' began Bahadir, the tone of his voice curt. He sat back in his chair and poured himself a drink.

'We bring greetings from Al-Gharib,' said one of the men and stepped forward, 'and a message.'

'A message from *"the Stranger"*? How interesting. What kind of message?'

'He's alive and well, despite the American air attack we believe you initiated.'

428

Taken aback, Bahadir looked up, surprised. 'What do you mean? I … I don't under...'

'Stand up!' barked the man, taking another step forward.

'*What* did you say?' asked Bahadir, surprised.

'You heard me. Stand up, you dog!'

Before the bodyguard could react to the insult, one of the men standing closest to him moved like lightning. He pulled out a gun from under his shirt and pressed it against the bodyguard's chest before he could reach for his own. 'You move, I shoot; clear?' he said.

The bodyguard nodded. The man then reached into the guard's holster, pulled out the gun, a Glock, and handed it to his companion standing next to him.

'Now stand up and put your hands behind your head,' continued the other man calmly, addressing Bahadir.

In a daze, Bahadir stood up slowly and did as he was told. 'Wh-what's all this about?' he stammered.

'Ibrahim el-Masri, you have been tried, found guilty and sentenced to death—'

'What do you mean, Ibrahim el-Masri?' Bahadir almost shouted, turning pale. 'I am Kemal Bahadir!'

'You are now, but in truth you are Ibrahim el-Masri, the despicable traitor working for the Great Satan, the Americans. There's no point in denying it … we know.'

'This is all a mistake,' protested Bahadir.

The man walked up to the desk, reached into his pocket and threw two photographs on the desk where Bahadir could see them. They were the photos Haddad had given to Al-Gharib, showing el-Masri on the operating table before his face operation. The other was a close-up of Bahadir's face after the operation.

Bahadir kept staring at the photographs, realising for the first time that this was all deadly serious and not some unfortunate mistake.

'What do you want?' he said, sounding hoarse.

The man began to laugh. 'What do we want? You think you can make a deal? Is that it? To be expected, I suppose, from scum like you. What we want is *justice.*'

'What do you mean, justice?'

'You will see soon enough. For now, this is what we'll do …'

The man pulled a piece of paper out of his pocket, smoothed out the wrinkles, and placed it on the desk. It was a rough plan of the Sultan's Table complex, showing underground passages leading in various directions through excavated sections of Constantine's ancient palace. The man pointed to a tunnel leading to an exit near the Hagia Sophia. 'This is where we are going.' The man held up the paper and showed it to the guard. 'And you will take us there – *now!* Understood?'

The guard nodded.

'If we meet someone, you clear the way – unless you want to drown in a bloodbath.' The man reached into his backpack, pulled out a grenade and held it up. 'Do you understand?'

The guard nodded again.

'You go first. I'll be right behind you. Act naturally and don't try anything stupid. Move!'

The tunnel leading from the restaurant to the Hagia Sophia exit was rarely used. After many twist and turns, navigating crumbling steps and climbing shaky, cobwebbed ladders, they reached the end of the tunnel with a padlocked, rusty door blocking their way. One of the men stepped forward, attached a silencer to his gun and shot the padlock clean off the door before pushing it open with his shoulder.

Two men, who had been waiting in the shadows under a tree, walked up to the man, embraced him and then helped him clear away the tree roots and other vegetation that almost covered the entire door on the outside.

'You have brought everything?' asked the man.

'We have,' replied his friend and pointed to two large backpacks on the ground. 'Come, I'll take you to the entrance I mentioned. It's just over there. What about him?' The man pointed to the bodyguard standing next to Bahadir. The man who had addressed Bahadir earlier said something in Arabic. His companion with the gun nodded, walked up to the bodyguard from behind and calmly shot him in the back of the head.

Feeling quite sick, Bahadir stared at the dead bodyguard lying on the ground, a wave of panic washing over him like a bad dream. The man standing next to him pointed to the bleeding corpse. 'He's the lucky one, trust me,' he said, laughing. 'All right, let's go inside.'

The concealed tunnel exit faced a small, deserted courtyard next to the Mausoleum of Selim II behind the Hagia Sophia, which towered above them in the dark like an ominous sentinel, guarding terrible secrets of generations past. One of those secrets was the brutal murder of Osman da Baggio's nineteen brothers the day his father had died, clearing the way for his older brother, Mehmed, to become sultan.

They entered the deserted church through a side entrance next to the Imperial Gate, used only by guides during the day. Surrounded by high walls and fences, the whole complex was in darkness and secured for the night. The elderly security guards patrolling outside had been bribed and would turn a blind eye to what was happening inside.

The two men with the backpacks seemed to know the huge church well. Working quickly and quietly to unlock doors and only using torches where necessary to show the way, they entered the staggering nave covered by a vast dome reaching fifty-six metres towards heaven.

Once inside, they quickly made their way towards the tall, ornate *mihrab* in the apse, pointing towards Mecca, where the altar used to stand. Flanked by two giant candlesticks brought back from Hungary by Suleiman the Magnificent to commemorate his conquest in the sixteenth-century, the death squad had decided the mihrab would be the perfect setting for the bloody drama to come.

Because the mihrab – a semicircular niche in the wall of a mosque – always indicates the direction of the Kaaba in Mecca, the symbolic significance of the chosen venue would therefore be clear to all Muslims. However, as the Hagia Sophia was now a museum and no

431

longer a mosque, no offence would be caused by what was about to happen.

The two men with the backpacks quickly went to work. They had brought all the necessary equipment, including batteries, lights and a high-quality camera to record everything for a video to be posted on social media in the morning. Once the lights directed at the mihrab had been switched on, crazy shadows began to dance across the stone floor, and then crawl up the walls towards the galleries, giving the huge nave a sinister appearance, like an arena preparing for a bloody spectacle to please the bloodthirsty mob cheering from above.

'What's all this about?' asked Bahadir, barely able to speak, fear clawing at his empty stomach.

One of the men held up the black IS flag, inspired by the black flag of the Prophet. Scrawled in white across the top was the Muslim profession of faith: "No god but God" with "Muhammad is the Messenger of God" inserted in black into a white circle below.

'It's about justice. Prepare yourself, you are about to die,' he said quietly, and then walked over to the mihrab and attached the flag to the back of the niche to form a dramatic backdrop.

The man who had earlier addressed Bahadir in his office pulled a black balaclava over his own head, stepped into the niche and faced the camera.

'They call me the Just One,' he said. 'This is how we deal with traitors. Bring him over here!'

Two men, also wearing balaclavas, dragged Bahadir over to the niche and made him kneel down in front of the Just One, but facing the camera. Having turned his back on Islam, Bahadir would die facing away from Mecca.

'This is Ibrahim el-Masri, aka Kemal Bahadir,' continued the Just One, 'the famous masterchef. He has betrayed Islam by becoming a slave of the Great Satan, America. The punishment for his betrayal is death. Hear this, my brothers. The final battle heralding the End of Days foretold in the Dabiq Prophesy is about to begin. Rejoice, the Mahdi is on his way. The Day of Judgement is near ...'

68

Colonel Riza was woken by an early morning phone call from his aide. It was just after four am. The aide told him there was something important that he should see. The colonel put on his uniform and hurried to his office on the floor below his room in the Gendarmerie General Command Centre.

'What is it?' he asked.

'This just came in,' said the aide and pointed to a computer screen. As a matter of routine, all IS social media sites were constantly monitored by the intelligence services.

'What am I looking at?'

'This here.' The aide called up a recorded video and pressed the replay button.

A man wearing a turban and a scarf covering his face, armed with a machine gun, stood in front of the smouldering wreck of a Toyota.

'I am standing in a field not far from Dabiq,' said the man. 'At five forty-five this evening, 25 June, a US fighter plane attacked three vehicles travelling towards the Turkish border, which is five kilometres from here.'

The man pointed over his shoulder.

'Four men were killed. One of them was Chief Inspector Naguib Haddad of the Turkish Gendarmerie. Here, let me show you.' The camera moved closer and the man pointed to another wreck a few metres away. Colonel Riza gasped as the camera zoomed in on a bloody corpse hanging out of the shattered windscreen of the twisted vehicle. The right arm was missing, but the face, while badly disfigured, was nevertheless recognisable.

'Naguib,' whispered the colonel, obviously shocked. 'How?' *What on earth was he doing in Syria?* he thought.

433

The camera swung around and focused once again on the man holding the gun.

'Al-Gharib, our illustrious leader, was the target, but the Americans killed one of their allies instead,' he said, raising his gun and firing into the air. 'Rejoice my brothers; this is a sign. The day of the final battle is near. Perhaps it has already begun; here, right now, as foretold by the Dabiq Prophesy. *Allah Akbar!*'

In a way it was all classic IS propaganda, but something told the colonel there was more to all this. First, the arrival of the Paris suicide bombers the night before, and now this. Coincidence? Hardly. Something was definitely going on. Something big.

The colonel turned to his aide. 'We are going into the Sultan's Table complex at first light. Get everything ready and tell the Americans we can't wait any longer. And tell Chief Superintendent Conti and Mr Rogan to come here as soon as possible for a briefing.'

Jack walked into the Gendarmerie's operations room in the basement an hour later. Conti and Cesaria were already there, waiting.

'When did you get in?' asked Conti, lighting a cigarette, his first for the day.

'Last night, late.'

'How was the funeral?' asked Cesaria, shaking her head. She still found it difficult to come to terms with Gambio's brazen assassination. 'Grimaldi told us you were there.'

'I was. Difficult to describe; a bit like a *Godfather* movie.'

'One down, two to go,' said Conti and slapped Jack on the back. 'Perhaps today's the day to make that three; what do you think?'

'Could be. We waited long enough for this.' Jack looked at Conti. 'I'm worried about Belmonte,' he said, lowering his voice.

'Why?' asked Cesaria.

'Well, no-one seems to have seen him since he arrived here, what, two weeks ago? A man like that, holed up in a restaurant? Come on ...'

'The place has been under surveillance 'round the clock.'

'Still ...'

'I know what you mean,' said Conti. 'I'm worried too.'

'We'll know soon enough.'

The atmosphere in the room was electric. The day everyone had been waiting for had arrived at last. The preparations had been extensive, and the waiting had stretched nerves and patience to the limit.

Colonel Riza stood in front of a large conference table surrounded by his team and was about to begin the briefing, when one of his men burst into the room. 'Sir, you have to see this – *now!*' he shouted, walking over to one of the monitors and turning it on. 'This just came in. Look!'

Almost instantly, a close-up of a man wearing a black balaclava came into view. 'This is Ibrahim el-Masri, aka Kemal Bahadir,' said the man and pointed to someone kneeling in front of him on the floor with his hands tied behind his back, *'the famous masterchef.'* The camera closed in on the kneeling man's face. Radiating terror, the eyes staring into the camera said it all.

Jack turned to Cesaria standing next to him. 'Can you believe this?' he whispered. Cesaria didn't reply and kept looking at the screen, mesmerised.

'He has betrayed Islam by becoming a slave of the Great Satan, America,' continued the man on the screen. 'The punishment for his betrayal is death!' The man paused, obviously for effect, and kept looking at the camera. 'Hear this, my brothers,' continued the man, raising his voice like a preacher addressing the faithful. 'The final battle foretold in the Dabiq Prophesy is about to begin. Rejoice, the Mahdi is on his way. The Day of Judgement is near ...'

'I know where they are!' shouted one of the men in the room. 'This is the mihrab in the Hagia Sophia; no doubt about it, *look!*'

'It is!' shouted someone else.

'Silence! Listen!' called out the colonel and held up his hand.

The man on the screen reached under his shirt and pulled out a large knife with a long, serrated blade, and held it up. Then he grabbed a handful of Bahadir's hair with his left hand and pulled back his head.

'*Allah Akbar!*' shouted the man and then quickly cut Bahadir's throat with one, deep incision from left to right. Blood gushed out of the deep wound in pulsating spurts as the camera moved in for a gruesome close-up.

The man then quickly made several further incisions along the side of the neck and at the back. Within moments he had expertly severed the head and held it up like some obscene trophy, as Bahadir's headless corpse fell forward and hit the floor.

'For this traitor, the Day of Judgement has already arrived!' shouted the jubilant man. '*Allah Akbar!*'

The camera closed in once more on Bahadir's bloody head – sightless eyes wide open, staring into eternity – before everything went fuzzy and then blank.

For a long, pregnant moment, everyone in the room stood still. Then Colonel Riza picked up the phone on the table and gave orders for a SWAT team to go at once to the Hagia Sophia to investigate. At the same time, he also gave orders for the commandos standing by, to take up positions at the Sultan's Table and wait for further orders.

The colonel put down the phone and looked around. 'You heard,' he said. 'Let's go!'

69

Belmonte had taken the news of Gambio's assassination very badly. He had first heard about it on the news the day before, like everybody else. Life had just taken a mega-shift, changing everything. Gambio's death couldn't have come at a worse time. The man who held his future and his fortunes in his hands, was no more. Belmonte was on his own, and on the run. When he had tried to talk to Bahadir about this, Bahadir gave him the cold shoulder and told him he had his own urgent problems. Instead of taking immediate action to find a way out of his predicament, Belmonte took to the bottle instead, and got terribly drunk.

The security guard who burst into his room below the restaurant found him asleep, still fully dressed, on his bed with an empty whisky bottle next to him.

'Wake up! We are being raided!' shouted the guard, shaking Belmonte with both hands. Belmonte opened his eyes and stared at the guard, sleep and alcohol fog clouding his brain. It wasn't until the guard repeated what he had just said on his way out that Belmonte sat up. 'What do you mean?' he growled.

'Police raid! Get out fast *now*! Use the cistern exit I showed you. It's the only safe way out of here.'

Within seconds, Belmonte's self-preservation instincts took over. As a man used to dealing with danger and the unexpected, he had the presence of mind to realise this was serious. He reached for his gun on the bedside table next to him and tucked it into his belt. Then he ran out into the corridor and down the stairs into the basement.

After breaking down the front door and securing all other known exits, the commandos entered the Sultan's Table just after sunrise.

Moving methodically from room to room, they began to secure the premises. This turned out to be more difficult than first thought. While there was no resistance as such and the few security guards and kitchen staff all cooperated willingly, the confusing, labyrinthine layout of the extensive underground chambers, tunnels and passages below the restaurant surprised everyone.

Conti, Cesaria and Jack had been told they were merely observers and must stay in the background. They were only allowed to enter the premises after the commandos had secured parts of the restaurant.

Colonel Riza had taken over Bahadir's office and was directing the raid from there. With Bahadir dead, a major problem had gone away and all that was left to do was to find the suicide bombers and mop up. The colonel was more interested in how IS had managed to get Bahadir into the Hagia Sophia, execute him there, film the whole thing, and then boast about it on social media. Questions would be asked about that, for sure. And he couldn't get Haddad's violent death out of his mind either. Belmonte and the Italian police weren't a priority.

Conti, Cesaria and Jack caught up with the colonel in Bahadir's command centre-like office full of high-tech equipment and CCTV screens that would have made a large department store proud. 'Any sign of Belmonte?' asked Conti.

'Nothing so far. It's a maze down there.' The colonel pointed to the CCTV screens on the wall, showing various parts of the underground complex. 'It will take some time to secure all this.'

Conti looked at Cesaria and shook his head. 'Do you mind if we have a look around and perhaps question the guards?' he asked.

'Go right ahead,' said the colonel. As far as he was concerned, the pressure was off and he was therefore prepared to cut Conti some slack.

'What's this? Here, have a look,' said Jack and pointed to one of the CCTV screens. A man was seen climbing down a series of ladders. As he reached the bottom, he turned around and for an instant faced the camera above his head.

'*Belmonte!*' shouted Cesaria. 'Over there, look!'

'You're right; it's him,' said Conti, becoming excited. 'Where's that?'

'No idea, but let's find out,' said the colonel and turned to one of the men searching the office. 'You there, bring the security guards in here *now!*' he bellowed. The man hurried outside and returned moments later with three men.

The colonel pointed to the CCTV screen showing the ladders. By now, Belmonte was nowhere to be seen. 'Where does this lead to?' the colonel asked the men. The three men looked at each other, but didn't say anything.

'I see. I can promise you, by the time we are finished here you will be taken in for questioning. *Severe* questioning, especially now that Kemal Bahadir is dead.'

'What do you mean?' asked one of the men, looking shocked.

'Bahadir was killed – executed would be a better word – during the night. Terrorists.'

The colonel sensed that resistance was crumbling and decided to press on. 'I will ask once more. Last chance. *Where does this lead to?*' he thundered. 'A little cooperation could make the questioning a lot less severe ...'

'The cistern exit,' blurted one of the men.

'Show me!' The colonel pointed to a piece of paper on the desk in front of him. It was a rough plan showing the layout of the restaurant premises he had used for the raid.

'It's not on here. It is – was – Mr Bahadir's—'

'Escape route?' interrupted the colonel, becoming impatient.

Obviously intimidated and eager to cooperate, the guard nodded.

'Show us where it is,' demanded the colonel. '*Now!*'

The colonel turned to Conti. 'I can't leave here, and I have no-one I can spare at the moment to go with you. Are you armed?'

Conti nodded. 'And so is Cesaria.'

'Good. Take the guard and go. Find Belmonte. I'll send someone as soon as I can.'

Smiling, Conti looked at Cesaria and Jack. 'You heard the colonel; let's go!'

Belmonte had never used the cistern exit before. It was only to be used in emergencies. To get in and out of the restaurant unnoticed – mainly for some gambling to pass the time – he had used another concealed side entrance during his enforced stay at the restaurant, which he had found so stifling. He had therefore only a vague recollection of what the security guard had shown him. But after climbing down several ladders, he managed to find the steel door in the basement that led into the tunnel. The tunnel was part of an intricate network of underground passages that once connected various parts of the Great Palace of Constantine.

Belmonte opened the door and stared into the dark, narrow tunnel smelling of nauseating sewerage and rat droppings. He reached for one of the torches kept on a shelf by the door and switched it on. The walls were covered in moss and the droplets of water clinging to the low ceiling glistened like precious gems in a secret pirate cave. Taking a deep breath, Belmonte closed the door behind him and stepped into the unknown.

'There's no light down there,' said the security guard and handed torches to everyone.

'Where does this go?' asked Conti.

'All the way to the Basilica Cistern on the other side of the Hagia Sophia.'

'And there's nowhere else he could have gone?' asked Jack from the rear.

The guard shook his head. 'No. This is the only way.'

'Then let's go and find him,' said Conti, eager to get started.

Wet, exhausted, and covered in slime and moss after having climbed down slippery ladders and crawled through wet passages barely wide enough to squeeze through, Belmonte reached what looked like a round drain cover no more than a metre in diameter. *Great,* he thought, *the end of the road,* and started pushing against the iron grate with his shoulder. At first, the grate wouldn't budge. However, after several attempts it began to move ever so slightly and then disappeared into the darkness on the outside and landed with a splash. *Fuck! Water. That's all I need,* thought Belmonte. He pushed his head through the opening, held up his torch and gasped. *What on earth is that?* he thought. An underground lake in a cathedral? With fish! He shook his head.

Conti stopped and held up his hand. 'Did you hear that?' he said.

'What?' asked Cesaria, who was directly behind him.

'A splash. I heard a splash.'

'I heard it too,' said the guard at the front. 'We must be getting close.'

'Close to what?' asked Jack, wiping his sweaty face with the back of his hand.

'The cistern,' replied the guard.

'Thank God! Hurry!'

Belmonte lifted himself out of the narrow tunnel and then quickly climbed down a rusty iron ladder leading to a ledge at the water's edge. From there he could jump across to a wooden boardwalk, which would be used by hundreds of visitors later that day to explore the cistern without getting their feet wet. Belmonte landed with a thud and looked around. That's when he thought he could hear voices coming from the tunnel. He switched off his torch and listened. The voices came closer. A cone of light coming from the opening above the ladder pierced the darkness and slowly crept along the water's edge like the probing finger of a giant, and then turned towards the boardwalk.

Careful not to make a noise, Belmonte moved forward on all fours, looking for cover.

The cone of light came closer.

Belmonte saw a huge column looming in the shadows in front of him. Just before the light reached his feet, he managed to crouch down behind the massive base of the column, only to find himself staring at a large stone face laughing at his predicament. It was the face of the famous Medusa, visited by curious tourists every day who came to marvel at the Gorgon's upside-down gaze. According to tradition, the head of Medusa had been intentionally inverted to negate the Gorgon's deadly gaze. Belmonte could only hope it worked.

'Wow! 'Look at that,' said Jack as he climbed down the ladder. He had visited the cistern several times before, but had never seen it deserted and in darkness. Radiating mystery and the promise of adventure, the silent, empty cistern beckoned with whispered stories of times long gone. It was a place where stones had voices and came alive. All one had to do was to listen ...

'He could be anywhere,' said Conti. 'What we need is some light.'

'I know where the switches are,' said the guard. He pointed to a set of stairs leading up to the entrance, lit up by one lonely light at the top. 'Up there.'

'Could you turn them on?'

'Worth a try.'

'Is there any other way out of here?' asked Jack.

'Not that I'm aware of, and the entrance up there is closed at the moment. Doesn't open for quite a while,' said the guard, eager to help, 'but the queues will start soon on the outside.

'I'll go with him,' said Jack and jumped across to the boardwalk. 'You and Cesaria stay here. Watch and listen.'

Belmonte checked his gun and the box of ammunition in his pocket. While he could see people moving about with torches and hear voices, he was too far away to risk a shot. His best option was to lie low for the time being, wait for the right opportunity to make a move, and not give himself away in the meantime. For the moment, Medusa's shadow and silence were his best cover.

Jack followed the guard along the boardwalk a few centimetres above the shallow, ankle-deep water full of carp swimming slowly in the dark, and then up the fifty-two stone steps leading to the entrance. As soon as they reached the top of the stairs, the guard went to a switchboard next to the gift shop. Moments later, the cathedral-size cistern below turned into a wonderland of coloured lights, illuminating a forest of elegant columns – each with its own unique history – arranged in twelve rows supporting the cross-shaped vaults and round arches of the lofty roof.

'We can't just stay here like sitting ducks,' said Cesaria as soon as the lights came on, 'and do nothing.'

'I agree,' said Conti. 'Let's go and look for the bastard. You go that way. I take the other side, but be careful. You know who we are dealing with.'

Conti pulled his gun out of his belt and jumped across to the boardwalk. Cesaria did the same. Momentarily overcome by the stunning beauty of the place, she looked dreamily along the illuminated colonnade rising out of the water like a silent army of stone warriors marching towards her out of the distant past.

Music began to fill the vast chamber. Softly at first, then becoming soulful as Turkish melodies echoed across the water, conjuring up images of Whirling Dervishes honouring their god, and old men smoking water pipes and drinking tea in the bazaar. The guard had accidentally switched on the speaker system.

Belmonte saw Cesaria coming slowly towards him, holding her gun with both hands in front of her. He also saw an opportunity. Hiding in Medusa's shadow, he waited for the right moment. He reached into his pocket and pulled out a couple of bullets. When Cesaria appeared to be close enough, he threw the bullets into the water. Cesaria reacted by turning towards the splash and pointed her gun in the direction of the sound, away from Belmonte standing in the shadows. Smiling, Belmonte pounced like a cat. He moved forward, put his arm around Cesaria's neck from behind and pointed his gun at her head. 'Drop it, sweetie,' he whispered, licking her ear, 'or I blow your tits off.'

Stunned, Cesaria dropped her gun and Belmonte kicked it quickly into the water before pulling her into the shadows.

'Listen, all of you!' Belmonte called out from behind the column. 'Game's up!'

Conti froze and then slowly turned around. Belmonte was standing in the shadows next to the Medusa column, holding a gun to Cesaria's head.

'Drop your guns *now* and hold your hands up, or she gets it in the neck,' continued Belmonte.

Conti dropped his gun on the boardwalk and raised his hands.

'Kick it into the water,' ordered Belmonte.

Conti did as he was told.

'You two up there, put your hands where I can see them and stay where you are,' shouted Belmonte.

Jack looked at the guard standing next to him and raised his hands.

'Now, that's a lot better. How quickly things can change. Listen carefully, this is what we'll do ...'

'Raffaele Bangarella, the Archangel of Palermo hiding behind a woman,' taunted Conti. 'I thought you were better than that.'

Belmonte began to laugh. 'Conti, is that you? Gambio told me you had returned and were up to your old tricks. Well, well ...'

'I've come to ask you a question.'

'Long way to come for a question. Fire away.'

'Did you kill my wife?' shouted Conti. He desperately needed an answer from the only man who could remove the nagging doubt that had tortured him since his wife's death two and a half years ago.

'That was a mistake. I was after you! And now, here you are,' replied Belmonte.

Conti closed his eyes for a moment and took a deep breath. A stone had been lifted from his troubled soul. *It was him! Just as I suspected all along,* he thought, feeling free for the first time since that tragic day in Palermo that had killed his happiness.

'You will all stay exactly where you are, and this young lady and I will walk to the exit up there and leave. I hope this is clear, because if not and you make a silly mistake, she dies; simple.'

'Not such a good idea,' said Conti. 'You will never get out of here alive, and even if you do, you will not stay alive for long.'

Belmonte began to laugh. 'I'll take my chances.'

'The reason you won't stay alive for long is as simple as it is compelling,' continued Conti, undeterred. 'Gambio is dead – I'm sure you knew that already. But what you may not know is that Bahadir is dead too; killed last night not far from here.'

'You're bluffing,' scoffed Belmonte, becoming angry.

'Why would I? You're holding all the cards. The reason you will not stay alive for long is something quite different: Giordano knows you killed his son. He will hunt you down, whatever it takes. You can count on that.' Conti paused to let that sink in. 'You have nowhere to hide.'

'Enough!' shouted Belmonte. 'We are going up now!'

Slowly, Conti began to walk towards Belmonte.

'Stay where you are!' barked Belmonte.

Conti kept walking. 'Let her go,' he said. 'This is between us. Take me instead. It will look a lot better that way, trust me. The Archangel hiding behind a woman is one thing, but taking Chief Superintendent Conti hostage and then walking out of a tight spot, well ... what do you say? Are you a man, or just the lowlife hitman everybody says you are?' said Conti calmly, throwing down a challenge he hoped Belmonte would find difficult to resist.

Belmonte stopped in his tracks. The insult had found its mark. 'All right. Come here,' he said after a while. Conti walked up to Belmonte with his hands raised and stopped in front of the man who had been haunting his nightmares for so long. 'I could kill you right now.'

'Only a coward would do that. Are you a coward? And besides, you need me alive to get out of here.'

'Turn around!'

Conti turned around and looked straight at the upside-down Medusa face in front of him.

Belmonte let go of Cesaria, put his arm around Conti's neck from behind and pressed the nozzle of his gun into his back. 'Now we're even,' he said.

'What do you mean?'

'I killed your wife by mistake, but I let this one here go as you asked.' Belmonte pointed with this chin towards Cesaria.

It was a bizarre explanation, but Conti knew better than to make a sarcastic remark. Instead, he nodded. 'Let's go. I'm ready.'

'Thank you,' whispered Cesaria, tears in her eyes as Belmonte and Conti began to walk slowly towards the stairs leading up to the exit.

Just before they reached the end of the boardwalk, a crashing noise could be heard coming from above. Moments later, two commandos, guns at the ready, burst through the upper gate, followed by Colonel Riza, and took up positions at the top of the stairs next to Jack.

'Not too late, I hope?' asked the colonel, catching his breath. 'What's going on?'

'See for yourself.'

Conti stopped and looked up at the commandos. 'How quickly things can change,' he said to Belmonte. 'The cavalry has just arrived. Bad luck.'

'Shut up and keep walking,' hissed Belmonte.

'I don't think so,' said Conti and turned around to face him.

'What is he doing?' asked the colonel.

'Don't know,' replied Jack, his eyes locked on the strange pair facing each other below.

The two commandos looked at the colonel, the question on their faces obvious. The colonel shook his head. 'Wait for my signal.' The commandos nodded and kept their guns trained on Belmonte.

'You're not listening,' hissed Belmonte, gritting his teeth in frustration. He raised his gun and pointed it at Conti's forehead. 'Keep walking!'

A smile spread over Conti's face. For the first time since his wife's violent death, he felt completely at peace. 'I've waited a long time for this.'

'What are you talking about?'

'Sending my wife's killer to hell' replied Conti and quickly dropped his arms. He managed to grab Belmonte by the shoulders and give him a push before Belmonte pulled the trigger, lost his balance, and fell backwards.

'*Take him out!*' shouted the colonel.

Hit by several bullets in the head and chest, Belmonte was dead before he hit the water. Blood began to flow from his body, turning the water crimson and scaring away the fish.

Screaming, Cesaria ran towards Conti lying on the boardwalk, blood gushing from his mouth. He was still alive, but could no longer see. She knelt down beside him – tears streaming down her face – cradled his head in her lap and stroked his hair. Moments later, he passed away.

Jack turned to the colonel standing next to him. 'A bad movie?' he said, shaking his head in disbelief.

'No, harsh reality. These walls would have seen a lot, but nothing quite like this.' The colonel put away his gun. 'I meant to tell you earlier ...'

'What?'

'Haddad's dead. He was killed yesterday near Dabiq in Syria.'

'Jesus! *How?*'

'I'll show you when we get back to my office,' said the colonel, sadness in his voice, and followed the commandos down the stairs. Just before he reached the bottom, he stopped and turned around. 'We've found something in Bahadir's office that concerns you,' he said.

'What?'

'Tell you later.'

PART V
OSDABIO

"The natural healing force within each of us
Is the greatest force in getting well."
Hippocrates

70

The Turkish security forces had moved quickly. All traces of the Hagia Sophia terrorist execution and the Basilica Cistern shooting had been erased before the popular tourist destinations opened in the morning. Sultan's Table had been temporarily closed, and the Americans had removed from the premises all potentially incriminating records and equipment linking them to Bahadir. Conti's body had been taken to the morgue and officers were on their way from Florence to collect it. Grimaldi had instructed Cesaria to wait for them in Istanbul and return to Florence with the body. Officially, nothing had happened. The all-important tourist dollar had been protected and was safe.

Colonel Riza had strongly suggested that Jack leave Istanbul as soon as possible and requested – for security reasons – that he not talk to the press. Jack agreed and decided to take the first available flight to Venice. In return, the colonel gave Jack something precious to take with him. In doing so, he had broken several rules, but felt that special circumstances warranted this.

Jack arrived at Marco Polo airport just before eleven in the morning and after spending almost an hour in a frustrating queue, finally managed to catch a water taxi.

As the taxi approached the Rialto Bridge and he could see the familiar facade of the Palazzo da Baggio in the distance, Jack began to relax for the first time since the horror he had witnessed the day before. So much had happened, but in a strange way the traumatic events seemed distant – almost surreal. He had spent half the night on the phone and had barely slept, but was very much looking forward to catching up with Tristan, Lorenza and the countess.

Jack stepped off the water taxi and then walked along a narrow, slippery stone ledge leading to the huge portal facing the canal. Pulling a thick chord to ring a bell inside, he wondered how Osman da Baggio would have felt doing the same four hundred years earlier.

Perhaps I should have called, thought Jack as he waited. Then the door opened. *Too late.* Coming straight from the kitchen and wearing an apron covered in flour, her hair pulled back with a headscarf tied at the back of her neck, Lorenza looked at Jack and froze. Then delight replaced surprise as she threw her arms around him and pulled him inside.

Tristan and the countess had arrived two days earlier. Tristan had made excellent progress and was no longer bedridden. Lorenza had collected her prize money and was busy making plans for a restaurant in the family palazzo, and the release of a cookbook. She was also in great demand for interviews and television appearances.

Jack's unexpected arrival caused quite a stir. Everyone gathered in the salon on the first floor and almost overwhelmed him with questions. Taking his time, Jack gave a step-by-step account of the turbulent events of the past few days, beginning with the Gambio execution everyone had of course already heard about.

'You were at the funeral?' asked da Baggio.

'I was there and saw it all.'

Lorenza looked at Tristan. 'Can you believe this?'

Tristan nodded. 'That's Jack,' he said, grinning. 'Always in the right place at the right time. Uncanny!'

Jack then told them how and where Haddad had been killed, but didn't show them the video posted by IS. But he did show them the gruesome Bahadir execution video and gave a graphic account of what happened in the Basilica Cistern.

When Jack finished, no-one stirred.

'Incredible!' said the countess at last. 'How could all this have happened in such a short time?'

'Destiny waits for no-one,' said Jack, 'and retribution is unpredictable, brutal and impatient.'

Tristan sat next to Lorenza. He was holding her hand and looked at her intently. 'What did I tell you?' he said.

Looking pale and quite shaken, Lorenza nodded.

Da Baggio turned towards his daughter. 'What does he mean?'

'Tristan told me this would happen ...'

The countess shot Jack one of her *do-something* looks.

Jack stood up walked to the door. 'I have a surprise for you,' he said. 'Back in a moment.'

Jack returned a few minutes later with a rectangular package under his arm, wrapped in brown paper and held together with string. He walked over to the wooden chest by the window. 'This is for you, Leonardo,' he said, and placed the package on top. 'And for you, Lorenza. Please open it.'

'For me?' Da Baggio began to untie the knots. '*I don't believe it!*' he whispered, carefully folding back the paper to expose what was inside.

'What is it?' asked Lorenza.

Da Baggio held up the package. 'Here, see for yourself.'

'Is that what I think it is?'

Lorenza stood up and walked over to her father. 'The recipes!' she cried out. 'My God, the recipes have come home!'

'How did you manage this?' asked da Baggio, shaking his head.

'The recipes were found in Bahadir's restaurant during a raid yesterday, together with a note from Gambio. The Turkish authorities kept the note.'

'Do you know what it said?' asked Tristan.

'Yes. Something like: "I kept my promise; I hope you will keep yours".'

'So, that's what this was all about,' said da Baggio. 'We know that Gambio was behind the abduction and the strange ransom demand ...'

'That made no sense at all at the time,' interjected the countess. 'The recipes ...'

'Now it does,' said Lorenza. 'This was all about *Top Chef Europe*. Kemal Bahadir was after the recipes.'

'Humiliation and pride,' said Jack. 'He couldn't accept his loss during the competition. As the self-proclaimed expert on Ottoman cuisine, he couldn't come to terms with losing to you, Lorenza.'

As the countess looked at Tristan sitting next to Lorenza on the lounge, she remembered his strange, almost prophetic words during the contest. *This victory will come at great cost.* She also remembered the expression on his face: troubled and sad. Now she knew why.

Da Baggio walked into the middle of the room and held up his hand. Slowly, everyone fell silent. 'As you just said, Lorenza, the recipes have returned home, the circle is complete. Let's close this painful chapter once and for all and move on. Thank God it's all over.'

Jack walked across to da Baggio and put his arm around his shoulder. 'Not yet, my friend,' he said. 'I'm afraid there is more, and it has to do with the recipes, and perhaps making history.'

'What on earth do you mean?' said da Baggio, a little annoyed.

Jack smiled. He was in his element. The storyteller inside him was bursting. 'Let me tell you,' he said, 'it's quite a story.'

Why am I not surprised? thought the countess and rolled her eyes, smiling.

Bemused, Tristan was smiling too and looked expectantly at Jack.

Jack walked over to the coffee table. He picked up his iPad, opened it and located a photo of the painting he had found in the Imperial Crypt in Vienna.

'Let's begin at the beginning,' he said and held up the screen for all to see. 'When I found this painting two years ago, I had no idea who this was, or the role the book he is holding in his hand was to play. But now we know. The man is Osman da Baggio – your ancestor who escaped from Constantinople as a young man, returned home here to Venice and became a famous physician.'

Jack turned around and pointed to the wall behind him. 'In fact, you told me the painting used to hang right here next to this delightful little portrait of Osman's mother, until the Nazis stole it during the war. We also know what book Osman is holding in his hand: it's *al-Qanun*, Avicenna's famous *Canon of Medicine*. But we had no inkling just how important this book was to become until you, Leonardo, mentioned the da Baggio family chronicles to me. Do you have them here?'

'Sure.' Da Baggio walked over to the chest by the window, took out a thin, leather-bound book and handed it to Jack. Holding it carefully with both hands, Jack held it up like a precious trophy, which in a way of course it was.

'This, my friends, contains a treasure-trove of information. As you know, I took copies of the chronicles back to Sydney with me. There I began my investigation with the help of a Jesuit priest, Father Connor, an expert in Church history and fluent in Latin. What we discovered was truly astonishing. We found out what happened to Osman and discovered clues pointing to the possible whereabouts of the book he was holding. To cut a long story short, our search took us to Rome, to the Vatican archives, where we located Osman's original annotated copy of *al-Qanun* buried in the Inquisition's records of his trial, and a lot more ...'

Jack paused to let this sink in. Mesmerised, everyone was hanging on his every word and following the extraordinary story with a mixture of fascination and disbelief.

'And this is where things become really interesting,' continued Jack, lowering his voice as he pointed to the bundle of recipes on the table. 'And it all has to do with this here.'

'The recipes?' asked Lorenza.'

'Yes.'

'In what way?'

'When we worked our way through Osman's copy of the book and the trial transcript that meticulously records all the questions put to Osman, and of course his answers too, we discovered something interesting ...'

'What exactly?' asked Tristan, sitting up and leaning forward.

'Osman recorded detailed information about his cases in the margins of the book with surprising detail and accuracy. He was a gifted observer of symptoms. Unfortunately, that's where the good news ends.'

'In what way?'

'He didn't record the treatment or the remedies he had prescribed for his patients, which appeared to have been so effective and successful – *miraculous* as the inquisitors suggested – and that was the problem. When questioned about this, he gave a very curious answer.'

'What did he say?' asked Tristan.

'He said that all treatments and remedies depended entirely on food; special recipes emanating from the East ...'

'Are you suggesting ...?' said Lorenza, pointing to the recipes on the table.

Jack nodded. 'But unfortunately, he didn't specifically talk about the recipes. All he said was it was all in his head. I believe he wasn't going to disclose his secret recipes. Much like the famous Ottoman cooks in the sultan's kitchens at the Topkapi Palace. They guarded their recipes with their lives. They were treasures, and I believe Osman treated them in the same way. The Inquisition wasn't satisfied with this answer and he was convicted of heresy. Without a satisfactory explanation, they suspected witchcraft was involved.'

Jack shrugged. 'With that, Father Connor and I reached a dead-end. It is hard to believe that this only happened a few days ago. Father Connor returned to Sydney with copies of various extracts of the original book, which contains the handwritten comments and annotations made in the margins by Osman himself. I had to go to Istanbul ... You know the rest.'

Jack paused again and put down the book next to his iPad.

'You also know why the Nazis were looking for this book and why Professor K was so interested in it. We've spoken about this before. But what you don't know is that certain information contained in the book may have present-day significance that could in fact hold the key to a possible breakthrough in certain cutting-edge medical research currently being conducted by Alexandra – Professor Delacroix – and her team at the Gordon in Sydney.'

'This is unbelievable,' said da Baggio, shaking his head.

'Sure is, but there's more ...'

'*More?*' asked the countess.

'Yes, and it has to do with the original recipes here.' Jack pointed to the table. 'You will remember when we decided to hand over the originals as directed in the ransom telephone call, and Clara came here from Florence and inserted a tracking device into the folder?'

'Yes, of course I remember,' said da Baggio, frowning.

'We took photocopies of the originals before we handed them over.'

'Of course. They are right here,' said da Baggio and pointed to the wooden chest.

'Could I see them?'

'Sure.'

Da Baggio went to the chest, retrieved the copies and handed them to Jack. Jack held up one of the recipes and looked for the original among the bundle on the table.

'Ah; here it is,' he said and held up both, the copy and the original.

'Perfect, right? In every respect.'

'Sure. What's your point?' asked da Baggio, becoming a little impatient.

'*Not so!* Here, have a look.' Jack turned over the original and pointed to a small symbol – exquisite Ottoman calligraphy – in the bottom right-hand corner. Then he turned over the copy and held it up. It was completely blank.

'How is this relevant?' asked Lorenza. 'This has nothing to do with the recipe.'

'*Oh, but it has,*' said Jack. 'Let me explain.'

Jack opened his shoulder bag, pulled out a piece of paper and held it up. 'This is an extract from the transcript of Osman's trial. As you can see, there are a number of symbols set out right here, and here. Osman was questioned rigorously about them by the Inquisition, because these symbols appear regularly next to his handwritten notes in the margins in the book.'

Tristan nodded and smiled. He could already see where Jack was heading. 'Instead of setting out the recipes themselves, Osman identified them through symbols.'

'Exactly,' said Jack. 'Each recipe has its own specific identification code – symbol – *on the back*. This only became clear to me yesterday, when Colonel Riza gave me the originals and I noticed the symbols on the back of each recipe. Without access to the originals, we would never have found out about this.' Jack paused and ran his fingers through his hair. 'This is the missing link, the connection that ties everything together. I called Alexandra immediately and told her the good news. As you can imagine, she became very excited. She had of course seen copies of the recipes before; copies that didn't have this important identification on the back – that missing, all-important clue.'

For a long moment there was a complete hush in the room, as the implications of what Jack had just said began to sink in.

'All right,' said da Baggio, breaking the silence. 'Let's take a step back. As I understand it, all of this may have a bearing on some important research currently being carried out in Sydney. But, does that really concern us here?'

'Oh yes, it does!' said Jack.

'In what way?'

'In a way you couldn't possibly imagine, and it has to do with the Vatican at the highest level.'

'Please explain,' said da Baggio.

'I can't,' replied Jack, the tone of his voice conspiratorial.

'Come on Jack,' said the countess, stepping in. She had seen Jack's antics before. 'This is too serious ...'

'You are right about that.'

'All right, why can't you tell us?' asked the countess.

'Because I gave my word not to talk about it to *anyone.*'

'Great. First you tell us all this, and then you just leave us ... *hanging there?*'

'Another one of your cliffhangers?' suggested Tristan. 'You are not writing a thriller here, Jack.'

'Of course not! And the good news is that you will only be left in suspense for a little while ...'

'How come?' asked Lorenza.

'Because tomorrow, all will be revealed – and it concerns you most of all, Lorenza.'

Looking confused, Lorenza shook her head. '*Me?* I don't understand ...'

'You will, trust me.' Jack paused and looked around the room. 'You will know exactly what this is all about when the cardinal gets here.'

'What are you talking about?' asked da Baggio.

'I spoke to Cardinal Borromeo at the Vatican this morning, and he asked me to prepare you for his visit.'

'*Cardinal Borromeo is coming here?* Isn't he the Dean of the College of Cardinals?'

'Yes, that's him,' said Jack cheerfully. 'He's the one who gave us access to the Vatican archives and helped us find the records. Nice guy.'

'You met him?'

'Oh yes, I did.'

Da Baggio looked at the countess and shook his head. She shrugged in silent reply. '*But why?* Why is he coming here?'

'Okay, my friends; that's as far as we can take it for now,' said Jack, brushing the question aside. 'Lorenza, any chance of some lunch? I'm starving. I haven't eaten anything proper for days. All that Turkish stuff just isn't me ...'

Lorenza turned to Tristan. 'Can you believe this man? First, he winds us up, and then he wants to *eat?*'

'That's Jack. Unpredictable and full of surprises,' said Tristan, laughing. 'But never boring.'

'I can see now why you two get on so well.' Lorenza stood up, threw back her head in a huff, and hurried towards the kitchen.

71

Looking at the tall, distinguished-looking elderly man in a black suit standing at the busy jetty where the water taxis came in to collect tourists who had just arrived in Venice, no-one would have guessed that he was the second most powerful man in the Vatican. And no-one would have suspected that the elegant man with the aristocratic bearing standing next to him, was the pope's personal physician.

Cardinal Borromeo looked at his watch and nodded. *Perfect*, he thought. *We are right on time.* For once, the plane from Rome hadn't been delayed as so often happened. For a busy man with a diabolical schedule like the cardinal, every hour counted. And what he was about to do was of the greatest importance, demanding his personal attention. It wasn't often that the Dean of the College of Cardinals travelled to see a young woman to ask for a favour. However, the gravity of the situation demanded such drastic action.

The cardinal, a practical, hands-on man, didn't believe in delegating something that concerned the pontiff's life. He could easily have sent someone else high-up to attend to this, but that just wasn't his way.

Jack spotted the cardinal first and waved. 'There they are,' he said to da Baggio and pointed to the jetty. Da Baggio manoeuvred the boat expertly through the busy traffic and pulled up.

For a man well into his seventies, the cardinal moved with surprising agility as he jumped on board and shook hands with Jack. 'This is Professor Montessori,' said the cardinal, as Jack introduced him to da Baggio.

'Your illustrious family is certainly no stranger to the Church and church business,' said the cardinal, standing next to da Baggio at the wheel. 'However, you must be wondering what this is all about, but I can assure you, it is of the utmost importance.'

'We are honoured, Eminence, and at your service,' said da Baggio as he pointed the boat towards the Canal Grande and put on speed.

Everyone in the palazzo had assembled in the salon and was waiting for the arrival of their eminent guest. All morning, the conversation had centred around guessing the reason for the cardinal's surprise visit. Despite a lot of teasing and prompting, Jack's lips had remained sealed.

Lorenza heard the engine noise first as the boat pulled into the mooring downstairs. 'Here they are,' she said, her cheeks aglow with excitement. 'How do I look?' Lorenza turned to Tristan, sitting next to her, as she adjusted her hair for the third time and fiddled with the pendant around her neck.

'Gorgeous as always,' said Tristan and gave her a kiss on the cheek. 'Don't fuss. Just be yourself.'

The countess looked at Lorenza and gave her an encouraging smile.

Everyone stood up as the cardinal and Montessori entered the room and da Baggio made the introductions. Used to being the centre of attention, the cardinal, obviously at ease, took control of the situation. He could sense the tension in the room and it wasn't difficult for him to guess the reason behind it. He therefore decided to come straight to the point and explain the purpose of his visit.

'I must apologise in advance for my haste,' began the cardinal, speaking perfect English, 'but I have to catch a plane back to Rome this afternoon. Therefore, there isn't much time, and we have a lot to talk about.' The cardinal paused, and looked around the room. He believed in the importance of first impressions. He had liked Lorenza and her father instantly, and was confident that his request, unusual as it may be, would be well received. Encouraged, he pressed on.

'To begin with, I must ask you all to keep everything you are about to hear confidential because I'm going to share something quite extraordinary with you. You will appreciate the reason for this request in a moment.'

The cardinal turned towards Lorenza. 'I have come here to ask you, Signorina da Baggio, for a big favour. And that favour concerns none other than His Holiness, the pope.' The cardinal paused to make a point.

'Sadly, His Holiness is gravely ill. In fact, he's close to death,' continued the cardinal, the tone of his voice solemn. 'A few weeks ago, the pontiff's medical advisers made contact with Professor Delacroix in Sydney and asked for her help. They turned to her because certain research she is involved in at the moment could have a direct bearing on the pontiff's illness, which has been very difficult to diagnose. This in turn has led to some unexpected developments. I think it would be better if you hear about that from Professor Montessori here, who has of course been closely involved with the pontiff's illness and treatment from the very beginning.' The cardinal turned towards Montessori and nodded.

'As you can imagine,' began Montessori, 'medical issues like the one we are dealing with here can be very complex and difficult to explain. Therefore, I would like to keep this as simple as possible and focus on just a few key points that will throw some light on why we are here.

'His Holiness is suffering from a rare and difficult to diagnose immune disease. The disease is destroying his red blood cells and platelets and destroying the lining of his large intestine. Unchecked, this will eventually be fatal. Various treatment options suggested by Professor Delacroix that may perhaps be available have been considered, but regrettably, due to the advanced nature of the disease and other complications, these options cannot be explored in the circumstances.

'However,' continued Montessori, 'Professor Delacroix and her team at the Gordon Institute in Sydney have just discovered a new, previously unknown gene in the pope's genome that may be the cause of the disease and could open up unexpected treatment possibilities—'

'In a way that I can only describe as providence,' interrupted the cardinal, 'a possible cure may be hidden in something Mr Rogan has just recently discovered in the Vatican archives.'

'Osman da Baggio's annotated copy of *al-Qanun*,' said Jack, stepping in.

For a long, tense moment the room was silent as the implications of what had been suggested began to sink in.

'As you know,' continued Montessori, 'several prominent doctors and scientists have been looking for this book for a long time now because they suspected it might contain valuable information about possible cures and ways to treat certain diseases – especially to do with the immune system, which is presently at the forefront of medical research around the world. Professor Delacroix, a Nobel laureate, certainly seems to believe that too. Mr Rogan, could you please elaborate?'

'After we discovered the annotated book in the Vatican archives – hard to believe that was just over a week ago,' began Jack, 'Professor Delacroix was able for the first time to have a close look at the entire book in its original form. As I explained yesterday, the book contains Osman's case notes he recorded in the margins. And that's where Professor Delacroix discovered something extraordinary. One of the cases described by Osman was an accurate account of an autoimmune disease just like the one His Holiness appears to be suffering from.'

Jack paused and glanced at the cardinal. He was trying to gauge whether to introduce something he had been thinking about all morning. Encouraged, he decided to go ahead.

'Your Eminence may not be aware that all of this began with the recent discovery of a painting that used to hang right here behind me.' Jack turned around and pointed to an empty space on the wall. The story behind the painting and of its discovery is extraordinary, but may have to wait for another time.'

Relieved, the countess took a deep breath and tried in vain to suppress a smile.

'The painting is currently in London, still being restored, but I have a picture of it right here.'

Jack opened his iPad, retrieved the photo of the painting and handed the iPad to the cardinal.

'The man in the painting is Osman da Baggio, and the book he is holding in his hand is none other than *al-Qanun*, the very book we found in the Vatican archives a few days ago. But just as interesting is the man in the bed, obviously a patient. We believe he is Cardinal Bettinelli, who later became pope and saved Osman from the ruthless clutches of the Inquisition. There is a great deal written about this case in Osman's book and this is in fact the very case that has aroused so much interest in medical circles. Professor Delacroix believes that Cardinal Bettinelli was suffering from the same immune disease as His Holiness.'

'Which Osman was able to cure?' interjected the cardinal, shaking his head and handing the iPad to Montessori.

'All the symptoms Osman describes in such detail strongly support this,' continued Jack. 'Professor Delacroix was first alerted to this by something she had discovered in Professor Kozakievicz's notes. He had come across certain extracts from Osman's annotations mentioned in later medical texts and was also looking for them for the same reasons. He too, suspected that they could contain valuable information about the immune system. Why? Because Osman claimed in the book to have successfully cured such a disease in a way that was quite unique and revolutionary, certainly at the time.'

'How?' asked da Baggio, following Jack's account with interest.

Jack looked at Lorenza. 'Remember what I told you yesterday about the symbols in the margin of the book and on the back of the recipes?'

'Yes,' said Lorenza, raising an eyebrow.

Jack turned to the cardinal sitting next to him. 'Your Eminence, the original recipes I mentioned to you on the phone yesterday are right here.' Jack pointed to the wooden chest by the window. 'I believe that's the reason you are here?'

'That's correct,' said the cardinal. 'The possible cure Mr Rogan referred to just now and Professor Delacroix was also looking at, relates directly to certain recipes, which, I believe you have ...'

'And we have now been able to link to the book through the symbols I mentioned yesterday,' Jack said. 'In fact, allow me to show you.'

Jack stood up and walked across to the chest. 'I took the liberty earlier this morning of going through the recipes and identifying the ones that specifically relate to the cure Osman claims to have discovered, and used so successfully on his famous patient in the painting. There are three of them.'

Jack opened the chest, took out three of the recipes and held them up. 'Here they are. The symbols here on the back match those shown in Osman's case notes in the margins of his annotated book. He claims to have cured the disease through diet. More specifically, through Ottoman dishes; these right here.'

'Is that possible?' asked da Baggio.

'According to Professor Delacroix, it is,' said Montessori. 'She's of the view that expression of the newly discovered gene I mentioned before, which appears to have caused the disease, could be switched off by epigenetic modification of the genome. Without becoming too technical here, this could come about through the use of certain foods that could stimulate gut microbes to produce a particular short-term fatty acid – Butyric acid – also called Butyrate. Butyric acid inhibits histone deacetylases, a class of enzymes that remove acetyl groups form histones, around which DNA is wound. Organosulfur compounds from garlic, as well as the isothiocyanates sulforaphane from cruciferous vegetables such as cabbage, cauliflowers, Brussels sprouts—'

The cardinal held up his hand. 'Please, Professor, stop,' he said, laughing. 'If this is what you call not becoming too technical – I'm sure you've lost everyone in here. You certainly lost me.'

'I'm sorry,' said Montessori. 'You are right, Eminence. What I'm trying to say is that certain foods could repress expression of this new gene in the gut and this may be possible through diet and certain special recipes. Dietary repression of this new gene might block the inflammatory bowel disease that is threatening His Holiness's life.'

Montessori paused and took a deep breath. 'In short, it could represent a cure, or at least a way to manage the disease, which could give our medical team some precious time to explore other, more permanent treatment options ...'

'Incredible! So, where to from here, Eminence?' asked da Baggio.

The cardinal turned to face Lorenza and looked at her intently. 'I – no – the Church, has a request,' began the cardinal, speaking quite softly. 'Would you be prepared to come to Rome and cook for His Holiness? Replicate the recipes that appear to have cured one of his predecessors?'

Speechless and quite stunned, Lorenza just stared at the cardinal as she tried to come to terms with what he had just asked of her.

'But-but why me?' she stammered. 'Couldn't one of the competent chefs at the Vatican do this just as well, perhaps even better than I? Especially as we now have the recipes?'

The cardinal smiled. He had been expecting something like this.

'No, it is *you* we need. Professor Montessori has just discussed this with Professor Delacroix before we left Rome this morning. Ottoman recipes like these here, are notoriously vague when it comes to precise measurements and even ingredients and cooking techniques. They are more like guidelines, leaving the final decisions up to the chef. This was done quite deliberately to protect the recipes. Osman would have had all of this in his head, just as he told the Inquisition.'

'But how could I be of help here?'

'Ah, because we believe you too have this in *your* head. As I understand it, cooking has been a long tradition in your family, handed down from generation to generation – right?'

'Yes, but ...'

'You see, according to Professor Delacroix, your *interpretation* of the recipes could well be the key here.'

Makes sense, thought Lorenza, squeezing Tristan's hand.

'You can do it,' he whispered and squeezed hers in reply.

'My daughter and I would be honoured,' said da Baggio, coming to Lorenza's assistance.

Lorenza nodded. 'When would you like me to start, Eminence?'

'I was hoping you would come back with us to Rome this afternoon and begin cooking tonight,' replied the cardinal. 'And I was also hoping that Mr Rogan would be able to accompany you. He has

466

the best grasp by far of all the relevant historical documentary material we may have to consider here as well.'

'Fine by me, Eminence,' said Jack.

'It's all settled then,' said da Baggio and stood up. 'However, before you go, gentlemen, you must have lunch with us. Lorenza stayed up half the night preparing it for you ... everything is ready. Please follow me.'

'With pleasure,' said the cardinal and stood up too.

The countess linked arms with Jack as they followed the others into the dining room. 'See, in Italy, it's all about food,' she said, a sparkle in her eyes.

'I got that,' said Jack. 'Lucky I haven't unpacked.'

72

'I must have been out of my mind to agree to this, Jack,' said Lorenza, carefully setting out the ingredients for her next dish on a wooden board, conscious that all the others working in the busy Vatican kitchen were watching her. Since their arrival the night before, and with the cardinal's parting words – 'You are His Holiness's last hope' – still ringing loudly in her ears, Lorenza had barely slept a wink as the enormity of the task she had so willingly undertaken began to dawn on her.

Back home in the family palazzo it had all seemed so exciting, with the cardinal and the pope's personal physician asking for her help. But now, standing in the Vatican kitchen where all the meals for the pontiff had been prepared for centuries, it was a different, daunting matter entirely.

Jack was sitting on a stool facing Lorenza's workbench and was recording everything: ingredients, precise quantities, cooking method ... As a keen amateur cook himself, he didn't mind and watched Lorenza with interest.

Alexandra had given Jack detailed instructions about this, as she was relying on the information to monitor and analyse what the pope was eating and what effect, if any, it would have on him. Because of that, accuracy was of the utmost importance.

'Don't worry, you're doing just fine,' said Jack.

Lorenza put down her knife and looked at him. '*Just fine?* I am preparing a dish based on an ancient Ottoman recipe that I have to "interpret" to save the pope's life, and all you can say is "I'm doing just fine"? This is crazy, Jack! What kind of pressure is that, eh? I don't know what got into me!'

'Calm down. I know it's been a long day and a long night, and cooking something in a hurry so late yesterday wasn't easy, but you are

468

pulling it all together. Come on ...' Jack got off his chair, walked over to Lorenza and put his arm around her shoulders. 'We have to finish this. We can't stop now. You know that.' Jack picked up the knife and put it into Lorenza's hand.

'By the way, this really looks like a fabulous dish.' Jack pointed to the recipe on the workbench next to Lorenza. It was a translation of the original, and the second recipe identified by Osman in the margin of his book next to the all-important case notes dealing with the immune disease.

'Hunkar Begendi, "Sultan's Delight" again,' continued Jack. 'You won *Top Chef Europe* with this dish, didn't you?'

Lorenza nodded.

'A dish based on a secret recipe that once belonged to Suleiman the Magnificent, as I recall it,' continued Jack, 'which may save the pope. Amazing.'

'A recipe young Osman brought with him from Constantinople when he escaped from the Topkapi Palace.'

'How romantic.'

'Yes, and one of my mother's favourites,' said Lorenza, becoming a little emotional. 'It was one of the first dishes I remember cooking with my grandmother in our kitchen in Venice. Generations of da Baggios have prepared it there for centuries.'

'Let's hope it can weave its magic here.'

Feeling better, Lorenza looked at Jack. 'Then we better get on with it,' she said and wiped away a few tears, 'or we'll never find out.'

Professor Montessori was personally overseeing everything to do with the pontiff's meals. He came into the kitchen several times throughout the day and accompanied the nuns who carried the meal tray to the pontiff's apartment. He also spoke with Lorenza about the dishes she was preparing, making sure they were served as soon as they were ready. He also made sure that Jack accurately recorded exact portion sizes and their weight every time a dish was taken to the pontiff.

It was already quite late in the afternoon when Montessori swept into the kitchen with a big smile on his face. He walked up to Lorenza and Jack at the workbench. 'I have good news,' he said. 'His Holiness seems to be improving!'

'So soon?' asked Lorenza, adjusting her apron.

'It's remarkable, but Professor Delacroix didn't seem surprised. She said if this was to work at all, improvements would become apparent very quickly.'

'Let's hope it continues,' said Lorenza.

'His Holiness's appetite has returned and he is enjoying the dishes. He is also sleeping better and there are other signs as well ...'

'That's great,' said Jack and pointed to a large pot simmering on the stove. 'So you think this is working?'

'Too early to tell for sure, but the signs are definitely encouraging. I haven't seen His Holiness so animated and in such good spirits for a long time. The pain in his abdomen seems to have eased too, and the fever has gone.'

'The bowel inflammation?' asked Jack.

'Looks that way. In fact, he asked for another portion of the dish we served for lunch,' said Montessori, obviously delighted. 'Another good sign.'

'Hunkar Begendi,' said Lorenza. 'It's not called the "Sultan's Delight" for nothing. We have plenty left.'

'If you could prepare a small portion now, I'll take it to His Holiness.'

'No problem.'

An hour later, Cardinal Borromeo came into the kitchen. Everyone stopped working and watched. To see the Dean of the College of Cardinals visit the kitchen was unheard of.

'You already heard the good news, I believe,' said the cardinal, walking up to Lorenza's workbench.

'We have, Eminence,' said Lorenza and wiped her hands on her apron. 'Very encouraging.'

'Professor Delacroix certainly seems to think so. I just spoke to her a moment ago.' The cardinal turned to Jack. 'Your notes are excellent by the way, she said.'

'Good to hear.'

'His Holiness has a request,' said the cardinal, lowering his voice.

'Oh? Something to do with the dishes?' asked Lorenza, frowning.

'No, to do with the chef preparing them.'

'Oh ...'

'He would like to meet you.'

Lorenza looked alarmed. 'When?' she asked.

'Right now. Please, come with me.'

Lorenza and Jack followed the cardinal through a maze of corridors to the papal apartments. Two Swiss Guards in full regalia stood in front of the pontiff's bedroom, their colourful uniforms lit up like beacons as shafts of afternoon sunlight reached through the windows like fingers of gold.

The cardinal stopped in front of the tall double doors. 'Wait here, please,' he said, then knocked and entered. He returned moments later.

'I will take you inside now and introduce you,' he said to Lorenza. 'His Holiness would like to see you alone.' The cardinal looked at Jack and shrugged.

'*Alone?*' said Lorenza, barely able to speak, a wave of panic washing over her. She looked pleadingly at the cardinal.

'There is nothing to worry about, trust me. You are about to meet an extraordinary man. Just be yourself; come.'

'Good luck,' whispered Jack as Lorenza walked past him, her eyes locked on the cardinal as he opened the door. Lorenza didn't reply and Jack wasn't sure if she had heard him.

Jack walked over to the windows and looked down into St Peter's Square, teeming with the faithful who had just attended mass in the basilica.

The cardinal joined him a short while later. 'I'm sorry,' he said, 'but His Holiness ...'

'I understand.'

'He definitely wants to meet you, but another time.'

'No problem.'

'She's an exceptional young woman.'

'She certainly is that, and she's been through a lot lately.'

'I know,' said the cardinal, 'and so does His Holiness.'

After the door had closed behind her, Lorenza stood perfectly still, unsure of what to do next. The windows were open and bright sunlight filled the sparsely furnished room, illuminating the magnificent paintings covering almost every wall. Apart from a single bed and a chair facing the door, a French antique desk by the window and a beautifully carved *prie-dieu* – a kneeler – at the foot of the bed, the large room was almost empty. However, the presence of the frail-looking man lying motionless in the bed with his eyes closed, seemed to fill the bedchamber.

He's asleep, thought Lorenza, listening to her own heartbeat pounding in her ears. Suddenly, the pope opened his eyes and looked at her. It was a look Lorenza would never forget. Someone was looking into her soul.

'Please, come closer where I can see you,' said the pope, his voice sounding distant but gentle, and pointed to a chair next to his bed. As Lorenza walked over to the chair, little did she know that the next fifteen minutes would transform her life.

Jack and the cardinal were chatting by the window when Jack noticed something out of the corner of his eye: the door to the pontiff's bedroom was opening slowly. 'Ah, here she comes,' he said, and turned towards the door.

For a moment, Lorenza stood motionless in the doorway, tears in her eyes, gazing at something in the distance only she could see. Then slowly, she closed the door behind her and looked around.

Jack walked over to her. 'How did it go?' he asked.

'Hold me, Jack,' whispered Lorenza, shaking all over.

Jack put his arms around her and held her tight.

'Could we please go into St Peters?' asked Lorenza.

'What, *now*?'

'Yes please.'

The cardinal, who had overheard the exchange, turned to one of the Swiss Guards and said something in Italian. The guard nodded and walked over to Jack.

'He will take you into the basilica,' said the cardinal, smiling. 'He knows a good shortcut.'

Jack and Lorenza entered the basilica through a side door close to the high altar where the pope had recently collapsed. Lorenza stopped and looked at the stunning columns of St Peter's Baldachin directly under the huge dome. Bernini's masterpiece – an inspired blend of sculpture and architecture –stood directly above St Peter's tomb. The stunning structure reaching towards Michelangelo's breathtaking dome was a visual link between the basilica's enormous size and the human scale of the papal altar beneath the canopy.

'Amazing, isn't it?' said Jack, looking up into the dome.

The basilica was almost empty by now as most of the faithful had left after the service.

'Give me a moment, please,' said Lorenza, her voice quivering with emotion, and then she walked ahead into one of the side chapels. She stopped by a small wrought-iron stand full of flickering candles. Slowly, she lit two candles of her own, crossed herself and then walked up to the altar and knelt to pray.

Jack stood in the shadows, watching. Strangely moved, his mind began to wander, taking him back to a mission station in outback Australia where as a boy he had spent a few months during a drought too awful to remember.

It all began with Brother Francis and that note, he thought, his mind racing back thirty years. *'If you follow my instructions, you will find all the answers, and a lot more ...'* *Was he right about that!* Jack shook his head as he remembered opening the grave in the little cemetery in Berchtesgaden on Christmas Eve many years later, and finding Brother Francis's diary hidden under the tombstone. And in a way, that had just been the beginning. And then came the Imperial Crypt in

Vienna and the discovery of the two paintings hidden in the sarcophagus. Incredible!

For a while, Jack watched Lorenza, head bowed and obviously deep in prayer, kneeling at the altar. Then his mind returned to the painting and how its restoration had uncovered the writing on the book – *al-Qanun* – which was at the very centre of the drama unfolding at the moment.

Jack shook his head. *Those breadcrumbs of destiny, again*, he thought.

Cardinal Borromeo walked up to Jack from behind. 'I thought I'd find you here,' he said quietly

Jack turned around, startled, and smiled. He pointed to Lorenza kneeling in front of the altar. 'Meeting His Holiness seems to have affected her deeply.'

'Not surprising. His Holiness has that effect ...'

For a while the two men stood in silence, watching Lorenza.

'I can see God's hand in all this,' said the cardinal. 'All the threads are coming together in unexpected ways. I firmly believe now His Holiness will pull through.'

'I call it following the breadcrumbs of destiny.'

'Perhaps we are talking about the same thing?' suggested the cardinal.

Then Lorenza crossed herself again and stood up. As she came closer, Jack noticed something remarkable: an expression of inner peace he hadn't seen before, and a radiating glow coming from somewhere deep within.

'I'll wait for you at the side entrance over there and take you back when you're ready,' said the cardinal and withdrew.

'Are you going to tell me what happened when you met?'

'His Holiness took away my grief.'

'I don't understand.'

'Mum and Antonio ... I was with them, just now. Right here. The wound has healed. I'm no longer grieving!'

'How did he ...?'

'He showed me the way.'

'How?'

'Love and faith.'

'Ah.' Jack nodded.

Lorenza took him by the hand. 'Don't look like a doubting Thomas,' she said. 'We have work to do! Let's go back to the kitchen.'

Jack noticed a new confidence and purpose in Lorenza's step as they followed the cardinal across a courtyard and then up some stairs.

'More Hunkar Begendi,' said Lorenza, putting on her apron. 'It seems to have become His Holiness's delight as well. He said as much.'

'Is that what you were talking about?' asked Jack, a mischievous sparkle in his eyes. '*Food?*'

'There was a bit of that,' said Lorenza cheerfully.

'Anything else?'

'Of course.'

'Care to tell me?'

'Later perhaps. But for now, let's cook! We are all instruments of God.'

'We are?'

'Even an incorrigible rascal like you, Jack Rogan; trust me. Where's your notebook?'

'You've been around Tristan and Katerina for far too long.'

'Could be. Come on, let's get stuck into it!'

'Yes, chef!'

THREE MONTHS LATER

Cardinal O'Brien's residence; Sydney

Despite her heavy, relentless workload, Alexandra made sure she was home in time to get ready for dinner. Since the Ethics Committee had cleared the path for the groundbreaking CRISPR trials in Australia, she realised the medical research fraternity in every corner of the globe was watching. If successful, this was a game changer. To Alexandra, however, it was much more than that. It was her friend and mentor's legacy: Professor K's final quest.

Not everyone approved, and many were sceptical. The pressure was therefore enormous, and Alexandra and her team had virtually worked around the clock for weeks to make sure there were no mistakes.

For the first time, CRISPR was being trialled on humans – real patients – at St Luke's Hospital directly next door to the Gordon. The Gordon and St Luke's had collaborated many times before, but never on something so revolutionary and controversial. CRISPR was definitely a world-first and would not have been possible without the support of the Catholic Church and the personal intervention of Cardinal O'Brien in the all-important ethics debate that had brought Alexandra's research almost to a standstill the year before.

The dinner had been arranged by Cardinal O'Brien to celebrate not only the pope's extraordinary recovery, but his highly acclaimed United Nations address in New York and his inspirational speech in the US Congress a few days later that had made headlines around the world. When the pope spoke, the world listened. However, due to the pope's illness, none of that could have gone ahead without Alexandra's groundbreaking research, medical advice and guidance.

Jack had just flown in from New York and was also getting ready. 'Lucky it still fits,' he said, adjusting his belt. 'I haven't worn this suit in years.'

'Let me have a look,' said Alexandra, smiling. 'Wrong tie.' She walked over to Jack's wardrobe and opened the sliding doors. 'Six ties? Is that it? You and your clothes! There's virtually nothing in here. Try this one.'

'You know I don't wear this kind of stuff ...'

'Come on, Jack, not even you can turn up at the cardinal's dinner party in jeans and a tee-shirt.

'Suppose so ...'

'Get on with it, or we'll be late!'

Alexandra and Jack were the first to arrive. Father Connor welcomed them at the front door and escorted them to the terrace next to the dining room for pre-dinner drinks. The cardinal was already there, talking to Mrs Kelly about the seating arrangements.

'I'm glad you could prise yourself away from your research, Professor Delacroix, albeit for just one night,' said the cardinal, a sparkle in his eyes. 'And thank you for travelling halfway around the world, Mr Rogan. I understand you came back to Sydney just to be with us this evening?'

Jack waved dismissively and took a sip of his gin and tonic. 'Couldn't miss this, Eminence,' he said, and took a bow.

Looking excited, but a little awkward, Ayah and Vimal arrived moments later. It wasn't often that two young research scientists were invited to a private dinner with their world-famous Nobel laureate boss, an acclaimed international writer, and a cardinal.

'Now that you are all here,' began the cardinal, looking at Alexandra, 'allow me to start by congratulating you on this marvellous article.' The cardinal held up a copy of *Science*, the peer-reviewed academic journal of the American Association for the Advancement of Science.

'Your Eminence is full of surprises,' said Alexandra. 'This only came out last week. You are more up-to-date than most of my colleagues.'

The cardinal smiled, acknowledging the compliment.

'Ah, the illustrious *Science* magazine,' said Jack. 'The Holy Grail of science journals. It's every researcher's dream to one day have an article feature in its hallowed pages.'

'True,' said Alexandra.

'Did you know it was founded in 1880 with financial support from none other than Thomas Edison, and later Alexander Graham Bell?'

'I didn't know that,' interjected Vimal.

'It has a chequered history. Due to lack of support it stopped publishing in 1882. It was resurrected a year later, but was soon in financial difficulties again and was eventually sold to a psychologist – James McKeen Cattell – for five hundred dollars.'

'You seem to know a lot about this,' said Father Connor. 'But then I shouldn't be surprised ... you seem to know a lot about, well, a lot.'

'I did a series of articles about the journal's history as a young journo in Brisbane,' said Jack, laughing. 'One of my first assignments. I thought it was the short straw at the time. Little did I know then ...'

'We have an almost complete set here in the library,' said the cardinal. 'I often pick up one of the early copies. Fascinating, I can tell you. Did you know there are articles in there by Albert Einstein about gravitational lensing, and Edwin Hubble about spiral nebulae? They have changed the way we see our world.'

'And an article on fruit fly genetics by Thomas Hunt Morgan,' Alexandra added, 'which has changed the way we look at genetics.'

'And now an article by Dr Alexandra Delacroix: "Is POMAX 16 the new KALM 30?" No doubt this is going to change something too?' asked the cardinal.

'Perhaps. Especially if we are successful with the new drug ...'

'*Osdabio*,' interjected Ayah.

'POMAX 16 and Osdabio? What's all this about?' asked Jack.

'You should read the article, Mr Rogan,' said the cardinal. 'I can lend it to you.'

'Why not hear it from the horse's mouth instead?' came Jack's riposte.

'Vimal, could you please help Mr Rogan here?' said Alexandra, and please, keep it simple.'

'Thanks. You mean *Science for Dummies*?' said Jack.

Alexandra gave Jack a coquettish look and shrugged.

'You will remember we recently discovered a new, previously unknown gene in His Holiness's genome,' began Vimal.

'Another "hidden gene", I think you called it,' said the cardinal.

'Correct; POMAX 16. A gene related to Professor K's KALM 30 gene that appears to block the action of the IL-10 brake system, allowing the "go signal" CD86 to stimulate autoimmunity,' said Alexandra.

'In the beginning, we called it the Holy Gene,' interjected Vimal, 'but thought that may not be such a good idea in the long run ...'

'In the lab we still do,' said Ayah, smiling.

Alexandra held up her hand. 'All right, guys,' she said, trying to keep the conversation on track. 'Enter Osman da Baggio and his notes ... Osman described this devastating inflammatory bowel disease in great detail and claimed to have successfully treated it with food; a diet.'

'The dishes we prepared for His Holiness,' said Jack. 'I was there with Lorenza ... we called it the Ottoman diet.'

'That was so successful,' continued Alexandra. 'And now we know why.'

The cardinal looked at her. 'You do?' he asked.

'Vimal, could you please explain?'

'As your Eminence will remember, we spoke about avatar mice not that long ago.'

'I do.'

'Well, we were able to successfully reproduce the mutations in His Holiness's genome in an avatar mouse and then breed a colony of mouse avatars we could use to pinpoint how the DNA difference has caused his immune system cells to go "rogue"—'

'And, most importantly,' interrupted Alexandra, 'how these ab-normalities could be corrected.'

'*You have discovered a way to do this?*' said the cardinal.

'We have.'

'How?' asked Jack.

'We discovered that expression of this new gene – POMAX 16 – can be switched off by epigenetic modification of the genome.'

'Please explain,' Jack said.

'We can do this through food; a specific diet.'

'The *Ottoman diet?*' asked the cardinal.

'Yes. Based on what Lorenza cooked for His Holiness. It's all in Osman's recipes.'

'Extraordinary!'

'Sure is. Professor K suspected something like this would work and referred to it in his notes. It all has to do with specific foods – vegetables, to be precise. In this case aubergine – or eggplant as you Aussies call it – and certain cruciferous vegetables mixed with some specific spices—'

'A balanced diet?' interrupted Jack again. 'Hunkar Begendi? The Sultan's Delight?'

'Among other things, yes,' said Alexandra.

'And this has been successful in the avatar mouse?' asked the cardinal.

'Yes, spectacularly. We even called the mouse HH, for His Holiness,' admitted Vimal, unable to resist.

'One of our lab jokes,' said Alexandra, stepping in. 'Strictly for in-house consumption only. Based on what we have found out so far, we are confident that a drug can be developed in due course to do the job here. Efficiently, and with certainty. It's all about personalised medicine. Pharmaceutical companies are circling already …'

'This is truly amazing,' said the cardinal.

'And you gave this drug a name already?' asked Jack. 'Osdabio?'

'Aha,' said Alexandra. 'Can you guess why?'

'Obvious, isn't it? After Osman da Baggio, of course.'

'Ah, I can see Mrs Kelly looking at me,' interjected the cardinal, pointing to the open terrace doors. 'I think dinner is about to be served. Let's go inside.'

'Beef Wellington,' said Jack, tucking into his second thick slice of perfectly cooked fillet steak with gusto. 'And what superb pastry. So light! Mrs Kelly must be congratulated. You are a fortunate man, Eminence, to have such a fine cook, right here.'

'Joining the Church has its advantages,' said the cardinal, smiling. 'You must tell her yourself,' he added, lowering his voice. 'Compliments can go a long way ...'

'I certainly will.'

'Don't be fooled, Eminence, 'Mr Rogan is an excellent cook himself,' said Alexandra.

'Wouldn't surprise me.'

'This beats Ottoman cuisine hands down,' said Jack, munching happily.

'Unless you are suffering from chronic bowel disease,' teased Alexandra, reaching for her wine.

'Then I would just take some Osdabio, and bingo?'

'One day, maybe.'

'But this will not cure His Holiness in the long run,' said the cardinal, turning serious. Having waited for just the right moment, he was guiding the conversation to exactly where he wanted it to go.

'No, I don't think it would. It will keep the bowel inflammation under control for the time being, but something more will need to be done.'

'Any ideas?'

Alexandra put down her glass and looked at the cardinal sitting at the head of the table. 'In fact yes, Eminence.'

'Oh? What?'

'CRISPR. Genome-editing.'

'Professor K's final quest?' asked Jack.

'Yes, exactly.'

Father Connor stood up and poured some more wine for everyone.

The cardinal was watching Alexandra intently. 'How would it work?' he asked, leaning forward.

481

'Based on the results of our clinical trial so far, I believe that genome-editing could correct His Holiness's defective LRBA gene in his own stem cells.'

'How?' asked the cardinal quietly.

'By using the new technology of CRISPR Cas9.'

'Have you discussed this with Professor Montessori?'

'I have, just the other day.'

'And?'

'His Holiness's medical team appear keen to try this – soon.'

Jack looked at the cardinal, expecting a reaction, but the cardinal's face remained impassive. However, Jack suspected that he hadn't been informed about this.

'And this could be done without having to be hospitalised?' asked the cardinal, frowning.

'Yes, I believe so,' said Alexandra.

'How would it work?'

'Well, how much detail would you like?'

'Enough to understand …'

'All right. Here we go: Step one. His Holiness's stem cells would have to be isolated from his blood after giving him several injections of a drug called "granulocyte colony stimulating factor", to mobilise his haematopoietic stem cells out of the bone marrow and into the blood.' Alexandra paused and looked around. 'Not the ideal dinner conversation, is it?'

'Never mind,' said the cardinal and held up his hand. 'Please continue.'

Alexandra pointed to Ayah sitting opposite. 'You know more about the next step than I do; please …'

'Next, His Holiness's stem cells would be injected with tiny amounts of sgRNA and Cas9 RNA and HDR template using electroporation. This would be done in tissue culture. In other words, in the lab.' Ayah paused and turned to the cardinal. 'And now comes the really ingenious bit,' she said. 'The sgRNA–Cas9 complex would cleave the LRBA gene near the site of His Holiness's inherited

GABRIEL FARAGO

mutation, and the HDR template DNA sequence would be designed to repair these cuts by pasting in the normal LRBA gene sequence.'

'Incredible,' said the cardinal.

'While all this is going on in the laboratory,' said Alexandra, 'His Holiness would undergo "conditioning for stem cell transplant".'

'How would that work?' asked Jack.

'With a course of chemotherapy to deplete his LRBA-defective hematopoietic stem cells and T cells.'

'And then?' asked the cardinal.

'As a final step, His Holiness would receive his own genome-edited stem cells as a transfusion. The wonderful thing here is this: the transplanted stem cells are his own in every respect except for the single letter in his genome that has been edited to correct his inherited misspelled copy of LRBA. And because the transplanted stem cells are his own, the stem cells won't be rejected and consequently pose no risk of graft-versus-host disease. Therefore, no need to be treated with powerful immune-suppressive drugs after the stem cell transplant. Quite simple and effective. Sounds complicated, but it really isn't.'

'My head's spinning,' said the cardinal. 'And you think this could buy His Holiness more time?'

'It could do more than that. It could be a cure.'

'I hope you didn't mind me bringing all this up in the middle of our dinner. Please forgive me,' said the cardinal, turning again into the polished, consummate host.

'Not at all,' said Alexandra, obviously pleased to have been asked. 'As Your Eminence can see, we are all very passionate about this.'

'Understandably so. But so much more is at stake here than just the pontiff's life,' said the cardinal, turning serious. 'When you suggested we try Osman's diet as a last resort, you did much more than buy His Holiness a little more time, Professor Delacroix. You made history.'

'Oh?' Alexandra looked at the cardinal, surprised. 'How?'

'As we know, His Holiness improved, surprisingly fast. So much so, that a few weeks later he was well enough to travel to the US and

483

attend two historic events: his speech in the United Nations, and addressing the US Congress. As a direct result of those two extraordinary events, a humanitarian ceasefire was negotiated, allowing thousands of trapped refugees to leave Damascus and Aleppo. According to reliable sources, this saved at least a hundred-thousand lives and opened the door for serious peace negotiations.'

The cardinal looked intently at Alexandra. 'As you can see, one voice can make a difference,' he continued quietly. 'And you made it possible for that voice to be heard when it counted most. And for that, I thank you – all of you.' The cardinal paused for effect. 'But I'm not the only one who would like to thank you,' he continued. 'Before Mrs Kelly serves her famous Peach Melba, I have a little surprise for you.'

The cardinal reached into his pocket and pulled out an envelope. 'I received this yesterday by special diplomatic delivery from the Vatican. Cardinal Borromeo has asked me to read it to you.'

The cardinal opened the envelope, pulled out a piece of paper and held it up for all to see, the crossed keys of the Vatican crest clearly visible at the top. 'This is a handwritten note from His Holiness, Pope Pius XIII.'

'To Professor Alexandra Delacroix,' began the cardinal quietly. 'Please accept the humble thanks of an old man approaching the end of his journey. I believe I had an appointment with destiny. You, and your dedicated team of researchers made it possible for me to keep it. And for that, I am forever in your debt.'

The cardinal paused again, looked at his guests and slipped the note back into its envelope. 'It's signed Pius XIII,' he said and handed the envelope to Alexandra. 'Sadly, looking around the world today, the cruelty of man appears to have no bounds,' continued the cardinal. 'Fortunately, neither does his ingenuity and capacity for good. Often, these matters hang in the balance and it is up to us to tip the scales.'

After a few moments of silence, Jack stood up slowly, breaking the spell. 'May I say a few words, Eminence?' he asked.

'By all means.'

'We have just witnessed an extraordinary event with far-reaching consequences. But I believe it is important to keep in mind where, and how, it all began. Looking back, I believe it all began with a vision and an inspired idea of a remarkable man – *Professor K.*' Jack paused and looked around the table. 'I would therefore like to propose a toast, if I may.' Jack reached for his glass and held it up.

Everyone reached for their glass and stood up.

'I give you Professor K and his final quest' said Jack. 'May his genius improve the journey of man and benefit mankind for generations to come. To Professor K.'

'To Professor K,' echoed the others, honouring the memory of an exceptional man who had dared to dream.

ONE YEAR LATER

I. *Sistine Chapel, Vatican*

Jack looked up at Michelangelo's *Last Judgement* behind the altar. He was trying to take in the monumental scale of the stupendous work as he remembered Goethe's famous words: "Without having seen the Sistine Chapel one can form no applicable idea of what one man is capable of achieving."

The invitation to attend Lorenza and Tristan's wedding had taken everyone by surprise. After making a full recovery from his injuries, Tristan had returned to France with Countess Kuragin to finish his degree at the Sorbonne. Lorenza had opened her restaurant in the family palazzo in Venice six months later and called it La Cucina di Osman – Osman's Kitchen. Tristan and Lorenza announced their engagement on the day the restaurant opened. But what came after that, no-one could have anticipated.

Jack, the best man, turned to Tristan sitting next to him in the front where the cardinals usually deliberated during conclave. 'Can you believe this, mate?' he whispered. 'A wedding in the Sistine Chapel officiated by the pope?'

Tristan shook his head and squeezed Jack's arm. 'I didn't see *this* one coming ...'

Before Jack could make another comment, the organ began to play and everyone stood up as His Holiness, Pope Pius XIII entered the chapel with his dazzling entourage.

One month after the engagement was announced – which had attracted a lot of publicity – Lorenza received a letter from Cardinal Borromeo that rocked the da Baggio household to the core. It was a personal invitation from the pontiff to come to Rome and be married by him in the Sistine Chapel.

Since the pope's almost miraculous recovery, Lorenza and Alexandra had become inextricably intertwined with the pontiff's life.

486

After the huge success of the Australian CRISPR trial, the pope's medical team decided to go ahead with the controversial treatment and have the pope's genome edited. This new, complex procedure – which was carried out at the Vatican in collaboration with Alexandra at the Gordon, but without the pope having to be hospitalised – was another great success and appeared to have returned the pontiff to robust health. So much so, he was able to undertake a historic trip to Jerusalem at Christmas and talk about peace in the troubled region.

Smiling, Cardinal Borromeo approached the groom and his best man. 'This way please, gentlemen, come,' he said and pointed to a spot in front of the pope. 'Please stand here and wait. The bride is about to enter.'

Jack and Tristan bowed towards the pope and turned around to face the small wedding party. Apart from trying to find a suitable date in the pope's busy calendar, it was a condition of the special wedding in the Apostolic Palace that it had to take place at nine am in the morning, before the Sistine Chapel opened to the public. Due to security reasons and logistical considerations, the wedding party had to be restricted to only a handful of family members and close friends. Every great honour has its price.

As Jack looked at Alexandra sitting next to the countess in the front, he remembered his private audience with the pope the day before. Faith and science had intersected in a dramatic way. The pontiff, who owed his life to cutting-edge medical research and the Nobel laureate who had made it all possible, discussing science and God was an encounter Jack would never forget.

Then the organ music changed tempo and became louder, signalling the arrival of the bride as the doors opened and da Baggio entered with his daughter. Wearing her late mother's simple wedding dress and carrying a lovely bouquet of yellow roses in her right hand, Lorenza looked stunning as she walked slowly down the aisle with her proud father, towards the pope waiting for her in front of Michelangelo's *Last Judgement*.

There were two bridesmaids – the countess's daughter, Anna, and Cesaria, who had forged a close friendship with Lorenza after Conti's tragic death in Istanbul – and one cute little page boy, Anna's son William, with his curly hair. As Jack watched Anna and little William come towards him he remembered that fateful day seven years ago in outback Australia when Anna's life had been hanging by a thread, and she and her baby were rescued. Jack and his friend Will had risked their lives to save them. Sadly, Will had sacrificed his during the rescue.

Walking slowly behind the bride and her father, Cesaria looked radiant as she approached the altar. *What a remarkable young woman,* thought Jack as he remembered Cesaria kneeling beside Conti in the Basilica Cistern after he had been shot. Seeing her again conjured up images of that terrible day of retribution in Istanbul etched into his memory, never to be forgotten.

Another moment of destiny, thought Jack as Lorenza and Tristan stood in front of the pope, exchanging their vows. The descendant of an Ottoman prince and the son of a Maori princess, joined in holy matrimony by the Vicar of Christ. Amazing!

Jack looked up at Michelangelo's iconic *Creation of Adam* on the ceiling above, a lump in his throat. *This is all about art and faith; the divine touching man,* he thought, savouring the exquisite moment: standing in the Sistine Chapel surrounded by one of man's supreme achievements. Yet, the reason His Holiness was able to be here at all was due to another, quite different achievement: man unravelling the secrets and complexities of nature. And that was about something else altogether: Michelangelo meets Professor K; art and faith meet science and reason. *Perhaps we need both if we want to make sense of it all,* mused Jack, as the pope pronounced Tristan and Lorenza husband and wife.

II. *Palazzo da Baggio, Venice*

It was all over in less than half an hour. Because of the intimate, private nature of the wedding ceremony and the logistical restrictions placed on it by the Vatican, da Baggio, as father of the bride, had suggested they should all return to the palazzo in Venice later that day and meet up with friends waiting to celebrate the occasion. As there were only ten in the wedding party, including the newlyweds and Lorenza's grandparents, this had been quite easy to arrange. Unfortunately, Cesaria, who had advanced rapidly in the Squadra Mobile after Conti's death, was on duty in Florence and couldn't join them.

The flight from Rome arrived on time. Dressed in his Sunday finest, the gardener was waiting for them at the jetty with the boat Tristan had so admired and two other vintage boats provided by friends, all decorated with colourful garlands, giving the ride home along the Canal Grande the festive air of a wedding procession Venice-style.

The restaurant had been closed for the day, and the chefs had prepared a wedding feast to remember. Lorenza had created a special menu – a blend of Ottoman and traditional Venetian dishes – that would be a true reflection of her family's heritage and history.

The guests were awaiting the arrival of the wedding party in front of the palazzo. As soon as the boats pulled up and Tristan and Lorenza stepped onto the jetty waving like film stars on the red carpet, everyone began to cheer and showered them with flowers from the balcony above.

'Better than a movie, don't you think?' said Jack as he helped Alexandra step off the bobbing boat.

'Beats working in the lab, I can tell you.'

After Lorenza had opened her new restaurant, she and Tristan had begun the long, difficult process of refurbishing the rest of the family palazzo to turn it into the exclusive boutique hotel it had once been.

By using many of the original furnishings, paintings and antiques that had been in the family for centuries, Lorenza was able to give the hotel a unique, personal touch that became an instant hit and was booked out for months in advance. Osman's Kitchen and Palazzo da Baggio were a perfect combination. Located on the Canal Grande close to the Rialto Bridge in the historic heart of Venice, the palazzo was a unique time capsule providing a priceless glimpse of the past through the lens of all the luxury trimmings a present-day boutique hotel had to offer, including an award-winning restaurant run by the current *Top Chef of Europe*.

'When are you going to do it?' asked Alexandra, turning to Jack sitting next to her at the dinner table.

'Later, I think. After all the guests have gone. This is a private matter; you know why ...'

'Good idea,' said the countess, 'but please, keep it short.'

'I will try.'

After the last of the guests had retired to their rooms or returned to their respective hotels, the family withdrew for a nightcap in the salon to reflect on the momentous events of the day. Feeling exhausted, Anna had gone to her room as well, to put little William to bed.

Jack glanced at Lorenza standing by the open window, watching the last of the guests leave by water taxi. 'May I have your attention please, for just a moment,' he said, tapping his glass with a small spoon. Jack paused until the room fell silent and then turned to face Lorenza.

'This is a day none of us will forget. Much of it is like a fairytale. First, a wedding in the Sistine Chapel officiated by His Holiness, followed by this splendid reception here in Venice, surrounded by your family and friends. It may be late, Lorenza, but it isn't over yet. There is one more surprise in store for you this evening ...' Jack paused and looked at Lorenza. 'Curious?'

Lorenza nodded, smiling.

'You won't be disappointed, promise! The surprise is all about one man: Osman, your illustrious ancestor,' announced Jack with a flourish.

He turned towards da Baggio and pointed to an empty space on the wall behind him. 'Leonardo, you told me that the only painting of

490

Osman was hanging on the wall right there next to the little portrait of his mother, until it was stolen by the Nazis during the war.'

'That's right,' said da Baggio. 'But that was well before my time. I have never actually *seen* the painting, only a couple of photos of it we have in one of the family albums.'

'Then it's about time you did,' said Jack and signalled to the waiter standing by the door.

'What do you mean?' asked Lorenza, walking over to Jack.

'You'll see in a moment ...'

Alexandra turned to the countess sitting next to her on the lounge. 'He's enjoying this,' she said.

'The storyteller in full flight; that's our Jack.'

Moments later, two waiters entered carrying a rectangular object with three legs that looked like an easel covered by a dark blue cloth, and placed it on the floor in front of Jack.

'Here it comes,' said Alexandra. 'Watch.'

'This is for you, Lorenza, and for you, Leonardo. It is only fitting that something that obviously belongs to your family, should return home on this special day.'

Slowly, Jack leaned forward, carefully lifted the blue cloth off the painting underneath it, and then stepped back.

For a long, tense moment, everyone gazed at the stunning painting, illuminated by flickering candlelight from the large candelabra on the chest next to it, the vibrant colours giving the faces in the picture a warm, lifelike glow. The restorers had done a marvellous job.

'This is my wedding present to you,' said Jack quietly, his eyes misting over. 'History in motion.'

Lorenza wiped away a few tears, walked over to Jack and kissed him tenderly on the cheek. 'Thank you,' she whispered. 'You are a true friend.' Then the room erupted as everyone crowded around the painting to get a better look.

Alexandra turned to the grandparents, examining the painting. 'Osman had quite a journey,' she said. 'You know the story, of course?'

'Yes, we do. It's truly amazing. Stolen by the Germans, and then hidden in a sarcophagus in the Imperial Crypt in Vienna all these years until Jack and Tristan found the painting and had it restored. They told us the story.'

'Jack and his breadcrumbs of destiny at work,' said Alexandra. 'I need another drink.'

'Me too,' said the countess.

'Anna looked lovely today, by the way,' observed Alexandra. 'And William is such a cute little boy.'

'She's certainly getting better. As you know, she and Tristan have a special bond.'

'I noticed.'

Da Baggio walked over to Jack and embraced him. 'I don't know what to say, Jack.'

'You've said it all already. Words are not the only way ...'

'You are right. So much joy in one day is almost too much, don't you think? It frightens you.'

'It's not our call, Leonardo, but it's up to us to embrace it all. Life is so short and unpredictable.'

'Look at those two,' said the countess and pointed to Leonardo standing next to Jack. 'I haven't seen Leonardo looking like this in years. He's been through a lot, but is no longer grieving.'

'Every moment of happiness is precious,' said Alexandra. 'We have to hold onto it the best we can, with both hands!'

'Yes, you're right.'

Jack held up his hand. 'My friends, *there is more* ...' he said, sounding almost theatrical as he began to tap his glass again with the spoon, like a magician introducing his next act.

'Here he goes again,' said the countess, laughing. 'He can't help himself.'

'A little too much champagne, you think?' suggested Alexandra.

'Not sure ...'

Tristan turned towards to Jack. 'What do you mean?' he said, surprised.

Jack put his arm around him. 'Can you *feel* something, mate? Any ideas?' he teased.

'None at all.'

'Serious?'

'Absolutely.'

'It seems I've succeeded at last. It would appear that this time, I will be able to surprise you all, and that includes Tristan here, who can usually sense what's coming, which can be quite deflating.'

Jack turned towards the painting and pointed to the book Osman was holding in his hand. 'In a way, the real mystery and importance of the painting all comes down to this book here – Ibn Sina's famous *al-Qanun* – and how Osman had tapped into some ancient knowledge and used Ottoman recipes to prepare dishes to cure his patients. Isn't that right, Alexandra?'

Alexandra nodded.

'In fact, it was only after we discovered Osman's original book in the Vatican archives and Alexandra made the connection between his case notes and the Ottoman recipes, that the true significance of what this book was all about became apparent.'

'Correct,' said Alexandra. 'And that's when it became clear to me why Professor K was so interested in it. The book was the missing link.'

'The original recipes have now safely returned home as well. You saw them earlier, prominently displayed on the walls of the restaurant,' continued Jack. 'After our audience with His Holiness yesterday, Cardinal Borromeo asked me to come back later in the day. He wanted to talk to me privately. You will remember I couldn't join you for lunch in the Piazza Navona. I went to see the cardinal instead.'

'Do you know what this is all about?' whispered the countess.

'No idea,' replied Alexandra, 'but I think we are about to find out.'

Jack paused and looked around the room, letting the suspense grow.

'The reason the cardinal wanted to see me was this ...' Jack turned towards the painting and pointed to the book in Osman's hand. *Al-Qanun.*

Jack walked over to a sideboard under one of the windows and picked up a small wooden box he had put there earlier. 'This is the final surprise for the day,' he said and handed the box to da Baggio. 'It's a gift from Cardinal Borromeo he entrusted into my care. He asked me to hand it over when the time was right. I believe the right time is now. Please, Leonardo, open it.'

Da Baggio opened the lid of the little box and gasped. Then he held it up so that everyone could see what was inside. It was Osman's annotated copy of Ibn Sina's *al-Qanun,* which had been presented by the Inquisition as evidence of witchcraft at Osman's trial four hundred years earlier, and would have remained buried in the Vatican archives forever, if Jack and Father Connor hadn't discovered it and brought it to light so it could shine again and improve the journey of man.

Afterword

Dietary repression of Alexandra's newly discovered POMAX 16 gene resulted in the development of a new drug – Osdabio – based on certain ingredients in Osman's ancient Ottoman recipes. Osdabio was a breakthrough because it successfully addressed the chronic inflammatory bowel disease that had been such a serious side effect in patients treated with new cancer drugs, like the hugely successful Yervoy used in cancer patients to block CTLA-4.

Autoimmunity against other critical organs like the pituitary gland or liver was another serious side effect of cancer drugs like Yervoy. Alexandra, together with her team at the Gordon, were able to demonstrate that inducing KALM 30 – Professor K's first 'hidden gene' – with Demexilyn, a drug based on a Mexican jungle plant, could focus the immunity on the cancer cells and not on healthy organs. This turned out to be the 'complete package' for cancer treatment, releasing an immune attack on cancer, but not the gut.

This was the lasting legacy of Professor K's final quest.

MORE BOOKS BY THE AUTHOR

JACK ROGAN MYSTERIES STARTER LIBRARY

So, what exactly is a STARTER LIBRARY? I hear you ask. Well, it's a way to introduce myself and what I do, to new readers, and create interest in my writing. How? By providing little insights into my world, and the creative process involved in becoming an international thriller writer.

The Starter Library consists of four short books:
1. *Letters from The Attic* – a delightful collection of auto-bio-graphical short stories;
2. *The Forgotten Painting* – a multi-award-winning Jack Rogan novella;
3. *The Kimberley Secret* – a much-anticipated prequel to the Jack Rogan Mysteries series;
4. *The Main Characters Profile* – provides some exciting background stories and insights into the main characters featured in the series.

The Starter Library is available right now, and can be downloaded for FREE by following this link: https://gabrielfarago.com.au/starter-library2/

Please share this with your friends and encourage them to download the Starter Library.

In 2013, I released my first adventure thriller –
The Empress Holds the Key.

THE EMPRESS HOLDS THE KEY

A disturbing, edge-of-your-seat historical mystery thriller

Jack Rogan Mysteries Book 1

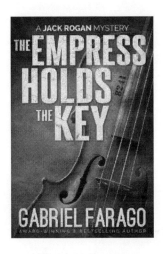

Dark secrets. A holy relic. An ancient quest reignited.
Jack Rogan's discovery of a disturbing old photograph in the ashes of
a rural Australian cottage draws the journalist into a dangerous hunt
with the ultimate stakes.

The tangled web of clues – including hoards of Nazi gold, hidden
Swiss bank accounts, and a long-forgotten mass grave – implicate
wealthy banker Sir Eric Newman and lead to a trial with shocking
revelations.

A holy relic mysteriously erased from the pages of history is
suddenly up for grabs to those willing to sacrifice everything to find
it. Rogan and his companions must follow historical leads through
ancient Egypt to the Crusades and the Knights Templar to uncover a
secret that could destroy the foundations of the Catholic Church and
challenge the history of Christianity itself.

Will Rogan succeed in bringing the dark mystery into the light, or will the powers desperately working against him ensure the ancient truths remain buried forever?

The Empress Holds the Key is now available on Amazon

Encouraged by the reception of *The Empress Holds the Key*, I released my next thriller – *The Disappearance of Anna Popov* – in 2014.

THE DISAPPEARANCE OF ANNA POPOV

A dark, page-turning psychological thriller

Jack Rogan Mysteries Book 2

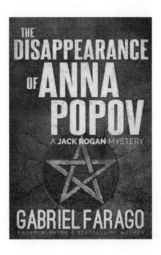

A mysterious disappearance. An outlaw biker gang. One dangerous investigation.

Journalist Jack Rogan cannot resist a good mystery. When he stumbles across a clue about the tragic disappearance of two girls from Alice Springs years earlier, he's determined to investigate.

Joining forces with his New York literary agent, a retired Aboriginal police officer, and Cassandra, an enigmatic psychic, Rogan enters the dangerous and dark world of an outlaw bikies gang ruled by an evil and enigmatic master.

Entangled in a web of violence, superstition and fear, Rogan and his friends follow the trail of the missing girls into the remote Dreamtime-wilderness of Outback Australia – where they must face even greater threats.

Cassandra hides a secret agenda and uses her occult powers to facilitate an epic showdown where the loser faces death and oblivion.

Will Rogan succeed in finding the truth, or will the forces of evil prevail, taking even more lives with them?

The Disappearance of Anna Popov is now available on Amazon

My next book, *The Hidden Genes of Professor K*, was released in 2016. Here's a short sample to pique your interest:

THE HIDDEN GENES OF PROFESSOR K

A dark, disturbing and nail-biting medical thriller

Jack Rogan Mysteries Book 3

"Outstanding Thriller" of 2017
Independent Author Network Book of the Year Awards

A medical breakthrough. A greedy pharmaceutical magnate. A brutal double-murder. One tangled web of lies.

World-renowned scientist Professor K is close to a ground-breaking discovery. He's also dying. With his last breath, he anoints Dr Alexandra Delacroix his successor and pleads with her to carry on his work.

But powerful forces will stop at nothing to possess the research, unwittingly plunging Delacroix into a treacherous world of unbridled ambition and greed.

Desperate and alone, she turns to celebrated author and journalist Jack Rogan.

Rogan must help Delacroix while also assisting famous rock star Isis in the seemingly unrelated investigation into the brutal murder of her parents.

With the support of Isis's resourceful PA, a former police officer, a tireless campaigner for the destitute and forgotten, and a gifted boy with psychic powers, Rogan exposes a complex web of fiercely guarded secrets and heinous crimes of the past that can ruin them all and change history.

Will the dreams of a visionary scientist with the power to change the future of medicine fall into the wrong hands, or will his genius benefit mankind and prevent untold misery and suffering for generations to come?

***The Hidden Genes of Professor K* is now available on Amazon**

My next book, *The Curious Case of the Missing Head,* was released in November 2019. Here's a short sample to pique your interest.

THE CURIOUS CASE OF THE MISSING HEAD

A gripping medical thriller

Jack Rogan Mysteries Book 5

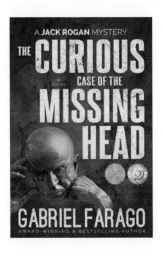

Gold Medal Winner in the Fiction Thriller - Conspiracy Thrillers Category!
2020 Readers' Favorite Annual Book Award Contest

"Outstanding Thriller/Suspense" of 2020
Independent Author Network Book of the Year Awards

A headless body on a boat. An international conspiracy. Can he survive a controversial scientific discovery?
Esteemed Australian journalist Jack Rogan is on a mission to solve the disappearance of his mother in the 70s. But when a friend needs help rescuing a kidnapped world-renowned astrophysicist, he doesn't hesitate. Struggling with more questions than answers, his investiga-

tion leads them aboard a hellish hospital ship, where instead of finding the kidnap victim, he's confronted with a decapitated corpse.

As the search intensifies, Jack bumps up against diabolical cartels with hidden agendas. And when his research reveals dubious experiments, a criminal on death row, and a shocking revelation about his mother's fate, he must uncover how it's all linked.

Can Jack unravel the twisted connections and catch the scientist's killer, or will the next obituary published be his own?

The Curious Case of the Missing Head is the fifth standalone novel in the page-turning Jack Rogan Mysteries series. If you like meticulous theoretical science, exponentially increasing intensity, and astonishing surprises, then you'll love Gabriel Farago's hair-raising medical thriller.

The Curious Case of the Missing Head
is now available on Amazon.

My latest book, *The Lost Symphony*, was released in November 2020. Here's a short sample to pique your interest.

THE LOST SYMPHONY

A historical mystery thriller

Jack Rogan Mysteries Book 6

A murdered tsarina. A lost musical masterpiece. A stolen Russian icon. Can Jack honour a promise made a long time ago, and solve an age-old mystery?

When acclaimed Australian journalist and author Jack Rogan inherits an old music box with a curious letter hidden inside, he decides to investigate. As he delves deeper into a murky past of secrets and violence, he soon discovers that he's not the only one interested in solving the puzzle.

Frieda Malenkova, a ruthless art dealer, and Victor Sokolov, a Russian billionaire with a dark past, will stop at nothing to achieve their deep desires and foil Jack's valiant struggle to uncover the truth.

Joining forces with Mademoiselle Darrieux, a flamboyant Paris socialite, and Claude Dupree, a retired French police officer, Jack enters a dangerous world of unbridled ambition, murder and greed that threatens to destroy him.

On a perilous journey that takes him deep into Russia, Jack follows a tortuous path of discovery, disappointment and betrayal that brings him face to face with his destiny.

Will Jack unravel the hidden clues left behind by a desperate empress? Can he save the precious legacy of a genius before it's too late, and return a holy icon revered by generations to where it belongs?

The Lost Symphony is the sixth standalone novel in the page-turning Jack Rogan Mysteries series. If you enjoy historical mysteries based on meticulous research, fascinating characters, and edge-of-your seat excitement, then you'll love Gabriel Farago's latest action-thriller.

The Lost Symphony is now available on Amazon

JACK ROGAN MYSTERIES
BOX SET BOOKS 1-4

The Jack Rogan Mysteries Box Set is now available on Amazon

About the Author

Gabriel Farago is the international, bestselling award-winning Australian author of the Jack Rogan mysteries and thrillers series for the thinking reader.

As a lawyer with a passion for history and archaeology, Gabriel Farago had to wait for many years before being able to pursue another passion—writing—in earnest. However, his love of books and storytelling started long before that.

'I remember as a young boy reading biographies and history books with a torch under the bed covers,' he recalls, 'and then writing stories about archaeologists and explorers the next day, instead of doing homework. While I regularly got into trouble for this, I believe we can only do well in our endeavours if we are passionate about the things we love. For me, writing has become a passion.'

Born in Budapest, Gabriel grew up in post-war Europe and, after fleeing Hungary with his parents during the Revolution in 1956, he went to school in Austria before arriving in Australia as a teenager. This allowed him to become multi-lingual and feel 'at home' in different countries and diverse cultures.

Shaped by a long legal career and experiences spanning several decades and continents, his is a mature voice that speaks in many tongues. Gabriel holds degrees in literature and law, speaks several languages and takes research and authenticity very seriously. Inquisitive by nature, he studied Egyptology and learned to read the hieroglyphs. He travels extensively and visits all of the locations mentioned in his books.

'I try to weave fact and fiction into a seamless storyline', he explains. 'By blurring the boundaries between the two, the reader is never quite sure where one ends, and the other begins. This is of course quite deliberate as it creates the illusion of authenticity and reality in a work that is pure fiction. A successful work of fiction is a balancing act: reality must rub shoulders with imagination in a way that is both entertaining and plausible.'

Gabriel lives just outside Sydney, Australia, in the Blue Mountains, surrounded by a World Heritage National Park. 'The beauty and solitude of this unique environment,' he points out, 'gives me the inspiration and energy to weave my thoughts and ideas into stories that in turn, I sincerely hope, will entertain and inspire my readers.'

Gabriel Farago

AUTHOR'S NOTE

I hope you enjoyed reading this book as much as I enjoyed writing it. I'd be very grateful if you'd post a short review on Amazon. Your support really does make a difference.

CONNECT WITH THE AUTHOR

Website
https://gabrielfarago.com.au/

Amazon Author Page
http://www.amazon.com/Gabriel-Farago/e/B00GUVY2UW/

Goodreads
https://www.goodreads.com/author/show/7435911.Gabriel_Farago

Facebook
https://www.facebook.com/GabrielFaragoAuthor

Made in the USA
Monee, IL
25 June 2021